I0670364

The Short End of the Stick

The Short End of the Stick

Henry Fiol

New York City

THE SHORT END OF THE STICK
© 1998 by Henry Fiol
All Rights Reserved

No part of this book may be reproduced, stored in a retrieval system, or transmitted in any form or by any means, including electronics. mechanical, photocopying, microfilming, recording, or otherwise (except for that copying permitted by sections 107 and 108 of the U.S. Copyright Law), without written permission from the Author.

ISBN: 978-1-7376688-0-0

9 781737 668800

Book Design: William Millán
For inquiries on this book contact: henry-fiol@henryfiol.com
Printed in the United States of America

Acknowledgements

Thanks to all my family and friends for their encouragement and support, and a very special thank you to my son, Henry Fiol Jr., whose patience and technical assistance made this project a reality. Also, a heartfelt thank you to my friend, William Millán, for all his technical help in bringing this novel to light.

Table of Contents

Chapter 1

It's Friday, the day before the big race, and as I walk out of the jock's room at the end of the day, I see my agent, Phil, waiting for me, leaning against the fender of his Lincoln.

"Hey, Joey boy, how's it hangin' kid?"

"What's up with you? You're usually gone by this time."

"Well, I figured I'd just stick around and have a little talk with you—that's all"

"Talk? About what?"

"Why don't you get in your car and follow me. I don't really feel like talking around here. Too many nosybodies."

I know something's up, but I'm not asking any questions though. I just get in my car to follow him as he leads me around to the main parking field on the backstretch and pulls in under a tree.

Most of the fans are gone by now, and there's only a handful of lonely cars dotting the big empty lot. I park next to Phil and take a few seconds to check out the sun as it turns golden yellow. It's quiet now, and all I can hear is the distant hum of the tractors harrowing the track and the chirps of a couple of birds. I light a smoke and sit by the hood of my car and stare out at the empty grandstand, bracing myself for what Phil has to say.

"Hey, did I tell you I put you on three lead-pipe cinches for tomorrow?"

"Yep, you told me. You told me this morning in the kitchen, and you told me again this afternoon in the tunnel outside the jock's room."

"Yeah, it's gonna be great. Mike Sheldon's filly and Harry Bickel's colt are mortal locks if I ever saw one. And then there's that other horse, what's-his-name, in the fifth. Fuhgeddaboudit, we're gonna turn the hat trick on Belmont Stakes day in front of sixty thousand fans. That's gonna be great for business. Can you Imagine the way all the....."

"Cut the shit, Phil. You didn't bring me out here just to talk about what I'm riding tomorrow. What's the deal?"

I cross my arms and wait, studying him as he pulls out his gold cigarette case and slips one of his Viceroys into his mouth. He seems to

1

be taking forever to light it up and blow out the first puff of smoke, so I know he's stalling for time, groping around in his brain for the right words to lay something really heavy on me. I feel my heart sink and my blood run cold.

"Joey" he says, flicking his lighter shut and sticking it back into his pocket. "First of all, I want you to know that none of this is coming from me. I got business associates. Now most of the time they stay in the background, behind the scenes, and they pretty much let me run the show. But sometimes a decision is made at the top, and.... Well, I just gotta go along with it, whether I like it or not. *Capish?*"

"C'mon Phil, spit it out already."

He reaches inside his jacket and pulls out a fat manila envelope and lays it on my lap. "Here Joey, this is for you. Twenty large. You can count if you want."

"Twenty thousand dollars! What are you giving me this for?!"

He doesn't answer right away; first he has to cough in his hand and spit out a blob of phlegm. "Like I said, this ain't coming from me, Joey. It comes from upstairs."

I don't have to ask what "upstairs" means, because I already know he's talking about his cousin Carmine and the rest of them creeps. "So, what's it all about?"

"Look, I'm just the messenger over here, but from what I understand, way too much early money has been bet on your horse, and even more is likely to come rolling in tomorrow."

"So?"

"Well, our bookies can't seem to find a lay-off outfit to cover it all. From what I hear, they usually use some people in Chicago for situations like this, but there seems to be some static between the families and this and that, and.... Well, they just can't handle it. That's it. So you're gonna have to do something."

"What do you mean 'do something'."

"C'mon Joey, you know what I'm talking about. You gotta do something. They don't want this horse to win, and that's all there is to it."

"But Phil, this ain't no thirty-five-hundred-dollar claiming race over here; this is the Belmont Stakes! How'm I gonna stiff Red Rebel in a race like this?! Are you fuckin' nuts?!"

2

He grabs the envelope and holds it up to my face. "That's exactly why they're giving you this. Twenty-fuckin'-grand. That's almost twice the jock's share of the purse, and it ain't chicken feed neither. Do you know how many broken-down bums you'd have to bring in to make this kind of money? C'mon, use your head for once in your life!"

I can't help staring at his ugly mug as he shakes the envelope in my face. His breath is giving off a nasty stink—as usual—and his eyes have the cold, dead look of a snake. I'm not buying this garbage about the bookies and the "lay-off outfit" for one second. It's just Phil's way of shifting the blame onto somebody else and covering his own back. Them beady, rat-bastard eyes are telling me the whole story; the whole, stinking scheme is coming straight from him. I know it. It's classic Phil: stiff the heavy favorite, bribe a couple of jocks to stay off the board, spread a mountain of money on the remaining contenders, and carry the winnings home in a wheelbarrow! We've pulled that shit lots of times—only I never thought he'd have the balls to ask me to do something like that in a big, important race like the Belmont.

On second thought, maybe these big-time bookies really *do* have something to do with it. After all, with the way everybody and their mother is betting on this horse, they'd stand to make a pretty penny if Red should lose. Aaah, who the fuck knows? All I know for sure is that this guy has got a lot of nerve to rain on my parade after all I've been through.

I've seen Phil pull some real low-life, scumbag shit since I first started working with him, but this is definitely the lowest of the low. How can he even *think* of asking me to do something like this? He knows how I feel about Red, not to mention Sam Cardone, his trainer, the guy who gave me my first break on the track, or Mr. Gargiulo, his owner, the guy who believed in me enough to give me a shot and let me ride the horse, instead of putting one of them veteran, big-money guys on his back. I can't do something like this to them—it ain't right.

And I can't do something like this to myself neither. This is my big chance, the Belmont Stakes, part of the Triple Crown. I've been dreaming of this ever since I was a little kid when I used to ride my bike around the reservoir in them make-believe races of mine. It's the chance of a lifetime. How can I intentionally mess it up? For what? For

3

money? Fuck that shit. I wouldn't do something like that for all the money in the world. I just can't, no fuckin' way.

But Phil looks like he don't want to take no for an answer, and the slimeball keeps closing in on me, shaking the envelope only a few inches from my face and talking a whole bunch of shit that I can't even hear anymore. It's like watching TV with the sound turned off; I can see his lips moving, but I can't hear a word he's saying. All I can see is the meanness, and the spite, and the jealousy on that skeevy mug of his. And I know where it's all coming from too. It just burns his ass that I got the mount on Red all on my own, through my own connections, and he had absolutely nothing to do with it. It's all about envy; he just can't stand the idea of me getting lucky for once in my life. And he just keeps on with his shit, coming, closer and closer, all the way up in my face, spritzing me with saliva and knocking me out with his fuckin' latrine breath. It's too much.

I can feel the veins throbbing in my head and my heart pounding away in my chest like a sledgehammer. My mouth is dry, and my arms and legs are trembling on me too. I'm trying my best to maintain my cool, but the disappointment is drowning me, and I keep sinking, deeper and deeper. It's already up to my eyeballs. I reach out to hold onto something, but there's nothing there. All I can feel is a blood-red wave, rising up from inside my guts, sweeping me away like a hurricane.

"Fuck you!" I yell, smacking the envelope out of Phil's hand and sending it flying into the bushes. "I ain't doing it! You can tell your fuckin' cousin Carmine, that ugly, hook-nose bastard, and the rest of them scumbags, that they can kiss my balls and both cheeks of my ass, 'cause I ain't stiffing this horse for no-goddamn-body! Ya hear?! For *nobody!*"

Well, now that I'm home and I've cooled down a little, I'm starting to feel like a real shithead for losing it and going off like that. I've been around long enough to know that I'm definitely going to have to pay the price for that little explosion—just don't know where and I don't know when. But as I pace up and down in my living room, trying to calm my nerves with a shot of booze, I get the answer to that question a lot sooner than I expected. The phone is ringing, and I'll bet anything it's Phil.

4

Right away I think he's going to start screaming and yelling and cursing me out and whatnot, but his voice is calm, almost friendly, and he sounds cool as a cucumber.

"Got a pencil, Joey?" he says, "I'm gonna give you an address, and I want you to write it down. Okay? Ready?"

"Yeah"

"Alright. It's 169 Thompson Street, the Villa Visconti Restaurant."

"Where the hell is that?"

"In Manhattan, one block up from Houston Street. My cousin Carmine wants you to be there at eight o'clock sharp."

"Tonight?"

"Yeah, tonight. When do ya think—next year?"

"What for?"

"You know what for. And I suggest that you be there on time too; he don't like nobody keeping him waiting."

"But Phil...I..."

Click. He hangs up the phone.

Well, maybe I was big-and-bad enough to blow a fuse with Phil, but I sure as hell ain't big-and-bad enough to throw a bomb on Carmine the Nose and not show up. Are you kidding? That would be like signing my own death sentence, and I ain't *that* stupid.

So, without thinking twice, I grab my car keys and fly out the door. It's already 6:45, and I know I only have an hour and fifteen minutes to fight the traffic, get into the city, and find this Visconti place before The Nose has a titty attack.

When I walk into the restaurant at 7:57, sweating bullets and shitting in my pants, guess who's waiting for me in the vestibule of the joint: Bobby Zito, "the King of the Bullies", the same Bobby Zito who made my life a living hell from the very first day I moved into the neighborhood.

Surprise, but no surprise. I guess while I was busy learning the ropes on the racetrack as an apprentice jockey, Mr. Shitface, must have been learning the ropes as an apprentice wiseguy. And it looks like he must've had some heavy connection all along that none of us knew about; a young guy like him don't get anywhere *near* The Nose—unless you're a nephew, a cousin, or some kind of blood-relative. Who knew?

5

Anyway, as soon as he lays eyes on me, he tries to play it off all tough and serious, but he still can't resist calling me by that stupid name he used to call me when we were kids.

"Well, look who's here, it's Shrimpy Gimp, the big-time jockey", he says, in his usual smart-ass tone of voice.

I'm so shocked to see his ugly mug after all these years, that I'm speechless. All I can do is give him a sneer and a dirty look. Of all the rotten luck! I can't believe that of all the people in the entire universe, I have to deal with this prick on top of everything else.

"Follow me."

I'm thinking he's going to lead me into the restaurant, but instead, he brings me over to a telephone booth off to the side in front of the men's room.

"Turn around and lift up your arms."

"What for?"

"Just do it. I got orders."

I raise my arms and feel his grubby paws frisking me up and down, grabbing around in my crotch and checking my legs all the way down to my ankles.

"What the fuck you frisking me for? I ain't packin' nothin'."

"Like I said, I got orders."

Satisfied that I'm not carrying a piece, or a shank, or maybe one of them little portable tape recorders that the FBI and the spies use—who knows what they're looking for—he leads me through the swinging doors and into the dining area.

I spot Carmine the Nose right away, sitting at a corner table at the far end of the room. He has two of his cronies next to him, that big bastard Nino with the twenty-inch neck, his chauffeur/bodyguard, and some skinny creep who I know by sight but not by name. Across from them are these two other guys. They're both fat and the one on the left is bald, but I can't see much else because they got their backs to me.

I feel my mouth getting drier and drier and my heart beating faster and faster as I follow my usher, Bobby Zito, and approach the table. Carmine the Nose looks up from his dish of spumoni for a second, but when he catches a glimpse of me, he makes believe he hasn't seen me, and he keeps right on eating. That sends a chill up my spine, because just from that split-second glance, I can tell my man is *pissed*.

6

As soon as the other guys see me, they stop with their dessert and start staring, flicking their eyes over to The Nose to see if he's noticed me too. But he's too busy enjoying his spumoni to look up at me—at least that's the way he wants to make it look anyway.

I know all about that move; Grandpa hipped me to it when I was just a little kid. He always used to say these *"gangisti"* guys like to act rude and crude with people, on purpose—just to let you know you ain't worth shit and you have no *"importanza"* whatsoever. It's a head game.

But now that The Nose is raising his eyes from his dish and locking them on mine, I'm really remembering Grandpa. He was always calling these guys *"the champeen from the dirty look"*, the dirty-look champs, and as I'm feeling that cold-blooded stare burning through me like a blowtorch, now I know first-hand exactly what he was talking about. If looks could kill, I'm already in the fuckin' morgue; that's the look of a stone-cold killer if I ever saw one.

Well, I guess The Nose must feel satisfied that he's seen enough fear on my face, because much to my relief, he's finally unlocking his eyes from mine and giving a little nod to my host, Bobby Zito. Shitface understands right away what the nod means, and he pulls a chair away from one of the other tables and pushes me into it.

From the look of things, I'd say this seat is the only courtesy I'm going to be getting. Nobody is offering me anything to eat, nobody is offering me anything to drink, nobody is shaking hands with me, and nobody is making no introductions neither. It's all part of the head-game. I'm being treated like a lousy little blob of dogshit because I'm supposed to *know* I'm nothing but a lousy little blob of dogshit, and I can be flushed away at any time—just like a turd.

But it don't bother me none; I know I ain't here to socialize. And besides, now that I've been able to scope out the two fat fucks sitting next to me out of the corner of my eye, I realize right away that I don't need no introductions anyway. I've seen these two at the track lots of times hanging around with Phil. They're Jewish guys. The bald one is Irv, and the other one with the red mustache is called Marty. I always knew they were big-time bookies, but I never knew until now just *how* big and *how* well-connected they are.

The Nose hasn't said peep to me yet, but I already know the deal. Phil has probably given him the whole scoop, word for word, including

7

the part about me cursing him out and calling him "an ugly, hook-nose bastard", not to mention the part about "kiss my balls and both cheeks of my ass". So, I know it's only a matter of time before the shit comes flying off the fan.

I just keep sitting here, shitting green and shaking like a leaf, while this creep ignores me on purpose and finishes his spumoni. He keeps poking at the ice cream with his spoon, real slow, stopping to pick out the little pieces of candied fruits so he can push them to the side. He's taking all his sweet time, trying his best to mess with my mind and make me feel twenty times more scared than I already am. What a scumbag.

While all this is going on, nobody at the table has dared to speak. All you can hear are the clinks of The Nose's spoon and the little grunts coming from Nino as he scarfs down an éclair. The silence is deadly, but now that the gigantic schnoz is rising up from the dish and them pencil-thin lips are opening to speak, I'm actually breathing a sigh of relief. I just want to get this shit over with, the sooner the better. I can't take it no more.

"So," he says, taking a swipe at his mouth and tossing his napkin on the table, "you know why I wanted you to come here tonight?"

"No."

"Hah? Speak up."

"No."

"Oh, you don't, hah? Well, for your information, I wanted to see with my own two eyes whether you're an ungrateful little prick, or whether you're just plain stupid."

I drop my eyes and look down at my hands, but once I notice how they're shaking, I hide them under the table right away, and start staring at the tablecloth instead.

The Nose reaches over and takes a toothpick out of this little glass thing in the center of the table and starts picking his teeth. "So, which one is it? Ungrateful little prick, or just plain stupid? You tell me."

I don't answer.

"Hah? I can't hear you. I said, 'which one is it?'"

"I don't know. Neither I guess."

"Neither, huh? Well, you know what I think? I think it's both—either that or you just got a real short memory."

8

All of a sudden, the waiter comes over, and the conversation hangs suspended in mid-air until every dish, spoon, and napkin is whisked away.

"Yeah," he says, in real sarcastic voice, "I guess that must be it. You probably just got a really bad memory—that's all. Maybe you got amnesia or something. Well, let me refresh it for ya."

I'm cringing already because I know what's coming next. But The Nose wants to drag the shit out and be all dramatic and whatnot, so he stops to pick a little piece of something off the tip of his tongue, and then, after he holds out his fingertip and takes all his sweet time looking at it, he wipes it on the tablecloth and keeps on talking. "Who took you on when you didn't have a pot to piss in and nobody around the track wanted to touch you with a ten-foot pole? Hah?"

"Phil."

"That's right, Phil. And why do you think Phil even got involved with you in the first place?"

"Because of you Mr. Carmine."

I guess that's the answer he's looking for, because I can see him nodding his head and turning his mouth down at the corners. "Ah! Ya see that?! Little by little, your memory seems to be coming back to you. Good! Now let me ask you another question. Who's kept you living like a king for the past year?—filling your pockets with more money than you can spend—cooling out that vacuum-cleaner nose of yours with the finest coke—and treating your puny, little dick to the best pussy money can buy. Hah? Who?"

"Phil...but I..."

"Phil and who else?"

"Phil and you, Mr. Carmine, but..."

"See that? It's all coming back to you now. Terrific! Now let me ask you another question. Why is it then, when I give Phil instructions to take you to the side and ask you for a little favor, one lousy, little sign of respect and gratitude, not only does he come back telling me that you refused, but he comes back saying that you had the nerve to curse him out, to curse me out, and to even use the words: 'ugly, hook-nose bastard'."

I close my eyes, bracing myself for the worst, but The Nose fakes me out. Out of nowhere, he lowers his voice and continues, all cool,

9

calm and collected, putting on this fake half-smile and talking down to me the way you'd talk to a little snot-nose kid. "Now Joey, you're a smart young man. Why would you do something like that? Ungrateful prick, just plain stupid? Or is it because you're a dirty little, piece-of-shit cripple, and you just don't give a fuck?!"

I want to grab that red candle-thing off the table and fling it right in his ugly mug, hot wax and all—'specially when I hear him use the word "cripple". But that'd be suicide, so I get a grip instead, bite my tongue, and keep staring at the sauce stains on the tablecloth.

"But I gotta hand it to you, though," he says, reaching over and patting me on the cheek. "You got a lotta balls, kid, a lotta balls. But that's the problem. I guess it must be the *Calabrese* blood; you're all bunch of hot-heads, stupid donkeys with too much balls and not enough brains."

I know I should probably stay quiet, but I figure this might be as good a time as any to try and cop a plea, 'specially since The Nose just patted me on the cheek. "Look, Mr. Carmine, I'm sorry if I flew off the handle like that and said all them stupid things. It's just that this horse ain't no ordinary horse—he's something special—and the Belmont Stakes ain't no ordinary race neither. It's the chance of a lifetime. You can understand that, can't you, Mr. Carmine?"

He just leans back in his chair and keeps picking at his teeth, sucking on them, and spitting out little splinters from the toothpick. "Yeah, I can understand that. That's why we tried to be fair with you and we offered you some nice compensation. Twenty large ain't nothing to sneeze at, ya know. But that's okay. Seeing as how you knocked it out of Phil's hand, you can forget about that now. I guess our money isn't good enough for you; maybe it's too dirty or something."

"No, Mr. Carmine, it ain't that. It's just that I've been through a lot with this horse, 'specially since he missed the Derby and the Preakness. I just wanna do the right thing—that's all."

"Oh! You mean you wanna do the right thing for the horse, but you don't wanna do the right thing for us? Is that it?"

"No Mr. Carmine, it ain't that," I answer, meeting his eyes and trying to level with the guy. "Look, if it was any other horse, in any other race, you know I wouldn't even think twice about helping you out. But

10

this is Red Rebel we're talking about over here. He's something special to me. I mean, he's the..."

"Yeah, yeah, save it kid. I know how much you love the fuckin' nag, and how you fought to save his balls when Cardone wanted to make a gelding out of him. You're a real Florence Nightingale—ya know that?"

Holy shit! How did he find out about that? I guess fuckin' Phil must've blabbed it to him—either that or he heard it through the grapevine. Aaah, it don't matter anyway. It's just like they say in the neighborhood: "The Nose knows"—and that's all there is to it.

Anyway, by now I can see my plea is falling on deaf ears, so instead of keeping on with the shit and making even a bigger jackass out of myself, I decide it's probably better if I just clam up and go back to looking at the tablecloth.

"'Ey!" he growls, leaning forward and nailing me with that bone-chilling stare of his. "You *look* at me when I talk to you! *Ya hear?!*"

I swallow hard and struggle to drag my eyes off the table and look up at his face again. But I guess I'm not doing it fast enough, because before you know it, this guy's blowing a fuse and going fuckin' apeshit on me.

"*Minchia!* You wasted enough of my time already, you little cocksucker! So you listen to me, and you listen *good*. I'm gonna say this one fuckin' time, so you better get it straight: This horse is not gonna win tomorrow. *Capish?!*"

"Yeah."

"Hah?!"

"Yeah!"

"Now I don't give two flying shits how you do it—that's your business—but you better do it, goddammit—'cause if you don't, I'm personally gonna turn *you* into a fuckin' gelding. Ya hear?! And if you think I'm bullshitting, you just try me, kid; I'll cut off them two little balls of yours and shove 'em down your throat faster than you can say your own goddamn name. Now get the fuck outa here!"

Then he slides his eyes over to Bobby Zito, and in a matter of seconds, I'm pushed through the restaurant and thrown out on the sidewalk like some deadbeat drunk who didn't pay his tab.

11

Chapter 2

So, as I lay here, tossing and turning, freaking out and worrying my ass off, I find myself going way back, thinking about my life, and how I wound up painting myself into this fucked-up corner.

I guess my story can be summed up with three little letters: L.L.D. It means Leg Length Discrepancy, and there's even a fancy, medical term for it too: anisomelia. I've had it from the day I was born. Don't know how, don't know why.

L.L.D. means I have one leg shorter than the other, and it's made me miserable my whole life. And even now, it still announces to the world, right off the bat, that I'm "different". I mean, now that I'm dealing mostly with adults, I don't get called "Gimp" like when I was a kid or when I was a teenager in high school. Adults are too slick for that. They're not as mean and cruel as kids can be, but I still never feel that people can just accept me as a regular guy, without first noticing my duck-waddle walk, or thinking about it, or looking at it—even while they're in the middle of a conversation with me. It's like when somebody is wearing a really bad wig. No matter how hard you try not to look at it, your eyes still keep drifting up to check it out.

Well, even though my L.L.D. was my main problem, it really was only one third of the shitty trifecta that God blessed me with. The other two parts were being short—I'm still only a little taller than midget size—and being skinnier than a toothpick. That's why a couple of the assholes on the block thought that the name "Gimp" wasn't good enough for me, so they added "Shrimp" to it, and started calling me "Shrimpy Gimp" instead. It took a pretty long time 'til the "Shrimpy" part got dropped, but after that, my official name on the block and all around the neighborhood became just plain "Gimp". In fact, if you asked anybody what my real name was, I bet you only Veronica, my neighbor, and my cousin Anthony would be the only ones who'd be able to tell you it was Joey. That's cause in my old neighborhood a nickname was like a tattoo. Once you got it, you were stuck with it forever, and it could never be erased. That's what happened to me. I got branded with

12

"Gimp", and I'm going to always be "Gimp", whether I like or not. Tough titties for me.

Most of the adults I deal with now know enough not to hurt my feelings by using words like "gimp" or "shrimp". But they know how to say "cripple" though. Yep, it's happened lots of times. Just let somebody get really upset or pissed off, and the word "cripple" comes flying out of their mouth like a dagger—just like last night with Carmine the Nose.

Ya know, not for nothin', but I never could understand why some people are born with both cheeks of their ass dipped in gold, while other people have to carry a heavy cross with them their whole lives— like being born blind, or deaf, or mute, or retarded, or paralyzed, or deformed, or with a harelip, or with an ugly birthmark, or without any parents, or dirt-poor,...or crippled—like me. That's why over the years, I was never able to believe in God or get into religion that much. I grew up hearing stuff like "God is love", and "God loves you". But even when I was a kid, I'd always think to myself: if "God is love", and if "God loves me" so much, then how come God ain't fair? How come God gives some people the ice-cream sundae with the whipped cream and the cherry on top, and other people get the short end of the stick? Well, it's taken me a long time to cut through all the bullshit, but If there's one thing I've learned for sure, it's that life definitely ain't fair. "Fair" has nothing to do with nothing. Never has, never will. You just gotta play the cards the way they're dealt.

But at least I can say I was lucky in something though: In spite of being cursed with my L.L.D., I always had my family, and they always had my back—everybody except my dad that is.

It's been a long time since I've seen him or heard from him, but I still remember him though.

His name was Joseph, and I was named after him. That's why everybody in the family calls me "Junior" and not "Joey" or "Joe". He was okay, I guess. He used to do the usual father-and-son stuff with me when I was little, like playing catch or having fake boxing or wrestling matches, but the thing I remember most is when we'd go "belly-whopping" together down that big, Fort George hill when it snowed. And he used to tell me some good stories too—like "The Golden Boy of the Golden River", and this other one that he probably made up

13

because he knew I loved horses so much: "The Horse of the Seven Colors". That was my favorite.

I guess I still miss him, even though he's been out of my mind for a really long time now. It really shook me up bad when he had that last big fight with Mom and slammed the door and never came back...but at least there was some peace after that. 'Cause let me tell ya, before he left, every day was World War Three in my house. They'd fight over anything and everything—non-stop. Big things, little things, anything. And I ain't talking only about screaming-and-yelling fights, I'm talking about *real* fights: smacking, and punching, and kicking, and choking, and smashing—even using knives. That's the one that scared me he most, the time when both of them were going at each other with these big, kitchen knives. I was little at the time, but I knew enough to grab the phone and call the cops. It was a bad scene, and as much as I loved my dad back then, I was actually glad to see him go.

One time I asked Grandma about him, and why he was the way he was, and she said he had a big complex about his height. According to her, his nickname was "Shorty", and at the time of World War Two, when all his buddies went to enlist, he tried to enlist too—only the army rejected him and classified him 4F because he was too short. Grandma said that the rejection did a big number on his head, and that's why he always wanted to fight with everybody—'specially with Mom—to show what a big man he was.

And he wound up doing a real number on my mom too. She's always been real nervous and emotional—that's just her nature—but looking back now, it's easy to see how those years she spent dealing with his bullshit really messed her up big-time. He left her completely high and dry, without any money, and without even a phone call or a letter to say he was alive or dead. She waited and waited, and kept hoping and praying for the longest time, struggling to make ends meet with the little she made as a beautician and from giving haircuts and "permanents" on the side to the ladies in our building. But when she got the news that the beauty parlor was closing down and she's was going to be out of a job, she got even more worried and depressed, and had no choice but to turn to Grandma and Grandpa for help.

That was probably one of the worst times in Mom's life, and even though I was only a little kid and didn't understand too much about

14

what was going on, I still knew something really bad was happening. But it turned out to be something good for me though, because it meant taking a trip downtown to Grandma and Grandpa's house, and anytime I was there, I was happy.

I remember that trip like it was yesterday. Not because there was anything special about visiting Grandma and Grandpa, but because that visit in particular turned out to be a real life-changer for everybody— 'specially me.

Mom had held out for a few days, worrying and sobbing alone in her bedroom. My guess was that she was probably waiting for the big Feast of Our Lady of Mount of Carmel that they celebrate every year in the middle of July, right there at the church on Grandma and Grandpa's block: 115th Street. That way she figured she could kill two birds with one stone.

She'd never miss the feast—I mean *never*. Every year we'd take the bus downtown, and she'd drag me with her through the whole hot, stinky procession, and then into the church, jam-packed with people, so she could pray and light candles to all the saints—and so I could get the "special blessing" of *La Madonna*. I guess both her and Grandma thought that the "special blessing" would spark some sort of miracle that would either cure my L.L.D., or at least help me grow out of it somehow. But it never happened.

The trip that year was a little different though, because besides scoring the usual "special blessing" for me, Mom was hoping to get some extra help from *La Madonna* for herself, so she could find a way out of her own dilemma: no husband, no job, and no money to pay the rent.

Anyway, as usual, the bus made its way down Amsterdam Avenue and across 125th Street, and, as usual, when we got to Harlem, I started asking Mom my usual questions about why the "brown people" had such fancy cars, and why there were so many Cadillacs, Lincolns, and Imperials all over the place, and why some of the men wore them silky, black handkerchiefs on their heads? But she wouldn't answer; she just kept telling me to lower my voice, and then she whipped out a pack of Charms candy and gave me one to shut me up.

It took more than an hour to get downtown to Grandma and Grandpa's house, and by the time we got off the bus, Mom said we were

15

running late and that we were going to miss the procession. That's when she started walking fast, dragging me along by the arm. I always hated that, because the faster I'd move, the bigger the dip in my limp and the duck-waddle in my walk. Sometimes people would stare, and that's when Mom would get snotty and say stuff out loud like: "What you lookin' at?!" or "Why don't ya put your eyes back in your head?!— *cretina bitch!* Fuhgeddaboudit, I'd get so embarrassed, I'd wish I could disappear into thin air, right there on the spot.

The only good thing that happened that day was when we got near the procession: I spotted one of them mounted policemen on a beautiful horse. He was probably there to control the crowd, but for me it was a big thing; that was the first time I'd ever seen a cop on a horse— in real life anyway.

"Junior! What are you doing?! Stop! Stop pulling me!"

"Ma, please! I wanna see the horse!"

"We don't have time now. Grandma's waiting for us, and we're gonna lose our place."

"C'mon Ma, please—just for a minute. Pleeeeease."

"Oh, you and your horses. Okay....but just for a minute."

I let go of her hand and circled the horse so I could see him from all sides. He was a bright, shiny bay, with a star on his forehead, a black mane, and a long black tail that he kept swishing from side to side, as he pranced in place sideways—almost as if he was dancing to the beat of the procession band.

While I was busy checking out the horse, out of the corner of my eye, I noticed that the Irish cop who was riding him had tipped his hat and was smiling down at Mom. "Top o' the morning to ya, ma'am. Looks like yer boy really likes his harses, don't he?"

"Oh yes, Officer," Mom answered. "He's nuts about 'em. Everything is horses, horses."

"Really now?" he chuckled.

"Oh yeah. When he's home, all he does is draw pictures of 'em. And he does a pretty good job for a kid; he puts in all the little details and everything."

"Ya don't say."

"Yeah, he's crazy about 'em. Say, that's a real nice horse you got there. He's bewdeeful."

16

"Oh yes, ma'am, he's a fine-lookin' animal he is—one of the best-lookin' harses on the force. He's part Thoroughbred ya know; I think that's where he gets his good looks from."

"That means he's part racehorse, Ma."

"My, my, sonny, for a little fella ya' sure know your harses, don't ya?"

I blushed and looked down on the ground, feeling a little embarrassed that I'd just stuck my nose into the middle of a grownup's conversation without being asked.

"Officer?"

"Yes, ma'am."

"Do ya think he could touch him?"

"Why, of course, ma'am, he's very good with children."

Mom reached down and grabbed me from under my arms and lifted me up so I could reach the horse's head. "C'mon Junior, the policeman's gonna let you touch the horse."

"Whoa, steady now, boy," said the cop.

First, I touched his nose—it felt soft and tickly—and then I patted him on his forehead, right in the middle of his white spot. He was nice, and I thought that he kinda liked me too.

"What's his name?"

"Well, son, they named him after the Yankee Clipper himself: Joe DiMaggio. His name is Joltin' Joe."

"Joltin' Joe?"

"Yep, Joltin' Joe, but I call him 'Joey' for short. Ain't that right, Joey me boy?" the cop said, giving the horse a couple of quick pats on the neck.

"Joey?! My name's Joey too!"

"Ain't that a kick in the head. Joey, ey? Well, nice to meet ya, Joey."

"Okay, c'mon Junior," Mom said. "Let's go, the officer's gotta get back to work. Say goodbye to the horse."

I rubbed his forehead and gave him one last pat on his white spot. "Bye, Joey."

"Well, thanks a lot Officer. You're very nice—God bless you."

"Oh, go on now, it's nothin' at all, ma'am. You be careful now, there's a big crowd out here today."

"Okay, thanks again, Officer. So long."

17

All of a sudden, I felt Mom poking me with her knuckle and whispering under her breath. "Say thank you to the policeman, Junior, where's your manners?"

"Thanks a lot, Officer."

"You're very welcome. Bye now, Joey."

"Bye."

Before I could peek over my shoulder to take one last look at "Joey", Mom started getting all excited because she'd spotted Grandma at the window, and she started pulling me hard to catch up to the procession that was already at the steps of the church.

"Look Junior! There's Grandma at the kitchen window—and Grandpa too."

I yelled out, *"Hi Grandma! Hi Grandpa!"*, as loud as I could, but it didn't look like they could hear me—what with the band playing so loud and all the noise and everything. Besides, they both seemed to be busy looking at the statue of *La Madonna* that was being carried into the church.

But Mom was one step ahead of the situation though, and she whipped out a big, red kerchief out of her pocketbook and started waving it real hard every time she saw Grandma or Grandpa look over in our direction.

"I don't think they see us, Ma."

She kept on waving it and yelling out, and then, *boom*, all of a sudden, Grandma spotted us. Right away she started waving like crazy and blowing kisses at us with both hands. And then, after she turned to Grandpa to point us out to him, he got into the act too, and both of them were smiling and waving their asses off.

"Hi Grandma! Hi Grandpa!"

Well, seeing as how the music was so loud, Mom and Grandma started talking to each other in sign language. Grandma held up her hand telling her to wait, mouthing *"aspetta"*, and then she patted herself on the chest and pointed downstairs to let us know she was coming down. Mom waved "okay" and then pulled me over to the side, out of the way of the people, so we could wait for her.

The sun was blazing and there was no shade at all, so we went over to Grandma's building to wait for her inside by the door. I breathed a sigh of relief because it was a little cooler in there. Mom leaned against

18

the wall and started fanning herself with the red kerchief, and then she took her glasses off and pulled out a tissue.

I loved to see Mom without them big, thick glasses she wears. She was real pretty back then. And she still is too—everybody always says so. It was just a tough break for her, because ever since she was a kid, she's always had really bad eyes. She even had to go to a special class called a "Sight Conservation Class", where they give the students these special, large-print books so that they're able to read them.

Anyway, as soon as I heard Grandma's footsteps coming down the hallway, I hid behind the wall next to the door so I could scare her when she came out. Then, when the door opened and I heard her say, "Celeste, where's my Junior?", I popped out from behind her like a jack-in-the-box and shouted *"boo!"* real loud. She grabbed her heart with both hands right away, and started huffing and puffing, trying to make believe she was scared.

"You little devil-u!" she said, grabbing my cheeks and giving me a whole bunch of kisses all over my face. "Why you wanna scare you Grandma? Ah? Why? *You little son-a-ma-gun!"*

Then, after she finished giving me all the kisses 'n' stuff, she threw her arms around Mom and gave her a big hug too.

"Celeste....*Celestina mia."*

They kept on hugging each other for a pretty long time, and when Grandma tried to break off the hug, Mom kept holding on and started mumbling stuff in Italian. She was probably crying too, because I could see her shoulders moving up and down.

"Celeste...c'mon,...*u-walyoona*. Come on."

I knew Grandma was talking about me—*u-walyoona* meant "the kid"—and when Mom couldn't stop crying, Grandma gave her another long hug, rubbed her on her back, and then handed her a crumpled-up tissue so she could blow her nose and wipe her eyes.

"C'mon Celeste, control you'self."

"Okay Ma."

It took a while for Mom to get a grip and compose herself, but once she was ready, we stepped out of the cool of the building and back into the street. The heat was like a smack in the face—it was *scorching*—and the idea of joining up with all them stinky people, pushing and squashing each other on the steps of the church, didn't appeal to me at

19

all. I figured it was probably going to take at least another hour just to get *inside* the place.

"Ma."

"What, Junior?"

"Do I have to go inside the church? Can't I wait upstairs with Grandpa? Please."

"No, I want you to get the blessing of *La Madonna*."

"C'mon Ma, pleeease? It's too hot. I don't wanna go in there."

I looked over at Grandma and gave her a look, as if to say, "help me", and, as usual, my "lawyer" jumped in to plead my case.

"Celeste, come on," she begged, turning on the sugar. "Why you no let Junior to go upstairs? He's too small, he no undastand this things."

"No, Ma, I want him to come with us. He's gotta learn sometime. And besides, I want him to get the blessing....you know."

As soon as Mom said, "you know", I knew right away she was talking about my legs and the stupid idea of *La Madonna* working a miracle so I wouldn't have to limp no more. Mom had her mind made up, and neither Grandma or me were gonna change it.

So, with me scrunching up my face and cursing under my breath, Mom grabbed me by the arm and pulled me into the hot, sweaty mob that was squeezing through the narrow doors of the church.

What followed after that was the worst. The antipasto was standing on this big, long line that went from the entrance all the way down the center aisle to the altar. And then, after we inched our way down to where *La Madonna* was, I had to kneel down with Mom and Grandma on both sides of me and wait forever for this weird-looking priest to come over and give us the "special blessing". Mom got real upset and started shaking and sobbing when the priest blessed me, and then, once he noticed how freaked-out she was, he moved over and put his hands on her shoulders, trying to calm her down. They started gabbing in Italian right away, and even though I couldn't understand everything they were saying, I knew they were talking about me. And I must have been right too, because Mom hadn't even finished telling him the whole story, before he came over to me again and plopped his hot, heavy hands on top of my head while he mumbled a whole bunch of extra prayers that were designed 'specially for me—and my L.L.D.

20

I made a quick sign of the cross and got up fast because I thought the main course was over and done with. But no such luck. Nope, now it was time for the dessert.

From the altar, Mom and Grandma dragged me into the "saint-room", where the statues of all of the saints were, so they could light a candle and say a prayer in front of every single one of them. And if that wasn't bad enough, they kept running into all these ladies that they knew, their long-lost buddies: *Cumara* This, *Cumara* That, Mrs. So-'n'-So from across the street, Mrs. Whats-'er-name from down the block, Mrs. Whatchamacallit's mother from downtown, Mrs. Whoochamacallit's sister from *"Brookculino"*, Mrs. Minetti's cousin's mustache's uncle from *"Bushawicka"*…. Fuhgeddaboudit, it took almost *two hours* before we could finally leave the saint-room, walk to back of the church, dip our fingers in the holy water, make the sign of the cross *again*, touch our knee to the floor *again*, and leave the church.

Mom finally let go of my hand, and I didn't waste any time running down the steps.

"Yippeee! Free at Last!"

After we hit the sidewalk and got away from the crowd, I asked Mom if she could take me to get a lemon-ice at Cincotti's bakery, but she said "later" because she was feeling dizzy and wanted to go upstairs to lie down for a while. But good ol' Grandma jumped in right away and said that if I went with her to get a "few things" on First Avenue, she'd buy me one on our way back.

I didn't think twice about tagging along, 'cause, let me tell ya, there was nothing I liked better than hanging out with Grandma. She'd always spoil me like crazy, and she was my "lawyer", like Mom would say, but she was my buddy too, my very best favorite buddy.

Ya know, not for nothin', but I'd always love walking with Grandma. She'd never walk too fast or too slow; she'd always walk just right. And she'd never say nothing about me keeping up with her neither. Nope, she'd always treat me just like a regular kid. That's what I liked best about Grandma. And if anybody would stare—ya know, 'cause of my limp and everything—she'd never get mad and make a big thing out of it; she'd just ignore their stinky behinds like they weren't even there.

21

Well, it looked like Grandma must have found me way too skinny, because she went on a mission to stock up on all my favorite goodies: cherries, watermelon, and honeydew, from the fruit store, ... "mootzarella bella bella", cappicolo, and all my favorite olives from the salumeria, ... fresh, crunchy bread from Maroni's, ... pumpkin seeds and pignoli nuts from the appetizer store, ... and then, finally, what I had been waiting for all day long: a big, ten-cent lemon-ice from Cincotti's.

We took our time walking home, licking away at our lemon-ice— and we even stopped at the feast for a while too. Grandma asked me if I wanted to go on the rides, but I was alone and felt funny about getting on a ride just by myself. And besides, I saw a bunch of kids from the block hanging around, and I was afraid that they might start making fun of me.

When we got home, I had a big shock: there was Grandpa sitting by the window in his undershirt. That's when I knew it must've been a record-breaking scorcher that day, because I don't think I've seen Grandpa in his undershirt more than four or five times in my whole *life*. Nope, even if he was at home and wasn't going no place, he'd always wear his Grandpa uniform: long-sleeve, white shirt, tie, vest (with his pocketwatch chain going from the third button into the little side pocket), gray pants, shiny black shoes, and these see-through, silk socks that he held up with them weird, elastic things called garters.

"Hello Junior," he said, "how's my big boy today—ah?"

I kissed him hello and felt his beard-stubble scratching my cheek. "Fine Grandpa."

"You have-a fun in the *festa*?"

"The church part was boring, but after that I went shopping with Grandma, and that was fun."

"That's-a nice."

Right away I started telling him about the beautiful horse that I'd seen, and the Irish cop, and how he'd let me touch him and everything. And when I got to the part where I told him that the horse's name was "Joey", just like me, he acted really surprised.

"*Madonna mia!* Boy oh boy-a, that's a big *coincidenza*—ah?"

22

I spent the next hour drawing a picture of "Joey" the horse with my crayons on a brown paper bag that Grandma had cut and flattened out for me. It came out pretty good, and when it was all finished, I wrote "Joey" on the bottom, left-hand corner, and "Joey" on the right side too. Everybody seemed to like it a lot, 'specially Grandpa, and even during supper, we all kept looking at it and talking about it because Grandma had taped it to the door of the kitchen cabinet.

As soon as I saw that Grandpa had smoked one of his half-cigarettes by the window—he used to cut his Old Golds in half because he thought he'd smoke less that way—I went to the bathroom to wash up right away to get ready to go with him on his *passegiata*. I didn't even have to ask if I could come along, because whenever I was visiting, I'd always tag along with him on his after-supper stroll.

When we were both ready, we went to the kitchen to kiss Mom and Grandma goodbye, and to see if there was any stale bread that we could take with us to feed the pigeons.

"Wow! That's a lotta bread Grandpa. Them pigeons are gonna have a feast tonight."

"That's-a right, we gonna make them fat."

A bunch of people from outside the neighborhood had come on the block for the feast, and they were still hanging around near the church. But we didn't pay much attention to them. The feast was nothing new to us—same thing every year—and besides, most of the good stuff, like the rides and the games and everything, were around the corner anyway. Grandpa held my hand as we weaved our way through the crowd and walked toward Pleasant Avenue. That's the way we'd always go to the park, the big park with the swimming pool in it.

When we got near the middle of the block, I noticed this fat guy sitting in front of the social club across the street. He was wearing one of them undershirts with no sleeves, and he was sitting on his chair backwards, the way the cowboys always did in the movies. I was surprised to see him out there—you hardly ever saw anyone hanging around in front of the social club—but I guess it must've been too hot inside.

23

I could never understand why Grandpa always made such a big fuss about that place. Nothing ever happened there. To me it looked sort of like a family club or something, because whenever anybody went in or out of there, I'd always see them kissing each other hello and goodbye—like they were brothers, or cousins, or relatives. But according to Grandpa, them social-club guys were bad men, and he'd always tell me to stay away from them and mind my own business. I think maybe that's why he put his big *basilico* plant on the left-hand side of the windowsill, so we couldn't see them, and they couldn't see us.

As we got closer to the club, I noticed these two men walking towards the fat guy sitting in the chair. One was a big, strong-looking guy, and the other one was a skinny, older guy with a big, gigantic nose. I didn't know their names or anything, but I'd seen them on the block lots of times. They both looked a little pissed off—'specially the one with the big nose. My guess was that they were probably mad because the street was all blocked off for the feast, and they couldn't drive their Caddy onto the block and park it in front of the social club like always.

As soon as the fat guy in the undershirt spotted his buddies, he jumped up, kissed both of them on the cheek, and followed them inside. I could feel Grandpa squeezing my hand, and I knew right away he was sending me a message not to be nosy and look. So, I just kept walking. Grandpa didn't even turn his head, and neither did I. We were minding our own business.

The air in the park smelled sweet, like grass and leaves 'n' stuff. It was a little too early to see the lightning bugs, but I knew it wouldn't be long before they'd be flying around all over the place, flashing on and off like a bunch of miniature Christmas-tree bulbs. Some of the teenagers were harmonizing and singing a song over by the pool, but I couldn't pick out the melody though.

Grandpa steered me over to his favorite spot. He called it his "church", because it was underneath these two rows of trees, and when you'd look up, you'd see the treetops touching each other and making an arch—like the inside of a church. It sure was a beautiful place, 'specially in the late afternoon when the sunbeams would pour through the leaves and paint these golden polka-dots all over everything.

24

Grandpa once said that his church was the most beautiful church in the world. And when I asked him why, he said that all the other churches were made by "the hands of men", but his church was made by "the hand of God."

"C'mon, Grandpa, take out the bread."

"*Aspetta*," he said, "there's no pigeon yet. When we see couple-a-them, then we feed. And then when they eat, all their friend gonna come. *Aspetta*, you gonna see."

Well, Grandpa sure had these pigeons pegged alright, because as soon as we spotted one or two and threw out a couple of crumbs, in nothing flat, a whole flock surrounded us, flapping their wings, cooing and gobbling, and fighting each other for food.

"Holy moly! Look at all the pigeons Grandpa! There must be a hundred of 'em! And look at all the different colors: gray, brown, white, brown 'n' white, gray 'n' white, dark gray, dark gray 'n' light gray, black, black 'n' white, everything!

"All the colors....*tutti i colori*"

"Yeah! Every color you can think of. And no two pigeons are the same neither; they all got different combinations and different marks on 'em."

"Just like people...*sunno tutti diferenti, tutti differenti*."

We kept throwing out the bread, but after a while, I started to notice that some of the pigeons kept hogging it all up, and some of the other pigeons weren't getting nothing. It looked to me like some of them were bullies, because they just kept bogarting everything in sight, and the other birds kept scattering and moving away—like they were sacred of them or something. Yep, every time a little crumb fell anywhere near another bird, these bully-pigeons would come running over, growling and pecking, and giving dirty looks, and before you knew it, the scaredy-cat pigeons would back off and leave everything to them.

Grandpa said the bully-pigeons are just like the men from across the street, the social-club guys. I didn't know what he meant by that, but I didn't bother to ask him to explain it or nothing; I was too busy checking out all the different-color birds.

When the bread ran out, Grandpa wiped his palms together, and held them up to the pigeons so they could see them. "Finish-a," he said. "No more bread today, it's all finish-a."

25

I guess the pigeons didn't get the message right away, because they kept sticking around, walking in circles, gurgling and cooing, and looking for more. But after a while, they gave up, and one by one, and a couple at a time, they just kind of wandered off and flew away.

Grandpa took out a scrunched-up half a cigarette from his pack of Old Golds, lit it, and then pointed to the sun over on the west side. Its bottom edge was just starting to touch the rooftops, and when he saw that I was checking it out too, he nodded and turned himself around on the bench to get a better view. I did the same, and we sat there watching as the big, watermelon ball sank behind the buildings and lit up the sky.

"Does your name mean anything, Grandpa? One time I asked Grandma about her last name before she got married, Belcuore, and she told me it means 'beautiful heart'. What does your name mean?"

He took a long puff of his cigarette and thought for a second. "Well, my first name Domenico, mean Sunday in *Italiano*."

"Sunday. Hmm....and what does Posella mean?

"I no think-a Posella mean nothing, Junior, it's just a name."

"Well, even though it don't mean nothin', I still like the way it sounds though. It sounds a lot better than *my* last name, Scalise. I *hate* my name. I mean, I like my first name, Joey, but I don't like Scalise—it sounds ugly"

"What you talk? Scalise is a very nice name. You suppose to like, it's you father name."

"Well, I don't like the way it sounds. Besides, I don't got a father no more anyway."

"What you mean, 'you no got a father'? You got a father, and he love you too."

I had to chuckle at that one. "If he loves me so much, how come he hasn't come around to see me? And how come he hasn't even called me or nothin'—not even for my birthday."

Grandpa didn't answer. I could tell he didn't know what to say, so he just stayed quiet.

"Ya know something Grandpa? Ya know what's a really nice name—Joey Posella. It has a real nice sound, don't it? Yeah...Joey Posella. Boy, I wish I had that name."

26

Grandpa said it was getting late and we should start heading home. I stood up and waited for him while he brushed the breadcrumbs off his lap, looked up to the sky, and made the sign of the cross.

"How come you made the sign of the cross, Grandpa?"

"Because, I leave my church, I gotta say goo'bye to God."

I made the sign of the cross too. Grandpa smiled and took my hand.

Chapter 3

I felt somebody kissing me all over my face, and when I looked up, I saw it was Grandma.

"Hey, sleepy head! C'mon! Get up! Get up or I gonna give you a big punch in the nose!"

I threw the sheet over my head and curled up into a ball, and right away Grandma started playing the punch-in-the-nose game with me: holding me down with one hand, while she gave me a make-believe punch in the nose with the other.

"Oh! You wanna punch in the nose, ah? Okay, I'm gonna give to you. I'm gonna give you a big, big punch in the nose. *Aspetta*."

I giggled and rolled around under the sheet so Grandma couldn't get me, but as soon as I covered my face, she went straight for my ticklish spot, my ribs.

"Stop! Stop, Grandma! Okay! Stop! Okay okay! I'll get up! Wait!"

"C'mon you!" she said, making a fist at me. "Get up, you lazy bum. Go in the bathroom and wash you'self, it's time to get up."

The thing I liked best about Grandma's house was the way she'd always keep the shades up —'specially in the morning. Yeah, when that fresh, happy light came bouncing through them lace curtains, the whole apartment would get filled to the brim with this warm, golden glow. It always was a real happy place to be in. Nothing like *my* house. My house was sad and dreary looking. Even in the summertime, Mom would always keep the venetian blinds pulled all the way down to the bottom, and with the walls painted that dull, ugly green color, I'd feel like I was living in a cave, a dark, gloomy cave.

When I walked in the kitchen, Grandpa was already sitting at his favorite spot, reading *Il Progresso*, the Italian newspaper. Grandma was over by the stove, cooking something, and Mom was sitting against the wall, hunched over a cup of coffee. Her eyes looked all red and swollen, and they had these dark circles under them—probably because she'd been crying again. But she looked to be in a pretty good mood though.

"Good morning Mister Junior," she said, in a nice, cheerful voice. "Wasn't it hot last night? Not even a little breeze or nothin'. How'd you sleep?"

"Okay," I answered, as I went over to the fire-escape window to see if the feast-people had hit the block yet.

Grandma came over and gave me another kiss. "Junior, you wanna some coffee?"

Right away Mom got all excited. "Mama! How you gonna give him coffee? Coffee's no good for kids."

"Celeste, stop. Just a little bit-a, I mix-a with milk."

Then Grandma reached over my shoulder and put a cup of coffee in front of me. It was more milk than coffee, but it still was fun to sit at the table and drink coffee from a cup like a grownup.

I could feel Mom staring at me. "Junior," she said, folding her hands and looking me straight in the eye. "I wanna ask you something."

"What, Ma?

"Well, I don't know if you've noticed, but I've been a little nervous and worried lately. It's because the beauty parlor where I work is going out of business, and pretty soon I'm gonna be out of a job. Understand?"

I looked up and nodded.

"Now you're a smart boy; you know that without a job, I'm not gonna have money to pay the rent and buy food and everything."

"Can't ya get another job, Ma?"

"Yeah, sure, sooner or later. But it can take time. Anyway, I was talking things over with Grandma and Grandpa last night, and they think it's a good idea if we move in with them, even if it's only for a little while—just until I find a new job. What do ya think? Ya think you'd like to live here with Grandma and Grandpa?"

"Are you kidding?! Sure I would! I'd *love* it! I think it's a *great* idea!"

Everybody started smiling, because they all saw how happy I was.

I leaned over and gave Mom a big hug and a big kiss. "Boy oh boy! Thanks, Ma, that's the best news I've heard in a *long* long time!"

"Whoa, hold ya horses, mister! This ain't gonna be a bowl of cherries, ya know. You're gonna have to go to a new school, and make

29

new friends, and be the new kid on the block. And let me tell ya, these little punks around here are a lot tougher than the kids uptown—some of 'em can be really mean."

"I don't care, just the idea of living with Grandma and Grandpa is good enough for me. Hey! Does Aunt Jean and the kids know about it?"

"Well, not yet. But they're coming over in a little while, and we'll tell 'em then."

"Oh boy! Wait 'til Anthony hears I'm gonna be right here all the time, and we can play together after school and on the weekends 'n' stuff. Why don't ya call Aunt Jean on the phone and we can tell 'em now?"

"No, Junior, they're coming over anyway; we'll tell 'em when they get here."

When I heard the doorbell ring, followed by a whole bunch of crazing banging, I went running to open it right away. I knew it had to be my cousins, and as soon as I opened the door, I saw I was right. Yep, there they were, Anthony and Carmela, huffing and puffing and all out of breath. I figured they must've had a race up the stairs to see who'd get to the door first.

"Hello, Junior!" they said, in a doofy, sing-songy voice, as I stepped aside to let them in.

Anthony stuck out his hand like he wanted to shake, but when I reached out for it, he pulled it back real fast and made the "out" sign like in baseball. "Gotcha!" he yelled, laughing like a stupid hyena, with Carmela laughing right along with him.

Anyway, after a minute or two, Aunt Jean walked in, holding little Frankie by the hand.

"Hi, Aunt Jean."

"Hello, Junior," she said, mussing up my hair and giving me a kiss on the cheek.

I bent down and made a face at Frankie and tickled him under the arm.

"Hi, Junior."

It looked like it didn't take Mom, and Grandma and Grandpa, too long to tell Aunt Jean the news, because I could already hear her shouting in the kitchen. "Well, *glory hallelujah!* It's about time! Boy, wait 'til I tell Rocco, he's gonna be so happy."

Then everybody came out into the living room where we were playing. "Hey, kids! Did ya hear?"

"Hear what?" Carmela said.

"Aunt Celeste and Junior are gonna move, and they're gonna come here to live with Grandma and Grandpa!"

"For real, Aunt Celeste?!" Anthony gasped.

Mom patted him on the head. "Yeah, Anthony, it's true."

"Oh boy!" he yelled, as he grabbed be in a headlock and gave me a noogie. "You're gonna be living here with us! Wow!"

Then he stuck out his hand again, and right away I thought he was gonna pull that "gotcha" shit again. But that time Anthony wasn't playing no more of his stupid games. Nope, he just shook my hand like a friend, and said: "Put 'er there partner, welcome to the neighborhood."

Carmela was happy too, and started jumping up and down and clapping, with little Frankie imitating her and doing the exact same thing. "Yippeee!" he yelled. "Yippeee for Junior!"

Aunt Jean grabbed a hold of Mom and started hugging her real tight, saying "thank God" over and over again. And Grandma jumped into the act too, and then all three of them were hugging, and kissing, and slobbering all over each other. I saw Grandpa lift up his glasses and wipe his eyes; I guess even *he* was getting a little teary-eyed.

Mom, Aunt Jean and Grandpa chipped in together and gave us some money to go downstairs to the feast. We went on a couple of rides, and for me that was fun, because at least I wasn't alone, and I could go on with my cousins. And after the rides, we even had enough left over to get a frozen-custard cone. Anthony pulled me over to the side, and as we sat there eating our ice cream, he took over the show and became my guide, pointing out everybody who passed by, and telling me all about the neighborhood. He lived on 111th Streeet , a few blocks away by the big gas tank on First Avenue; but seeing as how Aunt Jean was always visiting Grandma and Grandpa, he'd always spend a lot

31

of time on my what was going to be my new block: 115th Street. He knew mostly all of the kids, and they knew him too.

"Junior, ya see that tall, skinny kid over there waiting to get on the big-swing ride? That's Googie. You gotta watch out for him; he's a real wiseass and he likes to pick on people."

"How'd he get a name like Googie?"

Anthony bit his cone on the bottom and start sucking his ice cream through the hole. "I don't know. I think his last name is Guglielmo, or something like that, but everybody calls him 'Googie' for short. See, Junior, around here practically all the kids got nicknames—'specially if there's another kid who's got the same name like you. Then they *gotta* give you a nickname so they can tell the two of yuz apart."

"Yeah," I answered, wondering how many 'Joeys' there were on my new block.

"But sometimes it don't got nothin' to do with your name; sometimes it has to do with how you look or with something you like to do—like we got 'Skinny Vinny' and 'Fat Vinny". Then we got two Peteys. We call one 'Petey Bubbles,' 'cause he's always got a big blob of bubble gum in his mouth, and we call the other one 'Petey YoYo' 'cause he's always playin' with his yo-yo. But after a while we got a little lazy and wound up dropping the 'Petey' part. Now we just call 'em 'Yo-Yo' and 'Bubbles'."

When the big-swing ride ended, that kid Googie came over with another short kid who Anthony told me was called Paulie. They were walking like they were all drunk and dizzy from the ride.

"Hey, Ant, that ride is a killer," Googie said. "Did you go on yet?"

Anthony tried to play it all cool and everything. "Yeah. It's okay. It ain't no Coney Island ride or nothin', but it's alright."

"So who's the gimpy kid?" Googie asked.

"He's my cousin—and don't call him that. His name's Joey. He's gonna be moving in with my grandparents, and he's gonna be living on the block."

"Oh yeah?" Googie said, wiping his hand on the side of his dungarees and sticking it out to shake. "How ya doin', kid? My name's Googie."

I reached out to take his hand—like a jerk—and as soon as I did, he snatched it back and played the same stupid trick that Anthony had pulled on me a little while ago.

"Gotcha!" he said, laughing like a shithead and pointing his finger at me.

Paulie chimed in too and started laughing and pointing right along with his buddy.

"Don't pay 'em no mind," Anthony said. "C'mon, let's get outa here."

As we got up and walked away, I could feel Googie and Paulie goofing on me, almost as if I had eyes in the back of my head. So right away I started using my tiptoe trick: walking on the toes of my right foot, my short leg, so it evened me out a little and stopped me from limping and waddling from side to side so much. But I knew they were probably snickering and ranking me out anyway.

"Hey, Anthony, "I said, giving him a quick pat on the back. "Thanks."

"Thanks for what?"

"Ya know, thanks for not calling me 'Junior' in front of the kids and everything."

"Aah, c'mon. I know 'Junior' is only for us in the family. I always call you 'Joey' when we're around other kids. Don't I? You know that."

And you know something? He was right. That's what he always did. And he'd never slip up or forget neither—not even once. Yeah, most of the time Anthony was a real pain-in-the-ass, but sometimes, in *some* things, he could be a pretty nice guy.

Seeing as how we'd spent all our money already, we just sort of roamed around the feast, checking things out, and Anthony kept on with his role as my official tour guide.

"See them three guys leaning against the car over there? They're Redwoods."

"What's a Redwood?"

"Redwoods, the *gang*, stupid."

"Oh. How'd they get the name Redwoods?"

"How the hell should I know? One of 'em must've made it up I guess. I think it's got something to do with them big trees they got in California—ya know, that the wood is so old, it's supposed to be all hard

33

like a rock. They probably figured they're hard and tough like a rock too. Who knows? But they sure like to act all rocky though."

"You know their names?"

"Well, the skinny guy combing his hair is Frankie Tee, and the big guy scratching his crotch is Ziggy."

"And what about the other guy?"

"They call him 'Rizz'. He don't try and act all tough and rocky like some of the other guys—he's alright."

"So, what do they do?"

"Who?"

"The Redwoods."

"Not much. Mostly they just hang around by the park, fooling around, goofing on girls, combing their hair a lot and acting all rocky 'n' stuff. But sometimes they rumble."

"You mean like gang fights?"

"Yeah, they're always fighting with the Spanish gangs on the other side of Third Avenue. In the summertime—like now—most of the fights usually get started over at the big pool in the park, but during the rest of the year, the fights always jump off by the high school down the block. See, the Redwoods got this thing that they try and make the Colored and the Puerto Rican guys pay 'protection money' to 'em, just so they can pass through the neighborhood and go back and forth from the high school without getting jumped. That's what starts most of the fights, 'cause after a while, the PR's and the Colored get tired of that 'protection' bullshit, and they figure they're better off just fighting it out."

"So that's all they do is hang around and have fights?"

"Yeah, pretty much. But sometimes they sing."

"Sing?" I asked, thinking to myself that it could've been them that I'd heard in the park last night with Grandpa.

"Yeah. They sing harmony 'n' stuff—mostly at night. Usually they like to sing in the hallways 'cause they like the sound of the echo, but in the summer, they sing on the corner, or over in the park behind the pool. Some of 'em even put together a real singing group—and they sound pretty good too. Frankie Tee over there is the lead singer."

As Anthony was explaining about the singing 'n' stuff, these three kids walked over to the Redwood guys and started talking to them. They

34

looked to be only a couple of years older than me and Anthony, and it was easy to see that the big guys didn't want to be bothered with them. And it looked like the younger kids got the message too, because after a minute or two, they just walked away, looking all stupid and embarrassed."

"Who are they?" I asked.

"Oh, them three. I call 'em 'The Three Stooges'. They're a big pain-in-the-ass; they think they're hot shit just 'cause they belong to the Baby Redwoods."

"What's the Baby Redwoods?"

"Well, the Redwoods got different divisions that go according to your age. You got the Senior Redwoods, the Junior Redwoods, the Baby Redwoods....and even the Redwood Debs too—ya know, for the girls and everything."

"So them three are Baby Redwoods?"

"They *say* they are, but I think it's more like they *wanna* be Baby Redwoods. Who knows? All I know is that I hate their guts—all three of 'em."

"What are their names?"

"Well, we used to call the skinny one 'Boney Tony', but now he wants to be called 'Toney Bones' 'cause he thinks it makes him sound all tough and whatnot. His real name is Anthony, like me, but since they started calling *him* 'Tony', nobody calls *me* 'Tony'. They just call me 'Anthony', or 'Ant' for short. I woulda liked 'Tony' a whole lot better, but what can ya do?"

"Hmm, and who are the other two?"

"The doofus with all the greasy stuff on his hair is called 'Jerry Grease'. He got called that 'cause he's always got a pound and a half of lard on his hair."

"And who's the other kid?" I asked.

Anthony took a long, sneery look at the third kid, and then spit on the ground. "Him? That's 'The Face-That-Only-a-Mother-Could-Love': Bobby Zito. But I got my own name for him, I call him 'Fartface'. He's the biggest pain-in-the-ass of them all, a real bully. He swears he's all tough and big 'n' bad, and he loves to pick on all the kids on the block—'specially anybody who's smaller than him. Everybody hates his guts."

35

"I can see why." I said. "I don't even know the guy, but he looks like a real creep."

Carmela and a few of her girlfriends came by a few minutes later, but I was too shy to say very much, so Anthony did most of the talking. He introduced me as 'my cousin Joey', and after we stayed with them for a while and we talked about what grade I was in and what school I'd be going to, all the girls chimed in together and said, "welcome to the neighborhood". Then they walked off and went on their way, sneaking peeks at me over their shoulders and giggling to each other.

"Hey, Junior," Anthony said, "How ya like that girl Angela? Real pretty, huh?"

"Which one was that?"

"The one eating the pumpkin seeds."

"Oh."

"A lotta guys like her; they say she looks like Annette from the Mickey Mouse Club."

As I was thinking to myself that Angela really *did* look a lot like Annette, all of a sudden, this big, fat guy sneaks up behind Anthony , grabs him in a choke hold, and starts rubbing his knuckles on his head— giving him these sliding noogies 'n' stuff.

"Get off!" Anthony yelled, slamming the guy with a real hard elbow to the stomach.

The kid let go and doubled over right away, moaning and groaning and holding his belly.

"Damn! What's a matter with you, Anthony, can't ya take a joke? I was only foolin' around over here!"

The guy was real, real fat, and the kid with him, who was chewing away on this big blob of bubble gum, was a little on the chubby side too.

"Oh, it's you!" Anthony said. "Sorry, Sally, I didn't know who it was." Then he looked over at the other kid. "'Ey, Bubbles."

"'Ey, Anthony."

"What yuz doin'?"

Bubbles kept chomping on his gum. "Nothin', just walkin' around the feast, same as you."

By now the fat kid had stopped rubbing his stomach and was standing up straight again, just kind of looking around and scoping

36

everything out. "This shit is getting boring already," he said, with a disgusted look on his face. "Everything is money, money, money. I spent everything *I* had three hours ago; now all I can do is walk around and look."

"Yeah, fuhgeddaboudit, money goes like water around here."

"Who's he?" Bubbles asked, pointing to me and blowing this big bubble that just kept growing and getting bigger, and bigger, and bigger.

Right away Anthony stuck a lightning-fast finger in the bubble, and after it popped all over Bubbles' face, he just laughed and said, "My cousin Joey."

"C'mon, Ant! What ya do that for?"

While Bubbles was busy picking all the sticky, pink gook off his nose and his mouth, the fat kid turned to me and nodded his head. "'Ey, Joey, my name's Sally, and the dingleberry over there with all the pink shit on his face is Bubbles."

I chuckled as Bubbles gave Sally a shot in the arm for calling him a 'dingleberry', and then I nodded back to both of them and said hi.

Anthony put his arm around me and said, "Joey's gonna be livin' on the block from now on; he's moving in with my grandparents."

"Cool."

By now Bubbles had his gum back in his mouth and was chewing away again. "Hey, there's some of the guys!" he said, pointing down towards the end of the block. "C'mon."

Bubbles and Sally ran to join the guys, but me and Anthony just followed along behind—ya know, 'cause I couldn't really run that fast. Most of the time, Anthony would remember about my limp and would stick with me, but sometimes he'd just run off and leave me behind. I couldn't really blame him though. I knew he didn't do it on purpose or anything; he was only a kid, like me, and sometimes he'd just forget.

"So, Junior, that's Petey Bubbles, the guy I was telling you about before."

"Yeah, I figured that was him—ya know, with the gum and everything"

"Yeah. And the other kid, the fat guy, is called 'Sally Pork'. I don't know if they call him that 'cause his father owns the pork store on First Avenue, or 'cause he's a big fat slob and he looks like Porky Pig. Take your pick."

We followed Bubbles and Sally and walked over to a bunch of guys who were sitting in the shade on a stoop near the corner. I could feel my heart pounding as we got closer, because I thought they were going to start goofing on my walk 'n' stuff. But they were busy talking to Bubbles and Sally, and it looked like they really hadn't noticed me. Anthony nodded to them and sat down on the stoop. I did the same.

Little Paulie and that shithead Googie were there, along with this other kid who was flipping a yo-yo. Right away I knew he was probably the "Petey Yo-Yo" guy that Anthony had told me about before. And while the group was just sitting there talking, these two other kids came over, nodded to everybody, and sat down. Anthony whispered to me that the kid with the short, crew-cut was Pasqualino—"Lino" for short—and the tall guy with him was called "Joey Vee".

Shit! I'd been hoping that all along I'd be the only "Joey" on the block. But what can I tell ya? I guess I just didn't have no luck—no luck at all.

Anyway, it didn't take long for everybody to get bored just sitting around bullshitting, and that was when that Googie guy started mumbling and grumbling. "Fuckin' feast," he said, giving everything and everybody the finger with both hands. "This shit is getting to be one big pain-in- the-ass—that's all I can say."

"Yeah," Sally said. "You can't even *move* around here no more; every square inch of the place is packed with wall-to-wall people. *Madon'*, I never knew there were so many jerks in this neighborhood."

All of a sudden, the tall kid, Joey Vee, chimed in, and I heard him talk for the first time.

"They ain't all from here," he said. "Most of 'em come from the outside. Ya got uptown assholes, downtown assholes, assholes from the Bronx, assholes form Brooklyn—they're from all over the place. Looks like every *paisan'* in the whole city of New York is here today."

Petey Yo-Yo wound up the string on his yo-yo and put his two cents in. "You ain't kidding. It's fun at the beginning—when you got some money to play the games and go on the rides 'n' stuff—but after that, forget it. You need the Chase Manhattan Bank for this shit—everything cost an arm and a leg."

"You tellin' me?" Paulie grumbled. "These feast-people are all a bunch of crooks. Like that lady selling lemon-ice over there; she wants

38

a dime for the same shitty little cup that cost only a nickel on First Avenue."

Well, little by little, and one by one, every kid took their turn to bitch and moan about the feast, and how the neighborhood was so crowded that there was no room for us to play, or move around, or do anything at all. It was like we were prisoners in our own neighborhood.

That's when Joey Vee got his bright idea. "So fuck this shit," he said. "Let's go on the other side of First Avenue. We got the whole block to ourselves over there. Let's play something, let's play ball or somethin'."

Everybody liked the idea, but it turned out that nobody had a ball, and nobody had no money to buy one neither. That's when Anthony remembered my brand-new Spauldeen.

"C'mon, Joey, let us use your ball. Look! Grandpa's looking out the window. Ya don't even have to go upstairs to get it."

I wanted to say no, but I figured that since I was the new kid, lending out my ball probably would be a good way for me to get to know the guys and to make friends with them.

Googie must've overheard me and Anthony talking, and right away he seemed to like the idea. "Go 'head!" he said. "You two get the ball, and the rest of us will check out the cellars and see if we can find a broomstick to use for a bat."

So, while the guys split up and went into three different cellars to look for a broomstick, me and Anthony went under the window and started calling up to Grandpa.

"Grandpa! Grandpa! Hey, Grandpa! Grandp…"

When he finally heard us, he looked down and said, "Whatsa matter?"

"Grandpa, do me a favor?"

He didn't answer, he just touched his fingertips together as if to say "what?".

"Throw me down my pink ball! It's in the box on the floor next to the Victrola! Please!"

He made the *aspetta* sign and disappeared inside. Then, a minute later, he stuck his head out the window, and keeping it real close to the building so he wouldn't bean anybody, he dropped the ball down to us.

"Thanks Grandpa!"

39

Anthony cupped his hand around his mouth to make his voice louder. *"Listen, Grandpa, we're going over on the other side of First Avenue to play ball. Okay? We'll be* back *later for supper!"*

Grandpa held up his hand and nodded his head.

"Bye Grandpa!"

By the time we walked up to the corner, the guys were all circled around Joey Vee who had stuck a mop-handle into a sewer and was twisting and jiggling it around, trying to pry off the metal tip, so we could use the rest of it for a stickball bat. He wasn't having any luck, but after Googie took over and gave it three or four tries, the metal tip finally came loose and plopped into the sewer.

"See?" Googie bragged, puffing up his chest and pointing to himself with his thumbs. "It takes a man to do a man's job."

Joey Vee gave him the finger. "Get the fuck outa here, Googie, you did it 'cause I loosened for ya."

"Yeah, right. Keep dreamin'."

Joey Vee didn't bother to answer, he just grabbed his crotch.

Well, after we got over to the other side of First Avenue, it took about a half an hour for everybody to argue back and forth and decide that Joey Vee and Googie were going to be the team captains. I knew it was going to be them two before the arguing even started. What a waste of time.

Anyway, after they picked odds or evens, Googie and Joey Vee, did the usual once-twice-three-shoot and chose up sides. And, as usual, I wound up being the odd-man-out because nobody wanted me. Nobody even seemed to notice, and as Joey Vee and Googie were about to choose for who's-up-first, Anthony had to step in and stop them.

"Hold it! Wait! What about my cousin over here?!"

"What about him?" Joey Vee said. "I don't want him. Let Googie take him."

"What am I gonna do with a gimpy little shrimp? He probably can't even run. *You* take him."

"Don't try pawning him off on me, Googie, I don't want him."

40

Anthony jumped in between the two of them, and this time he was really pissed. "Wait a minute, that ain't fair! It's his ball, ya know! If it wasn't for him, none of yuz would be playing!"

"I don't care," Googie said, "I don't want him on my team; all he's gonna do is make outs and help us lose. How's he gonna run the bases? The gimpy little bastard can hardly *walk*—how's he gonna run?!"

"Well fuhgeddaboudit then. If he ain't playing, I ain't playing neither!"

"So don't play Anthony!" Googie yelled. "Who gives a shit!"

"Alright, so then we're leaving. Gimme the ball."

Right away Paulie walked over to Anthony. "Aw, c'mon, Ant, now *none* of us can play. Don't be like that."

"Yeah," Bubbles said, "It ain't fair. It ain't fair for nobody."

I tug on Anthony's shirt, and when he bends down, I whisper in his hear: "Maybe I could be official pitcher for both teams. That way everybody can play, and we don't have to break up the game."

Anthony stepped back and looked me in the eye. "You sure?"

"Yeah, I don't mind."

It took another round of arguing to convince Googie and Joey Vee that I knew how to pitch on one bounce—like for stickball—and when they finally accepted the idea, we were finally ready to start.

"*Chips on the ball! Twenty-five cents!*" Anthony yelled. "*That's my cousin's ball! You lose it, you pay!*"

I pitched it good to Anthony's team, nice and slow, right over the plate, and they got a lot of hits. I pitched it good to the other team too—to everybody except Googie that is. When he'd be up, I'd grab the ball between my thumb and my middle two fingers, and flick it, sidearm style, with a little English on it, so it would take all these crazy hops after it came off the bounce.

Ya know, not to blow my own horn or nothin', but when I'd throw them sidearm, knuckle balls of mine, hardly nobody could hit them. Googie had been trying his ass off, but he just kept striking out, again, and again, and again. He hit nothing but air, three times in a row, and

41

he was getting pissed. He kept cursing me out and calling me all kinds of names, but I just stayed quiet and kept dishing out my knuckle balls.

"C'mon, ya shrimpy little prick, pitch it over the plate! And stop putting that spin on the ball, I can see what you're doin'."

Swish!

"Oh, ya think you're slick, huh? What'sa matter, you afraid? Afraid I might send it down the block on ya? C'mon, shrimpy-gimpy boy, pitch it nice and slow, the same way you been pitching it to the other team. I dare ya."

Swish!

"Hey! Stop fuckin' around!"

"Wha'? I ain't doin' nothin'."

"Yeah, right! You better knock it off, you crippled little midget. Give me a decent pitch over here!"

I couldn't have cared less about Googie—I didn't like that creep from the first minute I laid eyes on him when he came out with that "gimp" stuff in front of the big-swing ride—but since his team was losing and falling farther and farther behind, the rest of the guys on his team started picking up on that "gimp" stuff too. And then everybody and their mother, even the guys the Anthony's team, were all calling me either "Gimp" or "Shrimp" or both.

Anyway, as I was fingering the ball behind my back, all of a sudden, I felt somebody sneaking up behind me. I spun around to see who it was, but before I could do anything, this kid grabbed my arm, ripped the ball right out of my hand, and started yelling *Saloogi!* at the top of his lungs.

It was that "Face-That-Only-a-Mother-Could-Love" guy: Bobby Zito. I remembered him right away from before, when Anthony pointed him out to me at the feast. He had his two buddies with him, "Tony Bones" and that skeevy "Grease" kid, along with some other tall kid who I didn't know.

Well, now that everybody saw what was happening, Anthony and Joey Vee both came running in from the outfield. They tried their best to get the ball back, but the four shitheads kept throwing it around, laughing and yelling *Saloogi! Saloogi!* and keeping it just out of reach of anybody who got near it.

Anthony got pissed and went right up into Bobby Zito's mug. "Give us the ball back!"

"Who's gonna make me? You and what army?

"Me, myself, and..."

Before Anthony could say the word "I", Bobby Zito pushed him so hard that he lost his balance and fell over backwards. Anthony tried to scramble back on his feet right away, but this Zito kid beat him to the punch, and stood over him with his fists clenched and this mean look on his face.

"C'mon, punk," he growled. "What ya gonna do? Hah? Ya think you're tough? Go 'head, try somethin'."

Anthony kept tryin' to get up, but Bobby Zito gave him a big kick in the stomach and knocked him back down again.

Joey Vee and Googie both ran over to help Anthony, but as soon as they did, Tony Bones, the "Grease" kid and the other one, came running over too. It looked to me like Googie and Joey Vee must've been scared or something, because when they came face to face with Bobby Zito's buddies, they just backed off and stayed quiet. And so did the rest of us.

At that point, the show was pretty much over. Nobody said nothing, and nobody did nothing neither. We all backed down, and once the four shitheads saw that they had won, it was time for them to celebrate.

That stupid-looking "Bones" kid, snatched the bat right out of Lino's hand, and we all stood by like dingleberries, while the four creeps took turns "taking shots" and hitting them out to each other. Everybody kept yelling, "Give back our stuff!", and "C'mon, finish already!", but they'd answer, "We'll finish whenever the fuck we feel like it, and if you don't like it, then do something about it!"

Well, even though we outnumbered these bastards two to one, nobody was about to do nothing. Nope, they were a little older, a little bigger, and a whole lot tougher than us, and everybody was scared of them. And they knew it too.

They took all their sweet time "taking shots" and finishing their stupid game, and after a while, the rest of our guys got tired of waiting around and doing nothing. So, one by one, like rats leaving a sinking

43

ship, they all cut out and went home. It was getting late, and me and Anthony had to leave too, but I wanted my ball back, so we just had to stay put and wait it out.

"C'mon!" Anthony yelled, "We gotta go, give us back our ball!"

Bobby Zito twirled the bat and tossed it to the tall kid, the one I didn't know. "Ten more minutes. Tommy gotta get his shots."

Well, them ten minutes turned into twenty minutes, and by then me and Anthony *really* had to start getting home.

"'Ey, c'mon already." Anthony begged, "Give my cousin his ball back. It's almost six o'clock, and he's gotta get home."

Bobby Zito held out the Spauldeen to me like he was holding out a carrot to a horse. "Ya want the ball, kid? C'mon, come and get it."

Well, since all I wanted was to get my ball back and go home, without even thinking—like a shithead—I started walking towards the guy, chasing after him and grabbing for it.

"Hey guys!" Zito yelled, "look at this little shrimp over here; the gimpy bastard can't even *walk!* 'Ey, Anthony what's a matter with ya cousin? What's he got—polio or what?"

I don't know what came over me, but when I heard that stupid asshole come out with that "polio" shit, I just couldn't control myself no more.

"Fuck you!" I yelled, limping closer and closer. "Gimme my ball!"

As soon as Bobby Zito's buddies saw me going off like that, they all made a circle around me and started sounding me out, making fun of me and imitating my limp. And the more pissed off I got, the better they liked it. They were having the time of their lives, laughing their asses off and pointing at me, like they were scoping out a freak in a goddamn freak show. I felt like crying, but was trying my best to hold it in. Anthony kept trying to pull me back, but it was no use; I'd already gone completely apeshit, and I just kept pushing him away and chasing after my ball, cursing and calling these creeps every name in the book. Bobby Zito kept holding the ball a few inches from my face, teasing me with it and holding it just a little out of my grip, and every time I'd make a grab for it, he'd toss it to one of his buddies. And then, when I'd get near that guy, he'd throw it to somebody else—just like a big game of saloogi, with me in the middle, running back and forth and making a real jackass out of myself.

44

Just when I couldn't take it no more and I was about to break down and cry, Bobby Zito took the ball and put it behind his back, waving me on and teasing me to come closer and closer.

"Hey, Gimp, you want the ball? Hah? Ya want it?"

"Yeah! Give it to me!"

"You sure?"

"Yeah!"

"Okay."

All of a sudden, he took this big wind-up, and before I could do anything to stop him, I saw my beautiful Spauldeen go sailing over the roof across the street.

Then he gave me an ugly smile and said: "Well, go get it."

Damn! I couldn't believe it. After me and Anthony waited around like two blobs of dogshit for almost an hour, just to get my ball back, this rotten son-of-a-bitch goes and roofs it on me. What a *bastard!*

But his buddies thought he'd just done the greatest thing in the world, and they were having one hell of a laugh—ha-ha-ha-ha-ha. And they kept right on laughing, slapping each other five, pointing at me, making faces, giving me the finger, and laughing some more, as they bopped all the way up the block and turned the corner.

I wanted to go up to the roof and get my ball right away, but Anthony talked me out of it. He said we were already a half an hour late for supper, and if we didn't get home right away, we were gonna get it.

As we walked home, I started to feel sorry that I'd even come downstairs in the first place. I probably would've been better off if I would've stayed upstairs and watched the feast from the window with Grandpa. 'Cause let me tell ya, you didn't have to be a genius to figure out that I was going to get stuck with that "Gimp" shit—just like the two Peteys got branded with "Yo-Yo" and "Bubbles". Yeah, I should've just stayed upstairs with Grandpa. At least I'd still have my real name...and my ball.

45

Chapter 4

Even though I had to deal with some bad stuff, I was still happy that we'd come to live with Grandma and Grandpa. I missed some of my school friends and some of the kids I used to play with in front of the house, but outside of them, I liked my new neighborhood, East Harlem, a lot better. That's because I was with my two favorite buddies, and every morning when Grandma would pull up them shades and let in that beautiful golden light, I'd say a little prayer and thank God for getting me out of that dark, miserable cave I used to live in. I hated that place—'specially with Mom and Dad fighting all the time.

Grandma and Grandpa would fight sometimes too, but it'd only be screaming-and-yelling fights—no slapping, and punching, and throwing things around. Well, maybe that wasn't true, because there was this one time when Grandpa got real mad about something just before we were about to sit down for supper, and he took this plate of fish and threw it against the wall. I didn't know what had gotten Grandpa so teed-off that he threw the fish, but he must've been really mad though, because after he threw it, he grabbed his hat and walked straight out the door. He didn't slam it hard the way Dad used too, but when he left all of sudden like that, I started to feel kind of scared and nervous. That's why I stayed glued to the window, hoping and praying I'd see him turn the corner and come walking back towards the building again. But after a couple of hours, Grandpa came back though. And after a couple of days, everybody forgot about the whole thing, and him and Grandma went right back to being friends again—just like nothing happened.

Thank God for that, because who was I going to pal around with after supper if Grandpa wasn't around no more? Yeah, going with Grandpa on his *passeggiata* was one of my favorite things. That's when we'd have a chance to be alone, just us guys, and that's when he'd answer all my questions and explain things to me—and tell me stories too.

I liked it best when he'd talk to me about Italy. Sometimes it'd be a little hard for him—he was a lot more comfortable talking Italian than he was talking English—but when he didn't know how to say something in English, he'd just say it in Italian, and most of the time I'd be able to understand it.

Anyway, half in English and half in Italian, as we'd feed the pigeons or scope out the river from the end of the pier, Grandpa would paint me word-pictures of *Italia*. It sounded like a real beautiful place, and I've always hoped that someday before I die, maybe I could get a chance to check it out.

One time he told me about his hometown, Borgia, in Calabria. He pointed to his shoe and explained to me that Italy is shaped like this big, long, high-heel boot, and that the instep of the boot was Calabria. But that wasn't good enough for me though; I wanted to know exactly where Borgia was, so I could find it in case I'd ever be in the neighborhood.

Grandpa laughed and pointed to the joint above his big toe and said: "That's Borgia."

When I asked him to tell me what it looked like, he said it's a small town of about five or six thousand people, it's very clean, and it's up in the hills on top of a mountain. Then he got this faraway look on his face and started remembering more and more stuff about it. He said the air smelled *"fresca e dolce"*, and even though it could get pretty hot in the daytime, in the evening, a cool breeze would blow in over the mountains to chase away the heat and make it feel nice and comfortable at night. Then he described the big hill at the entrance of the town, and the little fountain and the *piazza* in front of the main church with these fat palm trees on both sides. It wasn't one of them fancy piazzas like in Rome, but he said that the church was nice—maybe a little dirty on the outside, but on the inside, it was *"veramente bella"*.

According to Grandpa, they got this life-size statue of *La Madonna* in there that was like one of them mannequin things that you see in the store windows. She was dressed in a black dress, made out of real cloth, and right in the middle of her chest, she had a big silver heart with seven daggers piercing it from all sides. Grandpa said the idea of the statue was to show how bad a mother feels when she loses a son—'specially the Virgin Mary because of the way Jesus got killed right in front of her and she had to watch it and everything. I asked him if he thought the women in the town dressed in black because they were copying *La Madonna* in the church. He said he didn't know, but he told me that

47

more than half the women in the town looked like nuns because they were keeping *"luto"* for a death in the family, and they'd always dress in black and cover their heads with these black shawls.

Naturally, being a kid, I wanted to know what it was like for him when he was little. He said he had a rough time because his teachers were so strict and mean. One time, just because he kept mispronouncing the word for harpoon in Italian, his teacher thought he was trying to be a wiseass, and he beat Grandpa so bad on his leg with a stick that they had to put these blood-sucker things called leeches on it because it had gotten infected.

Yeah, it looked like Grandpa must've had it pretty rough as a kid, what with his mother dying and having to take care of his little sister—and all them mean teachers and whatnot. But he said there were still times when he could play with his friends and have fun like a regular kid. He didn't have no toys or nothing, but he said the kids would always make up games and find some way of having a good time—like going to the olive grove at the edge of town and playing *"banditi."* I took a guess and said that the game sounded like it was probably an Italian version of cops and robbers, and Grandpa said I was right, because that's exactly what it was.

Talking with Grandpa was fun; he'd always come out of nowhere with some real interesting stories, and nine times out of ten, they were always about some of my favorite stuff. Like for instance, he knew I loved to draw and paint, so he was always telling me stories about all the great Italian artists—like Leonardo Da Vinci, Michelangelo, Raffaello, Bellini, Donatello... I forget all the names. But Grandpa would tell me all about them.

Yeah, I got hand it to Grandpa. He was only a tailor, and he didn't have too much schooling, but he knew all about painting, and sculpture, and opera, and all the big stars like Caruso and that Toscanini guy he liked so much. See, to Grandpa, the greatest honor in the world was to be a great artist. He really admired the hell out of them people—'specially if they were Italian.

One time I asked him what he thought about Rocky Marciano, because he was big and famous and was Italian too, but Grandpa just chuckled to himself and called him a *"cafone"*. I could never figure out why he said that.

48

Anyway, there was this one story he'd tell me about this famous painter called Giotto. I still don't know if it was really true, but according to Grandpa it was. It went like this:

Once upon a time, the Pope sent word out to all the best artists all over Italy for them to come to *"Roma"*, because he needed a great artist to do a big, important job for the Church. So, they came from all over, and when they got to Rome, they all lined up in this place called the *"Vaticano"*, so they could talk to the Pope and try and convince him that they were the "man for the job". Each of them brought along either a painting or a sculpture as a sample of their work, so the Pope could get an idea of how good they were at drawing, and painting, and sculpting 'n' stuff. Well, as usual, the Pope took all his sweet time, but little by little, one by one, all the artists moved up on the line, and finally, each one got their chance to bullshit with the Pope for a few minutes and show him their stuff.

Anyway, at the end of the line was this little guy called Giotto, and when the Pope asked him to show him his work, he told him he didn't bring nothing because he's Giotto and he don't have to prove how good he is to nobody. Well, as soon as the people standing around hear him say that, they all break out laughing and start goofing on him and pointing their fingers at him like he's the biggest jackass on the face of the earth.

The Pope thought he sounded kind of weird too, so he says: "'Ey, Giotto, what'sa matter you? You crazy, or what? How can I give you the job if ya didn't even bring nothin' to show me over here?"

Giotto just stands there, cool as a cucumber, and while everybody is laughing their asses off and goofing on him like crazy, he turns to the Pope, and in a very polite voice, he asks him if he may please have a piece of paper and a pencil.

"Sure!" says the Pope, snapping his fingers at one of his servants. And before you can say *Dominus vobiscum*, one of the Pope's boys comes running back with a pencil and paper.

Giotto says *"grazie"* and stands up real straight. And then, after he gives a dirty look to all the people who were goofing on him, he takes the pencil in his hand, and ba-da-*bing!,* with one flick of the wrist, he draws a *perfect circle* and hands it to the Pope without saying a word.

49

When the Pope sees how perfect that circle is, his eyes pop right out of his head and his jaw drops straight to the floor. *"Madonna mia!"* he gasps, "I think I just find the man for the job!"

Yeah, that was one of my favorite Grandpa stories. He had a whole bunch of them like that, about a whole lot of different things. Usually they were about Italy, but since I'd moved in and was already part of the neighborhood, he started telling me a lot of stuff about the men across the street, the social-club guys. I guess he figured it was his duty to open my eyes so I wouldn't be *"pidyatu pe' fesso"*, taken for a fool.

See, according to Grandpa them guys across the street were nothing but a bunch of *"gangisti"* (that's how you say gangsters in Italian), and they're all *"ingordi pe' i sordi"*, greedy for money. He said they're like them bully-pigeons in the park, the ones who'd always have their beaks in everybody else's food and would want to bogart everything for themselves by pecking at the other birds and giving them dirty looks. Grandpa used to say that the dirty look was their favorite weapon, because all they had to do was hurt a couple of people real bad, every once in a blue moon, and then, after the news spread around from mouth to mouth, all they needed after that was one of their professional dirty looks, and everybody and their mother would just shit in their pants. That's why he'd always call them the "Champeen-a from the Dirty Look", the Dirty-Look Champs.

But I think the thing that really used to tick Grandpa off about these guys, is the way they always throw the word *"rispetto"* around all the time, like they really know something about it.

Grandpa would say that they're all a bunch of *"ipocriti"*, hypocrites, because, according to him, they wouldn't know what respect was if they got hit over the head with it.

See, to Grandpa, respect means that you show kindness and consideration to everything and everybody, no matter how big or small they are, because "in the eyes of God, the elephant and the ant are both the same size". Back then I wasn't so sure I understood exactly what that "elephant and ant" stuff was all about, but I learned one thing though: all that kissing and hugging them guys were always doing didn't fool *me* no more. Uh-uh, Grandpa taught me that stuff is nothing but a big, phony show, and when push comes to shove, none of them got no respect for nobody—not even for God on the cross. The only thing those

50

guys care about is making money, "bisinissa", and if you're good for business then you're their friend, but if you're bad for business, or if you get in the way of business, then you're like a stone in their shoe and they got to "take you out". At first, I didn't understand Grandpa when he came out with that "take you out" stuff, but when he took his finger and slid it real slow across his throat, I got the picture right away.

But respect wasn't the only thing that bugged Grandpa about these guys, he'd always make a big stink about that *"onore"* stuff too. That would really burn Grandpa's behind like crazy—'specially when these guys would have the nerve to call themselves *"uomini d'onore"*, men of honor. He'd always say that a real man of honor doesn't go around stealing, and killing, and hurting people and doing bad things like they do. To him, a man of honor is a man who is three things: *"buono, rispettoso, e onesto"*, good, respectful, and honest. And of the three things, I think the one that was most important to Grandpa was the third one: honesty. Yep, Grandpa was real big on honesty, and he was big on keeping your word too. See, because to Grandpa, a real man is someone who always speaks the truth, and who always, always, always, keeps his word, all the time, with everybody, no matter what. That's a real man. He'd say a man gives his word because he's going to keep it, and if he doesn't keep it, then he ain't really a man. This was a really big thing with Grandpa. Are you kidding? He couldn't *stomach* people who'd say one thing, and then go and do something else. To him that was a big, big *"vergogna"*, a big disgrace.

I think that was probably the main reason why he didn't like the social-club guys. That's because their word is only good when it's good for business, but when things change and it ain't good for business no more, then their word goes straight down the toilet. That's why he'd always keep telling me to stay away from them, because they say one thing today, and then tomorrow it don't mean shit. They can never be trusted.

"Duva li lasha, no li trova", that's what Grandpa would always say: "Where you leave 'em, you don't find 'em."

He'd call them "two face", because they're always wearing a fake mask to cover up what's really going on inside their brains. This is how they fool you and catch you off guard. He'd say they're all a bunch of

51

Academy-Award actors, and every last one of them is as phony as a three-dollar bill.

Grandpa would say that in Calabria, where he came from, real men don't bother with shit like that. Like for instance, if a guy is really mad at you and he wants to kill you—like for a *"vendetta"* or something like that—he'll go right up to your house, knock at your door, curse you out, and tell you to come outside and fight it out, face to face, man to man. But these social-club guys never do stuff like that. Nope, if they want to kill you, they do just the opposite: they sweet-talk you and get all buddy-buddy and chummy-chummy with you. Sometimes they even take you out and buy you supper to make you think that you're their favorite friend in the world, and then, when you're nice and happy, sipping coffee, eating dessert, and you got a nice, creamy piece of *cannolo* in your mouth, *BAM!,* they whip out a gun and blow your brains out all over the table. Grandpa would say that only cowards and sneaky snakes do stuff like that. That's why he'd always tell me not to fall for the "I'm your buddy" routine, with the phony smile and the pat on the back, because with these guys, the same place where they pat you on the back, is the same place where they "stick the knife".

But then he'd say that the "I'm your buddy" stuff wasn't the only thing to watch out for. They have another slick move that they use all the time: giving you gifts and doing you favors. Yeah, Grandpa would always tell me never to be a damn fool and accept no gifts or favors from these guys; that's how they trick you and suck you into doing business with them. Because when you don't take no gifts or favors, then you're both equal, but once you're stupid enough to take a gift or accept a favor, then you ain't equal no more. Nope, now they're higher than you, and you're lower than them—like they're your boss and they *own* your stinky ass. And these guys never let you forget about it neither; they'll hold that shit over your head and rub your nose in it for the rest of your life. Then, God forbid, somewhere down the line they ask *you* to do something for *them*. Fuhgeddaboudit, there's no way in hell you can say no to them then. You're stuck forever and ever—and there's no getting out neither.

Grandpa would say that's the worst part of the whole thing, because once you get in too deep and you know too much about their "dirty *bisinissa*", then you're dangerous to them because you can talk and rat them out. That's why he'd always keep drumming it in my head every chance he'd get: never take no gifts or accept any favors from these guys—no matter what.

But then he'd pull it back a little: "You no need this people to be you friend...but you no need this people to be you enemy. That's why when you say 'no' to them, you gotta use you head and say 'no' in a nice, polite way, *diplomaticamente*. You undastand?"

I could understand pretty much everything Grandpa had to say about them social-club guys, but when he'd whip out them big, fourteen-karat words like "diplomaticamente", that's when I'd get a little lost. But I knew one thing though; every time Grandpa would get into one of his lectures about the social-club guys, he'd always finish it off with the same exact words, every single time: "*Medyu sulo e no mal acompagnatu*"—you're better off by yourself than with bad friends.

And you know who else had a big thing about bad friends? Grandma. Only with her it was like a broken record: over and over and over, day in and day out, every single day.

See, Grandpa would always be busy doing his usual Grandpa stuff, but Grandma would always be paying real close attention to who I was hanging around with—and she'd always have something to say about: this kid, that kid, the other kid, this kid's brother, the other kid's father.... Fuhgeddaboudit, if I would've let Grandma weed out my friends, there would've been nobody left to play with in the whole damn neighborhood!

And she had names for them too: this one's a *"fetente"*, that one's a *"scustumatu"*, the other one is a *"mascalzone"*, the one from down the block is a *"strunz'"*, the one from around the corner is a *"lazzarone...*. She had names for everybody—even for Bobby Zito. Yep, she really hated his guts ever since she seen him trying to steal my scooter one time. From that day on, every time she'd see him, she'd make this ugly sound in the back of her throat—like she was trying to cough up a phlegm ball—and then she'd spit on the ground and call him *"Faccia 'e Merda"*—Shitface.

But besides watching out for me getting mixed up with bad friends, her main mission in life was to fatten me up and make me grow. She tried everything—even this stinky, cod-liver-oil stuff that tasted like it came from a dead fish that had been lying out in the sun for a couple of weeks. And none of it worked—not even that "Super Grow" junk that she brought home from the drug store one day. Nope, I just stayed skinny as a toothpick and short as a midget. She'd say it was because I had a "nervous stomach", and she was probably right, because when September rolled around and it was time for me to go to my new school for the first time, that "nervous stomach" started kickin' my ass like crazy.

It was bad enough that I had to go to a new school with new kids and everything—that scared the shit outa me—but with my rotten luck, I got assigned to the class of the meanest teacher in the whole school: Mrs. Samuels. I hated that bitch from the very first day I laid eyes on her. She was tall and ugly, with this blue-gray hair that she combed back into a DA, like a man, and with that big, hook nose of hers and them little beady eyes, she looked just like a vulture. That's why all the kids called her "The Beak".

But I had my own name for her; I called her "The Voice from Hell". That's because she had this real loud, harsh-sounding voice that sounded just like that lady singer I hated, Ellen Bourbon, the one that always sang: "There's *no* business, like *show* business". Yeah, she sounded just like Ellen Bourbon—only *louder*. And if that wasn't bad enough, whenever she'd get excited or pissed off, she'd get these milky, cheesy strands of spit at the corners of her mouth. *Eeuuwww!* Forget it, when she'd get them spit-strings in her mouth, I'd have to turn my head and look the other way; that was way too gross for me.

And on top of all that, she always had this big bug up her ass about people talking with their hands—'specially *me*. Yeah! I couldn't figure it out. Every time she'd call on me and I'd have to answer out loud, she'd make me sit on my hands before she'd let me open my mouth.

"I don't know what it is with you people," she'd say. "This is the United States of America. You must all learn to express yourselves without using your hands. Using one's hands is a very crude and vulgar form of communication."

I really hated that sitting-on-my-hands bullshit, because the whole class would always laugh at me and I'd get really embarrassed. That's why I stopped raising my hand altogether, and even if I knew the answer to a question, I'd just stay quiet and keep it to myself. And I wouldn't

54

ask no questions neither. Nope, if there was something that I didn't understand, I'd just try and figure it out on my own, or I'd ask one of the other kids to help me. Forget it, the only time I'd even open my mouth in that class was when "The Voice from Hell" would call on me—otherwise I'd just keep my trap shut and mind my own business.

Anyway, little by little, as I started to feel more comfortable in school, my "nervous stomach" seemed to calm down. I mean, I still had to go running to the toilet to toss my cookies every once in a while, but at least it wasn't happening every day like it was during the first few weeks of school. Thank God for that, I was starting to feel like "Vomit Boy" over here.

Grandma must've noticed it too, because after a month of shoving that "Super Grow" junk down my throat, she finally decided to ditch that shit and go back to her original plan: feeding me all my favorite things. But that didn't work too good neither, because as soon as I'd take a couple of bites of something, I'd get a pain in my stomach and then I'd feel full right away.

I guess Mom was getting a little worried too, because she took me to see this doctor for a checkup. He said that I had a "high metabolism"—whatever the hell that meant—and that I probably was just a "late bloomer" and would start "shooting up like a beanstalk" in no time.

Well, I sure hoped that doctor knew what he was talking about. I was getting tired of worrying, and believe it or not, I was getting tired of Grandma shoving food down my throat and pressuring me to eat all the time—even if it was the best food in the universe. And that's what nobody could figure out. How could I have Marietta Posella for a grandmother, one of the world's greatest cooks, making me all my favorite things every day, feeding me like there was no tomorrow, and still be a shrimpy little bag o' bones? It didn't make no sense, no sense at all.

But Grandma wouldn't give up. She was on a mission and she wasn't going to stop until she saw results. And when Thanksgiving rolled around, she didn't waste any time getting ready to cook her ass off for the big day.

Thanksgiving in our house was like The World Series of Eating. But it wasn't just your normal, all-American pig-out, it was a double-barreled, Italian-American pig-out. The reason why I called it "double-barreled" was because nobody could decide whether they wanted to be American or Italian. Nope, nobody knew if they wanted the regular American Thanksgiving dinner—with the turkey and all the trimmings— *or,* if they wanted our usual Italian holiday dinner. But Grandma always had the perfect solution: she'd cook *both!*

Anyway, Aunt Jean, Uncle Rocco and my cousins were late coming over, as usual, and while we were waiting, I couldn't resist picking on the antipasto: first a green olive here, then a black olive there, then a slice of bread with *caponata* over here, a roasted red pepper with a slice of *mootz* over there, a couple of anchovies, a slice of salami... Fuhgeddaboudit, by the time the doorbell finally rang to let us know that the gang had arrived, not only was I stuffed, but I was already worrying how I was going to bullshit my way through the rest of the meal without eating nothing.

Everybody started digging in and eating like crazy, but I just picked, and pushed food around in my plate, trying to bluff my way through course after course. It didn't take long for Mom to catch on to what I was doing though, and she started giving me the evil eye and pinching me under the table.

"Ah-*ha!*, she said, "I bet you were picking on the antipasto while we were waiting for Aunt Jean to come, weren't you?"

I looked down and picked on one of my fingernails. "No"

"Don't lie to me, Junior, I know you too good. Here we are, we just started eating, and you're already full—right or wrong?!"

"Right."

Grandma jumped in right away. "Celeste, c'mon-a. It's-a Thanksgiving. *Lasha l' stara*, leave him alone. He gonna eat. After he rest for a little time, he gonna eat. *Aspetta.*"

Aunt Jean was already smiling, and when I lifted my up eyes, she said: "Boy, Junior, good thing you got your lawyer with you, otherwise you'd be in some pretty deep trouble, hah?"

Mom looked down at her plate, trying to keep a straight face. But from the way the corners of her mouth were twitching and trembling, I could tell she really wanted to laugh. And I was right too, because when

56

she looked up and caught Aunt Jean's eye, she couldn't control herself a second longer and started cracking up all over the place.

Everybody else joined in the laughing, and right away Uncle Rocco lifted up his glass and made a toast. *"Buon appetito!"*

Well, you were going to need more than just a *buon appetito* to get through that meal—it was going to be a *marathon!*

I had no idea where everybody put it all—'specially the grownups. They had just finished eating a big holiday dinner, Italian style, *plus* a complete American turkey dinner with all the trimmings, and there they were, sipping coffee and gobbling up *cannoli* and *sfogliatelle* like it was goin' outa style. And when I saw Uncle Rocco splitting an éclair with Aunt Jean after he'd already knocked down a couple of pastries by himself, I figured he might be the right person to ask.

"Hey, Uncle Rock," I said, taking a lick of cream off the end of my *cannolo*, "how do you grownups eat all that food? I got full after a little antipasto and a couple of bites of lasagna. I didn't even have no room for no turkey or nothin'. What's the trick to it?"

Uncle Rocco chuckled and wiped his mouth. "Well, Joon, there's no real trick to it; you just gotta pace yourself—that's all."

"You gotta *what* yourself?"

"Pace yourself, Joon—pace yourself."

"What's that?"

"Pace—like in a horse race for example. See, the most important thing in a horse race is not who runs the fastest at the *beginning* of the race, it's who crosses the finish line first at the *end* of the race—that's what counts. 'Cause a lotta times the horse that goes out in front and opens up a big early lead winds up tiring himself out, and then, when they get into the homestretch where you gotta put up or shut up, he runs outa gas and drops out of it—that's 'cause he's already burnt up all his energy. *Capish?"*

"I guess. But what does that have to do with that 'pace' thing, and what does the 'pace' thing have to do with eating?"

"Well, let me finish, Joon, that's where the pace part comes in. See, the jockey's job is to put on the brakes a little and control the speed of the horse, or in other words, to *pace* the horse, so he don't burn himself out in the beginning and he's got something left for the end of the race."

57

"Oh, I get it! Ya mean if I woulda ate a little less antipasto and a little less lasagna, maybe I woulda had some room left over for some turkey, some sweet potatoes, some fruits 'n' nuts, and maybe even another piece of pastry or something?"

Uncle Rocco looked around at the other grownups and laughed, shaking his hand as if he'd just burned it on the stove. "*Madon'*, I never knew this guy was so sharp; I betcha when God gave out brains, Mister Junior over here must've been first on line!"

Before I had a chance to say anything, Mom stuck her nose into the conversation. "Yeah, he's *too* smart—that's the problem. He thinks he's a real wiseguy."

Grandma poked Mom in arm and said, "*Lasha l' stara.*"

"'Ey, Uncle Rock, how'd ya learn so much about horse races?"

"Well, 'cause I'm a racing fan, that's my favorite sport."

"*Really?!* Wow, I never saw a real horse race before—except on television. But I love horses though; they're my very best favorite thing in the whole wide world!"

Right away Mom pointed to my horse drawings that were hanging on the closet door. "Can't ya tell?"

"Oh wow!" Uncle Rocco said, as he walked over to get a better look at them. "Hey, Cel, these are really good! I mean, for little kids' drawings. Look at the way he put in all the little details and everything. Boy, you must really love horses—hah, Joon?"

"I told ya, Uncle Rock, that's my very best favorite thing: horses!"

"Well, ya gotta come with me to the track someday then. I usually go on Mondays when the restaurant is closed. You'd get a big kick out of it. If you love horses, you'd *love* the racetrack."

Aunt Jean leaned over and gave Uncle Rocco an elbow in the ribs. "Rocco! How's he gonna go on a Monday? He's got school! And besides, that's no place for a kid; there's gambling 'n' stuff over there—and there's a lotta bums and lowlifes that hang around there."

"What are ya talkin' about? 'Bums and lowlifes'. I'll have you know that some of the best people in the world are racing fans. You get a much better class of people at the track than ya do at them baseball games or them boxing matches—that's for sure. What are ya kiddin'? Ya know, Jean, they don't call it the 'sport of kings' for nothin'. Where do ya think the Queen of England, and the Whitneys, and the

Vanderbilts, and all them fancy people go when the wanna relax a little and have a good time? To the track."

"Yeah," Aunt Jean said, taking a bite of her éclair, "and that's where big-shot Rocco Marino goes to lose the money he works so hard to earn waiting tables six days a week—'to the track'! Ya know, Rocco, that's what's keepin' us in the poorhouse over here—you and them stupid horses."

"Aah, come of it, Jean. You don't even know what you're talkin' about. So I save a few dollars from my tips, and I go out to the track, play a couple of bucks, pass some time, relax. What'sa matter, can't a guy enjoy himself once in a while?"

"Yeah, right. I don't know who ya think you're fooling over here, Rocco, 'cause it ain't me. I wasn't born yesterday ya know—and I ain't no little baby sucking on a nipple neither."

"So when we goin', Uncle Rock?"

Uh-oh, I guess I got so excited about the idea of going to a real racetrack, that I didn't even realize that I'd interrupted a grownups' conversation. Mom gave me a dirty look, and showed me the back of her hand, in case I hadn't noticed.

"Well, Joon, we can't go for a while now 'cause the season is almost finished. There's no racing in New York in the winter months; it gets too cold for the jockeys and the horses. That's why they all go down to Florida, or out to California to race—ya know, where it's nice and warm and everything."

"So when do they come back?"

"In the springtime, when it starts getting a little warmer."

I thought for a second, and then I said, "'Ey, maybe we can go some Monday when I'm on Easter vacation, huh, Uncle Rock?"

Uncle Rocco coughed in his hand and took a look over at Mom. "Well, we'll see. We gotta ask your mother first. But if we don't go at Eastertime, don't worry, 'cause we got the whole summer to go to the races—just you and me. How's about that?"

"Great! Boy oh boy! I can't wait!"

Well, I guess I was going to have to keep on waiting. Yep, four long months had passed since Thanksgiving, and after Mom dropped the bad news on me, I knew I was going to have to wait even longer. She said

59

that the only available appointment with the "leg specialist" was the only Monday of my Easter Vacation. Boy, what a disappointment that was. I felt like crying. And I did too. But I cried in the bedroom, real quiet, and I didn't let nobody see me or hear me or nothing—not even Grandma and Grandpa.

So, after I'd been dreaming of going to the track with Uncle Rocco for such a long time, boom, there I was, sitting with Mom in that stupid doctor's office—just so he could put me up on the table, measure my legs, and say the same exact thing he'd always say: "L.L.D., Leg Length Discrepancy." I knew all about it. I'd been hearing that same shit for years already: "Joseph's right leg is still approximately two inches shorter than his left". Then Mom would ask the same ol' question about the "shoe lift" and the special "corrective shoe", and the doctor would give her the same answer about how the shoe is "very expensive", and how it didn't make sense to get it for me then, because I was a still a kid and my foot was still growing, and how it would be better to wait 'til I was fifteen or sixteen, because then my foot wouldn't be growing no more, and I could wear it for a long time and she could her money's worth out of it. That was it. Same ol' story. I knew it by heart already. And for this broken-record bullshit, I had to miss out on a chance to go to the racetrack and see some real live racehorses.

Well, there were only three things I could tell myself then: that's the way the cookie crumbles...that's the way Niagara falls...and that's the way the Tootsie rolls. It was just tough noogies for me, and I had to lump it.

60

Chapter 5

Well, better late than never, right? I had to wait more than an entire *year* until school finished and I was on summer vacation. But the big day finally came, and there we were, me and Uncle Rocco, breezing down the highway in his green Chevy on our way to the *racetrack*.

"Hey, Joon," he said, reaching up and adjusting the rear-view mirror, "ya know somethin'? Maybe it was good in a way that we didn't get to go to the track around Eastertime when they were running over at Jamaica."

"Why's that, Uncle Rock?"

"Well, because—now don't get me wrong—Jamaica's a nice track and all, but it's a little small, and the place where they saddle the horses is under the stands, and it's kinda dark under there and you can't really see 'em that good. But now, for your first trip to a racetrack, you're going to one of the most bewdeeful tracks in the whole world: Belmont Park, *'La Bella Belmont'*."

"Ya mean that's where we're goin'?"

"Yeah, Belmont Park. You're gonna love it. The paddock is big, and it's behind the stands, under the trees, and we can go back there and see the horses real close up."

"Wow, sounds great, but what's a 'paddock'?"

"The paddock is where they bring the horses before each race to get 'em ready. First they put the saddles on 'em, and then they bring 'em out into the walking ring. That's where the jockeys get up on 'em. You'll see when we get there."

"Hey, Uncle Rock, how come Anthony didn't come with us? He don't like the track?"

"Naa, he thinks it's boring. I took him with me a couple of times, but he gets bored right away and starts runnin' around and makin' a pest outa himself. He says he likes to see the horses run, but he thinks there's too much time in between races. You know how Anthony is, he's too restless. Nothing can hold his attention for more than two and a half seconds. I guess that's why he goes in more for the action sports: like boxing, and wrestling, and football 'n' stuff."

61

"Well, I know I won't get bored—not if there's horses there."

When we got to *"La Bella Belmont"*, Uncle Rocco grabbed me by the hand, and we walked towards this big awning with fat, green-and-white stripes all over it. In front of the awning, there was a fancy, U-shaped driveway with this big, round thing in the center with lots of flowers and bushes 'n' stuff. Off to the side, there was a big bunch of shiny, Cadillacs and Lincolns, all lined up in a row, and each car had a Colored guy watching it, all dressed up in a fancy uniform with a cap and everything. Most of them were just leaning up against the cars, smoking, talking to each other, and reading the paper 'n' stuff, but a couple of them were busy polishing their cars in the shade with these big rags. I asked Uncle Rocco who they were, and he said they were chauffeurs, and they worked for the bigshots who were in the clubhouse.

"What's the clubhouse?"

"Well, ya see that big, green-'n'-white awning over there? That's the entrance to the clubhouse. That's the part of the track where the rich people, and all the big-provolone horse owners go to watch the races—plus the trainers, and the jock agents, and all the other people who work with the horses."

"And what about the regular people, where do they go?"

"They go to the grandstand, on the other side of the track."

"Is that where we're goin'?"

"Well, yeah. We're gonna go *in* from the grandstand side, but then we're gonna cross over to the clubhouse side. One of the guards near the paddock is and old, high-school buddy of mine, Don, and he always lets me into the clubhouse for free."

And that's exactly what we did, we walked around the side of the clubhouse, following the fence, 'til we came to a smaller green-and-white awning that said "Grandstand" on it. Uncle Rocco had to pay to get in, but the man in the booth just told me to duck under the turnstile—like I always do with Mom when we take the subway 'n' stuff.

62

As soon as we got in, Uncle Rocco bought two programs, and I followed him past the big trees 'til we got to another green-and-white awning with a man in a uniform standing under it.

As we got closer, Uncle Rocco told me to stick my hand under this purple-light thing, and to keep right on walking without stopping or nothing.

"Hey, Don, what's goin' on?!" Uncle Rocco said, as he walked up to the man.

"Rocco!" he answered, making believe he was looking at our hands as we stuck them under the purple-light machine. "How ya doin'? Feel lucky today?"

"Yeah, I got my lucky charm with me, my little nephew over here."

The man bent down and shook my hand with a big smile on his face. "Hi, sonny, ya like the track?"

"Yeah," I answered, feeling a little shy 'n' stuff.

"Well, you two have a good time now. Hope you pick a couple of winners."

"I hope so too. Thanks a lot, Don."

"Take care, Rock."

As soon as we walked into the clubhouse, I could see that it looked a lot fancier than the grandstand did. All the men were wearing suits and ties, and some of them had these big, binoculars-things hanging around their necks. The ladies were all dressed up too, in fancy dresses and high-heel shoes, and some of them had on these big hats with fake flowers and fruits 'n' stuff. Everything looked all hotsy-totsy in there, and that's when I knew why Uncle Rocco showed up wearing a suit-jacket and had told me to wear one too.

"So," he said, leaning over and talking out of the side of his mouth, "how does it feel to be a big provolone, Joon, and to rub elbows with all the other provolones here in the clubhouse?"

"Great, Uncle Rock. I like it."

"C'mon, let's go to the paddock and see the horses for the first race."

We walked over to a nice, shady spot under a tree, and we leaned against this black, iron fence to wait for the horses. Uncle Rocco got quiet because he started reading this big newspaper he'd brought with him with lots of little numbers on it.

63

When I asked him what the paper was, he said, "This here's the horseplayer's bible, The Morning Telegraph. This is where ya get the dope. Without this, ya don't really know who's who and who's gonna do what. *Capish?*"

"Dope?! I thought dope was drugs—like the junkies use."

"No, Joon, this is a different kinda dope. 'Dope' is just a slang word for information—that's all. That's what ya get here in the Telly: information, information on the horses. See? Like look here. Ya see this first horse? Okay. Here it tells ya his name, Blazing Comet, and over here it tells ya his color, how old he is, and all about his breeding. See?"

"What's breeding?"

"Breeding is just a fancy word for his family—that's all. Over here it tells ya his sire's name, Bolero—that means his daddy—and here it tells ya his dam's name, Shooting Star—that's his mama's name—and over here it tells ya his grandpa's name, Olympia. So now we know his breeding, and you'd say it like this: Blazing Comet, by Bolero out of Shooting Star by Olympia. Hey, ya know somethin', Joon? This horse must be a speedball, he's got speed on both sides of his family, top and bottom."

"Does that mean he's gonna win?"

"He's got a chance," Uncle Rocco said, concentrating on all these little numbers in the paper. "He's got speed and goes to the front, but usually he runs outa gas. The last time he won was back in April at Jamaica. But speed's always dangerous, and he's got a new jockey riding him today, Sidney Brookhouse. He's excellent with front-runners. He gets 'em out of the gate good, and he keeps 'em rolling in the stretch when they wanna chuck it. Hey, Joon, look, here come the horses!"

When I looked up, I saw them coming towards us down this shady lane. Each horse was walking with a man who was holding it by the bridle. Most of the horses were walking nice and slow, but there were a couple of them who were prancing sort of sideways-like, tossing their heads up and down, like they couldn't wait to start running.

"Uncle Rocco," I said, pointing to the first horse, "What do ya call that color?"

"That's called 'bay', that's the most common color in racehorses."

"How many colors do they come in?"

64

"Well, there's gray, like that second horse there. And some of the gray horses have these spots on 'em called dapples. Pretty, huh? Yeah, I like them grays, and I've had a lotta good luck with 'em too. I've clicked with some nice, gray longshots."

"What's a longshot?"

"That's a horse that not too many people are betting on, and when they win, the payoff can be really big, 'cause the odds are nice 'n' juicy."

"What are 'odds'? I don't understand that part, Uncle Rock."

"Forget about that for now; that has to do with betting. You got plenty of time to learn about that stuff." Then he pointed to the next horse in line. "Hey, look at that one. Now that's what I call a real beauty. Ya see that rusty, reddish, orangey-brown color that looks sorta like copper? That's called chestnut. That's my favorite horse color. Ya like that color?"

"Yeah. And what do ya call that white stripe on his face?"

"That's called a 'blaze', but when it's skinnier, it's called a 'stripe' or a 'strip'. And ya know how some horses just have a white spot on their foreheads? That's called a 'star'. And ya see the white he has on the bottom part of his legs?"

"Yeah."

"Those are called white stockings. Wow, that sure is a nice-looking animal alright. Look at all them bright-red highlights on his coat."

"Wow. I think chestnut is my favorite horse color too."

"'Ey, Joon, ya know who was a chestnut? Man o' War, the greatest racehorse of all time. He was a bright-red chestnut; that's how he got his nickname, 'Big Red'."

"Did ya ever see him run?"

"No, he was before my time, but I saw his son, War Admiral, run. He was one of the great ones too."

"Was he a chestnut like his sire?"

"Whoa, did you say 'sire'? 'Ey, Joon, you catch on fast—that's good! No, he wasn't chestnut; he was a little, dark brown horse—almost black. He had a lotta heart and was dead game—and, boy! could he run."

Uncle Rocco pushed his reading glasses up on his nose and folded the horse-paper so he could read it better. "Okay, Joon, now you look at the horses while I study the dope here in the Telly. I need a few minutes to see if I can come up with a winner—alright?"

65

So, while Uncle Rocco was busy burying his face in the 'Telly' and studying the 'dope', I was busy studying the horses and scoping out everything that was going on. I saw these guys come out with these little saddles and these white, cloth things with big, black numbers on them, and then, I watched as each horse got saddled in these separate stalls. I had some questions about some of the stuff I was seeing—like why some of the horses had to get their tongues tied, and why some of them had these hoods on—but I could see that Uncle Rocco was busy, so I figured I'll ask him later.

Anyway, after all the horses got saddled, I saw the jockeys come trickling in from this small, red brick building with white windows; and I put two and two together and figured that must be the jockey house or the jockeys' dressing room. A few of them walked out alone, but most of them came out two or three at a time, talking and joking together. I was surprised at how short and skinny they were, and how all of them were wearing the same white pants with the same black boots with a strip of brown at the top. But each one had a different-color cap and a different-color shirt though, and all their shirts had different designs on them: a white shirt with red polka-dots and a red cap,...blue 'n' yellow diamonds with a yellow cap,...black cap with a pink shirt with black stripes on the sleeves,...light purple and sky blue,...green and gold,...pink 'n' white,...blue 'n' orange—lots and lots of different colors. On their right sleeve, each jockey was wearing a number, and each one of them was carrying a whip. One jockey kept twirling his whip like the way a cheerleader twirls a baton, and another guy was smacking his against the side of his boot and swinging it like a golf club, clipping off the tips of a few blades of grass as if he was aiming at some make-believe golf ball. But most of the jockeys weren't fooling around with their whips; they were just standing there, waiting for their horses, real business-like, holding their whip under their arm, chewing gum, and fixing these thick, rubber bands that they all had on the cuffs of their shirts. I liked the way they looked—they were cool.

"Look, Joon," Uncle Rocco said, putting his paper down and pushing his glasses up, "here come the horses. Take a good look and tell me who you like."

66

"Gee, Uncle Rock, they all look good to me. But my two favorites are Blazing Comet, the one you said has all the speed, and that nice chestnut horse you were talking about before. What's his name?"

Uncle Rocco took a quick look at his program. "He's High Flame, and he's the chalk—that means he's the favorite."

Just then, the horses slowed down from walking around the ring, and Blazing Comet's "groom" stopped him right in front of us and I could check him out from up close. His coat was all shiny, and silky-looking, and even though he was 'bay' and not gray, I could see these little spots on it—like them "dapple" things that Uncle Rocco was talking about before. He sure looked good. A little jumpy maybe, but not nervous though. It looked to me like he was just anxious to get out there on the track, because he kept pawing the ground, and making this weird grinding sound by chomping down on this chain that was running across his nose and into his mouth.

"Junior, look! Here comes Brookhouse. Ya see him? Over there— the one with the green-and-gold silks."

Uncle Rocco pointed to this short, pudgy jockey heading toward Blazing Comet. A tall, skinny man wearing a suit and a straw hat—who I figured was probably the horse's trainer—was walking alongside him. He had his arm around the little guy's shoulder and was talking to him out of the side of his mouth—like he was telling him a big secret or something. This Brookhouse guy kept nodding his head like he was listening and paying real close attention, but he didn't look up at him though. He kept his eyes straight ahead, glued on Blazing Comet. Then, when I heard someone yell "riders up!", the trainer guy gave Brookhouse a quick, smooth boost up into the saddle, and Blazing Comet danced away, swishing his tail and tossing his head.

"C'mon, Sidney!" someone yelled from the crowd, "wire to wire! Wire to wire, Sid baby! This one's all yours!"

Number two, the gray horse, followed next. He wasn't as lively as some of the other horses, but he looked nice and calm, holding his head high and looking down at everybody, like he was a king or a prince or something, and we were a bunch of nobodies.

But the next horse, number three, was the one I *really* liked, that good-looking, chestnut horse with the 'blaze' and the four 'white stockings'.

67

As he went by, Uncle Rocco pointed to his jockey. "I bet ya know who he is," he said.

"Uh-uh, who's he?"

"Junior, that's Vinny Vaccaro! He's the most famous jockey in the country—probably even in the whole world! He's one of the all-time greats. Vinny Vaccaro?! Are you kiddin'? Joon, you're lookin' at a legend over here, a living legend. And guess what? He's Italian too."

"Wow!"

As this Vaccaro guy passed by, standing up in the saddle, tightening a strap and fixing his stirrups, out of nowhere these people across from us in the grandstand started calling out to him.

"'Ey, Vinny boy, start the day off with a winner! C'mon, you got the horse!"

"There he is, ol' Elephant Ears! C'mon, give us a break, don't stiff this one!

"Hey Vin, bring him in!"

"Give it all ya got, Vinny!"

Well, I was new to horse racing, but from the way all the people were yelling at him, it was easy to see that this horse, number three, was probably the favorite. And I was right, because when I asked Uncle Rocco, he said he was "six to five."

I didn't understand what "six to five" meant, but I figured I'd ask Uncle Rocco about it later, because right then I was busy scoping out High Flame. Now that was what I call a *horse!* I liked the way he was curving his neck and carrying his head sort of cocked to the side, pulling it in close to his chest. And I liked the way he moved too, with his 'white-stocking' feet touching the ground, two at a time, but only for a split second—like he was stepping on hot coals or something. I just stood there with my mouth open as he went dancing sideways through the shady part of the walking ring. And then, once he moved out of the shade, I watched as the sunlight hit his shiny, red-orange coat, and lit it up like a match, making it catch fire and burst into a bright, burning flame. He didn't get the name, High Flame, for nothing—I'll tell ya that much.

I pointed him out to Uncle Rocco, and he looked up from his paper and admired him too. "Yeah, he's a beauty alright, a real picture horse—like one of them horses in a painting. But why should I take such a short price on this horse? Because he's pretty as a picture? 'Cause Vinny Vaccaro's on him? Well, he may be a picture horse, but he looks more like a sucker horse if ya ask me."

"What's that, Uncle Rock?"

"A sucker horse is a horse that looks like a winner, but always finds some way to lose—'specially when it's the big, heavy favorite. I can't deny the horse looks like a million bucks, but ya know somethin', Joon?"

"Wha'?"

"This ain't a beauty contest, it's a horse race. Now put on your thinking cap, and let's see if we can find somebody to beat this sonuvagun."

As we followed the horses from the walking ring, all the way around the side of the clubhouse, under the big awning and down the ramp to the track, I had to really struggle my ass off to keep up with Uncle Rocco. It wasn't easy for me, because we were walking on these little gray pebbles, like gravel or something, and my feet kept sinking down into it with each step. But once we hit the track and Uncle Rocco showed me the post parade, it was all worth it.

It was easy to see why they called it the "post parade", because that's exactly what it looked like: a parade—a beautiful parade of shiny horses—bay, brown, gray and chestnut—each one coiled like a spring and ready to run, with their jockeys sitting on their backs, like knights from the olden days, all dressed up in them crayon-colored silks. Boy, I'd never seen nothin' like that before—not in real life anyway.

"Okay, Joon, there they are," Uncle Rocco, said, folding up his paper and putting it in his pocket. "Take a real good look at all of 'em, and tell me who ya like?"

I studied the horses as they galloped up the track, but they all looked so good, I couldn't make up my mind.

"C'mon, Joon, who ya' like?"

I scratched my head and looked down at my program. "Gee, I don't know. I guess I like High Flame the best, but I like the number one too, and the five... Oh, and the gray horse, number two, looks good... And you yourself said that we can't throw out the seven.... It's hard to pick Uncle Rock, I guess I like 'em all! Well, all except the six, I don't like the six."

"Jeez, you're a big help. We got seven horses in the damn race, and you like six of 'em! Alright, let me help ya. Let's use the process of elimination and narrow it down a little. First thing we gotta do is throw out that sucker horse, the three—and that six-horse too, the one you don't like. Okay? Now, out of the horses that are left, who do you like the best?"

It took me a while to answer Uncle Rocco's question because it was hard for me to choose between all them beautiful horses. But after I thought about it for a few more seconds, I looked up at him and said: "Number one, Blazing Comet."

"I *knew* you were gonna say that! Blazing Comet with Sidney Brookhouse, wire to wire, stealing the race, leaving the rest of 'em choking in the dust. Okay, Joon, now listen, I'm gonna go inside to put a couple of bucks on this horse, and I want you to wait for me right here on this bench. Okay? Don't move from here. I'll be right back, and then we can go upstairs, and you can watch your first horse race from up in the stands, where you can see everything good. Okay?"

"Okay, Uncle Rock."

Well, maybe I was Uncle Rocco's "lucky charm", but *I* didn't have no luck at all. I only got to see *half* of my first real-live horse race! Yeah! I mean, I saw the beginning of the race, and how Blazing Comet was the fastest breaking out of the gate and how he took the lead right away and opened up and everything, but when they made the turn into the homestretch, I couldn't see *shit!* All these stupid people in front of me stood up to see better and root for their horses, and by time I was able to scramble and stand up on my seat, the race was almost *over!*

And Uncle Rocco wasn't much help neither. He got excited and stood up too, slapping his program on his hand and cheering like crazy: "Attaboy, Sidney! That's it! *Now!* Step on the gas! C'mon with this horse! All the way! All the way, baby!"

But I *was* able to see some of the last part though, and, boy, that was exciting. I could see that Blazing Comet was getting tired, and I thought the other horses were going to catch up to him—'specially High Flame—but that's when Sidney Brookhouse crouched down real low and started riding his ass off, pushing and pumping, kicking back with his heels, smacking his horse on the behind and on his shoulder, shaking

70

the whip alongside his head and begging him to hang on for just a few more strides.

"He won! He won, Uncle Rock! He *won!*"

That's when Uncle Rocco went quiet; he just rubbed my head and smiled, and we watched together as the rest of the horses staggered past the finish line like a bunch of drunken sailors.

"I can't believe it! He won!" I said, jumping down from my seat. "Did ya see that! He won! Oh boy! Blazing Comet! What a horse!"

"And what a jockey too. That was some ride."

"I know! Did ya see the way he kept him goin' at the end?"

"Yeah, Joon, that was one helluva ride, one helluva ride."

All at once I heard this lady in back of us let out a scream, and when I turned around, she was jumping up and down and looking at this ticket in her hand, kissing it, swinging her arms around in the air, and making a real jackass outa herself.

Well, maybe *she* was happy, but the other people in the crowd sure weren't. Everybody else had on a real long face, and I could hear a lot of them mumbling and grumbling, tearing up their tickets, and cursing out Vinny Vaccaro for losing—'specially these two men behind us.

"Did ya see the way that bum got left at the gate? I can't believe it. That horse was a cinch, the best bet of the day, and look, he runs like a piece of shit."

"Yeah, Vaccaro probably did it on purpose; looked to me like he stiffed him good—the little creep"

"Hey, that's Vinny the Guinea for ya—greasy little wop bastard. What else can ya expect from these people? Whenever there's something sneaky and crooked goin' on, them greaseballs are right in the middle of it—every single time."

"Ya tellin' me?"

Uncle Rocco couldn't help overhearing these guys, and he turned around real slow and gave them both a mean dirty look. He didn't say nothing, but I guess they got the message, because they shut up fast.

"See that, Joon? Uncle Rocco said, turning back around and taking me by the hand. "Some of these bums got no class. No class and no respect. And ya see that lady over there, the one that was jumpin up 'n' down, screamin' 'n' yellin', and acting all stupid 'n' whatnot?"

"Yeah."

71

"Well, she ain't much better that these two jerks. See, Joon, when ya come to the track, ya gotta have a little class—ya know what I mean? Ya gotta know how to be a good loser, and ya gotta know how to be a good winner too. 'Cause that's the name of the game over here: ya win some and ya lose some—that's horse racing. And let me tell ya, mosta the time it's a lot easier to be a good *loser* than a good *winner*. A good winner is hard to find; those are the people who got the *real* class."

"What do ya mean, Uncle Rock?"

"Well, all I can say is this—and it's very important, so don't ever forget it: Ya gotta win with class, and ya gotta lose with class. That's the code of the racetrack. Remember: Win like your *used* to it...and lose...like it *never happened*. Understand?"

"Yeah."

"Good," Uncle Rock said, giving me a little pinch on the cheek. "C'mon, let's go downstairs, I gotta cash this ticket."

It didn't take long for Uncle Rocco to come back from cashing his ticket, and I could see he was feeling good. He had this sneaky, little smile on his face that reminded me of the way Sylvester the Cat always looks every time he catches Tweedy Bird—ya know, the canary in the cartoons 'n' stuff.

Uncle Rocco wanted to give me a "deuce" because he said I was his "lucky charm" and I'd helped him pick the horse. I didn't want to take it, but before I could say anything else, he shoved the two dollars in the side pocket of my pants, and then he patted me on the cheek.

"C'mon, Joon, take the two bucks. Use 'em for something special. Okay?"

"Well, alright. Thanks a lot uncle Rock."

"Forget it, you're my partner over here. Hey, Joon, ya feel hungry?"

"Yeah, I guess so. I didn't eat anything 'cause I was too excited about coming to the track."

"Well, c'mon then, you're in for a treat. I'm gonna take you to try Chicken Bessie's southern fried chicken. You can't come to Belmont Park without having some of Bessie's chicken. Everybody eats it: the trainers, the grooms, the jockeys, the agents, even some of the big-provolone horse owners—everybody. C'mon!"

72

As we walked away, I figured it was a good time to ask Uncle Rocco the questions I had about some of the stuff I'd seen and heard that I didn't understand that good. Well, I guess it was good timing, because Uncle Rocco answered all my questions. And he explained everything in detail too: like what blinkers were, what a shadow roll was, what a furlong was, what a tongue-tie was, what run-down bandages were, what the Widener Chute was, what a turf race was—everything. The only time he hesitated and tried to brush me off was when I asked about that word "gelding" that I heard the track announcer say.

"Well," he said, coughing in his hand and looking a little embarrassed for some reason, "a gelding is a boy horse, or a colt, that's had this operation where they remove his private parts. That's what a gelding is: a boy horse who had an operation. Understand?"

"I don't think so, Uncle Rock. I mean, how can the horse take a leak if they cut off his private parts?"

"Well, Joon, they don't cut off his—ya know his pee-pee or nothin'—they only cut off the other part of his privates...the testicles."

"Tessicles? What are tessicles?"

"His balls, Junior. They cut his balls off."

"*Cut his balls off?!*—why they gotta cut his balls off for?"

"Well, that's a little hard to explain. See, some of these colts can be hard to handle, 'cause they got their minds on the fillies, the girl horses, instead of having their minds on racing. Every time they see a filly that they like, they get all hot 'n' bothered and all excited, and it's hard for the grooms and the stable people to control them. They get studdish. That means they get mean and nasty—they wanna act like a tough guy. All they wanna do is bite, and kick, and make a big pain-in-the-ass outa themselves. And some of these colts are just plain mean too; they don't wanna behave, and they don't wanna cooperate with their trainers and learn what they need to learn to be racehorses."

"I can understand that part, but I still don't understand why they gotta cut their *balls* off"

"Well, for some reason, after they cut their balls off, a lot of these hard-to-handle colts start to settle down, and they become a lot tamer and a lot easier to work with. They start goin' along with the program more and keeping their minds on their business, which is running and

73

winning races—not chasing fillies, and biting and kicking, and all that other stuff. *Capish?*"

"I guess so, but I don't think it's right though."

"Why not? They do it all the time. It doesn't hurt the horse much, and some of these rogues, these real pain-in-the-ass nut-jobs, can really turn into some top-notch racehorses after they get gelded. Look at Exterminator, the horse they used to call 'Ol' Bones'. They made him into a gelding, and he turned out to be one of the all-time greats."

"I don't know, Uncle Rock. I still say it's wrong. How would you like somebody to cut *your* balls off?"

"*Ouch!* Junior, please! Don't even *say* something like that!"

"Well, what's the difference? It's still the same thing, ain't it?"

"No, Joon, it's not. First of all, I'm not a horse—I'm a human being over here. And a human being is a human being, and a horse is a horse. There's a very big difference."

"Okay. If you say so, Uncle Rock. But to me, I still say it's wrong, 'cause a horse is made by God, and the way I figure it, only God should be allowed to mess around with its private parts."

"Whoa! Hold it right there, Joon. Now you're getting a little too deep for me. Why don't we talk about this some other time, okay? Right now it's time to eat some chicken. Ya see that Colored lady over there by that little food stand?"

"Yeah."

"Well, that's Chicken Bessie. She makes the best southern-fried chicken in the world."

Uncle Rocco took my hand and led me over to this little table in the shade of the trees, over by the back part of the paddock near the red-brick jockey house. Standing behind the table was a fat, dark-brown Colored lady with glasses. Her gray hair was pulled back in a bun, and she wore a clean, white blouse, and a clean, white apron. As we got closer, I could see she was studying her program and writing stuff in it with a pencil that she stuck into the front part of her hair when she was finished with it. I thought that was kind of weird, because I'd never seen nobody stick stuff in their hair like that, and for it to stay stuck in there without falling out.

The table in front of her was covered with a red-and-white tablecloth, and on it was a big pan and a big pot that were both covered with a long, cloth napkin that looked like a towel. And next to the two pans, was a basket filled with slices of French bread, two pies, a big metal pot with a lid on it, and another smaller basket full of hard-boiled eggs.

"How ya doin', Bessie?" Uncle Rocco said, as he got near the table. "Any luck so far?"

"No, sir, no luck at all. I go and wheel Vaccaro's horse in the double like a damn fool, and he winds up second—just got beat. Oh, Lord almighty! I guess I'm just off on the wrong foot today. Anyway, no sense cryin' over spilt milk now. What can I get'cha?"

"Couple of pieces of chicken."

"Ya want the leg or the breast?"

"I'll take a leg," Uncle Rocco answers. "What about you, Joon—the leg or the breast?"

"Leg."

"Two legs."

Bessie lifted up the cloth on the big pan full of chicken, and after she picked out a couple of nice pieces, she wrapped each one in a napkin with a slice of French bread and handed them to Uncle Rocco. "Ya'll want som'n to drink with that, sir?"

"Yeah, Bessie," Uncle Rocco said, "I'll take two lemonades. I wanna give my nephew here the royal treatment. He's my lucky charm; he just helped me hit this winner here in the first."

Bessie took the lid off the big pot and filled up two paper cups with lemonade. "You got that winner in the first race? Oh Lord! I wish I woulda had that hoss. How much he pay anyway?"

"Thirty-eight dollars."

"Thirty-eight dollars?! Ooo *wee!* I sho' coulda used a nice winner like that to start the day off right. And ya know som'n? I liked that hoss. Mista Lawrence, the trainer, give a tip on him yesterday, but I forgot all about it 'til the race was over. Then, that's when I looked at my program and remembered."

"Oooo, that hurts," Uncle Rocco said, taking a cup of lemonade from Bessie and sipping some off the top so it wouldn't spill.

"Sho' do! But knowin' me, I probably wouldn't have played him anyway. See, befo' the race, Vaccaro's valet comes outa the jock's room, buys a piece of chicken, and tells me I can bet the whole damn

75

farm on Vinny's hoss. He be sayin' it was a 'sho' thang', and that Vinny himself liked him a whole lot, and everybody in the jock's room was playin' the hell outa him. So what do I do? I wheel him in the double, and I forget all about Mista Lawrence's hoss. Ain't that som'n?

"Yeah, ya gotta watch out for them 'sure things'; there ain't no sure things in this game."

"Now ain't that the truth."

While Uncle Rocco and Bessie were busy talking, I already started diggin' into the chicken. And let me tell ya, I never tasted no chicken like *that* before. The outside was crispy and crunchy, and the inside was all tender and juicy. Mmmm, the perfect combination. Yep, Uncle Rocco was right again; Bessie's chicken really was the all-time best.

"Ooo *weee!*" Bessie chuckled, as she gave Uncle Rocco his change and saw me gobblin' up her chicken. "Looks to me like there's a young fella 'round here that likes ol' Bessie's chicken. Don't ya now, sonny?"

"Yep," I answered, without even lifting my head, "it's the best chicken I ever ate in my whole life."

Right away Bessie bowed to me and did one of them curtsy things. "Well, thank you, sir. I'm mighty glad ya like it." Then she shook her finger at me, and with a make-believe angry look on her face, she said: "Now don't you be givin' all them longshot winners only to your uncle now. Come 'round here and give ol' Bessie a winner every now and then. Lord knows she needs one, ha-ha-ha-ha-ha! Don't be hoggin' up all them winners by ya'self now—ya hear?"

"Okay, I won't."

Bessie laughed and wiped he hands on her apron. "Good. Ya'll enjoy that chicken now while I take care of this here gentleman. Oh, Mista Hamilton! How are you today, sir?"

A tall man dressed in a fancy, light-blue suit, looked over the food on the table. "Fine, Bessie, I'm doing quite well. And yourself?"

"Well, right now I got me a case of the hossplayer's blues, but I'll get over it soon enough. What can I get'cha, Mista Hamilton? Some chicken maybe? Came out real good today, sir."

"No no, Bessie, I'm afraid I've been eating a little too much of your chicken lately," he said, patting his stomach. "I think I've been putting on a few pounds. Perhaps it's time to...cut back a little. I'll just take one of these eggs and a piece of that bread if I may."

76

Bessie hands the man a paper plate and a napkin. "Help ya'self, sir. Would ya care for some lemonade with that, Mista Hamilton?"

"Why yes. Thank you so much, Bessie."

As Bessie was getting the lemonade, Uncle Rocco bent down and whispered close to my ear. "Junior, ya know who this guy next to me is?"

"Who?" I asked, chomping on a mouthful of chicken.

"That's Mr. Hamilton. He's one of the big provolones I was tellin' ya about. He owns the Belvedere Stud, and he's even part owner of the track too. Boy, there's been a whole lotta champeen horses that've raced in his colors—that's for sure. Ya see, Joon, it's like I told ya, everybody and their mother stops to grab a bite at Bessie's food stand. They all come down to the paddock to sit in the shade and eat Bessie's chicken—and they give her tips too."

"Ya mean like extra money 'n' stuff?"

"No, Joon, not *money* tips; I'm talkin' about tips on the *horses*—tips from the people on the inside: the owners, trainers, jockeys, grooms, jock agents, valets, everybody. Problem is, she gets so many tips, from so many different people, she gets confused. She knows she can't bet on all of 'em, so every day she makes the same mistake: she throws out the good tips, bets on the bad ones, and then kicks herself in then head for the rest of the day."

"Gee, that's too bad."

"Yeah, this poor lady is gonna wind up in the poorhouse 'cause of them tips—either that or she's gonna make herself sick. But win or lose, Bessie always shows her class. Yeah, good ol' Bessie. Ya see that bewdeeful old pine tree over there in the walking ring?"

"Yeah."

"Well, Bessie's like that tree. She's part of this track, and she belongs here. Ya know, in all the years I've been coming here, I don't think I've ever seen her lose her temper, or say somethin' nasty, or be a sore loser or nothin'—not even once. Nope, when Bessie loses a big bet, she just brushes it off, smiles, makes a joke, and says: 'We'll get 'em next time'. And you'll never see Bessie cursing out a jockey, or a trainer, or a horse, or nothin' like that. Okay, she may only be a poor old lady who's tryin' to make a buck by cooking some chicken at home and bringin' it to the track and sellin' it and whatnot. But if you ask me, I'd

77

say she's got a lot more class than a lotta these rich bastards walkin' around here—and a lot of other people I know too. Remember, Joon, class ain't got nothin' to do with money; class is something *inside* the person. Either you got it or you don't. Understand?"

Uncle Rocco decided that he wasn't going to be a "damn fool" this time, and he wasn't going to keep betting the rest of the races and wind up giving his winnings "back to the track". So, he folded up his Telly, put it in his pocket, and spent the rest of the day just hanging out with me, scoping out the horses, pointing out the jockeys and the top trainers, watching the races and having a nice quiet time. He told me about everything and everybody, and I soaked up every word like a sponge.

But when the last race rolled around, he couldn't resist putting a "few bucks" on a horse he liked called Syncopated Sam. The horse fought it out through the whole length of the stretch and wound up winning by a nose. It was really exciting to watch, and Uncle Rocco was happier than a pig in shit, because his horse was a big longshot and was going to pay a whole lotta money. But all of a sudden, just as he was tasting the win, the "inquiry" sign lit up, and after Uncle Rocco sweated it out for more than twenty minutes, his horse got disqualified for "interference in the stretch".

I felt really bad for him, but Uncle Rocco just played it off like it was nothing. And as we walked to the parking lot, he put his arm around me, called me his "lucky charm" again, and kept talking about what a great day we had together. I guess he knew how to follow the code of the racetrack: He won like he was *used* to it, and he lost...like it never happened.

78

Chapter 6

Ever since I got my first taste of the racetrack, it's been my very best favorite thing. Yep, me and Uncle Rocco have been going almost every Monday, and little by little, he's been teaching me practically everything there is to know. He even showed me how to read The Morning Telegraph too. It wasn't all that hard—once you got to know what all the little numbers and the symbols mean—and after I practiced for a few weeks, I started to get hang of it. And that was great, because then I could get the dope on the horses all by myself, and it made going to the track twenty times more interesting than before.

Mom still wasn't too crazy about the idea, and when she snagged me lying on my bed and reading the "Telly" one night, she threw a fit.

"Look at this!" she yelled, "They already got the kid readin' the *scratch sheet* for cryin' out loud. Next thing ya know he's gonna start saving up his candy money and making *bets* over here!"

Yeah, she really caught a titty-attack when she saw me reading the Telly, and if it hadn't been for Grandma, my lawyer, stepping in and pleading my case, she probably would've put her foot down and stopped me from going to the track altogether.

"Celeste," Grandma said, "he no do nothing wrong-a. He just like the hoss—that's all. C'mon, leave-a him alone. *Lasha l' stara.*"

Not for nothin', but if there was ever anyone who really understood me, deep down inside, it was Grandma. She could see right through me, straight into the center of my heart, almost as if she had X-ray vision. Yeah, I sure was lucky to have Grandma in my corner; her and Grandpa were definitely in a "dead heat" for being my very best buddies in the whole wide world.

Only problem was, they were grownups, and what I really needed then were some friends my own age—ya know, kids that I could play with and pal around with 'n' stuff.

See, even though I knew practically all the kids on the block by that time, there still wasn't anybody who I was buddy-buddy with, somebody who'd knock on my door and call for me every day, or look up at my window and yell: "Hey, Joweee, when ya comin' down?!"

79

I've never been lucky enough to have a best friend—not even in my old neighborhood. And even in my new neighborhood, it was pretty much the same thing. I'd usually just look out the window and see who was playing downstairs, and if I saw some of the kids I got along with—like Sally Pork, or Yo-Yo, or Nicky Specks, or Bubbles, or Lino—then I'd go down and sort of join in with whatever they were doing. They'd treat me okay most of the time, but I wasn't ever one of the popular kids on the block. It was more like if I was there it was cool, and if I wasn't, that was cool too. I guess I was more like a spare-tire friend, or a pinch-hitter friend to some of them guys, someone to hang around with when none of their main buddies were around. I hated that, it would hurt my feelings and make me feel shitty. Because sometimes I could be hanging around with one of the guys—playing a nice game of Chinese, or marbles, or flipping baseball cards or something—and then one of his best pals would come around, and *boom,* he'd just leave me flat, just like that, and I'd find myself standing there, alone, like a stupid dingleberry.

Boy, let me tell ya, it wasn't no fun getting dumped and having somebody leave you flat. No fun at all. It'd make you feel messed up. That was why I'd never do that to nobody because I knew how it felt. And besides, I believed in following the Golden Rule: You should never do nothing to nobody that you don't want being done back to you. That's why the other kids might've called me different names sometimes, but you'd never hear nobody calling me a "flat-leaver". Uh-uh, I wouldn't do that to a dog. It's just plain wrong, and it would always make the other person feel like one big blob of shit on a stick.

And what was even worse was when I'd get left flat by all the guys on the block, all at once, all at the same time. See, sometimes we could all be playing something together in a group—like red-light green-light, or what's-in-the-ice box?, or marbles, or skelly—and all of a sudden, one of the guys would get the bright idea to go to the park to play basketball, or to choose up a game of two-hand-touch football, or ring-a-leevio—or one of the other games that I couldn't play that good because of my legs—and everybody would jump up and shout, "Yeah! that's a great idea", and before I even knew what hit me, every last one of them would be running down the block, and I'd be left standing there, all my myself, holding a big bag of shit.

80

Every once in a blue moon, one of the guys would remember about me, and as the whole gang would be hustling away, he'd turn around and say, "Hey, Gimp, ain't ya coming?". But I'd answer, "Naa, I gotta go to the store for my mother", or "I gotta take a wicked leak", or "I gotta take a wicked dump", or any one of a hundred excuses that nobody really believed anyway. Then the guy would just shrug his shoulders and say, "Okay, see ya later", and I'd look down at the ground and say, "Yeah, see ya".

Then I'd always do the same thing: I'd wait a little while 'til the guys were all gone, and then I'd go upstairs, bring down my scooter, and go for a scooter ride—and I'd just keep riding my scooter around the block, over and over again, 'til I'd forget about everything and everybody.

I loved riding my scooter. And you know why? Because when I'd be riding my scooter, nobody could tell that I got one leg shorter than the other! And you something else? Scooter riding is one of the few things where having one leg shorter than the other can actually come in handy. For real! I'd put my right leg, my short leg, on the bottom part of the scooter, and I'd use my left leg, my long leg, for pumping. Maybe that's why I was so good at scooter riding: I was built for it. Yeah! I mean, I don't want to brag or nothing, but I was the best scooter-rider on the whole block. 'Cause let me tell ya, whenever we'd have them scooter races—one lap around the block—nobody could beat me, nobody. I was the scooter champ of 115th Street.

And I had a real nice scooter too. I made it myself with a milk crate, a two-by-four, and an old skate split in half. I painted it all black, and I spelled out my name, Joey, on the front with lots of different-color bottle caps. And sometimes I'd make believe that my scooter was a beautiful black horse, and when I'd make the turn from Pleasant Avenue onto the block, I'd crouch down real low, and start pumping and whipping and driving, just like the jockeys do at the racetrack.

And you want to know a secret? I was always hoping that someday some of the kids would notice me riding my scooter all the time, and instead of calling "Joey Gimp", or "Gimp", or "Shrimpy Gimp" and all that other stuff, maybe they'd start calling me "Joey Scooter", or just plain "Scooter"—like that Phil Rizzuto guy from the Yankees. I figured if Bubbles and Yo-Yo could get their names from what they did all the time—why couldn't I?

Well, you can lead a horse to water, but you can't make him drink. Nope, because no matter how many times these kids would see me riding my scooter up and down the block, I don't think any one of them ever even *thought* about calling me "Joey Scooter". I could've ridden my scooter right under their nose a zillion times, and I could've prayed to Jesus, *La Madonna*, and every single saint there is, and nothing was ever going to change. It was hopeless, and I knew it. The only way I was ever going to get anybody to stop calling me "Gimp" was to move off the block or *die*.

But there was one kid who never called me none of them stupid names: Ronnie. Yeah, I guess you could say Ronnie was the closest thing I ever had to a best friend. Only problem was, Ronnie was a girl.

Her real name was Veronica, but only her family, and some of the old people called her that. Everybody else called her "Ronnie". She was a year or two younger than me, and she lived right downstairs from us on the second floor. I got to know her right away, because Grandma would always watch her and her little sister, Dee Dee, whenever Ronnie's mom had to go to the hospital to take care of Ronnie's grandpa.

See, Ronnie's grandfather had this serious sickness called "Alzheimer disease". That's when your brain gets all weak and you can't remember stuff no more. And Ronnie's grandpa had it bad. Most of the time he couldn't remember his own name, and he couldn't even recognize his own daughter, Mrs. Spinale, or Ronnie's dad, Mr. Spinale, or Ronnie, or DeeDee, or nobody. And sometimes he'd even forget how to eat and go to the toilet 'n' stuff, and Ronnie's mother would have to feed him and clean him up and everything—just like he was a little baby. Yeah, I really felt bad for him, and for Ronnie's whole family too. They had it rough; it definitely wasn't no picnic taking take of Ronnie's grandpa—I'll tell ya that much.

Anyway, while Mrs. Spinale would be busy taking care of Ronnie's grandpa, Ronnie and DeeDee would always come upstairs to stay with us. I'd love it when Ronnie would come over, because it was nice having another kid to play with—even if she was a girl.

It wasn't fun being an only child. I hated it. I mean, I'd watch TV, draw pictures, play with my toys, look out the window, and talk with Grandpa 'n' stuff, but it was always better to have another kid around

82

to play with. It would make everything a lot more fun, even something simple like watching TV was a lot more fun when you had another kid to watch it with you.

Little DeeDee could be a pain in the ass sometimes though—'specially when me and Ronnie would be playing something like Monopoly, or Parcheesi, or checkers, or cards, or something like that. She'd always start touching stuff and messing things up, and that's when Ronnie would grab her hand and drag her into the kitchen so Grandma could stay with her and get her out of our hair for a while.

Sometimes, 'specially in the fall when it'd be nice and windy, me and Ronnie would go up on the roof and fly kites together. Grandpa would always come with us though—he didn't like us playing up there by ourselves—but he'd never bother us; he'd just sit off to the side and smoke and read the newspaper. Yeah, we'd have a ball flying them kites. We'd get them suckers up so high, that after a while you couldn't hardly even see them no more. They'd just look like two little dots in the sky, far, far away,...and we'd just sit there for a really long time, with the wind in our faces, smelling the fresh air, flying our kites and watching the sun sink lower and lower 'til everything turned golden red.

It was fun having a friend like Ronnie. Too bad she was a girl though, because sometimes we'd be playing downstairs together, and the guys would notice us and tease us 'n' stuff. They'd make them stupid smooching sounds, and start singing: "Ronnie and Gimp, sittin' in a tree K-I-SS-I-N-G". I hated that shit; that's why I liked it better playing with Ronnie in my house or flying kites up on the roof. Nobody could see us then, and I wouldn't have to hear no stupid wisecracks or nothing.

Only problem with us being friends was that Ronnie was a girl, and I was a boy. Yeah! I mean, even though I liked doing *some* things with her, she'd still want to play girl-stuff with the girls—like jump rope, or dolls, or potsy—and I'd want to play boy-stuff with the guys—like marbles, or skelly, or flipping baseball cards 'n' stuff. That's why I couldn't call her my best friend, because real best friends are always playing together all the time, like two buddies that like all the same things.

But I couldn't complain though; I was lucky to have a friend like Ronnie—even if she was a girl. She was a good friend to me, and she'd always share stuff with me. Like even if she'd be playing near the stoop

83

with the girls, and I'd be playing in the middle of the street with the guys, she'd always come over to give me a lick of her lemon-ice, a bite of her jelly apple, or a handful of her Good 'n' Plenties—without me even asking her or nothing. And I'd always share with her too. Like whenever I'd get one of them nickel ice-pops with the two sticks, I'd never eat a whole one by myself; I'd always smack it up against the corner of a building and give one stick to Ronnie. Or like when I'd get my favorite soda, Mission grape, I'd always give her a big slug or save her some in the bottle, and then, after I'd get one of them skinny pretzels with the two-cent deposit, I'd always break that in half too so we could both sit around together and make believe we were smoking cigars.

We'd always be sharing stuff together, and I ain't just talking about candy, and soda and ice-pops. Nope, we'd share practically everything—even our thoughts, and our feelings, and things like that. I know it sounds all doofy and corny and whatnot, but me and Ronnie would talk to each other, and sometimes we'd tell each other stuff—ya know, like private stuff, stuff you didn't talk about with nobody—secret stuff.

Usually we'd hang out and talk on the fire escape—'specially on them hot summer nights. Nobody would mind us sitting out there; Mom knew where we were, and Mrs. Spinale knew that Ronnie was safe because she'd be sitting right outside her own kitchen window. Sometimes they'd even forget about us, and we'd stay out there 'til ten thirty or eleven at night, just talking, looking up at the moon, feeling the breeze, and listening to some of the Redwoods who'd usually be harmonizing across the street by the corner of Pleasant Avenue.

I'd love to hear them sing, and so did Ronnie. They were good—'specially the lead singer Frankie Tee; he had one hell of a voice. My favorite song was "When I Woke Up This Morning", the one where the background guys would start off: "langa-langa-langa-langa-lang, zoom-zoom-zoom, bop-bop-bop-bop". And then Frankie Tee would come in on top of them, real smooth, and sing: "When I woke up this morning, I looked for you...".

Ronnie liked that one too, but her favorite was "Little Star". She was crazy about that song, and every time they'd sing it, she'd snap her fingers and sing along. I liked it too—'specially the part where Frankie

84

Tee would go: "oh-oh-oh-ohoooh-radda-tadda-tadda-tooo...". Forget it, that was the coolest.

I remember one time me and Ronnie were sitting out on the fire escape listening to the Redwoods singing "Little Star", and I don't know if it was one of them coincidence things, but that night there wasn't a cloud in the sky, and you could see millions and zillions of stars all over the place. For some reason Ronnie picked one out and pointed to this real bright one that was shining up in the top part of the sky over towards the Triborough Bridge.

"'Ey, Joey, do you believe in wishing on a star?" she said, looking over at me with a dreamy sort of look on her face.

"Naa," I answered, "I don't believe in stuff like that."

"Why not? Don't you remember that Walt Disney movie when Jiminy Cricket sang that song—ya know, the one about wishing on a star and dreams coming true 'n' everything?"

"Yeah, that was in Pinocchio, I seen that movie lots of times. But I don't believe on wishing on a star 'n' stuff like that."

"How come?"

"'Cause."

"'Cause why?"

"'Cause...I figure wishing is pretty much the same thing like praying, and I've already prayed lotsa times, for lotsa different things, and nothin' ever happened. It's just a big waste of time if ya ask me."

"But Joey, prayin' is prayin, and wishin' is wishin'. It ain't the same."

"To me it is. What's the difference? It's just a different word, that's all."

"No it ain't. Prayin' is when ya ask God, or Jesus, or Our Lady, or one of the saints to step in and make something happen. But wishing is different. Wishing is more like hoping—ya know, like dreaming and hoping for something to happen. It don't got nothin' to do with God."

"It don't?" I asked, a little surprised at myself for not ever thinking about it like that.

"Nope. I'm tellin' ya, it's different."

"Well, if it's really different, then maybe I should try it. Whatta ya think?"

"Sure, go 'head. I do it all the time."

85

"So, does it work? Did all your dreams come true, like the way the song says?"

"I don't know yet," she said, "it takes times for dreams to come true. I mean, it's not like you wish for something and, all of a sudden, your dreams come true right away—like putting some Bosco in a glass of milk and stirring it up, and then, boom, one-two-three—ya got chocolate milk. It don't work that way, ya gotta wait. Ya gotta have patience. Why don't ya try it, Joey?"

"I don't know. I don't think wishing is the...."

"Aw c'mon, what do ya got to lose? Go 'head,...wish. It can't hurt nothin'."

I was too shy to do it, but Ronnie wouldn't give up, and she kept trying to convince me. She even said the that she'd go first, and when I asked how many wishes we'd get, she said we should make it three wishes each—just like that Aladdin guy, the one with the magic lamp.

Ronnie didn't seem to need too much time to think of her wishes. She just coughed in her hand, cleared her voice, and pointed to the same bright star that she'd seen before, the one that was sparkling high in the sky, real far away.

"My first wish is for my grandpa," she said. "I wish he gets better real soon, and that someday he'll be able to remember who he is, who I am, and who everybody else in the family is too."

I didn't say nothing. I just listened to Ronnie and kept looking at that bright, shiny star, and wished right along with her. I figured that if two people wish for the same thing, it probably doubled the chances of it coming true.

"And my second wish is for my family. I wish for us to be happy again—like the way we were before Grandpa got sick."

I kept my eyes glued to the star and wished right along with her. "So, what's ya third wish, Ronnie?"

"Well, I guess my third wish would be for when I grow up. I wish I could be a doctor, so I could help all the sick people and make 'em better. But if I can't be a doctor, 'cause I'm a girl, then I wish I could be a nurse or somethin' like that—ya know, so I could still help the sick people in some kinda way."

I looked over at Ronnie and smiled. "Those are some really nice wishes. I hope they all come true."

"Thanks," she said. "Okay, c'mon, now it's your turn. What are ya gonna wish for?"

I already knew what my first two wishes were; I been wishing, and hoping, and praying for the same two things for such a long time, I knew them shits by *heart* already.

"Well," I said, looking up at the same star that Ronnie picked out, "my first wish would be to see my dad again—or at least to get a phone call or a letter from him or somethin'. And my second wish would be for my right leg to grow a little bit longer and match with my left leg, and for me to grow and to be just as tall as a normal person, so nobody would ever call me "Gimp" or "Shrimp" again for the rest of my life."

Ronnie didn't say nothing, but I could tell she was wishing right along with me. I could see her out of the corner of my eye, staring up at that faraway star and holding her hands together like she was praying or something.

Then she sat there real quiet, waiting for me to make my third wish, but my third wish never came. I couldn't think of nothing else to wish for!

"Joey, c'mon, make your last wish."

I frowned and scratched my head. "I can't think of nothin', Ronnie."

"Sure ya can, it's easy. Why don't ya make your last wish about something ya wanna be when ya grow up—like I did."

"I don't know, it's not easy for me."

"Why not? Don't ya know what ya wanna be?"

"Yeah, I guess."

"So? What's the problem then? C'mon already."

"Well, okay," I, said, looking back up at the star. "If I don't grow up to be as tall as a normal man, and I stay short and skinny like I am now, then I wish that someday I could be a jockey."

"A jockey?!"

"Yeah, a jockey—what's wrong with that?"

"Nothin'. I mean, I just never heard of nobody wanting to be one before—that's all. Most boys wanna be a policeman, or a fireman, or a baseball player, or somethin' like that."

"So?"

"Sew buttons! If ya wanna be a jockey, great! There ain't nothin' wrong with it. I mean, hey, I bet you could be one of the very best most

87

famous jockeys that ever lived—'specially with the way you love horses and everything."

"Yeah," I said, feeling myself blush a little, "I guess I really do love horses. And I think I could be a pretty good jockey too. But if I could choose between being a jockey or growing up to be as tall as a normal person, I'd take growing any day. I'd only wanna be a jockey if my second wish don't come true—ya know what I mean?"

Ronnie didn't answer. She just looked up at the star again, and after she stared at it for a while, she closed her eyes and folded her hands. "Please," she prayed, "make Joey's second wish come true. Make him as tall as he wants to be—even as tall as Paul Bunyon or the Jolly Green Giant—but if ya can't help him with that, then make him the best jockey that ever lived."

Well, that was pretty much the way it was with me and Ronnie. She'd always understand how I felt about stuff, and she'd never laugh or make fun of me or nothing. But the thing I liked best was the way she'd always call me by my real name, and not none of them stupid nicknames. It was like music to my ears, and sometimes, when she'd call out to me by name, I'd even play deaf and make believe I didn't hear her—just so I could hear her say "Joey" over and over again. I guess it wasn't right to do that, but I couldn't help myself; I just loved the way she'd say my name—and she had a real nice voice too.

But even though she was my buddy, there was still one bad thing about her: she couldn't keep a secret to save her life. Nope, I couldn't understand what was so hard about it. I mean, every time she'd tell *me* a secret, I'd keep it to myself and wouldn't say nothing to nobody. But whenever I'd tell *her* a secret, forget it, sooner or later she'd go blabbing it to one of her stupid little girlfriends, and before you knew it, everybody and their *mother* knew my business. Jeez, I hated that. That's why I stopped telling her my secret stuff altogether.

Grandpa said I shouldn't stay mad at her though. He said that even though she was only a little girl, she was still a woman, and women can never keep a secret—no matter how hard they try. He'd say it's easier to hit the Italian lottery than to find a woman who can keep a secret. Well, I didn't really know much about girls, or women, or lotteries, or none of that stuff, but I figured if Grandpa said so, it was probably true.

88

But I gotta be fair to Ronnie; when she did leak out some of my secrets every now and then, a lot of times she did it not to hurt me, but to help me. Like take them three wishes we made out on the fire escape, for instance. Well, I got this funny feeling that she told her dad about my second wish, because you know what he went and did? He took these regular pair of roller skates and fixed them up in the metal shop where he worked, 'specially for me—and then he gave them to me for Christmas.

Boy, not for nothin', but them skates were definitely the very best present I ever got in my whole life. Mr. Spinale put in this special platform on my right skate, so that when I'd put on both skates, my right leg would be just as long as my left, and I'd be all evened-out—and I could skate like a champ. And let me tell ya, Ronnie's father must've worked really hard to fix up that right skate. That platform-thing was all carved out of wood and shaped just right so it fit perfect and it wouldn't wobble or nothing when I'd ride on it. He even painted the sides of it black, so that it would blend in with the color of my shoes and you could hardly even notice it. But that was nothing, the *real* hard part must've been putting in them extra pieces of metal on both the back and the front part of the skate, to lift it up and make it higher, and then to attach the front part to them fancy Chicago clamps. He did a real good job on that too, because when I'd tighten them up with my skate key, those clamps would grip my foot nice and tight. The whole thing must've been hard to do, but Mr. Spinale said it was no big deal. He said he was a welder, and welding stuff was his "specialty".

Well, maybe it wasn't a big deal to him, but it sure was a big deal to *me*. With my new skates, I could skate as good as anybody—without limping or nothing. It was like having a pair of them special "corrective shoes" that the leg doctor was always telling Mom about—only on *wheels!*

Yeah, them skates were cool. I must've thanked Ronnie's dad more than a hundred times, but every time I'd thank him, he'd just smile and blush a little, and say: "Aah, fuhgeddaboudit, it was nothin'. I'm glad ya like 'em."

Mom and Grandma kept thanking him over and over again too, and they even made him a special batch of *stuffoli*, the little Christmas

89

cookies, and a big bunch of homemade *zeppole* too, all smothered in honey—just for him.

And Grandpa was happy about my skates too. I'll never forget how he went over and hugged Mr. Spinale when I opened up that package and pulled out them skates on Christmas morning. I think he was even happier than *me!*

See, Grandpa would usually just shake hands with Ronnie's father, but when he saw them custom-made skates and how happy I was to get them, he walked right over to Mr. Spinale and gave him a great big hug. Then he took off his glasses and started wiping them, and when he finished, he blew his nose and wiped his eyes too. It looked to me like Grandpa wanted to cry, but he was trying to hold it in—ya know what I mean?

But there were no tears in my eyes though—only a big, happy smile, as I ran downstairs to try out my new skates. They worked great, and even though it was colder than a witch's tit outside, I spent the whole morning skating up and down the block 'til Aunt Jean, Uncle Rocco and my cousins showed up for Christmas dinner. Boy, you should've seen the look on Anthony's face when he saw me skating around like a pro on my brand-new skates. He couldn't believe it, and neither could I. Nope, because there I was skating...just like a regular kid.

Chapter 7

It's funny how a little thing like a pair of skates can change your life, but that's exactly what happened to me. Because once I could move around on my skates, I could keep up with the other kids a lot better, and I wasn't getting left flat and left behind all the time, like before. I mean, I still couldn't play handball, or softball, or stickball, or tackle football, or two-hand touch, or basketball, or stuff like that, but I could play hockey though. In fact, I was one of the best hockey players on the block, and when they'd choose up sides, I'd be one of the first guys to get picked. Yep, "Joey's my name and hockey's my game", that's what I would say—thanks to Mr. Spinale and my special custom-made skates.

We didn't play *real* hockey though—like with ice skates, and gloves, and masks, and real equipment. We'd just play regular street hockey. All you needed was a pair of roller skates, a hockey stick, a roll of tape to use as a puck, and you were in business. We'd use the manhole covers in the street for the goals, but if somebody had a piece of chalk, sometimes we'd mark off the lines for the face offs 'n' stuff. It wasn't no big thing, but I loved it though; because when it came to playing hockey, I was just as good as anybody on the block. Maybe even better—and all the kids knew it too.

That's why I say them pair of skates changed my life. Because once the guys on the block saw how good I was at playing hockey, something changed. I mean I'd still get called "Gimp", and I'd still get left out of a lot of games—because of my legs and because I couldn't run so good — but something felt different: I was starting to feel like I belonged there.

That's because after a couple of years on the block, I knew everybody, and everybody knew me. I wasn't "the new kid" or "that crippled kid" no more; I was part of the block. Like when we'd have them big, water-balloon fights in the summertime against the kids from around the corner on 114th Street, I'd always be right in the middle of everything, fighting to the end, right along with the rest of the guys.

And it was the same thing with water-guns, pea shooters, snowballs, and them homemade slingshots that we'd use to shoot little rocks and paper clips. We'd have these big wars, one block against the other, and we'd always win. Yep, nobody messed with us. That's because we'd always stick together, and whenever we'd go up against one of them other blocks, we'd have everything all planned out and organized, just like an army or a team or something.

I was still trying to get rid of that "Gimp" shit though, and I tried skating my ass off all the time, thinking that maybe I could get called "Joey Skates" or "Skates". But that turned out to be a blip. Riding my scooter all the time didn't work and skating all the time didn't work either. Nope, thanks to that shithead, Googie, I was always going to be the "shrimpy-gimpy boy".

He was one of the only kids on the block that I never could stomach. And it wasn't because I had a grudge against him because of that "Gimp" shit neither. I just didn't like him from the first minute I seen his ugly mug at the feast, and after I got to know him better, I liked him even less.

Googie was the kind of guy who liked to hurt people, just for the fun of it—for kicks. Like the time me and Lino, and Bubbles, and Joey Vee were sitting on the stoop playing poker for pennies. Right away Googie came over and bogarted his way into the game—without even asking or nothing. That's the way he was; he'd never ask, he'd just bogart. Like if you had a soda, for example, you think he'd say, "thumbs up" or "can I have a slug?", like everybody else? Noooo, not Googie, that would be way too civilized for him. He'd just grab the bottle right out of your hand, and then, after he'd take one of them big, long, monster slugs that would kill practically half your soda, he'd hand whatever was left back to you, and belch right in your face.

Anyway, like I said, Googie didn't even ask if he could play cards with us; he just plopped his shitty ass down and said: "Deal me in". I didn't mind him playing with us, but after he lost a couple of hands at poker, he wanted to change the game on us. He started saying, "poker is for pussies", and he wanted to play this game called "knucks" instead. None of us wanted to play knucks, but when Googie finally won a hand of poker, he had the right to pick the next game, and it was just tough titties for us—we were playing knucks.

The whole idea of the game was to make matches and get rid of your cards as fast as you could, because when it was all over, the last guy holding any cards, had to get one "knuck" from everybody else in the game for each card he had left in his hand. A knuck was when'd you hold out your hand and make a fist, and then everybody would hit you on the knuckles with the deck of cards. Them knucks could hurt like hell. And you couldn't flinch neither, because if you got caught flinching, you had to get fifty-two knucks from each guy in the game, one for each card in the deck.

The only good thing in the game was that before you'd start getting your knucks, all the cards in the deck would get spread out in front of you, face-side down, and you'd get a chance to pick for "soft" or "hard". That gave you a fifty-fifty chance of getting soft knucks or hard knucks. If you were lucky and picked a black card, then all your knucks would be soft—just a little tap on the knuckles—but if you picked a red card, fuhgeddaboudit, kiss your ass goodbye, because you were getting some *hard* knucks—and them hard knucks hurt like a bitch.

Well, to make a long story short, we played a game of knucks—just to shut the creep up—and at the end of the game, guess who was left holding the bag of shit. You guessed it: me.

And when all the cards in my hand were counted, I was gonna be getting seventeen knucks from each guy in the game—one knuck for each card I had left in my hand.

Googie was happier than a pig in a latrine full of diarrhea, counting my cards in slow motion, one by one, with a big, ugly smile on his face. "Oooo!" he said, "looks like somebody's gonna get a few little knuckies over here! Seventeen! Seventeen knucks for Shrimpy Gimp. Awww, poor little shrimpy-gimpy boy. You're not gonna cry when ya get 'em— are ya Gimp?"

But as Googie was "warming up", smacking the deck against his leg a few times to "loosen up", all of a sudden Lino stepped in. "Hold it!" he yelled, "ain't ya even gonna give him a chance to pick?"

Then Bubbles chimed in. "Yeah! What'sa matter with you, Googie? You know the rules."

"Oh yeah," Googie answered, with a stupid smirk on his face. "I forgot"

"You 'forgot' my *ass!*" Joey Vee said. "You're in such a hurry to give Gimp his knucks, ya didn't even wanna give the poor guy a chance to pick. Ya know, not for nothin', Googie, but you're a real sick bastard—I swear to God."

93

"Wha'?! I told ya! I forgot! Come off it already, Joey."

"Yeah, yeah, we know."

So Googie spread the cards, face-side down, on a step of the stoop, and then, with a fancy flick of the wrist, he said: "Here. Go 'head, Gimp. Pick. Be my guest."

Silently, in my mind, I said a quick, little prayer to Saint Francis, my favorite saint, begging him to help me pick a black card and not a red one. But I guess he must've been out in the forest talking to the animals, or in his cave praying, or in the toilet, or out having lunch or something, because when I picked a card and flipped it over, it was the three of hearts.

Yesssss!" Googie hissed, "seventeen *hard!* Seventeen hard knucks for the shrimpy-gimpy boy. C'mon, Gimp, stick out ya hand."

As Googie took all his sweet time, trying to make me suffer even more, I did a little quick multiplication in my head. It came out to sixty-eight knucks altogether, combined, from all four guys. What the hell was I gonna do?!

Well, one thing I *definitely* wasn't going to do was flinch. Forget about that, I wasn't about to risk getting no fifty-two knucks from each guy. And I made up my mind I wasn't going to cry neither. I had enough problems without everybody calling me "faggot" and "crybaby".

So, as Googie laughed and danced around, scratching his crotch, spitting on the ground, wiping his mouth with the back of his hand, fixing the deck, smacking it against the side of his leg and loosening up his arm like a batter in the on deck circle, I just stood there, still as a statue, with my fist sticking out and my eyes open, trying to look as brave as I could, waiting for Googie to give me my first knuck.

Whack! Holy shit! It hurt like hell. I wanted to pull my hand back and shake it and rub my knuckles, but I knew better than that. That would've been flinching, and I wasn't going to flinch for nothing.

"How did that feel?" Googie asked, showing them crooked teeth and that big, ugly smile of his. "Good? Did ya like it? Huh? Want another one? Well, get ready 'cause there's sixteen more where that came from."

I didn't answer. I just stood there and stared him in the face. Fuhgeddaboudit, I couldn't believe how happy this guy was to be giving out knucks—like he'd died and went to heaven or something, laughing, and drooling, and licking his chops, like he was having the time of his life.

Whack!

Googie grinned and tilted his head. "How'd ya like that one, gimpy boy? Hah? Well, get ready 'cause there's fifteen more to go."

"Aw c'mon, Googie," Joey Vee said, "Cut the shit already, just give the guy his knucks and let's get this stupid game over with. I wanna get back to playin' poker."

"Yeah, c'mon, Googie" Bubbles shouted. "Just give him his fuckin' knucks and cut the bull."

"Keep ya shirt on, I'm givin' him his knucks. I just like to take my time and enjoy 'em."

Whack!

"How about that one, Gimp?"

Whack!

"Huh? Did ya like that one?

I could see that Googie was trying his best to make me suffer as much as he could, dragging everything out and talking a lot of shit after every single knuck he dished out. I knew he wanted me to cry, but I wasn't going to give him the satisfaction, so I held it in with all my might.

Well, I guess maybe my quickie prayer might've worked after all, because all of a sudden, outa nowhere, I got lucky. It happened when Googie was giving me my eleventh knuck.

"Hold it!" Joey Vee yelled, as he jumped up and grabbed Googie by the arm, ripping the deck right out of his hand. "What'sa matter with you?!—you fuckin' crazy or what?! Them last two knucks were over the shoulder!"

"Over the shoulder? What are you talkin' about? They wasn't over the shoulder."

"Oh yes they were, Googie, they were way over the shoulder."

"Get the fuck outa here! You need glasses, Joey, none of them were over the shoulder!"

"I saw it with my own two eyes, ya got a little carried away."

Well, as Googie argued with everybody about whether or not he'd gone over the shoulder. I took a breather and tried to get myself together. I was about to cry, and Googie knew it too. That's why he

95

probably lifted his arm a little too high on them last couple of knucks, trying to really lay into me hard to see if he could get me to break down.

But Joey Vee didn't wanna hear it, and he spread the cards out on the stoop. "Alright, let's cut the crap already. Go 'head, Googie....pick."

"*Pick?!* Why do I gotta pick for?"

"C'mon, Googie, don't play dumb. You know the rules. You went over the shoulder, and now ya gotta get fifty-two from everybody. So shut up and pick."

"I ain't pickin' shit!"

"Oh, what'sa matter? Googie the little pussy can dish it out, but he can't take it. Is that it?"

"Who you callin' a pussy?"

"You, that's who. What ya gonna do about it?"

Googie and Joey Vee kept cursing each other out and pushing and shoving for a pretty long time, 'til Bubbles and Lino jumped in and broke it up—otherwise it could've turned into a real fight. I didn't do nothing though, because I was too busy rubbing my knuckles, blowing on them, and shaking my hand to try and get it to stop hurting. But after all the arguing was over, Googie had no choice but to give in. Everybody saw him go over the shoulder, and now everything had boomeranged, right in his face. And by the look on his mug, it was easy to see he was shitting in his pants as he reached down to pick for hard or soft.

"*Fuck!*" he yelled, as he peeked at the card and then threw on the ground with all his might.

It was the jack of diamonds, and that meant he was going to get fifty-two knucks from each of us, for a total of two hundred and eight hard knucks. Oh my God! What was Mr. Big-'n'-Bad gonna do now?

Well, Googie surprised the shit outa me that time; he didn't beg, or cop a plea, or try and weasel his way out of it. He just stuck out his hand and took his knucks. He started with his eyes open, but after Joey Vee hit him with about a dozen real hard shots, he closed them, and it wasn't hard to see that he wanted to cry.

Anyway, after he got his fifty-second knuck, he opened his eyes again, and when he saw Joey Vee pass the deck to Lino, he tried to pull the woof. "Go 'head, Lino" he said, giving him a cold, dirty look, "give me fifty-two. I dare ya. Give 'em to me and I'll kick your fuckin' ass."

But Lino didn't buy none of that shit, and he didn't get scared neither. He just took the deck from Joey Vee, and without blinking an eye, he gave Googie fifty-two hard knucks—boom-boom-boom—just like a machine.

Googie didn't even try to woof out Bubbles; he was hurting way too bad by then to try and fake any dirty looks. His bottom lip was trembling like Jello, and in spite of all the messed-up shit he'd done to me, I couldn't help feeling sorry for the guy.

I guess Bubbles must've felt a little sorry for him too, because he didn't hit Googie as hard as Joey Vee or Lino had. But no matter how you sliced it, Bubbles still gave him fifty-two hard knucks, and when he finished, Googie's whole hand was bright red and raw, and each knuckle was all scraped and bleeding.

Joey Vee took the deck out of Bubbles' hand and held it out to me. "Here. Go 'head, Gimp, it's your turn."

I looked down at the deck of cards and over at the bloody fist. And then, when I looked up at Googie's face, I saw him blinking and wiping his nose like he was about to bust out crying any second.

Joey Vee shoved the deck into my hand, "C'mon, Gimp, give him his knucks."

"Naa, forget it," I said, handing the cards back to Joey Vee. "I don't wanna, I'll pass."

"What are ya talkin' about 'pass'? You can't pass in this game. We ain't playin' *dominoes* over here, we're playin' *knucks* for Godsakes. Here, now take the cards and give him his fuckin' knucks already. C'mon!"

"I told ya, I don't wanna—just fuhgeddaboudit."

"*Fuhgeddaboudit?!* What's wrong with you, Gimp? You crazy or somethin'?"

"Naa...it's just that...."

"Time out," Joey Vee said, as he put his arm around my shoulder and pulled me over to the side so nobody could hear. "What'sa matter, Gimp, you scared of this guy?"

"*Hell* no, I ain't scared of him. I just don't wanna give him no knucks—that's all. I didn't even wanna play this stupid game in the first place—remember? Besides, the guy's practically cryin' over here. Look at him. Look at his hand, he's bleedin' all over the place."

97

"I don't believe it, now I've heard everything. Gimp, what'sa matter with you? A few minutes ago, this sick fuck was happy as a pig in shit, giving you knucks like there was no tomorrow, and now you wanna feel *sorry* for the guy. Are you fuckin' nuts?!"

"He had enough already, Joey. Let's just forget it, okay?"

"Well, ya can't just 'forget it', it's too late for that. Do you think for one second if the shoe was on the other foot, this scumbag would give two flyin' shits about *you?!* C'mon, Gimp, don't be a mammaluke over here. Give the rat bastard his knucks and let's get this shit over with!"

Well, I gotta admit, Joey Vee was right. This creep never cared about me, so why should I care about him? And I knew it probably would've looked like I was scared if I backed out. So, I had really no choice; if I didn't want to get called "pussy", and "faggot", and "chump", and "chicken", and "punk, and every other name in the book, I had to give this shithead his knucks.

I really didn't wanna do it, but I took the deck of cards anyway, and then I walked up to Googie and started smacking his hand. What else could I do?

At first it was easy; each time I came down on that bloody fist, I just thought about all the mean names and all the mean things he'd done to me ever since I moved into the neighborhood. But after a while, I didn't want to hit him no more. Naa, I'd always heard that revenge was supposed to be sweet, but once I actually got a taste of it in my mouth, it didn't taste so sweet—it tasted kind of sour if you ask me. I mean, I've got to admit that it felt good to get back at Googie and give him them first ten or fifteen knucks, but after that, I started to feel like a creep, almost like me and Googie were changing places. I didn't like the feeling. It was like I was wearing somebody else's clothes and nothing fit.

Anyway, Googie took his two-hundred-and-eight knucks like a man. He didn't flinch, and even though he came close, he didn't cry neither. And when it was all over, he wrapped his handkerchief around his bloody hand, sat back down on the stoop, and couldn't wait to keep playing cards so he could win a hand at poker, play knucks again, and get his revenge.

Well, I guess it was just tough noogies for Googie, because we must've played at least fifteen hands of poker, and he couldn't win not

98

even one. Boy, was he pissed. Every time he'd lose another hand, he'd throw the cards on the ground, turn all red, and start cursing up a storm. He even tried to stop Bubbles from going home for supper when it started to get late, just so he wouldn't take his deck of cards with him and break up the game. But Bubbles wasn't going for none of that shit; when it came time for him to leave, he just scooped up his cards and cut out, leaving Googie sitting there, dingling and dangling like a dingleberry.

Ya know, come to think of it, maybe the priest at Mount Carmel was right all along when he'd say: "God works in mysterious ways." That's because from what I've seen, it doesn't pay to be mean to people and to be a bully. Nope, sooner or later it all catches up to them, and in the end, they all wind up covered in shit from head to toe—just like a Raisinet.

"Sooner or later, every dog gets his day." That's what Mom would say all the time, and she really hit the nail on the head with that one. Yep, I'd seen it happen over and over again—like the time it all caught up to Bobby Zito, the King of the Bullies. Well, I didn't exactly see *all* of it. I mean, I saw the first part, but I didn't see the second part though— and from what I heard that was the good part. That's when Shitface got a taste of his own medicine.

It all started one day when me and Nicky Specks, and Bubbles, and Sally Pork were playing marbles on one of them manhole covers down by the corner of Pleasant Avenue. We were down on all fours, concentrating on our game, just minding our own business, when all of a sudden, out of the corner of my eye, I saw The-Face-That-Only-a-Mother-Could-Love sneak up in back of Sally Pork, squirt something on the seat of his pants, light a match, and throw it right at Pork's behind. I tried to warn him, but Bobby Zito did the whole thing so damn fast, before I could even open my mouth, flames were shooting out of Sally Pork's ass.

"Pork!" I yelled. *"Look! Turn around!"*

"What?" he said, sniffing the air like he smelled something burning. "What'sa matter?"

"Turn around! Ya pants are on fire!"

99

"My pa..... *Holy shit!*" he screamed, as he shot up in the air and started running around like he had an army of killer bees up his ass.

Well, what can I tell ya? While Sally Pork was jumping around like a chicken without a head, screaming and yelling and whacking his can, trying to put out the flames, Bobby Zito and his two asshole buddies, were laughing so hard, not even a sound was coming out of their mouths. They were all doubled over, rocking back and forth and staggering around like three stupid hyenas that were so drunk from laughing that they couldn't even stand up straight.

Me, Nicky Specks and Bubbles, were too shocked to move; we just stayed there, frozen, kneeling in the gutter, with our mouths open and our marbles in our hands, staring at the flames that were coming out of Sally Pork's ass.

"*Sit on it, Pork!*" Bubbles yelled. "*Sit on it!*"

"*Sit down, Sally!*" Nicky screamed. "*Sit! Sit!*"

Bobby Zito looked at his two buddies and fell over onto the hood of a car, holding his stomach and laughing like a wild maniac. "Yeah! Go 'head, Pork, *sit on it!*"

Well, as Sally Pork plopped down on the ground and started rolling his ass around, I whipped off my tee-shirt and started swatting at the flames. I guess it must've done some good, because after a few seconds, it looked to me like the fire was all out.

"I think we got it, Pork," I said. "Go 'head, stand up so I can get a better look."

Pork stood up, and while I smacked at a piece of the back pocket of his pants that was still smoldering a little, all of a sudden, he let out a scream that shocked the shit outa me.

"*Owww! Oh! Jeez! Put it out, Gimp! Put it out! Put it out!*"

"Wha'? It's already out, Pork!"

"*No it ain't! Put it out! My fuckin' ass is burnin'*"

"Bubbles!" I yelled, "run into the candy store and get some water! *Hurry!*"

I kept on swatting away at Pork's behind with my tee-shirt, but he kept jumping up and down like a Mexican jumping bean, yelling that his ass was on fire.

"*Put it out, Gimp! Put it out! Ow! Owww!*"

100

"Pork, I'm tellin' ya—it's out! I don't see nothin', it looks like it's all out to me."

"Well it ain't!" he screamed, as he turned and started tearing ass down the block. *"My underwears are on fire over here, they're smoldering inside my pants!"*

"Stop and take ya pants off, Pork! Take 'em off!"

"I can't!" he yelled, and he kept on running as fast as he could, with me limp-running behind him, all the way down the block and across First Avenue, dodging cars and trucks and buses, 'til we reached the awning of his father's pork store and flew inside.

"Sally! What'sa matter?!" his father gasped.

Pork didn't answer, he just made a bee-line straight for the bathroom in the back of the store, unzipping his fly and dropping his pants as he ran.

"Quick!" I shouted, "get some water! They set fire to his pants, and his behind is burning!"

Pork's father and his older brother, Angelo, both ran to the sink in the bathroom and started splashing water all over Pork's behind. And then, after they'd put out the smoldering underwear and everything was under control, Pork's father dried him off with a towel and ran his fingers across these two ugly burns on the right cheek of his ass. Eeeeuuuww, that shit looked *nasty.*

"Angelo," he said, "bring me some butter from the front. Hurry up."

"We ain't got no butter, Pop."

"Then bring me some lard or some pork fat—anything! C'mon, we gotta put something on this right away! Jeez, what a bad burn. Who did this to you, Sally?"

"It was that big bully, Bobby Zito."

"Bobby who?"

"Bobby Zito, ya know, that ugly creep, the one that's always hangin' around the candy store on Pleasant Avenue with his two stupid friends."

"Oh, that *strunz.* It figures. So how did this happen anyway?" he asked, taking a big blob of pork fat off Angelo's fingers and spreading it all over the cheek of Pork's behind.

"I don't know, Pop," Pork answered. "We were just playin' marbles in the street, and all of a sudden I smell something burning, and when I turn around, the seat of my pants is on fire."

101

Pork's father turned to me, wiping the lard off his hands and onto his blood-stained butcher's apron. "What about you, sonny? Did you see what happened?"

"Yeah, I seen the whole thing."

Angelo bent down a little and looked me in the face. "So how did these bastards do this to Sally?"

"Well, like he said, me and him and these two other kids are playing a game of marbles, when all of a sudden this Bobby Zito kid, sneaks up on Sally while he's busy taking a shot and he has his behind sticking up in the air, and then he whips out this can of something-or-other... (I'm pretty sure it was that Ronson lighter-fluid stuff 'cause I recognized the blue 'n' yellow can.) Anyway, he takes this can of lighter fluid, squirts it on Sally's behind, and then he lights a match and throws it on his pants, and before we can do anything, the whole back of his pants is on fire!"

"Sonuvabitch! *Sonuvabitch!*" Pork's father yelled, as he grabbed one of his big butcher knives from behind the counter and stormed out the door. "Angelo, watch the store."

Angelo chased after his father. "Pop, where ya goin'?!"

"I'm gonna find that little sonuvabitch and cut his goddamn *balls* off—that's where I'm going! Don't worry about it—just watch the store!"

Pork's father was mad as hell, and he ran out of the store so fast, he forgot to take off his apron. Then he went barreling down 115th Street, wearing his bloody apron and carrying that butcher knife, with his face all red and his eyes bulging out like one of them pyscho-killers in the horror movies. Lucky for him there were no cops around, otherwise he probably would've got himself locked up or thrown into Bellevue in one of them straight-jacket things.

Anyway, Pork's father hustled down to Pleasant Avenue as fast as he could, looking for Bobby Zito along the way, but when he got to his hangout, the candy store, Shitface and his two buddies were nowhere to be found. Ya know, not for nothin', but this guy must've been born with both cheeks of his ass dipped in gold, because no matter what he'd do, he'd always seem to disappear into thin air, just at the right time, and he'd never get caught doing nothing.

Well, maybe he was lucky then, but his luck ran out later that afternoon when Angelo and Pork's older brother, Vito, went looking for

102

him. After they'd combed the entire neighborhood, they finally caught up with him on 111th Street over by the big gas tank. Like I said before, I didn't see all of what happened with my own two eyes, but 111th Street was my cousin Anthony's block, and he told me all about it the very next day.

According to Anthony, Bobby Zito never had a chance. He said that Vito and Angelo snuck up on him from behind, real sneaky-like, and before he could try and make a run for it, each one of them big, monster guys, grabbed an arm and practically lifted him off the ground. Then, with Bobby Zito cursing, and yelling, and pedaling his legs in the air like he was riding some make-believe bicycle, they actually carried him up First Avenue like that all the way to the pork store. Anthony said it was a pisser, because every time Shitface opened his mouth to say something, Vito and Angelo would yell, "Shut the fuck up!", and then they smacked him in the head so goddamn hard, you could hear that shit from half a block away.

Yep, the King of the Bullies, was finally getting a taste of his own medicine alright. And he had nobody to help him neither. Anthony said three of his buddy-boys, Tony Bones, Jerry Grease, and Tommy Salami, were all there with him when Vito and Angelo came along, but once they got a look at how big Pork's brothers were, all three of them punked-out and tore ass like a bunch of pussies.

Boy, that scuzzball must've really felt like shit on a stick then. He had to feel cheap—"cheap like a broken-down jeep that goes beep-beep in the middle of the street"—because there he was, all alone with nobody to help him and nowhere to run, and as Vito and Angelo hustled him up First Avenue smacking him and kicking him, you *know* he had to be shitting some king-size bricks.

Well, Anthony didn't know what happened once they got him inside the pork store, but Sally Pork was there, and he picked up the story from where Anthony left off. Pork didn't want to give us too many details because he was told not to talk about it, but from the little he told us, it sounded like his father and his two brothers practically *killed* the guy. He said they made him cry, pee in his pants, and wish he'd never been born. And after they smacked him around and scared the shit out of him—Pork's father had pulled down his pants and threatened to cut his balls off with his butcher knife—they threw him

103

in the meat freezer and left him there for the longest time. Then, when they finally pulled him out, Pork said he had icicles hanging from his nose, he was shaking and shivering, his teeth were chattering, and he looked just like a "frozen shitsicle".

Yeah, they must've scared that guy *real* good, because after that, Shitface kept his distance from Sally Pork, and wouldn't go anywhere near the pork store neither. He stayed away from that whole family like they had smallpox or leprosy or something. And if he'd see any of them coming his way, he'd duck behind a car, jump into a hallway, or walk all the way around the block, just so he wouldn't have to bump into them.

Well, maybe he learned his lesson not to mess with Sally Pork, but it didn't stop him from messing with the rest of us. Nope, he was still the King of the Bullies, and he kept right on picking on everybody, 'specially the kids that were smaller than him—like me.

The thing I hated the most was when him and his boys would sneak up on you and fuck with you in the wintertime when there was snow on the ground. They'd throw you down in the snow, rub your face in it, squish it under your neck, stick it down inside your jacket and under your stocking cap, and then, when they were all finished, they'd shove it down your throat and make you *eat* it. Jeez, I hated that. It wasn't too bad when the snow was fresh, and it was nice and clean and soft, but after a few days when it would get all hard and icy, it would really hurt like hell to get your "face washed". Your face would get all red and scraped up, and it didn't get much better when the snow would start to melt and it would get all gray, and dirty and slushy. Forget it, I would've rather been a Sumo wrestler's *diaper* than to get my face washed in *that* shit.

But the worst was when they'd throw you down into a patch of that *yellow* snow—*on purpose! Yiccchh!* That creep Booby Zito wouldn't stop grinding you face in that disgusting yellow stuff 'til it was all in your mouth, and up your nose, and in your eyes and everything. Ughh! Fuhgeddaboudit, just the idea of knowing that you had frozen dog-piss in your mouth was enough to make you want to puke your guts out right there in the middle of the street.

I remember the time it happened to me. I had to run upstairs and scrub my face about twenty times, and I kept washing my mouth out over and over again with that nasty-tasting, Listameen stuff, 'til it

104

burned my mouth so bad, I finally had to stop. I didn't go back down to play in the snow for the rest of that day—or for the rest of that *week* neither. Nope, it wasn't worth the risk, and I waited 'til every drop of snow was gone before I even *thought* about going outside again— thanks to the King of the Bullies and them stupid friends of his.

And that really bothered the hell outa me; because I really loved the snow, and I loved to play in it too. But you could never enjoy yourself when you had to be looking over your shoulder all the time, watching out for Bobby Zito. Him and his asshole friends spoiled the whole thing for everybody.

But after a while, I just said "the hell with it", and I blanked them stupid shitheads out of my mind and went out to play. I wasn't going to let them creeps mess up *my* fun. Later for that shit.

Yeah, I really loved the snow. It would always make me feel a little sad though—ya know, because it would remind me of Dad and how we'd always go belly-whopping together. But outside of that, it was always the very best part of the winter.

Those big, snowball wars we'd have against the kids from around the corner or the guys from the other side of First Avenue were always a blast. But my all-time favorite snow game was playing "king-of-the-mountain". I loved that game.

See, any time it snowed a lot, these big snow-plow things would clear off First Avenue and push all the snow into these big mounds that looked like miniature mountains. That's where we'd play king-of-the-mountain. We'd pick the biggest mound of snow we could find, make believe it was a real mountain, and go charging up the sides of it 'til one guy got to the top. Then the guy who got to the top first would plant his feet in the snow, stand up straight, bang on his chest like Tarzan or King Kong, and yell "I'm king of the mountain!", while the rest of us would do everything we could think of to drag his stinky ass down and knock him off.

Well, once you'd fought your way to the top, you weren't about to let nobody pull you down. Forget about that shit. You'd push, and shove, and kick, and bite, and step on the other guys' fingers, kick snow in their faces, bomb them in the head with these big boulders of snow and ice, and use every trick in the book to stop anybody from pulling

105

you down. 'Ey, you were "king of the mountain" and you wanted to *stay* king for as long as you could.

For me, the best thing about the game was that my limp hardly mattered at all. That was because in the deep snow, everybody limps and loses their balance, and trips, and falls over frontwards and backwards and every which way—there was no way around it. We were all in the same boat for a change, and that always felt good, 'specially to me. But the thing I really liked best about king-of-the-mountain was that there were no teams or nothing: no teams, no captains, no choosing up sides, no "once-twice-three-shoot", no "eeney-meeney-miney-mo", no "one-potato, two-potato", no fighting, no arguing, no getting left out, no feeling all shitty and stupid,...*none* of that stuff! Nope, when we'd play king-of-the-mountain it was every man for himself, and that suited me just fine.

Yeah, that game was the best. We'd spend all day charging up them snow mounds, fighting our asses off like a bunch of wild dogs just to get to the top—only to get knocked off balance a few feet from the top, and come rolling, and tumbling, and crashing down to where we started from. But you didn't stay down for long though. You'd get right back on your feet, brush yourself off, jump back on that mountain, and start climbing, over and over again, time after time, all day long, 'til the sun sank behind the buildings, and the snow would turn lavender-blue—like the color of one of them violet candies.

I'd never get to be "king" too often, but when I did, it would feel great. It'd be worth every second of all that climbing, and struggling, and fighting that it took to get up there, because let me tell ya, when you stood at the top of that mountain of snow, you felt like you were sitting on top of the world. Usually you wouldn't get to stay up there too long—what with everybody attacking you and fighting like crazy to pull you down—but while you were up there, even if it was for only a minute or two, you were "king of the mountain" and you'd feel like a million bucks.

One time a funny thing happened while we were playing king-of-the-mountain though: Every time I happened to look over toward the house, I kept noticing Grandpa watching me from the living-room window. I waved to him and yelled, "Hi Grandpa!", and he smiled and waved back at me, flicking the ash off his cigarette like he always did.

106

At first, I didn't think nothing of it, but then, every time I'd look, there was Grandpa, leaning out the window, watching me. I found it a little weird because it was really cold that day, but Grandpa just stayed there with his head out the window, smoking and scoping me out.

I found the whole thing kind of strange because Grandpa never paid no attention to none of our games or nothin'. So when I went upstairs for supper, I asked him about it.

"'Ey, Grandpa," I said, rubbing my red, wrinkled hands together over the radiator, "how come you were watchin' us playin' in the snow today?"

Grandpa didn't answer; he just shrugged his shoulders like he didn't have no special reason. But then, after he took this long, dreamy look out into the street, he pushed up his glasses, frowned, and then, tilting his head to the side a little, he said, "Junior, what's the name from this game you play in the snow today?"

"Oh! That's called king-of-the-mountain. It's a lotta fun Grandpa; that's my favorite snow game."

Grandpa rubbed his chin and screwed up his face like he was thinking to himself. "Hmm, *il re della montagna*, ah?"

"Yeah, king-of-the-mountain. Did you see me, Grandpa? I got to be king three times today. Well, I didn't get to stay up there too long 'cause the other guys pulled me down right away, but still, I made it up to the top three times in one day."

"*Bravo*, Junior," he said, nodding his head and smiling. "Yeah, I watch-a you play. You gotta have lotsa *coraggio* to play this game."

"Yeah, it ain't easy fightin' your way up to the top, Grandpa. And let me tell ya, once you get up there, it ain't easy to stay up there neither, 'cause everybody and their mother is always tryin' to pull you down—ya know what I mean?"

"This game is just like *la vita*."

"Whatta ya mean, Grandpa?"

"No you worry. When you get more big, you gonna *capisha*."

The whole thing sounded crazy if you asked me. I mean, what could a stupid kid's game like king-of-the-mountain have to do with life—"*la vita*". But, hey, I wasn't going to waste my time thinking about it—I was too busy having fun.

107

Chapter 8

Well, I finally caught a lucky break when my Easter vacation rolled around, and I finally got the chance to check out the Jamaica Racetrack with Uncle Rocco. It was a nice track and I liked the look of it, but it didn't measure up to Belmont though. That was like comparing a hamburger to some filet mignon.

Uncle Rocco was right about the paddock. It was located under the stands and it was kind of dark in there and I couldn't see the horses that good. But outside of that, it was cool.

The track itself was shaped sort of like an egg—the clubhouse turn was a lot tighter and sharper than the far turn—and I found that weird. But Uncle Rocco liked it though. He said Jamaica was a "speed track", and all day long he bet nothing but front-running, "speed" horses. And he did pretty good too; he scored with three winners, and one of them was a hefty longshot that put a big smile on Uncle Rocco's face.

I had a great time, as usual, and everything was fine and dandy— until two days later. That's when Mom found a two-dollar win ticket in the pocket of my pants, and Holy Mother of God did she throw a fit.

"What's this?" she said, staring me straight in the eye with a cold, hard look.

"A ticket."

"What *kind* of ticket?"

I looked down and the floor and didn't answer.

"What *kind* of ticket?! Answer me, Junior! Don't play dumb!"

"A ticket from the track."

"What was the promise that you made when you begged me to let you go to the track with Uncle Rocco?"

"That I wasn't gonna get mixed up with betting and gambling."

"Well, you can forget all about it now! You're never goin' back to that stupid racetrack ever again!" she screamed, tearing the ticket into little pieces and throwing them in my face. "I knew this was gonna happen! I knew it! I *knew* you were gonna get involved with gambling sooner or later; that's why I didn't want you goin' there in the *first*

108

place! For what?! So you can wind up like your uncle and turn into a pathetic horse-junkie like him?! Hah? Is that what you want?"

Boy, was she *mad*, smoke was coming out of her ears, and as she paced up and down, throwing her arms around, and screaming and yelling like a wild maniac, I could see she was getting more crazy and hysterical by the minute. She even wanted to call up Uncle Rocco at the restaurant to give him a "piece of her mind" and start a fight with him over the phone.

That's when I started to get scared, and worried too. Uncle Rocco had always been real cool with me, and I didn't want to get him in hot water with Mom just because I messed up and forgot to throw away that stupid ticket.

See, the truth was that every time Uncle Rocco hit a winner and made a nice score, he'd usually bet a couple of bucks for me on a horse I liked in one of the following races. I was always careful to throw away all my losing tickets, but I guess I must've slipped up that one time, and with my luck, *boom*, I got snagged.

Anyway, there I was, up to my eyeballs in shit. Mom kept carrying on and getting hotter and hotter by the minute, and I knew if I didn't do something quick, she was going to call Uncle Rocco on the phone, get loud with him, and then I'd never see the inside of a racetrack again 'til I'd be old enough to *drive* there by *myself*. I definitely had to do something, and I had to do it *fast*.

Well, as luck would have it, while I was sitting there, racking my brains out and trying to come up with some story or something to cover up for me and Uncle Rocco, Grandma, my lawyer, overheard what was going on, and before you could hum the opening line of the "Perry Mason" theme song, she was already rolling up her sleeves and getting down to work. The first thing she did was to help Mom get a grip on herself, and to stop the pacing up and down and all the screaming and yelling. And then, after she'd calmed her down a little, she took her by the hand, sat her down at the kitchen table, and sweet-talked her into at least listening to my side of the story.

Back then I hardly ever lied, and I wasn't very good at it neither, but I knew I had to come up with something fast, so I crossed my fingers behind my back where Mom couldn't see them, and after I took a deep breath and put on a real innocent face, I looked her straight in the eye

109

and gave it my best shot. I felt like a creep doing it, but what else could I do?

"Ma, listen to me. I wasn't betting on no horses—I swear to God. Uncle Rocco gave me that ticket to hold for him—like for good luck 'n' stuff—that's all. He's got this thing that I'm his lucky charm, and that's why sometimes, after he buys his ticket, he rubs it on my head, and then he gives it to me to hold for him—ya know, to see if I can help him get lucky and hit a winner. That's all there is to it, Ma—honest to God! See, after his horse lost, I guess I probably forgot to throw away the losing ticket, it stayed in my pocket, and that's how you found it. For real, Ma—I'm telling ya the truth!"

Well, I didn't know how convincing I was with my bullshit story, because with Mom it was always hard to tell. She'd never say a word; she'd just keep staring and staring at you, burning a hole straight through your forehead like she was trying to read something written on the inside of the back of your skull. She was really giving me the creeps, but I knew I had no choice but to keep staring right back at her. Yep, because if I didn't, if I flinched and looked away, or if I looked down at the floor, or if I blinked too many times, or rubbed my nose with my hand, or coughed, or blushed, or did anything that looked a teency bit suspicious, fuhgeddaboudit, it would've been all over for me. That's right, then she'd know I was lying, and it would've been goodbye racetrack, and hello *strap*.

Mom was just like Grandpa when it came to that honesty stuff; she had a big thing about it. If she'd even *think* I was lying, she'd go straight to the closet, whip out the belt, and give me the beating of my life. Yeah, she didn't fool around when it came to telling the truth and being honest 'n' stuff; there was nothing she hated more than a liar or a sneak. That's why I was shitting bricks. I knew I was taking a big gamble, and I knew it could backfire and blow up in my face.

Well, just as I was about to look down at the floor and give myself away, Mom finally stopped the staring contest and did something: She came out with the ol' feet-of-Jesus routine. That's the way we'd swear to stuff in my house, Italian style, and just the thought of it made me take a long hard swallow.

"Oh no!" I said to myself, "not the feet of Jesus. What the hell am I gonna do now?"

110

Mom locked her eyes on mine again and crossed her middle finger over her pointer finger, making them look like the feet of Jesus on the cross; and then she held them right in front of my face, so I could see them real good and understand what they meant.

"Ya know what this is, don't ya?"

"Yeah."

"What?"

"The feet of Jesus."

"That's right, and I want you to think real good before ya go swearing to things that aren't true. Understand?"

"Yeah."

"Alright then, if you're tellin' the truth...then kiss the feet of Jesus."

Well, I was in too deep, and there was definitely no turning back then, so I held my breath, prayed to God to forgive me, closed my eyes, and kissed Mom's fingers.

"Good," she said. "And now I want ya to make a promise."

"What?"

"I want ya to promise me that if I give you another chance and let ya keep goin' to the track, you're not gonna touch no betting tickets—not even to hold them for your uncle or nothin'—you're not gonna go near no betting windows, and you're not gonna have nothing to do with betting or gambling. Ya promise?"

"Yeah, I promise."

"Alright, kiss the feet of Jesus."

I started to lean over to kiss Mom's fingers again, but before I could, she pulled them back and said: "Don't go makin' no promises you're not gonna keep. This is a holy thing over here, so if you're gonna make a sacred promise on the feet of Jesus, you better mean it, mister."

I didn't say nothing, I just leaned over, sighed a deep sigh, closed my eyes, and kissed Mom's fingers again. I didn't know whether I could keep the promise or not, but if that's what I had to do to keep on going to the track, I'd promise anything—even on the feet of Jesus. May God have mercy on my soul.

Well, I couldn't believe it; Mom went for my story and let me off the hook—without giving me a beating, or a punishment, or a lecture, or nothing—and without calling Uncle Rocco and get him mixed up in the shit neither. It was way too good to be true. The only bad thing was

111

that I was left with this real shitty feeling—not only for having lied, but for swearing on the feet of Jesus too. And the shitty feeling didn't go away; it kept burning inside of me, fizzling and sizzling in my brain and eating away at my guts, like Drano—'til I just couldn't take it no more.

I went to confession that Saturday afternoon and told the priest all about what I'd done. He gave me three Our Fathers and three Hail Maries, and a big, long lecture about lying. I went up to the altar and said my penance, but when I was leaving the church, I *still* felt like shit on a stick. Yeah, I knew I was sorry, and I guess God knew I was sorry too, but deep down inside, we both knew that if I had to do the same thing again to keep going to the track...I would.

Well, you win some and you lose some—that's the way the Tootsie rolls, right? Sometimes Mom would listen to your story and let you slide, and other times she'd go straight for the belt and start whipping your ass—without even giving you a chance to explain or nothing. It would all depend on the mood she was in and what you did.

But let me tell ya, if you got caught doing something dangerous or something against the law, fuhgeddaboudit, you might as well kiss your ass goodbye—like that Fourth of July when she found all them firecrackers, and ash-cans and cherry bombs in my toybox. Boy, did I catch a beating that day. Not even my "lawyer" could help me get out of *that* one; I got the shit kicked out of me.

I've got to be fair though; Mom wasn't always that strict *all* the time. I mean, if you did something bad, okay, you could pretty much expect to get your ass kicked. But if you didn't do nothing bad, and you didn't mess up in school, and you didn't lie, or curse, or show nobody no disrespect or nothing like that, she could be the sweetest lady in the world. For real!

And she could be fair too, and she'd even give you the benefit of the doubt sometimes—like the time she took my side against a teacher. I never thought something like that could ever happen, but it did.

It all started a few weeks before Easter vacation, and it all had to with the word "lodge". That's because in our house, the word "lodge" and the word "large" sounded exactly the same. No difference. You

112

couldn't tell one from the other. I know I couldn't, and neither could Mom.

Anyway, one day my teacher, Mrs. Greenberg, was up in the front of the room blabbing away about the stupid "Plains Indians" or something, but I wasn't listening at all. I was busy looking out the window, staring at this puffy, white smoke that was coming out of this smokestack over by the gas tank on 111th Street. I was making believe that the smoke was these beautiful white horses, and in my mind, I could see them real clear, as they came tumbling out of the smokestack and went leaping across the sky, tossing their heads and snorting the wind, running wild and free in one big, snow-white herd.

Well, I guess I must've got a little carried away with my daydream, because I didn't even hear Mrs. Greenberg when she started asking the class questions.

"Joseph! *Joseph Scalise!*" she shouted, as I turned away from the window and saw her coming down the aisle, straight towards me with a mean, ugly look on her face. "Sorry to interrupt you, Mr. Scalise, but would you please answer the question?"

I mumbled and fumbled and stumbled out of my daydream, looking around at the kids nearby, hoping that one of them might mouth the question or the answer, or give me some kind of clue about what was happening. But none of them helped me out; they just stared at me, giving me that same stupid, blank look that a dog gives you when it's crouching down and taking a shit in the middle of the gutter.

"Answer the question, Joseph. What is a lodge?"

I didn't have the foggiest idea what she was talking about, so I just blurted out the first thing that came into my mind. "Uh... uh... well... It's a size. It's the size that comes after medium—ya know, like... small... medium... and large."

Well, I don't know what was so funny about my answer, but everybody in the class thought it was the most hilarious thing they ever heard in their lives, and they all started laughing and howling like a bunch of crazy hyenas. Yeah! I couldn't believe it, it must've taken Mrs. Greenberg a good thirty seconds of clapping her hands, yelling and stomping her feet, just to get everybody to pipe down and get a grip on themselves.

"Thank you, Joseph," she said, staring me down, "thank you very much for disrupting my lesson. I'll see you after class young man."

When the bell rang at three o' clock, everybody was dismissed except me. I was pretty sure I was going to get a big, long lecture, or maybe a punish assignment—like when you have to write something on the blackboard a hundred times 'til your hand falls off and plops on the floor. But this time Mrs. Greenberg faked me out; she didn't give me a lecture, and she didn't give me a punish assignment neither. Nope, she gave me something worse: a letter to take home to my mother.

Holy shit, what was I going to do?! I knew how Mom was; all I had to do was show her a letter from the teacher, and she'd go running straight to the closet to get the strap—without even reading it or asking questions or nothing. Yep, my only hope was to have a little talk with my "lawyer" before Mom came home from work.

As it turned out, Grandma believed everything I said, and before Mom could read the letter and find out for herself what the whole thing was all about, good ol' Perry Mason cut her off at the pass, grabbed her by the arm, and forced her to sit down and listen to my side of the story first.

So, as Mom sat there with a real suspicious look on her face, drumming on the kitchen table with her fingertips, I told her everything that happened at school that morning. And I didn't lie about nothing neither; I told her the whole truth, exactly like it happened. I admitted that I was daydreaming and that I hadn't been paying attention to the lesson, but I swore to her that when I answered the question, I wasn't trying to be a wiseguy or nothing like that.

"All the kids laughed, Ma, and I still don't even know why."

Mom tilted her head and frowned. "Well, what was this question?"

"The teacher asked what a 'lodge' is. So I told her, I said it's a size—ya know, like small, medium and large—like that."

"So?" she said, shrugging her shoulders and looking over at Grandma. "What was wrong with this answer? It makes good sense to me."

Grandma raised her eyebrows and shrugged her shoulders too. "It make good sense to me too: small...*mezza-mezza*...and lodge! What'sa matter this?!"

"I don't know," Mom said, tearing off the end of the envelope and pulling out the letter. "There's gotta be something more to it than that."

Well, Mom read the letter, and after she read it, she went straight to the closet, whipped out the strap, and gave me a real good beating for daydreaming and not paying attention in class. And then, when I thought everything was all over and done with, she turned around and gave me four or five extra whacks because Mrs. Greenberg said in her letter that I'd been "disrespectful" and had acted like a "whizzenhaymer" or a "weisenheimer"—whatever the hell that means.

There was nothing new about Mom giving me a beating for messing up in school; it's what she did *after* she gave me the beating that surprised the shit outa me. She read Mrs. Greenberg's letter a couple of times to herself, very carefully, and then she sat down at the kitchen table and started writing a big, long letter back to her. And she spent practically all night working on it too, crossing things out, looking stuff up in the dictionary, tearing it up, writing it again.... Fuhgeddaboudit, it was like she was writing to the President of the United States or something. For real! And when my bedtime rolled around, she was still right there at the kitchen table, writing her ass off.

When I woke up the next morning, I was curious as hell to find out what Mom had written. So, as we were all sitting around the table eating breakfast, I dunked a piece of toast in my coffee-milk, and without even looking at Mom, I said, "Hey, Ma, what was it that you wrote in that letter to Mrs. Greenberg anyway?"

"Hay is for horses, how many times I gotta tell you."

"Sorry," I mumbled, sticking a soggy piece of toast in my mouth. "So?"

"Sew buttons."

"Aw c'mon, Ma, what did ya write?"

"Well, if ya gotta know, the first thing I said was that I was very sorry for you not paying attention in class,...but I told her I had a long talk with you about it, and that it wouldn't be happening again."

"Yeah, right," I thought to myself, "some 'long talk'; I had a nice, long talk with the *strap*—that's the 'long talk' I had."

Mom stirred her coffee and took a sip. "But then, after I told her that, I had to straighten her out about a couple of things she said in her letter that I didn't like."

115

"Like what, Ma?"

"My, aren't we nosy this morning?"

"C'mon, Ma! Tell me! Like what?"

"Well, for one thing, she said a lotta things about you that just weren't true. She said you were 'disrespectful', and that you were looking for attention from the other kids, and that you were trying to be 'comical' and be the 'class clown' 'n' whatnot—plus a whole bunch of other stuff that didn't sound like you at all."

"So, what did ya say?"

"Junior, I'm not tellin' you what I wrote; that's between me 'n' her."

"Yeah, but just gimme a rough idea—like more or less."

"Look, I believed you when you said that you weren't tryin' to be funny or nothin'. I know you pretty good, mister, I bet you were probably dreamin' about the racetrack or some horse or somethin', and when the teacher caught you off guard, you just blabbed the first thing that came into your head. But I'm pretty sure you didn't say what ya said to be 'disrespectful', or to be funny, or to be a 'whizzenhermer' or whatever that Yiddish word was. That's not you. Besides, your answer to the question made pretty good sense to me; I didn't find nothin' wrong with it. So I told her, I says, 'yes, my son probably *was* daydreaming and not paying attention, but I know my son, and my son was not raised to be disrespectful. He just tried to answer your question as best he could; he wasn't tryin' to be a smart-aleck, or a wiseguy, and he *definitely* wasn't tryin' to make the other children laugh and call attention to himself'. 'I know my son', I says, 'and I'm tellin' you, you're wrong. And by the way, Mrs. Greenberg, in the future, if you have anything to say about my son, please say it in *English*.'"

"Wow!"

"'Wow' what?"

"Wow, Ma! You really wrote that?!"

"Yeah, why not? The truth is the truth, and what's right is right."

"Wow!"

"What are you 'wowing' about?"

"Wow, you never stuck up for me with no teacher before."

"Well, there's a first time for everything. C'mon, hurry up, it's already eight fifteen over here—you're gonna be late. Move it!"

116

I killed my juice in one big gulp, and after I kissed Grandma and Grandpa goodbye, I leaned over to Mom, kissed her on the cheek, and gave her a great big smile. "Thanks, Ma."

She kissed me back and pointed to the clock. "Let's get a move on—look at the time!"

"Okay. Bye, Ma."

"Bye. And don't forget to give that letter to the teacher—ya hear?"

"Don't worry," I yelled, as I grabbed my books and ran out the door, "I won't!"

Well, let me tell ya, I don't think I've *ever* been as happy to go to school as I was that morning. I couldn't believe it, for the first time in my life, my mother was actually taking *my* side against a teacher. Forget it, I was in such a hurry to give the letter to that cranky, old witch, I ran all the way there.

When I finally handed the letter to Mrs. Greenberg, she just took it without saying a word, and stuck under the corner of that big blotter-thing on her desk. I thought she at least was going to read it in front of me, so I could get the satisfaction of watching her turn all red when she got to the part where Mom said she was "wrong". But she didn't even look at it. I felt gypped.

I thought she might've even forgotten about it too, 'til she pulled me over at dismissal and handed me *another* letter. "Joseph, please give this letter to your mother for me."

Well, before I even knew what hit me, I found myself right in the middle of The Battle of the Poison Pens! Yep, for an entire week, Mom and Mrs. Greenberg kept writing letters back and forth to each other, each one trying to outdo the other by coming up with these long, complicated meanings for a simple-dimple word like "lodge". Fuhgeddaboudit, after a while I was starting to feel like I was in the middle of a ping-pong tournament or a tennis match. For real! First it was "lodge" this, then it was "lodge" that, then it was "lodge" the other, 'til the whole stupid mess got so crazy and confusing, I don't think even *they* knew what they were arguing about anymore.

Ya know, not for nothin', but sometimes these grownups can act more like kids than us kids do. 'Cause let me tell ya, you'd never see no kids getting into a big argument about the meaning of some stupid word. We got *better* things to do with our time than to waste it fighting

117

about some dumb shit like that. I mean, okay, maybe we *might* bounce it around for a while, but after that, we'd just say "fuck you", or "get the fuck outa here", or "you don't even know what the fuck you're talkin' about", and that would be the end of it. Yeah! Then we'd go to the corner to get a soda or start a game of boxball or single-double, and we'd forget all about it.

But not these "adults", they'd keep stirring and stirring the shit, over and over again, 'til it would stink so goddamn bad, you'd have to get yourself *gas mask!* I'm serious!

'Ey, I still didn't know nothing about none of them fancy meanings for that stupid word they were fighting about—and I couldn't have cared less neither. But I knew one thing though: by the time the end of the week rolled around, the whole stupid mess had turned into one "lodge" pain-in-the-ass.

Chapter 9

Mr. Grasso, the barber, put that scratchy, tissue-paper stuff around my neck, patted me on the shoulders, and looked at me in the mirror. "So, Joey my boy, what are we gonna have today—the usual?"

"Naa," I answered, blushing a little, "I wanna try somethin' different."

"Like what?"

"Well, I don't wanna have the part in my hair no more. Ya think you could cut it so that I could comb it back and wear it in a DA?"

"Sure I can, Mister Joey, anything you say. You're the boss. One DA comin' up."

I liked Mr. Grasso, he was cool. A little cheap with his lollipops though; he'd give you the cheap, junky kind. But it didn't matter anyway; I stopped taking lollipops after my haircuts a long time ago—that was for little kids.

Anyway, while Mr. Grasso hummed along with the radio and started clipping away, I kept my eyes glued to the mirror with a worried look on my face. I guess I was a little nervous, because deciding to get a DA was a big decision for me. I spent practically the whole summer thinking about it, because there I was, getting ready to start the seventh grade, and I still looked like a doofy, little kid. I was still the shortest guy on the block and in my class, and between the part in my hair and my stupid-looking baby face, I looked like a fourth or fifth-grade dingleberry.

That's why I figured I had to do something fast, and that's why I decided to get a DA. I was hoping it would make me look a little older, and with any luck, maybe a little cooler too.

See, around my neighborhood you had two different kind of guys: "goody-goody boys" and "rocks". The goody-goody boys all had parts in their hair, and the rocks all had DA's—that was just the way it was. You'd never see a rocky guy wearing a pair of tan chinos, with a plaid shirt and brown penny-loafers, and you'd never see a goody-goody guy, with the sleeves of his tee-shirt rolled up, wearing a garrison belt, and combing back the sides of his DA neither. It would never happen in a million years.

I used to think hairstyles didn't matter much, but that summer, my hair started to become kind of important to me. I mean, I didn't even bother to comb my hair except when Mom or Grandma told me to, but little by little, I found myself spending more and more time in front of the mirror every morning, combing it over and over again before I'd leave for school.

It probably had something to do with the big crush I had on Angela, the girl that looked like Annette from the Mickey Mouse Club. I liked her from the first minute I laid eyes on her at the feast, and ever since then, my crush has been growing and growing—'specially when I'd see her at school or at Mass on Sundays.

There were a couple of other girls who were starting to look kind of cute too—like Roseanne Totino, and that new girl, Linda What's-'er-name. But when you came down to it, none of them could compete against Angela—not for good looks anyway. Naa, Angela definitely kicked their asses; she was the champ.

Anyway, getting a new hairstyle probably wasn't no big thing or nothing, but at the time, it was one of the most important decisions I ever had to make in my whole life. I was almost a teenager, and it was time for me to decide whether I was going to be a goody-goody boy or a rock. I knew I couldn't stay in the middle no more, so I had to pick one or the other.

Well, it was easy to see what side of the fence I wanted to be on. I went with the rocks. I didn't want to get all super-duper rocky or nothing; I just wanted to get the part out of my hair so I could blend in a little better—so I wouldn't stick out like a sore thumb and get called "doofus" or "flunky".

Well, as soon as Mr. Grasso blobbed the usual green, gooky stuff on my hair and started to comb it, I knew right away I'd made the right move. Yep, first he slicked back the sides, and then he made this cool pompadour in the front—just like a DA. No more part, no more dingleberry boy.

I squinted and looked in the mirror to take my first look at the new me. I noticed I had a few hairs sticking up like a porcupine in the back, but Mr. Grasso said all I had to do was "train my hair" and brush it back with a hard, stiff brush and it would be fine.

"Thanks a lot, Mr. Grasso."

"You bet, Joey."

I slipped Mr. Grasso the dollar and a quarter Mom had given me for the haircut, and then I took another quick look in the mirror and patted the sides of my brand-new DA. I was happy, and as I walked out of the barber shop, I felt a whole lot cooler than when I walked in. It was almost like I got baptized, and that was the first day of the rest of my life.

As soon as I walked in the house, I could see Mom wasn't too happy with my haircut.

"What kinda haircut is that?"

"It's a DA, Ma—ya like it?"

"I *know* it's a DA. Who told ya to get a haircut like that?"

"I don't know, I just thought I'd try somethin' different—that's all. What'sa matter, ya don't like it?"

"*Ma!*" she yelled, calling to Grandma in the kitchen. "Come in here and look at this!"

Grandma hustled in, licking the sauce off her cooking spoon. "What'sa matter?"

"Look, Ma, I give him good money to get a haircut, and this is what he comes back with. He wants to copy his little hoodlum friends and be just like them."

Grandma didn't say nothing; she just started walking around me in a slow circle, looking at my head from different angles, like she was looking at a statue or a sculpture in a museum.

"And while Grandma was busy, checking out my hair, Mom was busy sticking her finger in my face and growling at me. "Go 'head, keep following your stupid friends, and you're gonna see where it's gonna get ya."

"But, Ma, it's only a haircut—what's the big deal?"

"The 'big deal' *is* that I gave you my hard-earned money to get a nice, decent haircut, and you come strolling in here looking like some juvenile delinquent that just got back from reform school—*that's* what the big deal is!"

121

Grandma turned to Mom and waved her away. "Celeste, what'sa matter you? He no look like *delinquente,* he look cute."

"*Cute?!* Are you crazy, Ma?"

Grandma slid her hand slowly along the sides of my hair and smiled. Then, after she grabbed the sides of my face with both hands and gave me a big, noisy smooch, she spread her arms out wide and looked up at the ceiling. "That'sa right, to me he look cute."

"Ya see? Grandma says I look cute."

"Oh boy," Mom grumbled, rolling her eyes and trying to squash a smile. "Yeah, real, real cute. I wanna see how 'cute' you're gonna look when you're behind bars, mister. 'Cause let me tell ya, keep on with that stupid monkey-see monkey-do attitude of yours, and you're gonna follow your little friends straight into *jail.*"

Grandma put her arm around me, and pulled me close, stroking the side of my face. "Celeste, *lasha l' stara*, leave my Junior alone. That's a very nice haircut. Whatta you talk? He look *bello, bello, bello.*"

Mom turned away and made believe she was looking out the window. She was trying to cover her face with her fist, but I could tell she was starting to laugh. "Gee, thanks a lot, Ma—you're a big help."

Well, maybe Grandma wasn't such a big help to *Mom*, but she sure was a big help to *me*. Yep, whenever the chips were down, my lawyer would always come through for me with flying colors.

So, as the last few days of the summer oozed by like honey off a spoon, I "trained" my DA with a "hard, stiff brush" and got ready for the seventh grade. I didn't know what was waiting for me around the corner, but I had this funny feeling it was going to be something good.

Well, I had that shit pegged, because as we lined up in the schoolyard, I found out right away what that "something good" was: For the first time in my life, I was getting a man teacher, and there he was standing right in front of me.

I liked him right away. He had a big smile on his face, and he didn't look all crabby and cranky, like them grumpy, old battle-axes I'd always get. He looked to be a pretty cool guy.

From his looks, I figured he was a Jewish guy, maybe about forty or forty-five, and he wore the same wire-frame glasses, like the kind Grandpa wore. His hair was kind of thin in the front, and he had a big

122

bald spot in the back, but he looked okay—except for that doofy-looking, bow tie he had around his neck.

But the real kick in the head was when he wrote his name on the blackboard in big letters: Mr. S-A-N-D-M-A-N. Holy shit! I couldn't believe his real name was Mr. Sandman—just like the song! Everybody started laughing their asses off, and right away a couple of the wiseguys in the back of the room started singing the "Mister Sandman" song out loud. It was a pisser.

But the guy was a good sport about it though. He just leaned back against the blackboard, cool as a cucumber, with his arms folded and a big smile on his face, just waiting for us to calm down and finish goofing on his name.

"What can I say?" he chuckled, rubbing his hands together and opening up his attendance book. "Ever since that song became a hit, my name always seems to get a musical reaction—especially from my students."

Well, this Mr. Sandman might've been a nice guy and everything, but he wasn't about to waste the whole morning letting us have a field day goofing on his name. Nope, after he took attendance, the first thing he did was to break up the "little clusters of friends", and he assigned all of us new seats in alternating rows of boys and girls. Right away I got excited and started hoping and praying that I'd get assigned to the seat next to Angela, but no such luck. He put me over by the window, and she got a seat over by the cloakroom. But it wasn't all that bad; with me on one side of the room and her on the other, I figured I could scope her out all day long and she wouldn't even know I was doing it. Yeah, in a way I was glad I didn't get seated next to her; that would've got me way too nervous and distracted, and I probably would've failed all my subjects.

But even though I wasn't lucky enough to sit next to Angela, sometimes I'd wind up next to her when we'd line up for lunch. And that's when she finally said something to me. She kept staring at me for some reason; so naturally, I got scared right away, and the first thing I did was to cover my face with my hand—ya know, in case I had a booger dingling down from my nose and it had caught Angela's eye or something. But as it turned out, she wasn't staring at a booger at all; she was checking out something else.

123

"Hey, Joey," she said, tilting her head to the side and wrinkling up her cute little nose, "Did you do somethin' different to your hair?"

Right away I felt my heart pounding and my mouth getting drier than the Mohave desert. "Yeah," I answered, "I started combin' it back."

"Hmmm, looks nice."

"Thanks."

Well, what can I tell ya, that one little word "nice" had me floating on air—and I kept right on floating for the rest of the day, the rest of the week, and the rest of the school year. Yep, I was happier than a pig in shit, knowing that Angela, the most beautiful girl in the world, liked my DA. Thank you, Mr. Grasso!

Anyway, as time passed and I got to check out Mr. Sandman in class every day, I got to like him even more than I did at the beginning. He definitely turned out to be the very best teacher I ever had. And it wasn't just because he was a guy; it was because of his personality and his style of teaching. He had this way of taking something really boring and twisting it into something really interesting. He'd show you pictures, and filmstrips, and movies, and take you on trips to museums and stuff like that. And he wasn't afraid to crack a joke and makes things funny and fun neither. Nope, he was the first teacher I ever had who had a sense of humor and wasn't all mean, and nasty, and grouchy all the time.

The whole class really liked him—'specially the boys. And we even made up a song about him too. Me, Richie Gamarella, Vinny Tornatore and a couple of the other guys put our heads together one day and came up with the words to it. We didn't need no melody because we already had one. Of course! What else? The "Mister Sandman" song! And when we sang it to him in the schoolyard one day, he didn't even get mad or nothing—he got a big kick out of it.

It went like this:

"Mister Sandman, please help me pass
Please stop my mother from kicking my ass
Sharpen my brain and give me some knowledge
and maybe I could even go to college

124

Mister Sandman, I'll try my best
Just leak the answers to all of your tests
I'll do homework every day
Mister Sandman give me an 'A'"

He cracked up and thought the whole thing was a pisser—all except for the word "ass". He said "ass" was a bad word. That's when Vinny Tornatore whipped out a dictionary and showed him that "ass" was right there in the dictionary—so it couldn't be a bad word. But Mr. Sandman didn't buy it though; he stuck to his guns and said that no matter how you sliced it, the word "ass" was still "vulgar".

Well, maybe it was "vulgar" for him, but it sure wasn't "vulgar" for us. Hell no. We kept our song exactly the way it was, and we weren't about to change a word of it for nobody—not even Mr. Sandman.

Boy, if he thought a lousy little word like "ass" was vulgar, I wondered what he'd say if he heard some of the other versions of the "Mister Sandman" song that some of the other kids would make up behind his back when they'd get pissed at him. I'm talking about stuff like:

"Mister Sandman, you piece of shit, you made my mother start throwin' a fit" or "Mister Sandman, you stupid prick, this math assignment is makin' me sick". Ya know, stuff like that.

Well, I never made up none of *them* kind of songs; not so much because they were vulgar, but because I never had no beef against Mr. Sandman. Nope, me and him always got along pretty cool. I liked him, and I got the feeling that he liked me a little too.

He seemed to really like the way I could draw and paint 'n' stuff, and he was always asking me to help him decorate the bulletin board or to draw stuff on the blackboard for him with them big Indian chalks. And he'd always make a big fuss about the pictures I'd draw too—'specially my horse drawings. He'd always tell me to color them in, and after I did, he'd hang them up in the big bulletin board in the hallway where the whole school could see them.

Yeah, Mr. Sandman really liked my artwork alright, and one day he even told me that I had a lot of talent, and that maybe I could even become an artist someday. But he said I should try and take some art lessons though, so I could develop the talent and make it better.

125

Well, when I told him my mother didn't have no money for no art lessons or nothing like that, you know what he went and did? He called up some friend of his at this place on the west side called The Riverside Neighborhood House, and he got me into these free art classes that they had for kids on Saturday mornings. Yeah, that Mr. Sandman was one hell of a nice guy, and having him for a teacher, was one of the luckiest things that ever happened to me.

Anyway, Mom thought it was a great idea, but she said she couldn't take me because she had to work at the beauty parlor on Saturday mornings. I told her that I could take the crosstown bus by myself, but she wouldn't go for it. She said I was too young to be getting on buses and crossing through Harlem alone. But as I walked away, feeling all sad, and shitty, and disappointed, guess who jumped in to save the day, just like Mighty Mouse: Grandpa.

"'Ey, what'sa matter me?" he said, "I no do nothing Saturday in the morning. I can take Junior to the class."

"You mean it, Grandpa, you'll really take me to the art classes?"

"Sure, I take you—why not?"

Well, it looked like everything was settled; not only was I going the art classes, but I was gonna be going with my very best favorite buddy: Grandpa.

The big day finally arrived, and there I was bopping down the street with Grandpa. I always liked going places with him, and I'd never feel awkward or embarrassed walking with him, like I did with Mom sometimes. I wasn't sure exactly why, but maybe it had something to do with him being a guy and me being a guy. Because it wasn't like: "Look! There goes little Joey Gimp limping along with his mommy". It was more like: "'Ey, there's a couple of guys walking down the street together"—no big deal.

Anyway, from the way Grandpa was acting on the bus, it looked to me like he was even more excited than *I* was about going to the art class. He kept fidgeting around like he was a little nervous— straightening his tie, shooting his cuffs, touching the brim of his hat— and every few minutes he'd whip out his pocketwatch to check the time to make sure we weren't going to be late. Grandpa hated to be late. He'd say that being late was a big disrespect to the person who was

126

waiting for you, and he'd always try his best to be right on time—no matter where he was going.

He was usually kind of quiet, but that day he kept talking and talking—like he ate a parrot for breakfast or something—and he kept patting me on the knee, smiling, and telling me that I was real, real lucky to be getting such a big *"opportunita'"*.

"Who know?" he said, "maybe someday you gonna be a big *artista*—like Michelangelo, or Raffaello, or Botticelli, or Bellini....or Giotto."

Well, maybe I had a shot at being as good some of them other guys someday, but I knew I'd never be as good as Giotto though. Are you kidding? The only way *I* could draw a perfect circle was if I used a compass, and even then, it would come out all egg-shaped and lopsided.

The art class turned out to be a dud at the beginning. The teacher, Miss Pels, was a pretty lady, and real nice too, but all she did was make us draw a bunch of fruits in a bowl with this black stick called "charcoal". She called it a "still life", but it was more like a "dead life", if ya asked me. But after we finished doing the assignment, she let us use the rest of the time for "free expression". That's the part I liked the best, because that's when I could make my horse drawings. Miss Pels liked them a lot, and one time she even held up one of my pictures so the whole class could see it.

And after a while, the class got better and better, 'specially when I "worked my way up" to using all the different materials they had there—like the pastel-chalks and the oil paints. That's when Miss Pels showed me how to mix colors and how to blend them together to make stuff look natural and "realistic".

Yeah, that Miss Pels really knew her stuff when it came to art, and I looked forward to the class every week. But what I liked even better than the class itself, was hanging out with Grandpa, just me and him.

I remember one day in particular when we decided to walk across Central Park to get to the east side without taking the crosstown bus. Grandpa got a little tired after a while, so we sat down to rest. It was

127

getting late, and the light was already turning yellow orange. He pulled out an Old Gold and lit it, and I sat next to him and stayed quiet. I don't know why, but for some reason, I thought that it might be the perfect moment to ask him a question that had been on my mind for a pretty long time.

"Hey, Grandpa, can I ask you a question?"

"Sure. What you wanna know?"

"I wanna know how come you never go to church on Sunday. I mean, ya know all about the saints, and ya know all about God 'n' everything, so how come you never go to church? Huh, Grandpa?"

"I go to Church, I'm in my church right now."

"Grandpa! This ain't no church, this is Central Park over here—what'sa matter with you?"

"Well, maybe for you it's Central Park, but for me it's a church."

"C'mon, Grandpa, you know what I mean. I'm talkin' about a regular church—like Mount Carmel or St. Ann's. Didn't you ever go to a regular church, not even when you were a kid?"

"Yeah, I go."

"So? What happened? Why'd ya stop goin'?"

Grandpa took a puff of his cigarette and looked at the sky, like he was seeing something far away. "Well, once in a time, long ago, when I was little boy, my father he get sick. He have heart attack. He was very sick, and my sister, Violetta, was very worry he gonna die."

"Yeah, so?"

"So, when we come from the school, Violetta wanna go in the church to pray for him and to light a candle for him. Oh boy, the way Violetta cry. She say to God, 'please no take my papa. You already take my mama, please no take my papa!' I no forget the way Violetta cry. I cry too."

"So then what happened, Grandpa?"

"The priest he come inside the church. He come and he stand in front from us and he says, 'Ey, what you do in the church?' So I says 'Patre, we come to pray.' Then he look to Violetta and he says 'What'sa matter you? You come to pray inside the house from God, and you no have nothing to cover you head?' So Violetta she says, 'Oh, Patre, I'm-a sorry. I forget, I come from the school, and I no have nothing to put on my head.'"

128

"So what did the priest do?"

"He look to me, and he says: 'Ey, what'sa matter you? Take you hankachifa from you pockets and give to the girl to cover her head.' I touch my pockets from my pants, but I no gotta hankachif. So I says 'I'm-a sorry, *Patre,* I no gotta hankachifa'"

"So then what did he do?"

"You wanna know what he do? The sonuvabitcha he says, 'You no have respect for God. Go from the church to you house and get something to put on you head.'"

"Are you kiddin', Grandpa? You mean he chased yuz outa the church just 'cause your little sister didn't have nothing to cover her head with?"

"That'sa right, the sonuvabitcha."

"So what did you do?"

Grandpa shrugged his shoulders and touched his fingertips together. "What I'm gonna do? The priest he say go out from the church, so we go out. That's all—*finisha.*"

"Wow, you must've been mad, huh Grandpa?"

"Sure I was mad, and before we leave the church, I look to the priest and I says, *'alla faccia tua!'*"

(I knew that meant something like "up yours" in Italian.)

"Holy moly! So then what did you do?"

"Well, me and Violetta we sit in the *piazza* in front from the church. Violetta feel bad, and she cry. So I says, 'You wanna pray to God for Papa? Look to the sky and pray. You no need church, you no need priest, you no need candle, you no need nothing. Close you eyes, and say what you feel in you heart, and He gonna listen to you. You gonna see.'"

Grandpa looked up at the clouds again and stayed quiet for a while, like he was thinking and remembering something from long ago. I just sat there and listened to the trees, as he took out his handkerchief, cleaned his glasses, and took a couple of quick swipes at his eyes when he thought I wasn't looking.

"So, you never went back to church after that?"

"Yeah, I go back. I go back for the *funerale* for my papa, I go back when I marry you Grandma, and I go back lotsa time. What'sa matter you? You no remember when I go to church for you, for you *confermazione*?"

129

"Oh yeah, for my confirmation. I almost forgot about that. Boy, not for nothin', Grandpa, but that was really weird seeing you in church."

"Well, sometime when you gotta go, you gotta go."

I chuckled to myself, remembering his corny joke about why going to the toilet and dying is like the same thing: "'cause when you gotta go, you gotta go". But then I just stayed quiet for a while, thinking, and smelling the breeze, checking out the sunset light as turned from pinkish-gold to bright, golden-orange.

"But don't you ever pray, Grandpa?"

"Sure I pray! What'sa matter you?

"Well, I never seen you prayin' or nothin'"

"Junior, when you pray, it's something between you and God. It's no for other people to hear, and it's no for other people to see—like to make show off. *Capisha?*"

Well, once we got on the subject of praying, Grandpa explained his own ideas about it—and he had a lot of them. He said praying was a real private thing, and instead of saying regular prayers like the Our Father and the Hail Mary, it's better to talk to God from your heart and to use your own words—not words that other people put in your mouth.

And when I asked him about repeating a lot of prayers all together, like you do when you say the rosary, he just chuckled and said: "God he no deaf, you no need to repeat a hundred time. God no want prayers by the pound. You only gotta say what you feel one time, from deep inside you heart—no a hundred time like a machine."

"Yeah, I never thought about it like that."

It started to get cold, and Grandpa said we should start heading back home. We climbed a steep, little hill on our way out of the park, and he stopped in his tracks for a second to take a rest. Then, almost like he forgot something, he turned around to take one last look at the trees, and the sky. I watched him as he lifted his head and took a deep breath, sniffing the air like he was smelling perfume. The breeze was getting a little stronger. I watched a red leaf as it danced down the hillside and landed next to a rock. It got real quiet all of a sudden, and all you could hear was the hum of the buses on Fifth Avenue, and the sound of the birds chirping. Everything was covered in a rosy-blue shadow, but across the street, the windows on the top floors of the buildings were still burning gold, reflecting the sunset—like an echo.

Chapter 10

A few months later something really weird happened to me. I didn't know what to make of it or how to explain it, but it all started on a Saturday night when I was taking a bath.

See, there I was, lying in the tub, soaking in the suds and humming a tune, when all of a sudden, I started to get this funny feeling in my crotch. I had no idea how it happened; I was just rubbing the soapy washcloth around in between my legs, and—boom!—before I knew what hit me, I saw the tip of my dick sticking up out of the water like it was the freakin' Loch Ness monster over here! For real! It shocked the shit outa me.

"Holy moly!" I mumbled, as I pushed some of the bubbly foam to the side to get a better look at it. "What the hell is this?"

I'd never seen my dick looking nothing like that before—usually it was kind of small and droopy looking—but all of a sudden there it was, all hard and stiff, sticking up straight in the air like a little pink stickball bat. The whole thing was freaky, because I'd never paid too much attention to my dick before. I mean, I always knew it was *there*, but I never thought about it or touched it or nothing. I figured it was just there for taking leaks—what else was I supposed to do with it?

Well, I knew different then. Yep, without even trying, I discovered something new. So I just leaned back, made the washcloth nice and soapy, and started rubbing it all around my crotch.

"Junior!" Mom yelled, banging on the bathroom door and scaring the shit outa me. "What'sa matter? You drowned in there or what?! C'mon! Other people gotta use the toilet over here!"

"Alright, Ma, I'll be right out."

Well, what happened in the bathtub definitely shocked the shit out of me, but in a funny way, it opened my eyes to a few things that had been bothering me for a while—like take that word "rape" for instance. I'd been thinking about it ever since I heard it in this John Wayne movie and got this half-assed explanation from Mom that left me even more

132

confused. I'd been wanting to ask some of the guys on the block about it for the longest time, but I'd always wind up chickening out; I guess I was scared that somebody would start goofing on me 'n' stuff. But after that thing happened to my dick in the bathtub, I just had to know more about it. I don't know why, I just had this feeling that there was some connection between the two things—ya know what I mean?

So, after a while, I finally got up the courage to ask a couple of the guys what it meant. Nobody really seemed to know except Joey Vee; he was a year or two older than the rest of us, and he always knew more than we did when it came to stuff like that. He made a real big production out of it, and after he finished with all his bullshit, he finally came out with it.

"Rape," he said, spitting through his teeth and scratching his crotch, "is when a guy forces himself on a broad and fucks her when she don't wanna get fucked. *Capish?*"

Well, I guess when Joey Vee saw all our blank, empty faces staring back at him, he must've known that we didn't *"capish"* too good. That's when he made a circle with the thumb and pointer finger of one hand, and then took the pointer finger of his other hand and started sliding it in and out of the circle real fast.

"Hey, you stupid shitheads, I'm talkin' about fucking! Don't tell me yuz don't even know what the word 'fuck' means?!"

We all chuckled and waved him away with our hands, as if to say: "Of course, we know what 'fuck' means—what are you kidding?"

Well, I guess we didn't convince Joey Vee too good, because he started in with us even more: "I can't believe it! I don't even know why I hang around with you guys. What a buncha stupid assholes, I swear. All day long, every other word outa your mouths is 'fuckin'' this, and 'fuckin'' that, and 'fuckin'' the other, and all this time none of yuz even knew what the word 'fuck' means. *Madon'*, what a buncha dingleberries—I swear to God."

We kept on saying that we knew what "fuck" meant, but Joey Vee wasn't buying it. So, after he goofed on us and made us feel like shitheads all over again, he called us into a huddle like a quarterback, and he finally whispered the definition we'd all been waiting for.

"The word 'fuck' means that a guy gets a hard-on, a big fuckin' boner, and he sticks it into a broad's cunt and starts humpin' away,

133

slidin' his dick in and out of her pussy 'til he comes and creams all over the goddamn place."

Lino got up and waved Joey Vee away. "Is that all? I knew that shit a long time ago."

"Yeah, me too," Nicky said. "Big deal."

"That's right," I added, "I knew that shit a long time ago too."

Joey Vee's middle finger popped up in a flash. "Get the fuck outa here, don't try and bullshit *me!* None of yuz knew *shit*—'specially you, Gimp. I bet you probably think the fuckin' *stork* brings babies down from heaven in his *beak* 'n' whatnot."

"Come off it already, Joey," I said, trying to look like I knew all about that stuff.

"*You* come off it. *You're* the one who came asking about the word 'rape'—not me."

"So big deal, so I didn't know what the word 'rape' means; that don't mean I didn't know what the word 'fuck' means—does it?"

"Save it, Gimp, none of you dumb, little bastards knew shit, and I betcha anything you're all gonna go home tonight and jerk off just thinkin' about it too."

I stood up and gave Joey Vee the finger. "Fuck you."

"Fuck *me?!* Fuck *you!*"

Well, I went home that night, but I didn't "jerk off" or nothing. How could I if I didn't even know what it *was*? But I *did* think about everything Joey Vee said on the stoop though. I've been thinking about it ever since, 'specially all them new words I'd never even heard before—like "hard-on", and "boner", and "come", and "cream". I put two and two together and figured that "hard-on" and "boner" were probably names for the thing that happened to me in the bathtub, but I still didn't know what none of them other words meant.

And to tell the truth, Joey Vee was right; I really *didn't* know where babies came from. I mean, I *knew* the stork didn't bring them—I wasn't *that* stupid—but I really didn't know too much else. Part of it was because I never had a sister or nothing, and even though I'd seen a lot of paintings and sculptures of naked ladies in the museum, and I had a pretty good idea about what tits and asses and all them V-shaped crotches looked like, I'd still never really seen a cunt or a pussy in real

134

life before—not even in a picture for that matter. That's why I wasn't too sure about where the babies came out from; I didn't know whether they came out from the cunt, or the pussy, or from the back—ya know, from the behind.

My best guess was that they probably come out from the back though because I'd always heard a lot of grownups using the expression "rear your children" all the time. So I figured that probably meant that babies came out from the rear—like from the ass. It made sense. I mean, why else would they say something like that?

But I still wasn't a hundred percent sure though. I guess I'd have to see a pussy up close, in real life, so I could compare the size of it with the size of an asshole. Because even though that "rear your children" stuff made a lot of sense, I still couldn't picture in my mind how a big thing like a baby could come out of somebody's behind.

Well, I guess I'm going to have to figure that one out for myself. I sure as hell wasn't going to ask Mom. What for? So she'd tell me only *half* the story and leave me even *more* confused, like she did when I asked her what "rape" meant? Forget that shit, I'd rather just keep things to myself. Only problem was, every single day I was coming across a whole bunch of new stuff that'd make me feel ten times more mixed up than I already was.

Like take them hard-ons for instance, I wasn't just getting them in the bathtub no more; I started getting them all over the place. I could be riding on the bus, watching TV in the living room, or just sitting at my desk doing my homework, and all of a sudden, I'd look down and—boing!—I'd see the 'Leaning Tower of Pizza" sticking up out of my lap. And to make matters worse, I think Mr. Sandman must've had hard-on radar or something, because every time I'd get one of them things and it would be kicking my ass, guess who he'd call on to stand up and read something, or to go up to the blackboard and do a math problem? Me! Fuhgeddaboudit, can you imagine how embarrassing it was to stand in front of the class and do some stupid algebra problem with a big, freakin' bulge in your pants? I'd want to turn into the "Invisible Man", 'specially when I'd see Angela and a couple of the other girls covering their mouths and giggling.

It was just a bad time for me; that's all there was to it. It was like I had a split personality, like that Doctor Jekyll and Mr. Hyde guy. For real!

135

Because one minute I could be getting a boner thinking about Jayne Mansfield shaking her ass in one of them skin-tight dresses, and the very next second I could be lying on the living room floor, playing make-believe stuff with my toy horses or my horse-race game—just like I always been doing since I was a little kid. The whole thing was crazy, and really confusing too. It's like I was half man and half boy, and I couldn't decide which one I was or which one I wanted to be. But I guess I just had to lump it though; all it probably meant was that I was growing up and turning into a teenager. Better late than never, right?

Well, thanks to good ol' Mr. Sandman, my final report card was a killer—I got an A in everything except math—and when I woke up on the morning of my birthday, there was a brand-new bike waiting for me in the living room with a big, red ribbon on it. Yep, I finally turned thirteen, and not only was I officially a teenager, but I was a teenager with *wheels*.

I loved my new bike—it was twenty times better than my scooter—and from the time I got it, I hardly even touched my scooter no more. Why would I want to ride around on a dinky, homemade scooter, when I could ride in style on my brand-new English racer?

But maybe it wasn't right to say that. After all, that little black scooter of mine helped me get through some pretty sad and lonely times when I first moved on the block and nobody wanted to play with me or nothing. Yeah, that scooter was almost like a friend to me then, and even though I hadn't been riding it since I got my new bike, I still didn't have the heart to throw it out. I've kept it sitting there in the corner of my room next to my toybox, and every time I'd look at it, it would remind me that, little by little, I was growing up,...and I would never be a kid again for the rest of my life.

Anyway, now that I had wheels, I figured it was time for me to start branching out and start spreading my wings a little. I knew I had promised Mom that I wouldn't ride in the street and that I'd stay around the block, but that was bullshit. How many times could you ride around the same block without getting bored and going bananas? I felt bad about lying and disobeying her, but what else could I do? It was summertime, and every day it would be the same ol' story.

136

See, every morning around eleven o'clock all my friends would meet on the block, and then, after they fooled around and bullshitted for a while, they'd always wind up going over to the Jefferson Pool, so they could spend the afternoon splashing around and beating the heat. But I'd never go with them though; I'd always stay behind. I'd just stay sitting on the stoop, all by myself, holding a big bag of shit, watching, while everybody else went bouncing down the block toward the pool with their towels under their arms, laughing and joking, and slapping each other five. I really hated being left out like that, but I had no choice. I'd *never* go to the pool in the summer. Nope, not to a pool, not to a beach, not to a lake—nothing. I wouldn't go anywhere near water, except when someone would open up the Johnny pump and I could get wet without taking off my pants or my shoes. But outside of that, fuhgeddaboudit. Who wanted to get stared at, and sounded out, and ranked on, just to splash around in some water and act like a duck for a couple of hours? Not me. Forget about that shit.

Anyway, while the all the kids from the block would be over at the pool, splashing around and having a good time, I'd get my bike and go on one of my long solo-rides. I called it going "exploring", because that's what I'd do; I'd go exploring different neighborhoods, scoping stuff out and giving myself a little change of scenery.

Most of the time I'd go riding over by the other the other side of Third Avenue; that was more or less the dividing line that separated our neighborhood from Spanish Harlem, or "Spictown"—like the guys on the block called it. But I never liked using the word "spic" though, so I made up my own name for the place; I called it "Puertoricanland".

Their neighborhood was only a couple of blocks away, but it was like a different world over there. You'd never see no PR's hiding in the shadows of some dark, gloomy social club, playing cards and listening to Frank Sinatra records. Are you kidding? Not in Puertoricanland. Over there everybody and their mother would be out in the street all the time, sitting on the stoops, or leaning against the cars, talking and laughing, eating and drinking, and grooving to that crazy, mambo music that was always blasting all over the place. And sometimes you'd even see some of the young guys, over by a park or a schoolyard, beating away on them bongo or congo drums, and having themselves a big, outdoor jam session. I really liked the sound of them drums, and

137

sometimes, when I could, I'd stop my bike and stand there with my mouth open, listening to the coon-coon-coon pap-pa-dap of them congo drums like I was hypnotized.

But the thing I liked best about Puertoricanland wasn't so much the drums; it was the girls. Hell yeah, some of them Spanish chicks were *fine.* Practically all of them had these real pretty faces, not to mention the bodies on some of them chicks. Hubba-hubba! And I'd like the way they'd dress too, 'specially when they'd go sashaying down the street, all sexy-dexy, wearing them tight skirts or them pedal-pusher pants they'd like to wear. Fuhgeddaboudit.

Yeah, I was getting a big kick out of riding around Puertoricanland. It didn't look as clean as our neighborhood—there was always a lot of junk and garbage all over the streets and on the sidewalks and everything—but I could tell you one thing though: In spite of how slummy and dirty the place looked, there was this nice, happy, friendly feeling around there. I couldn't put my finger on what it was, but I knew I liked it.

Well, maybe Puertoricanland *looked* like a nice place in the beginning, but after I rode around and checked it out for a while, I found out it wasn't as friendly as I thought it was. I had a close call one day on 100th Street when a bunch of guys threw a bottle at me.

"Get the fuck off the block, ya guinea bastard!" somebody yelled, as the I heard the *swish!* of a bottle only a few inches past my ear.

I didn't even turn to look; I just pedaled my ass off to get out of there as fast as I could. I guess it was probably my own fault though, because everybody knew that block was one of the worst, and I should've had the sense to stay away from it. Sooner or later I knew someone would probably peg me for a "guinea", but I guess I thought it would be later and not sooner.

But I wasn't sorry I started to explore Puertoricanland. It was fun while it lasted, and you'd be surprised all the stuff I learned just by riding around and scoping shit out. Like take them drug addicts for instance. In my neighborhood, you'd always hear a lot of talk about "junkies", but you'd never really see too many of them though. But after touring Puertoricanland for a while, I learned how to spot them creeps a mile away. Hell yeah, you'd see a lot of them over there, and every single

138

one of them had that same skeevy-looking, junkie walk—all hunched over, knees bent, touching their noses all the time, staggering down the street with some raggedy, folded-up newspaper under their arm. They'd swear they were all cool and whatnot, but to me they just looked like a bunch of stupid assholes—'specially when you'd see them all shot full of drugs, nodding out on some stoop, or standing right there in the middle of the sidewalk, all doubled over, with their eyes half closed, and their eyeballs rolled back inside their heads, drooping their half-open mouths down at the corners, while they'd go reaching for their noses and rocking back and forth like they were going to keel over any second. Yiiiicchhh, them junkies looked like pure shit on a stick if you ask me; that's why every time I'd see one on the street, I'd always thank my lucky stars we didn't have too many of them scuzzballs around where I lived.

Yeah, from what I could see, there sure was a lot of them junkies over in Puertoricanland, but from what I heard, there was even *more* of them up in Harlem, in the Colored neighborhood. But I'd never go up there though. There was no way I'd be able to blend in and not get noticed around there. See, the PR's came in all different colors, and a lot of them were light-skinned or white. That's why I'd take the chance because I figured I could pass for Puerto Rican. But I *knew* I could never pass for Colored though; that's why I'd never even *think* of riding around there. Are you kidding? I'd stand out like a piece of lint on a black velvet suit.

Well, that was pretty much the way it was. I *knew* I couldn't go riding around the Colored part of Harlem, and after I almost got my ass handed to me down by 100th Street, I wasn't going to go riding around Puertoricanland no more neither. So, I decided to check out a different neighborhood: Yorkville.

There wasn't too much to see around there though, and after a while it got a little boring—'til one day I found myself all the way over by Madison Avenue, and I got the idea of riding over to Central Park and checking it out. That turned out to be a great idea, and ever since I found a safe way to get there, without having to pass through Puertoricanland, I started going there all the time.

My favorite part of the park was the reservoir. It was this big lake with a running track that went all the way around it, and lots of people

139

would ride their bikes there. And did I too, only in my mind I wasn't riding around no dinky reservoir; I'd make believe I was in Belmont Park and I was riding in the third leg of the Triple Crown: the Belmont Stakes, and I'd pretend I was Vinny Vaccaro, or Sidney Brookhouse, or Rick Donato, or one of them big-time jockeys, and I'd make believe I was riding Citation, or Whirlaway, or War Admiral, or one of them all-time great, Triple Crown winners too. And then, to make the whole thing even more exciting, I'd always make believe that my horse already had the Kentucky Derby and the Preakness under his belt, and we were the odds-on favorite to breeze through the Belmont Stakes and clinch the Triple Crown.

Naturally, I'd have to call the race, so after I'd tighten my grip on my make-believe reins and give my horse a little pat on the neck, I'd clear my throat and imitate Lou Taravella, the announcer at Belmont: "Good afternoon racing fans," I'd say, talking through my nose just like he would, "It's a beautiful day here at Belmont Park for the 85th running of the Belmont Stakes. The crowd of sixty-five thousand fans is starting to move a little closer to the rail, and that means only one thing: *riiing!* It is now post time. Yes, it's post time. None of the field of eleven top, three-year-olds seem to be kicking or acting up, and we should get a break momentarily. Yes, they're all in line.... *And they're off!*"

I'd always hold back in the beginning because the Belmont Stakes is a long, mile-and-a-half race, and I'd have to make sure I'd still have some gas left in the tank for the run down the homestretch. I'd just sit chilly around the first turn and down the backside, biding my time, rating my horse on the lead, getting him to relax and save his energy. And then, when we'd hit the turn, I'd "pull the trigger" and crouch down real low on my bike and start pumping on the handlebars, clucking to my horse, trying to hold him together for the run to the wire. That's when I'd cock the tree branch I'd always use for a whip, and start whipping and driving, pedaling my bike faster and faster all the way down the straightaway 'til I'd hit the finish line by the other end of the reservoir.

"Citation!" I'd mumble, standing up on my bike the way the real jockeys stand up in their saddles at the end of the race. "The winner by twenty lengths!"

140

Fuhgeddaboudit, I'd have a ball riding my bike in them make-believe races. And I'd go to the reservoir almost every day to do the same thing, over and over again. I felt a little funny about doing it, because I was thirteen, and there I was playing the same doofy, jockey game that I always used to play on my scooter when I was a little kid. But I just kept doing it anyway. Why not? It was fun, and besides, since I couldn't go to the track no more, I guess I missed it a lot.

See, me and Uncle Rocco had been going to Belmont every Monday ever since school finished, but ever since freakin' August rolled around, there was no racing in New York no more. That's because every August they'd move the whole kit 'n' kaboodle all the way upstate to that pain-in-the-ass, Saratoga place. I already hated the guts of that joint because it would always mess up my summer, but Uncle said that August in Saratoga was a tradition that went back a long time, and there was nothing we could really do about it. According to him, it was the oldest track in the whole country—and probably the most beautiful too. But Uncle Rocco told me not to feel bad though, because there was something really special coming right around the corner: the grand opening of the brand-new Aqueduct Racetrack, "The Big A".

I couldn't wait for opening day. I knew they'd been building it ever since they tore down the old Aqueduct a couple of years ago, but I couldn't believe it was actually finished already. It was the "talk of the town", and all you'd hear on the radio and TV were advertisements for the new track. And there'd been a lot of write-ups about it too—'specially in The Morning Telegraph and the Daily News. Yep, everywhere you'd look, you'd see these big, blue-and-white billboards that said: Coming soon...the Big A...opening day September 14th.

Well, as soon as I found out the date for opening day, I went running straight to the calendar to see what day of the week September 14th was going to fall on. And when I saw it fell on a Monday, I was tickled pink. But I only stayed happy for a second or two, because as soon as I remembered about school, my heart sank straight to the floor like a lead balloon.

"*Shit!*" I grumbled, pounding the wall with my fist. "I'm already in school on the 14th!"

I kept banging on the wall and mumbling "fuckin' school, fuckin' school" until I saw the two most beautiful words I'd ever seen in my

141

whole life: Rosh Hashanah. That was the Jewish holiday, and it meant there was no school. Nope, I'd be free as a bird.

I felt so happy and grateful to this "Rosh" guy, that if there would've been a Jewish church in my neighborhood, I would've marched my ass right in there, kneeled down in front of him, and said ten Our Fathers and ten Hail Maries—and I would've lit up one of the big, tall, dollar candles and put it right there at the foot of his statue too. I hoped Saint Francis wouldn't get mad or jealous or nothing, but right then, my favorite saint was "Saint Rosh".

So, at least I had something to look forward too. And good thing for that, because thanks to that stupid Saratoga bullshit, the whole month of August had turned into one big blob of shit on a stick. The only thing that would break up the monotony were my solo-rides and my reservoir races, but outside of that, it was the same ol' shit.

But there was something that happened that I could never forget— not in a million years. It was the first time that Grandpa ever got *really* mad at me.

It happened on one of them cloudy days when the guys from the block hadn't gone to the pool. Me, Sally Pork, Bubbles, and Nicky Specks were playing a game of single-double off the point right in front of the house, when all of a sudden, I hit a shot that took some crazy bounces. It was one of them hard, line-drives that had come right off the tip of the point, real solid and everything. Bubbles tried to catch it, but he couldn't get to it in time.

"Hindu!" he yelled, as I watched my new Spauldeen ricochet off the side-view mirror of one car, pop up, hit the tail fin of a Caddy, and go rolling straight inside the door of the social club across the street.

"Do-over!" Sally hollered, with his hand cupped around his mouth. "That was a hindu!"

Nicky came running in from the outfield on the other side of the street. "Fuck the hindu, Pork, didn't ya see where the ball went?"

"No, where'd it go?"

"It rolled straight into the fuckin' social club for Chris'sakes."

Sally waved Nicky away with his hand. "Get the fuck outa here. How could it have gone in there? They always keep their door closed."

142

"Well, it's open today, and the ball rolled straight in there. I'm tellin' ya! I seen it with my own two eyes."

I started backpedaling from where I was standing. "It's true, Pork, I seen it too. C'mon, let's get outa here."

"Hold ya horses, Gimp," Sally said, "Why do we gotta cut out? We didn't do nothin' wrong. It was just one of them crazy fuckin' hindus—that's all. Go 'head, Bubbles, go in and get it."

"Why me?"

"'Cause ya can't fuckin' *catch*, that's why! If ya woulda caught the ball, it wouldn't have gone in there in the first place!"

Bubbles grabbed his crotch with one hand and gave Pork the finger with the other. "Fuck you! Let Gimp go in and get it, he's the one that hit it—not me!"

Well, to make a long story short, we argued our asses off for a pretty long time, but after all was said and done, Bubbles wasn't going to budge. Nope, he kept insisting that I had hit the hindu, so it was up to me to go in there and get the ball.

Well, I could've kept on arguing 'til I was blue in the face, but it wasn't going to do me no good. If I wanted to get my ball back, there was only one way to get it; I was going to have to go in there and get it myself.

I was scared shit, but I really wanted my ball, so I let the guys egg me on 'til I finally said: "fuck it". What could them social-club guys do to me, eat me alive, just because my ball took a crazy hop and got knocked into their club? The most they could do is say "get the fuck outa here", and that would be the end of it.

So, after I took a deep breath and made the sign of the cross, I threw my shoulders back and started walking towards the club with all the guys cheering me on.

"Go 'head, Gimp, don't be afraid."

"Yeah! They ain't gonna do nothin' to ya. Just be polite—that's all."

"Tell 'em it was just one of them freaky hindus—they'll understand."

"It ain't no big thing, Gimp. Go 'head."

I stopped right in front of the door of the club and sort of peeked inside. It was real dark in there, but I could see a couple of men playing cards all the way in the back. My heart started racing and pounding a

143

mile a minute as I walked into the little entrance space and lifted up my hand to tap on the glass. I was just about to knock, when all of a sudden, I heard Grandpa's voice.

"Junior!"

I spun around real fast and saw Grandpa leaning all the way out of the living-room window. His face was all red, and he looked really mad. He waved me over, so right away I ran across the street and stood under the window, looking up.

"Ma chi cazzu fai?!" he hissed, touching his fingertips together and growling through his teeth. "You crazy? What you gonna do over there?"

(He was *really* mad because what he said in Italian meant "what the fuck are you doing?")

"My ball went in there, Grandpa. I was just tryin' to get it back—that's all."

"Come upstairs."

"But Grandpa, I'm in the middle of a game over here!"

"Come upstairs *now!*"

I ran upstairs as fast as I could, and when I walked into the living room, I found Ronnie and DeeDee sitting there watching cartoons. I wasn't surprised because Grandma's been babysitting for them a lot lately ever since Ronnie's grandfather wound up in the hospital again.

"What'sa matter you?! Grandpa yelled, "How many time I tell you to keep away from this place?! *How many time?!"*

"Sorry, Grandpa, I was just tryin' to get my ball."

"Oh! So for a piece-of-shits, twenty-five cents ball, you gonna get mix up with bad people?! To you this make sense?! Ah?"

I didn't answer, I just stood there and looked down at the floor while Grandpa gave me a big, long lecture. He was pissed, and he kept saying that I should show more respect, because when he told me to stay away from the club, he was looking out for my own good.

"You Grampa tell you this because he love you, and he wanna protect you. *Capisha?"*

I didn't answer, I just kept my eyes glued to the floor, feeling all sorry and stupid for even *thinking* of going in that place.

And then, to make matters worse, while Grandpa was chewing me out, Ronnie kept teasing me and making faces 'n' stuff. I was getting

144

pissed because I could see her out of the corner of my eye, sitting there giggling and stroking one finger against the other as if to say "shame, shame." That's when I reached over and bopped her in the head with my baseball glove when Grandpa wasn't looking.

I'd never seen Grandpa that mad before. He hardly said a word at supper, and after he smoked his cigarette by the window and put on a fresh shirt and his hat, he left for his *passeggiata* without even saying goodbye or asking me if I wanted to go with him or nothing. I felt cheap. I mean, I was already used to getting in trouble with Mom—that would happen almost every day—but getting in trouble with Grandpa was something different. It made me feel all sad and shitty inside.

Mom gave me a couple of smacks when she heard that I almost went into the social club, and she didn't let me go downstairs after supper neither. So, I wound up sitting out on the fire escape with Ronnie, just to get some fresh air and listen to the radio. I felt a little embarrassed hanging out with her—'specially after she just finished seeing me get bawled out by Grandpa and smacked by Mom—but Ronnie was almost like family, and she'd seen me get in trouble and get smacked around lots of times, so it really wasn't *that* big of a thing. Naa, before you knew it, we'd forgotten all about it, and we just started talking, and fooling around, and singing along with the radio.

Opening day at the "Big A" turned out to be a beautiful, clear, sunshiny day, and the brand-new track didn't disappoint me one bit. Nope, it was all that it had been cranked up to be—and more. The thing I liked best was the sunken paddock right in front of the stands. And from whatever spot you were standing at, you could see everything, real clear, without going back and forth from the paddock to the front side and then back again—like you had to do at Belmont.

Yeah, the Big A was cool. I liked it a lot better than Jamaica, but the look of it wasn't as nice as Belmont though. It was all new, and shiny, and modern and everything, but it didn't have none of them big, beautiful trees in the paddock, or them ivy-covered walls, or them black, iron railings, or none of them big, green-and-white awnings like Belmont had. Uncle Rocco would always say, "They don't call it *La Bella Belmont* for nothin'", and he was definitely right. Yeah, Aqueduct was all new, and exciting, but it couldn't compare with Belmont though.

That would be like comparing a brand-new Ford Fairlane to a Rolls Royce. The Big A was new and flashy, but Belmont still had the class.

But Uncle Rocco liked Aqueduct a lot. He kept saying "speed is the key at Aqueduct", and I guess he was right too, because every one of his winners had gone wire to wire, "on the Bill Daley", in front every step of the way. He had a really good day—and so did I—and I couldn't wait for the next school holiday to fall on a Monday so I could go back again.

Well, thanks to school and the end of the racing season, I didn't get a chance to go back again 'til winter ended and spring came around again. I couldn't wait for Easter vacation to finally get a chance to go back to the track, and while everybody else was getting "spring fever" and "baseball fever", I'd caught a bad case of "racetrack fever".

That's why as soon I smelled spring in the air on the first warm day, I got the bright idea of riding my bike over to Randall's Island. I knew they had a running track over there that was just like the one they have in the Olympics, and I thought it would be ten times more fun to have some of my make-believe races in Downing Stadium on a real honest-to-goodness track. I knew it would probably be a little dangerous because the ramp that leads to the Triborough Bridge and Randall's Island was up on 125th Street, and I'd have to pedal through five or six blocks of Colored Harlem to get there, but I figured that once I got there, it would be well worth it.

Well, once I got there, it turned out to be a great idea. I had the time of my life, slipping my jet-black English racer into top gear, zipping and zooming around the track, leaning into the turns, and pretending I was Vinny Vaccaro riding in the Kentucky Derby. I rode around the track a whole bunch of times, and after I knocked myself out, I sat up in the stands for a while to catch my breath, rest my legs a little, and soak up some sun.

I guess everything was too good to be true, because all of a sudden, out of the corner of my eye, I spotted these three Colored kids sneaking towards me. They looked kind of suspicious, so right away I jumped up and tried to ride away. But before I could even hop onto my bike, the three of them beat me to the punch and had me surrounded.

"Yo, kid," the biggest one said, "let me get a ride on ya bike."

146

I started shitting bricks right away. "Sorry, I don't give no rides."

"C'mon, man, don't be like that. Let me get one little ride around the track?"

Well, before I could even say no again, this scuzzy bastard grabbed the handlebars of my bike and tried to pull it away from me.

"Hey! Get your hands off my bike!"

"C'mon, Shorty, just one little ride."

"No!"

I pulled back with all my might, and so did the big kid, and while we were having this big tug of war, all of a sudden, his two friends jumped in. I tried my best to fight off the three of them, but out of nowhere, one of them threw a punch at my face and knocked me down. I tried to scramble up onto my feet as fast as I could, but by the time I got up, the big kid was already riding away on my bike with his two friends running right behind him. I started tearing ass right away to try and catch up with them, but they were way too fast for me—'specially with my limp and everything.

"Hey, stop! Give me back my bike! Stop! Help! Somebody! Those kids are stealin' my bike! Help!"

I kept chasing after them, screaming and yelling my ass off, but they just kept getting farther and farther away from me. They hotfooted it out of the stadium and made a beeline straight for the ramp that led to the bridge. I knew they were trying to get back to Harlem where they could get lost in the streets and disappear—the rat bastards. I tried yelling for a cop, but there was none around. And I tried to wave down some of the passing cars, hoping that somebody would stop and help me, but they just kept whizzing by.

"Stop! Help! Police! Stop! They're stealin' my bike! Help!"

I kept screaming my ass off, but I was so out of breath, I couldn't even yell no more. I just kept huffing and puffing and struggling my ass off, but no matter what I did, I kept falling farther and farther behind. And by the time I got halfway across the bridge, I could see them way ahead of me, scooting down the ramp onto 125th Street and getting lost in the traffic along Second Avenue. Fuhgeddaboudit, them moolie bastards were long gone, and my beautiful English racer was long gone too. I knew I could kiss that sucker goodbye—it was history.

147

The walk back home was definitely the longest, saddest, lonliest walk of my whole life. From the moment I left Randall's Island, my heart was dragging on the ground, ten steps behind me. And by the time I passed Patsy's and was back in the neighborhood again, I felt like one of them lambs on the way to the slaughterhouse. I'd been trying to calm down and get a grip on myself, but no matter what I did, I couldn't stop the tears from rolling down my face.

I was hoping there would be an outside chance that Mom would feel sorry for me and understand that the moolies had ganged up on me all at once, and there was no way for me to stop them or fight them off. But I knew that was wishful thinking. I knew Mom better than that; I was gonna get the shit kicked outa me. Forget it, no matter how you sliced it, the whole thing was one hundred percent my fault. I never should've gone up to Randall's Island in the first place, and I knew it.

As soon as I got home, I knew everything was going to go down exactly like I expected. I was going to get the beating of my life, not only for sneaking off to Randall's Island, but for losing my bike too.

Mom didn't even bother to go to the closet to get the strap; she just started punching and pounding me all over the place, hitting me in the head, on the arm, on my back, on my legs, everywhere. She just kept flailing away like a wild maniac. I tried to cover my face and my head and curl up into a ball, but it didn't do much good.

"I *told* ya this was gonna happen, *didn't I?* I *told* ya not to go riding around outside the neighborhood on that goddamn bike, *didn't I? Didn't I?* I *told* ya they were gonna steal it on you. But did you wanna listen? *No!* 'Cause you wanna be a *stonehead*, that's why! You wanna be a *wise*guy, and a *smart* aleck, and a *know*-it-all, and ya wanna be little *sneak* too!

"Who told you to go ridin' through Harlem all the way to Randall's Island? Who told you? Hah? Who?!

"Well it serves you right, mister. That's what ya get for doin' things behind your mother's back! Sneaky little liar. I hope you're proud of yourself, 'cause look what ya got now—*nothin'!*

"*Nothin'!*

"Ya know, I can't believe it, like a jerk I saved up my hard-earned money for six months to buy you that bike, and now some stupid black

148

bastard is probably having the time of his life, ridin' it all over Harlem, right this very minute, laughing his face off and taking us all for a bunch of damn fools over here.

"Well, I hope ya learned your lesson this time, Mister Smart Guy. And if you think for one second that I'm gonna buy you another bike, you're crazy! You had your chance and you blew it! So now you can stay with *shit!*"

When Easter vacation came, there was no racetrack for me. Nope, thanks to my stupid, Randall's Island number, not only did I miss out on going to the track with Uncle Rocco, but I missed out on going outside too. That's because as a punishment for losing my bike, I got grounded, and had to spend the entire Easter vacation trapped in the house, staring at the four ugly walls. Man, talk about cruel, that was definitely the cruelest, meanest, coldest punishment Mom had ever dished out, 'specially the part about not letting me go to the track—that was hitting below the belt, if you ask me.

But then, to make matters worse, when I'd finally gotten the acceptance letter from Music 'n' Art High School, the school I *really* wanted to go to, Mom deep-sixed that too, with only three little words: "fuhgeddaboudit".

"But why, Ma?"

"What'sa matter with you? Didn't ya learn your lesson when they stole your bike?"

"What does *that* have to do with anything? We're talkin' about where I'm gonna go to high school over here!"

"It has a *lot* to do with it, 'cause if you go to Music 'n' Art, you're gonna have to take the bus every day and go back 'n' forth across 125th Street."

"So."

"So?! That's right through the center of Harlem for Chris'sakes!"

"C'mon, Ma, that ain't no big thing; I'm old enough to travel on a bus by myself."

"The problem is not *you*, the problem is the Colored and all them juvenile delinquents and gang members. They love to pick on anybody who looks like 'easy pickins' for them. Look at what they did to you on Randall's Island. And look at what they did to that Donald Fanning kid

149

up in Highbridge Pool. The kid was only fifteen years old, crippled in a wheelchair, and now he's dead—stabbed to death!"

"But, Ma, I'm not gonna have nothin' to do with no gangs; I'm just gonna get on the bus, get off the bus, and go to school—that's it."

"Well, I'm sorry, mister, you'll be much better off goin' to Benjamin Franklin. It's only half a block from the house; you don't have to take no buses, and you don't have to go through Harlem neither."

"But, Ma, Music 'n' Art is a special school for kids that got talent! Benjamin Franklin is just a regular, ordinary high school. It's an all-boys school, and all the tough kids from the neighborhood go there—plus the PR's and the moolies from Harlem too."

"I don't care who goes there, it's half a block from the house, and ya don't have to take no trains or buses or nothin'. Besides, Anthony goes there, and he's never had no problems."

"But I ain't Anthony. I wanna study art, so maybe I could be an artist someday. Music 'n' Art is the place for that—not stupid Benjamin Franklin."

"Don't worry, they got art classes at Benjamin Franklin too."

"But, Ma! How can you say som....."

"*Junior! Stop it already!* My mind is made up, you're goin' to Benjamin Franklin—and that's *final.*"

Chapter 11

My graduation from elementary school was a very happy day—for a lot of different reasons. Mom, and Grandma and Grandpa were all there for the ceremony, and they were as proud as a peacock—'specially when the principal, Mr. Weiss, called my name for me to go up and get the "Excellence in Art Award". Mom must've used up a whole roll of film, just taking shots of me going up the aisle to get the medal, not to mention all the pictures she took out in the schoolyard with Grandma and Grandpa, my teacher, and some of the kids in my class. Fugeddaboudit, I must've said "cheese" so many times, my *cheeks* were starting to hurt.

As a special treat, Mom took us all to have lunch at my favorite Chinese restaurant down by 86th Street. It turned out to be a pisser because Grandpa and Grandpa hadn't been to a Chinese place too many times before, and from the way they were botching up all them Chinese words, it was easy to see it wasn't just Chinese—it was *Greek* to them. Mom had to explain every dish to them in detail, and it must've taken more than half an hour before we were ready to place our order. Both Grandma and Grandpa settled on the lo mein, because once Mom told them it was "Chinese spaghetti", they both figured it was probably their best bet.

Boy, not for nothin', but if that Marco Polo guy could've seen Grandma and Grandpa digging into that lo mein, twirling it on their forks like they were scarfing down *spaghetti a la marinara*, he would've been so proud of himself, he would've busted his buttons.

Anyway, after we'd finished eating and we were just sitting around cracking open our fortune cookies and reading our fortunes 'n' stuff, all of a sudden, Mom reached into her purse and pulled out an envelope.

"Here," she said, kissing me on the cheek, "this is for you. Happy graduation."

Right away I figured it was probably a graduation card with some money in it, but when I opened the envelope, I found a letter inside. It looked like one of them fancy, certificate type of things, like the kind

151

that comes from the court or from a judge or something. I tried my best to read it, but it was all written that real complicated lawyer-language.

"This is to...certify...that under the juris... Forget it, Ma, I can't read this! What does it say?"

"Well, it says that your name has been legally and officially changed from Joseph Albert Scalise to Joseph Albert Posella."

"Whatta ya mean?"

"Look," Mom said, pointing to the bottom part of the letter, "it's all right here in black 'n' white. See? Your new name is Posella ... Joseph ... Albert ... Posella. Are ya happy?"

Right away I gave Mom a big hug and a kiss, and then I leaned over the table, kissed Grandma and Grandpa, and held their hands. My tongue was stuck in the back of my throat, and I could hardly even speak.

"Well," Mom said, grabbing my hand and squeezing it, "are ya happy?"

"Are you kidding, Ma? This is the happiest day of my life."

Well, since the Labor Day weekend was right around the corner, all I could do was sit by the window, think about what the first day of school was going to be like, bite my nails, and worry.

See, in PS 102 at least there were kids in the lower grades that were younger and smaller than me, and I didn't feel so much like the low man on the totem pole. But in high school, 'specially an all-boys school like Benjamin Franklin, there weren't going to be no short little girls and younger kids behind me. Nope, I could forget about being the shortest kid in the class, because in a few days I could have the honor of being the shortest kid in the *whole damn school.*

Just thinking about it tied my stomach into a big, nauseous knot. I didn't know what to expect, and I had no idea what I was going to do neither. All I knew was that I'd better wear some heavy-duty, rubber bands on the bottom of my pants—otherwise it was gonna be "plop-plop, get the mop".

But at least I had one thing to look forward to: hearing people call me by my brand-new name. I'd been wanting to get it changed for the longest time, and since Mom had finally done it, I couldn't wait for the first teacher to call out my new name in the roll call, just so I could raise my hand with pride and say "Here!". Yeah...Joseph Posella. It sounded twenty times better than Joseph Scalise did—I'll tell ya that much.

Sometimes I'd feel guilty about getting it changed though—I'm pretty sure Dad wouldn't like it if he ever found out about it—but, hey, what was I supposed to do, sit around like a stupid dingleberry, waiting for this guy to show up and start acting like a father to me? Forget about that shit. As far as I was concerned, I didn't have a father no more. My family was the Posella family, and I even had their name to prove it too. That was it, case closed. And if Dad or anybody else didn't like it, it was just tough noogies for them.

But I had to admit I was a little worried though—ya know, about what the guys from the neighborhood were going to say when they'd notice that, all of a sudden, I had a different last name. That's why I talked it over with Mom, just in case anybody got a little too nosy, and started asking too many questions.

"Just tell 'em ya got adopted by your grandparents," she said. "That's all they gotta know. You don't have to go giving no explanations, and ya don't have to go sayin' nothin' about your father leavin' us and disappearing and this 'n' that—that's nobody's business."

So that was what I decided to do. If anybody would ask me anything, I was just going to answer, "my grandparents adopted me", and they'd probably say "oh", and that would be the end of it—at least that's what I *hoped* anyway. But maybe nobody would even bother to ask me about it at all—that would be even be better!

I figured that maybe only my old classmates, Richie Gamarella and Vinny Tornatore, would be the only guys to notice it. That's because the only place where anybody would even *use* your last name was in school, otherwise everybody would just know you by your first name or your nickname. And that's another thing that had me worried: my nickname. I was hoping that since I was going to be starting in a new school with a new bunch of guys, maybe the slate would be wiped clean, and that "Gimp" shit would get dead and buried once and for all. Yeah, with any luck, these new guys might start calling me by my real name, "Joey", or maybe even "Joe". Yeah, "Joe". That sounded cool—and a lot more grown up too.

153

Well, I guess it was just more wishful thinking, all over again, because on my very first day at Benjamin Franklin, all the dingleberries who knew me from around the way busted my dream-bubble right in my face. Yep, before I even had a chance to introduce myself as "Joey" or "Joe", all the shitheads from the neighborhood kept coming around shouting: "'Ey Gimp, wait up!", or "Gimp, who ya got for homeroom?", or "Yo, Gimp, I'll see ya later at lunch", or "Gimp" this, or "Gimp" that, to the point where guys I hardly even *knew* were already calling me fuckin' "Joey Gimp" over here! I'm serious!

'Ey, what ya gonna do? I guess that's just the way the Tootsie rolls. I mean, I couldn't really blame them; that's what they've all been calling me ever since I moved into the neighborhood. How could I expect them to drop my nickname all of a sudden just because we were in high school? And besides, none of them really called me that to be mean, or to hurt my feelings, or embarrass me or nothing. Naa, most of the time they'd say it a friendly way, and even as much as I hated it, I couldn't really get mad and make a big thing out of it.

The only one who really got on my nerves with that "Gimp" shit was Googie. He was a sophomore at the school—that was one of the reasons I didn't want to go there—and every time he'd see me walking the halls or eating lunch, he'd always yell out, "'Ey, how's the shrimpy-gimpy boy?!", at the top of his lungs, so everybody and their mother could turn around and start staring at me. Jeez, I hated that shit. I mean, getting called "Joey Gimp" or "Gimp" was bad enough, without this stupid jerk embarrassing me in front of the whole freakin' school with that "shrimpy- gimpy" bullshit. What a shithead—I swear to God!

Well, besides Googie being the big, pain-in-the-ass that he always was, Benjamin Franklin wasn't really half as bad as I expected it to be. I definitely would've liked it a lot better if it would've been coed and they had some fine-looking girls floating around the place, but what can you do—you can't have everything, right?

But at least I felt at home though. It was almost like Benjamin Franklin was the district high school for East Harlem or something, because practically all the guys from the neighborhood were all with me there at "Ben Frank". (That's what we'd call it for short.) There were a few Irish, German, and Polish guys who'd come up from Yorkville, and a few Chinese guys too, but outside of them, mostly all of Ben Frank was Italian—well, except for the moolies and the PR's that would come in from Colored Harlem and Spanish Harlem. There weren't that many of them though—maybe about fifteen or twenty percent of the school— but there were still enough of them to make a problem.

See, a lot of the Italian guys hated their guts—'specially creeps like Googie and some of them crazy bastards from the Redwoods. They were always calling them "spics" and "niggers", and they'd use any chance they'd get to sound them out and pick fights with them. I felt sorry for them because they were really outnumbered, and they had to take a lot of shit off these guys.

A lot of the fights would get started because of the trail of garbage that the PR's and the moolies would leave behind them on their way back and forth from Ben Frank. They'd just throw their shit all over the place—bags, wrappers, bottles, food—right in front of everybody like they had no respect or nothing. That would be when a lot of the neighborhood guys, and even some of the grownups, would get really pissed off and start yelling stuff at them:

"Hey, you! Ya stupid black bastard, ever heard of using a garbage can?!"

"Yeah! What do ya think this is—Harlem over here?!

"Pick up that paper, you greasy spic! What'sa matter, ain't they got no garbage cans in Pawda Rico?!"

"'Ey, this ain't the jungle over here! Why don't ya try and act civilized for a change, ya fuckin' monkey bastard!"

Boy, not for nothin', but I've seen some real ugly fights get started over something as stupid as a candy wrapper, or a little, potato-chip bag. One time, only a few weeks after school started, I seen Butchie from the Redwoods and this big, Colored guy swing out on the corner of Pleasant Avenue, right in front of the school. It didn't last too long before it got broken up, but while the shit was on, fuhgeddaboudit, that had to be one of the dirtiest street-fights I'd ever seen: kicking in the balls, hitting with garbage-can covers, biting... For real! When this moolie guy was struggling to get out of Butchie's headlock, all of a sudden, he grabs a chunk of his arm in his teeth and bit the shit out of it—just like a wild dog in a freakin' dog fight or something. Eeuuww! That's was disgusting! I'll never forget seeing them big teeth marks and

155

the blood rolling down Butchie's arm, running in between his fingers, and dripping down into the gutter. Good thing the *moolinyan* didn't have no rabies or nothing, otherwise Butchie could've gotten really screwed. *Hell* yeah, he could've even *died* from that shit.

But I never thought the thing about the PR's and the moolies throwing their garbage around was the real reason for all the static. That was just an excuse, the *real* reason had to do with the way they'd dress, the way they'd walk—and the way they acted too.

See, a lot of the guys from the neighborhood—'specially the Redwoods—didn't go for nobody coming into their turf, bopping hard, and acting all big-and-bad and whatnot. Nope, that would burn their asses, and every time they'd see one of them Puerto Rican jitterbugs, or some diddy-boppin' moolinyan come strolling down the block—ya know, dragging one leg behind the other,…strutting with that little hop and that little dip, … cupping one hand under the sleeve of his belted-back jacket, … fixing the pearl on the side of his stingy-brim hat, … sporting a pair of wrap-around shades and one of the square-back haircuts, … wearing them pegged, high-water pants two inches above the ankle so you could see his black, silk socks, and his shiny, roach-killer shoes, … blowing smoke-rings and twirling his stiletto-tip umbrella like it was a cane or one of them fancy, walking sticks…. Fuhgeddaboudit, them Redwoods would have a titty-attack just *looking* at the guy. *Hell* yeah, that was like waving a bright red flag in front of a bunch of bulls, because before you could even say the word "diddy-bop", them crazy bastards were already crossing the street, making a beeline straight towards the guy to make trouble and start something—usually by knocking off his hat or snatching his umbrella.

'Ey, that's just the way these guys were; they couldn't *stand* to see no "spics" and "niggers" diddy-boppin' in their neighborhood. And God forbid, one of them shitheads would be stupid enough to go anywhere *near* Jefferson Park, forget it, that's when the shit would *really* hit the fan and all hell would break loose.

See, the park was the Redwoods' hang-out and their headquarters, and the only time they'd let any PR's or moolies go anywhere *near* it was in the summer, in the daytime, when the pool was open, and everybody and their mother would be coming in from all over the place and they couldn't really stop them anyway. But outside of that, you

156

could pretty much forget it. And at night, you could *really* forget it, because nobody from the outside *ever* came into that park at night—not when the Redwoods were around.

But I never could really understand why some of the guys would get so bent outa shape, just because a few moolies and some PR's would pass through the neighborhood. I mean, it was true, some of them really did act like a bunch of pigs and slobs, throwing all their garbage around, but it wasn't such a big thing to be fighting with them all the time and doing all them means shits to them—like squirting them with water guns filled with piss and stuff like that.

Yeah, the PR's and the moolies had it rough. And it wasn't really fair neither, because I had a whole bunch of them in my class, and not one of them ever messed with me or bothered me, or nothing. Nope, in fact, I got along with them pretty good. Serious!

The Puerto Rican guys would all call me "Pepito" (that meant "Little Joe" in Spanish), and the Colored guys mostly called me either "Joey Joe" or "Little Man". I guess I probably liked getting called by them names, because by that time, any name that didn't have "Gimp" or "Shrimp" in it was like music to my ears. And to tell the truth, most of the Spanish and Colored guys treated me a hell of a lot better than my own people did. A lot of the Italian guys were always bunking into me in the hallway or in the lunchroom, pushing me out of the way, shoving me around, and saying stuff like, "Watch it, Shorty" or "Get outa the way, Shrimp", and shit like that. But the Spanish guys would never pick on me though. I don't know why, but they never did. They'd never sound me out, or make fun of my limp, or my height or nothing. Nope, they were always cool with me, and I was cool with them.

Most of my teachers were cool with me too. Mr. Di Salvo, my science teacher, was my favorite though. He was the first Italian teacher I ever had in my life, and I got along good with him. He reminded me a lot of Mr. Sandman, because he had a good sense of humor and was always cracking jokes and making us laugh—like the time he came out with that corny riddle about the solar system. I was the only guy in the whole class who came up with the answer and got the joke; everybody else just sat there all cross-eyed with their mouths open—like he was talking Greek or Chinese or something.

157

"Of all the planets in the solar system, which is the planet where the sun never shines, and it stinks like hell?"

"Uranus!" I shouted.

"Very good, Joseph," he said, patting me on the shoulder. "I'm glad that *somebody* knows his *ass* when it comes to the solar system."

Yeah, that Mr. Di Salvo was a pisser; he was a real down-to-earth, regular kind of guy. And with his corny jokes and wisecracks 'n' stuff, he took something really dry and boring like earth science, and he'd twist it into something really interesting. I did pretty good in his class, and on the first report card, he gave me a ninety-something.

I did really good in art class too. But that was no surprise, because ever since I could remember, art was always my favorite subject—and my best. The art teacher was this skinny, bald guy named Mr. Hoffman. He was a nice guy too, and as soon as he saw how good I could draw and paint, he asked me right away if I'd ever had any "special art training". I told him I'd been going to them Saturday art classes, but that I had to stop because I was in high school and those classes were only for grammar-school kids. That's when he told me about this place downtown called "The Art Students League". I would've really liked to go, but it was expensive, and I knew Mom had no money for stuff like that. But Mr. Hoffman was cool, and once I told him that my mother couldn't afford no special art classes, he started letting me stay after school, so I could get in some extra time drawing and painting while he'd be cleaning up the art room.

Besides some of the teachers, most of the guys at Ben Frank were cool too. And coolest of them all turned out to be my own cousin: Anthony. He really had my back, and he helped me to get to know people and fit in. At that time, he was a sophomore, like Googie, and from the first day of school, he took me under his wing and tried to show me the ropes 'n' stuff. He would bring me around to all his friends, and some of the teachers too, and he'd always introduce me as "my cousin Joey", and he'd never call me "Gimp" or "Shrimp" or none of them stupid names. Yeah, I had to hand it to the guy, he really went out of his way to help me get off to a good start at Ben Frank—and I owed him a lot.

158

See, Anthony was a pretty popular guy around the school—for a sophomore. He had really sprouted up over the last couple of years and had gotten big and strong, and because he was a good athlete, practically everybody knew him. He even joined the Redwoods too.

Uncle Rocco didn't know nothing about it though. Are you kidding?!—he would've kicked Anthony's ass big time if he would've ever found out. And I wasn't about to go blabbing nothing to him neither. Hell no, there was no way I was going to rat on my own cousin—'specially after all he'd done to help me and everything. But it was true: Anthony was a Redwood.

From what he told me, it all got started at the end of last summer when the guys from the Junior Redwoods asked him to play on their football team. Anthony already knew most of them from playing ball in the park and from the Boy's Club, so it wasn't no big thing when he joined their team and started hanging out with them.

He even told me how they initiated him. He said that one night when all the guys were hanging out at the park, shooting the shit and sneaking sips from a paper bag with some cheap wine in it, all of a sudden, somebody decided it was time to give Anthony "the ol' Redwood initiation", and they all took off their garrison belts and made him go "through the mill". That was when everybody would line up in a straight line, and then they'd make you crawl under their spread legs on your hands and knees, while they'd all smack the shit out of you with their garrison belts as you'd pass under them. Anthony said it didn't hurt *that* much, because most of the guys didn't hit him with the buckle. But a few of the really sick creeps, like Butchie and Sammy Dee from 112th Street, really laid into him good, buckle and all. He got a couple of bad welts on his face, his neck, and on the back of his head, but, according to him, it was all worth it, because now he could say he was an "officially initiated" member of the Redwoods.

Anthony sure was proud about being a Redwood alright, and he was proud of being on their football team too. But as proud as he was, he couldn't enjoy the kick of wearing one of them cool, black-satin jackets with that fancy red lettering on the back that said: Redwoods. Are you kidding? If Anthony ever strolled into the house wearing a Redwood jacket, Aunt Jean would've probably had a heart attack and dropped dead—right there on the kitchen floor. And forget about Uncle

159

Rocco! After he'd kick the shit out of Anthony for joining a gang, he'd probably rip the jacket right off his back, slice it to shreds, and then *burn* it—right in his face.

Chapter 12

Once school was over, me and Uncle Rocco were right back at my favorite place: Belmont Park. I felt a little guilty keeping the secret from him about Anthony joining the Redwoods, but I had to back up Anthony—'specially after the way he'd helped me at Ben Frank. I mean, he was my cousin and all, but ever since I came to live in the neighborhood, he'd been more than that: he'd been my friend too.

Anyway, no matter how many times I'd come back to Belmont, it was always like seeing stuff for the very first time. I'd never get tired or bored with it, and I was always at my happiest, just hanging around with Uncle Rocco under the shade of the trees, feeling the breeze, and watching the horses as they'd go dancing around the walking ring.

"Hey, Uncle Rock," I said, as I watched the jockeys come bopping out of the jock's room, twirling their whips and fixing the rubber bands on their cuffs, "I been thinkin'."

"Thinkin' about what, Joon?"

"Well, I been thinkin' that maybe I wanna be a jockey."

"A jockey?"

"Yeah! I mean, I gonna turn sixteen next week, and from the looks of things, I don't think I'm gonna be growin' too much more, so I....."

"Don't say that, Joon, you don't know what's gonna happen. Maybe you're just a late bloomer—that's all. You could still grow."

"Aw c'mon, Uncle Rock, don't tell me you're gonna start with that 'late bloomer' stuff too? I ain't gonna grow no more—let's face it. I'm gonna stay short, just like my father. That's all there it to it."

"I don't know, it's still too early to tell. I've seen a lotta guys sprout up after they...."

"Please. C'mon, Uncle Rock, I ain't nobody's damn fool. I'm almost sixteen over here, and I'm only five feet tall. How much am I gonna grow in the next couple of years? An inch? Two inches tops? Even if I am a late bloomer like you say, and I start growing a little, I'm pretty sure I'll still wind up short enough to be a jockey."

"Well, I don't know. It really don't go by your height, it goes by your weight. How much you weigh anyway?"

161

"About ninety five, ninety six pounds."

"Yeah?"

"Yeah! I'm tellin' ya, I could be a jockey. And I've made up my mind already, that's what I wanna be."

Uncle Rocco took a long drag on his cigarette, and as the smoke poured out of his nose, he picked a couple of specks of tobacco off his tongue and turned to the side to spit. It looked to me like he must've been thinking because it took him a pretty long time to say something.

"Joon, look.... I know you love the track and you love the horses and everything, but lovin' horses is only part of what ya need to become a jockey. It takes a lotta skill. You gotta know horses inside and out—and ya gotta know how to *ride* for Chris'sakes. Ya think these guys just woke up one morning and *ba-da-bing*, all of a sudden, they're jockeys? It takes a lotta time, a lotta time and a lotta hard work. See, most of these guys are country boys; they grew up around horses. Some of 'em have even been ridin' since they were little babies. A city kid like you has to work double and triple hard just to catch up to these guys."

"Yeah, but I could do it, Uncle Rock. I read this article in a magazine about Tod Garretson, and it said that he was a city guy, just like me, and when he first went to the track, he didn't know the front end of a horse from the back. But he learned. I could learn too. And what about that other top jock that rides over in Jersey—that Walter Staub guy?"

"What about him?"

"Well, I read that he grew up in Brooklyn, and he didn't even get on the back of a horse 'til he was in high school, when he first tried riding over at the riding academy in Prospect Park. Hey, if these guys can do it, so can I."

Uncle Rocco didn't say nothing; he just took the last drag of his cigarette, dropped the butt and stepped on it. Then he folded up his Telly, pulled his reading glasses off, and looked me in the eye. "Junior, do you know the kind of sacrifices you gotta make to be a jockey? Some of these guys haven't had a decent meal in years; they practically starve themselves just to keep their weight down—not to mention all the time they spend sweatin' their asses off in them hot-boxes. Are you willing to go through somethin' like that? That's *torture* for Chis'sakes!"

"Not all jocks gotta do that, Uncle Rock—only the bigger guys. The real short guys like Dan McCarthy and Paulie Tompkinson don't gotta

162

worry about their weight that much; they stay at their regular riding weight naturally, without hardly doin' nothin'. I figure I'm probably short enough and light enough to be like one of them guys. I'm tellin' ya, Uncle Rock, I been readin' about it. I know practically everything there is to know about bein' a jockey."

"Oh yeah, smart guy? What about all the danger, huh? Did ya read in them books how every year a couple of riders get killed out there on the track? Did you read how some of these guys get paralyzed for life, and how they break one bone after another, and get all banged-up from all the accidents and all the spills 'n' whatnot? Hah? Did you read about that?"

"Yeah."

"Well for Godsakes, Joon—use your head! Bein' a jockey is some real risky business over here. Outside of bullfighting, or maybe auto racing, horse racing is the most dangerous sport there is! It's the only line of work where an ambulance follows you around while you're doin' your job. Think about that."

"I know, I know, Uncle Rock. But I don't care. I rather die young doin' somethin' I love, than live to be a miserable old man doin' somethin' I hate. Life's too short for that bullshit."

"Yeah, but, Joon, you're so smart—and so talented and everything. What about your artwork? I thought you wanted to do somethin' with that?"

"I don't know. I'm starting to realize that it ain't so much the drawing and the painting that I love—it's the horses. That's why ever since I was a kid, the only thing I wanted to draw were pictures of horses, and nobody, not even my teachers, could ever get me to draw nothin' else. I guess I figured if I couldn't be around horses in real life, the next best thing was to make pictures of 'em—ya know what I mean?"

"Yeah, I think I do."

As we were talking, the paddock judge shouted, "riders up!", and one by one, all the jockeys got a "leg up" and bounced up onto their horses, real smooth, like a bunch of alley cats jumping on a backyard fence.

"Ya know, Joon, there's no such thing as a 'jockey school'. If you're really serious about learnin' to be a jockey, you gotta start at the

163

bottom. You gotta walk hots, and muck out stalls, and pick up horseshit, and do anything you gotta do, just so a trainer or somebody in the know will give you a couple of minutes of their time and teach you something."

"I know, Uncle Rock, that's why I thought maybe you could talk to that trainer friend of yours, Sam Cardone. Maybe he could give me a job as a hotwalker—ya know, just for the summer—just so I can get my feet wet and see how I like it 'n' whatnot."

"Well, I could talk to Sam, but I'll tell ya right now: the problem ain't gonna be with Sam, it's gonna be with your mother. I don't know if she's gonna go for the idea of you workin' at the track. And by the way, have you ever talked to her about this jockey stuff?"

"No."

"Well, you better get started, mister, 'cause let me tell ya, it's gonna be easier to sell her the *Brooklyn Bridge* than to sell her on the idea of you becoming a *jockey*."

"Yeah, this is true. I guess I'll just have to cross that bridge when I get to it."

The horses were already parading around in the shade of the walking ring. I stayed quiet and watched as the sun streamed through the trees, lighting up bright patches of color on the jockeys' silks and splashes of yellow on the grass. Uncle Rocco took a quick look at the odds board and at his program, and then he looked over at me with a puzzled look on his face.

"You're really serious about this jockey business—ain't ya?"

"Never been more serious about anything in my whole life."

I'd always heard that a girl's sixteenth birthday was something special—they call it "sweet sixteen"—but for us guys, there ain't nothing sweet about it, at least not for me anyway. Nope, it was more like *"sour* sixteen", because when my birthday finally came, it turned out to be nothing but one big disappointment after the other.

First of all, a few days before my birthday, Uncle Rocco called to tell me that he'd spoken to his friend, Sam Cardone, the trainer. He said Mr. Cardone told him that if I could show up at the Aqueduct stable gate at five thirty in the morning on Monday, with working papers and a social security card, he'd give me a shot at being a hotwalker.

164

I was excited when I got the news, but once I started explaining everything to Mom, I knew it was going to be exactly like Uncle Rocco said it would be—maybe even worse. Yep, he really hit the nail on the head when it came to Mom's reaction. She didn't wanna hear shit, and before I could even explain to her what a hotwalker was, she deep-sixed the whole idea with a wave of her hand and her two favorite letters in the alphabet: N O.

"But, Ma, this is somethin' that's really important to me. I already made up my mind that I wanna be a jockey, and I gotta start working at the track now, so I can start learnin' stuff."

"A *jockey?!*" she yelled, touching her fingertips to her forehead and then spreading them up toward the ceiling, "Are you crazy, or what?!"

"I ain't crazy. I been thinkin' it over for a long time already, and I figure that with my size and the way I love horses and everything, bein' a jockey would be the perfect thing for me."

"Oh my God! Now I've heard it all! Now he wants to break his neck riding a bunch of stupid horses. What'sa matter with you, don't ya know you can get *killed* doin' that?!"

"C'mon, Ma, I ain't gonna be ridin' no horses anyway; I just wanna be a hotwalker for the summer—ya know, like a summer job 'n' stuff—that's all."

"What the hell is a 'hotwalker' anyway?"

"A hotwalker walks the horses around the stable so they can cool off after they come back from their morning workouts."

"Well, it sounds pretty dangerous to me; those horses can kick, and bite, and trample you and everything. And how would you even get there? You don't drive, you don't have a car."

"The subway, Ma. The A-train takes you straight to Aqueduct."

"*The A-train!* Are you *serious!* You wanna ride the A-train at four in the morning?! You're nuts! And besides, that train cuts right through a very bad section of Brooklyn called Bedford Stuyvesant, and that's all Colored over there. It's even worse than Harlem for Chris'sakes!"

Jeez, not for nothin', but these moolies were getting to be one big pain-in-the-ass. First, I couldn't go to Music 'n' Art High School because the stupid bus went through Harlem, and then I couldn't work at the racetrack because the stupid train ran through Bedford Stuyvesant. Fuhgeddaboudit, every time there was something I really wanted to do, there was always a bunch of eggplants in the middle of everything, making my life miserable and stopping me from doing what I really wanted to do. *Madon'*, not even if I lived in fuckin' *Africa* over here!

Well anyway, me and Mom argued about me working at the track all night long, but no matter what I said, she wasn't about to change her mind for nothing. Nope, I tried everything: reasoning with her, sweet-talking her, nagging her, begging her... But it was no use; her mind was made up, and that was that.

As a last resort, I tried asking my lawyer, Grandma, to step in, thinking that maybe she could plead my case for me and convince Mom to change her mind and give me a break. But when I asked her to help, she just shook her head and said: "I feel sorry for you, Junior, but to be jockey is too dangerous. You mama she right."

Well, what can I tell ya? Ever since I was a little kid, Grandma had always taken my side and stuck up for me against Mom, but when my whole future was at stake, and I really needed someone to be in my corner, she turned her back on me. Gee, thanks a lot, Gram.

And Grandpa wasn't much help neither. When I explained to him that I'd been doing a lot of thinking, and I finally decided that I wanted to be a jockey, he just lit up a cigarette and gave me a big long speech about how I was too smart and had too much *"talento"* to do something stupid and dangerous with my life like riding horses. Gee, thanks a lot to you too, Grandpa. Yeah! There I was, looking for somebody to give me some backup and help me out a little, and all I got was a freakin' lecture.

I was starting to realize that the only two people in the world who understood how much I wanted to be a jockey and how much it meant to me, were Uncle Rocco and Ronnie. That's it. And good thing I had them two, otherwise I *really* would've felt like shit on a stick.

Yeah, thank God I had Ronnie. She'd been growing up, right along with me, and she wasn't no silly little girl no more. I talked with her out on the fire-escape that night after I got tired of arguing with Mom, and she seemed to understand everything pretty good. She told me never to give up on my dream, and never to let anyone stop me from doing what was in my heart—not even my mother. But she said I needed to

166

have a little patience though, because, according to her, "Rome wasn't built in a day".

"Don't worry," she said, putting her arm around me and rubbing my back, "you'll get another chance. Maybe next summer when ya get a little older. Maybe then your mother will understand things a little better and change her mind."

"I don't know, Ronnie, I sure hope so. But I don't think anybody will ever *really* understand how I feel about the whole thing."

"What's there to understand, Joey? You love horses and you wanna be a jockey. What's so hard to understand about that?"

"It ain't that simple, Ronnie, there's more to it than that."

"Like what?"

"I don't know,...it's kinda hard to explain. Aah, let's just forget it, you wouldn't understand anyway—nobody does."

"C'mon, Joey, don't be like that. Why don't ya explain it to me? I'm your friend."

I could feel part of me shutting down and closing up, while another part of me wanted to open up and say what I really felt inside, so I could get it off my chest, once and for all, and feel free of it. The tug of war in my mind lasted for a few seconds, and then I just said, "fuck it".

"Well, it's like this feeling I got deep inside—like an intuition, or one of them 'premonition' things. I just *know* that once I get up on the back of a racehorse, I'm never gonna feel like no doofy, little shrimp no more for the rest of my life. I'm gonna feel like I'm ten-feet tall, like I'm just as good as everybody else. Ya know what I mean?"

Ronnie didn't say nothing; she just sat next to me with her head in her hands, staring up at the sky, and even though she didn't look over at me, I could tell she was really listening and understanding every word I was saying.

"And ya know something else, Ronnie? Ya know my leg problem and this stupid limp that's been messing up my life and making me miserable ever since I can remember?"

Ronnie nodded her head.

"Well, once I climb up in that saddle...it ain't gonna mean shit."

Mom nixing the idea of working at the track wasn't the only disappointment that was waiting for me on my birthday; the other one

167

was not getting a pair of them "special shoes". See, for years I'd been hearing the leg doctor go on and on about how, when I got to be sixteen, it would make sense for Mom to "invest" in a pair of "corrective" shoes, the kind with the "lift" on the right shoe, to even out my legs so my limp wouldn't be that "pronounced". According to him, my feet should have reached their "full adult size" by then, and Mom didn't have to worry no more about me outgrowing the shoes and not getting her money's worth. I knew those shoes had to be "custom made" and were probably really expensive, but I was still hoping and praying I might get them.

Well, what can I tell ya? I guess Mom didn't catch all the hints I'd been dropping—either that or she still didn't have the money. But I didn't want to make her feel bad though, so when she handed me a birthday card with twenty dollars in it, "to buy clothes", I tried by best to fake a smile and play it off like I was happy.

The main reason I wanted the shoes so bad was because I'd become a teenager, and I wanted to do the things that teenagers do— like going to dances, listening to music, hanging out, or maybe even having a girlfriend or something. Yeah, having those shoes would've been a big, big help to me. I'd already become super self-conscious about my looks, and I was even *more* self-conscious about my limp, and if them shoes could've evened me out a little and cut down on my "duck-waddle", that would've been like hitting the jackpot.

I'd already been to a couple of dances—like them CYO things over at Mount Carmel—but things never went too good for me. It would take me a long time to get up the courage to ask a girl to dance, and nine times out of ten, they'd always turn me down. They'd give me that split-second once-over, and as soon as they'd see how short I was, they'd give me one of them half-assed smiles and say, "no thanks".

And I really started to catch a complex behind that shit, 'specially when the same girl who'd just brushed me off would go out and start dancing with somebody else, right under my nose—like it was nothing. I hated that. I mean, I could understand if a girl didn't want to dance with me because she felt tired, or because she wanted to go to the bathroom with her girlfriends, or because she was thirsty and she wanted to get a soda or something—or whatever. But when the same exact broad would start grinding her ass off with some guy she didn't even know, right in front of my face, only two seconds after she'd just

168

finished turning me down, forget it, no matter how I'd try to explain it away—that shit hurt.

That's because a lot these girls were selfish, and they didn't think of nobody but themselves. But if I were a girl, I'd never do nothing like that to a guy; I'd try and show a little more consideration. Like if I turned down a guy for a dance, I'd make it a rule: never to go out and dance the same record with nobody else until the song is completely finished. 'Ey, guys have feelings too—ya know what I mean?

Anyway, part of my problem was that I was always too self-conscious about my limp to go out on the floor and do "the slop" or none of them fast dances. And then, when the slow records would come on, the girls would always turn me down because I was too short for them. I could never figure out what it was with these chicks. I mean, it wasn't like we were getting *married* or nothing; it was only a lousy, three-minute dance for Chris'sakes. So you dance with a guy who's a couple of inches shorter than you—big shit.

Well, maybe them couple of inches were no big thing for me, but I guess it must've been a really big thing for them girls though. Yep, because hardly none of them would ever dance a slow record with me. I didn't know what they were so afraid of—that I wouldn't be tall enough to hold them the right way, and my face would get buried in their tits or something?

Sounds crazy, but that shit actually happened to me one time. For real! That's when I learned never to ask a girl to dance if she's sitting down—no matter what.

It happened over at Mount Carmel. I saw this girl sitting by the corner of the parish hall, sort of curled up in a ball, with her arms wrapped around her legs. I couldn't really tell how tall she was, but she looked kind of cute and a little lonely too, so I asked her out to dance. Well, as soon as she said "okay" and stood up, I knew right away I'd made one hell of a mistake. That girl was *huge!* But what could I do? It was too late for me to change my mind. And besides, I had a feeling from the way she was sitting alone, and all curled up, that maybe she had a complex about her height, just like me—only in reverse. So, with a shy, nervous grin, and a big lump in my throat, I took her by the hand, led her out onto the dance floor, and started slow dancing with her.

169

Madon', I couldn't believe it, this girl was so goddamn tall, my face only got up to her *chest* for Chris'sakes. And before I knew what hit me, there I was, staring right in the middle of these two big honeydew melons. For real! Jeez, talk about embarrassing, I *really* didn't know where to put my face that time.

Anyway, at first, we both felt kind of shy and nervous about the whole thing, so we just held each other at arm's length, and danced all stiff and whatnot. But little by little, as we both started getting into the record, we closed our eyes and started dancing closer and closer, 'til before you knew it, my happy little mug was cuddling smack-dab in the middle of the Honeydew Valley, feeling the soft, fuzzy fur of her pink, angora sweater rubbing against my cheek, smelling her perfume, and wishing that the song would never end.

Good thing Father D'Amiano came along in the nick of time, and said, "Okay, let's leave a little room for the Holy Ghost over here", otherwise things could've gotten a little embarrassing for me—if ya know what I mean.

But, hey, what can I tell ya? That was definitely the exception. Ninety-nine percent of all the other times, those dances would turn into one, big, humiliating mess. Who wanted to stand around and watch, like some lonely little dingleberry, sipping on a coke and holding up the wall, while everybody and their mother were out there on the dance floor, hugging each other and grinding up a storm? Not me—I'll tell ya that much. Nope, forget *that* shit, I rather not even go. And that's what I did: I stopped going.

Chapter 13

All the disappointments of the summer and my "sour sixteen" birthday left me feeling like shit on a stick, and when school started, I was in a really bad mood. I didn't feel like doing nothing or being around nobody; all I wanted was to be left alone.

"Lay off, Chickie!"

"Damn! You a touchy little lame, ain't ya?"

Chickie was this big, tall moolinyan that was in my new homeroom class. His real name was Charles Lee, but everybody called him "Chickie" for some reason. I didn't know why, and since I didn't like the ugly, rat bastard anyway, I never asked nobody no questions about it neither.

See, Chickie was one of them real skeevy moolies, the kind that would never bother to use a handkerchief when they had to blow their nose. What for? They'd just block off one nostril with their thumb, lean over, and shoot their slimy snot-rockets straight to the floor, or the sidewalk, or the street—or wherever the fuck they happened to be at the time.

Anyway, this scuzzball really thought he was hot shit. He'd always be bopping around school with a cigarette behind his ear, a toothpick dangling from his lip, and this dirty, black doo-rag hanging out of the back pocket of his pants that he'd use to cover up his greasy "process"— only he'd call his "marcel". He'd never wear the doo-rag in class though—Doctor Morello, the principal, didn't allow no hats, caps, or doo-rags in school—but as soon as he'd leave the building at three o' clock, the first thing he'd do was to tie that stupid black rag around his head, pull it real tight on the sides, and then fluff it up in the front 'til he looked like some kind of chocolate Elvis or something. What a slimeball.

There was always something about this guy that rubbed me the wrong way. You can call it "instinct", or "sixth sense", or "intuition", or whatever the fuck you want, but from the very first minute I laid eyes on this skeeve, I knew me and him were gonna be like oil and water.

And I guess Chickie must've felt the same way about me too, because he didn't waste no time before he started picking on me,

171

sounding me out all the time, and making me the laughing-stock of the whole freakin' class. He started in on me right away, on the very first day of school, when he first came out with that "lame" bullshit.

See, Chickie would always be talking that moolie jive, and with the exception of the word "mothafucka", his favorite word was "lame". Every other word out of his mouth was "lame" this, and "lame" that, 'til you felt like saying: "Give it a rest already for Chris'sakes!".

Well, I personally didn't give a shit *what* word he liked to use, as long as he didn't go using it on me. But that was the problem with this creep; he didn't want to leave me alone for nothing!

Nope, every day it would be the same ol' story: As soon as we'd be in the hallway, walking to the lunchroom, him and his stupid buddy, Derrick, would follow along two feet behind me, and start goofing on me and coming out with all these mean wisecracks about my limp 'n' stuff. I'd usually mind my own business and ignore them, but sometimes they'd get a little carried away.

"Man, this little ofay mothafucka ain't just lame, he *really* lame."

"Shit yeah, that sho' is one lame-ass mothafucka alright. Check out the way my man be walkin'; he be waddlin' just like a mothafuckin' duck."

"Tell me about it. I betcha when God gave out legs, this mothafuckin' lame musta been takin' a shit or som'n, 'cause by the time he wiped his ass and got back on line, all he got were the leftovers and the second-hand rejects 'n' shit."

After each wisecrack, I'd hear laughing and then the sound of skin hitting skin from Chickie and Derrick slapping each other five. I wish I could've said that their smart-aleck remarks didn't hurt my feelings, but I couldn't, because they did—specially on that bad day when I wasn't in the mood for that shit. I kept telling myself to take a deep breath, calm down, keep walking, and play deaf; that way, if I didn't give them the kind of reaction they were looking for, maybe they'd get bored with the shit and drop it.

Well, that idea didn't work too good because they just kept on and on, getting louder and louder, and meaner and meaner by the second. I tried my very hardest to control myself, but it got to be way too much.

"Why don't the two of you monkey bastards go back to fuckin' Africa and leave me the fuck alone already?!"

172

"Why don'tcha make me? Ya cripple-ass wop mothafucka."

I felt like kicking that scumbag right in the balls, but I knew I didn't stand a chance against him and the other Watusi, so I figured I better just lump it, turn my ass around, and keep on walking. So that's what I did, but the two bastards just wouldn't leave me alone! They stayed two steps behind me, ranking me out and making a big scene in front of everybody. And if that wasn't bad enough, out of nowhere, fuckin' Chickie started doing this stupid, Walter Brennan imitation, hopping around on one leg and flapping his arms around, trying to make fun of the way I'd walk 'n' stuff.

When we walked into the lunchroom, it got even worse; the two shitheads were so loud, they had everybody and their mother staring at me and laughing their asses off right along with them. That's when Chickie exaggerated his Walter Brennan routine even more and put on a really big show for his audience.

I didn't know where to put my face, and as I took a tray and got on the lunch line, I could feel myself turning redder than a ripe tomato. And then, to make matters worse, who comes up right behind me? Googie.

"Hey, shrimpy-gimpy boy", he chuckled, "you don't look so good. What'sa matter, ya can't take a joke or what?"

I didn't even bother to answer, I just gave him the finger and moved away.

The whole lunchroom was still staring, and as I walked toward the table where Chickie and Derrick had sat down, I could feel my heart beating a mile a minute. I didn't know where to put my eyes, so I just kept looking down at my tray, hurrying by as fast as I could so I could find a seat and get out of everybody's line of vision. But before I could get by Chickie's table, the stupid prick stuck out his foot to try and trip me. He didn't get me that good. I felt myself stumble a little, but, luckily, I didn't fall flat on my face or nothing—only a container of milk wound up falling off my tray. I gave him a dirty look, and as I bent down to pick up the milk, the rat bastard gave me a quick kick in the ass, sending me, my tray, and everything on it, crashing all over the place.

I had no choice but to pick everything up, piece by piece, and after I wiped myself off, I got back on my feet again. A big hush fell over the lunchroom. Every eye in the place was staring straight at me and every

173

mouth was wide open. I could feel the blood rushing up to my head and flooding my brain. Enough was enough.

Without blinking an eye, I stepped towards Chickie and smashed him right in the face with my tray. He fell over backwards, but before he could get up, I grabbed a chair and started belting him over the head with it. I wanted to kill that scumbag, and if I couldn't kill him, I wanted to fuck him up real bad. I could hear whistles blowing and everybody yelling "fight! fight!", but I didn't stop for nothing; I just kept swinging the chair at his head, trying to get a good shot at his ugly mug, so I could bust a couple of teeth, or at least break his nose or something.

I felt somebody grabbing me from behind, trying to pull me away. I couldn't see who it was, and I didn't give a fuck; I just wanted to give this sonuvabitch another good shot in the face.

"Here! Take this, you ugly piece of shit!"

I could feel myself getting pulled away, and then I heard: *"Hey! Hey, Joseph! Stop! Stop!"*

As mad as I was, I could still recognize the voice. It was Mr. Di Salvo.

He got me in a half-nelson right away, and while I was struggling to get loose, Chickie scrambled to his feet and made a lunge at me. Officer Castro, the school cop, jumped in between the two of us, but before he could pull Chickie off me, the rat bastard grabbed a hank of my hair, and got off a shot to my face. I swung right back at him, but by this time, everybody and their mother had jumped in and were pulling us apart. I felt something trickling down my lip, and when I went to wipe it, I saw it was blood.

"I'm gonna get you!" Chickie yelled, as Officer Castro gave him a shove and hustled him out of the lunchroom. "Just wait 'til three o'clock, mothafucka! Your crippled little honky ass is *mine!*"

I was taken straight to the nurse's office, and as I sat there holding my head back to stop my nose from bleeding, I could see Chickie out of the corner of my eye, sitting in the next room with an ice pack on his forehead. I didn't know exactly what I'd done to him, but I must've gotten in a couple of good shots though, because this ugly, black bastard looked fucked up.

Well, after I'd calmed down and had gotten a grip on myself, the reality of the situation started to close in on me like a dark, gloomy

174

thunderstorm. Things weren't looking too good, and I knew it was only a matter of time before the shit *really* hit the fan.

See, the way I figured it, I was going to catch two beatings: one from Chickie at three o'clock, and the other one from Mom once she found out I'd been fighting in school and had gotten myself in a whole bunch of trouble. And then, if I survived the two beatings, I was pretty sure I was going to get suspended, or maybe even expelled. I didn't know if there was some way of getting off the hook; I just had to put on my thinking cap and try and come up with something. But in the meantime, I figured a little prayer to Saint Francis couldn't hurt.

Whoa! Saint Francis must be clutch saint, because now that my back was *really* nailed to the wall, it looked like he finally might be coming through for me. Yep, if I heard what I *think* I heard, that little prayer I sent out got through loud and clear. That's because the assistant principal, Mr. Epstein, and Officer Castro had been talking to each other in the next room, and from the bits and pieces I was able to overhear, it sounded like they had decided to let Chickie go home early. Mr. Epstein said that it would be the best way to "de-fuse a volatile situation with a minimum of trouble", and let me tell ya, I agreed with that decision one hundred percent.

Well, I still wasn't exactly sure what was going to happen, but as I sat there, worrying my ass off and twirling a Q-tip in my nose, I looked out the window and what I saw surprised the shit out of me. It was Chickie walking out of the building. He had a big bandage on the right side of his forehead, and I could see him touching it and wincing from the pain. But that didn't stop him from putting on his doo-rag though. Nope, just like clockwork, as soon as he reached the bottom step of the entrance of the school, he whipped it out of his back pocket. Then, once his stupid black rag and his make-believe pompadour was in place, he pulled a cigarette from behind his ear, lit it, and bopped towards 116th Street. I kept on watching, even after he turned the corner; I didn't trust that skeevy bastard for one minute. I knew he wasn't going home. He was probably right around that corner somewhere, leaning against a car and sipping on a soda, just laying low and killing time, waiting for three o' clock so he could pounce on me and kick my ass in front of the whole freakin' school.

Mr. Epstein gave me a big, long speech about "unacceptable behavior", and when he finally got finished, he turned me over to Mr. Jarema, the guidance counselor. Mr. Jarema tried to pick my brain for almost an hour, nagging me and trying to get me to talk about what happened between me and Chickie, but I didn't tell him shit. I wasn't about to tell my personal business to no sneaky teacher, and I just kept giving him short, one-word answers like "yes" and "no", and when I didn't feel like answering at all, I just looked down at the floor and stayed quiet.

After a while, Mr. Jarema gave up, and when the three o'clock bell rang, he left the room and handed the baton back over to Mr. Epstein. Epstein looked angry, and after he said he was gonna hold me in school for an extra fifteen or twenty minutes "for my own safety", he handed me a piece of paper that looked like one of them appointment-slip things.

"This is an appointment for a hearing with Doctor Morello. You'd better be here tomorrow, young man, at ten o' clock sharp *with* your mother—otherwise your days at Benjamin Franklin are going to be over."

As soon as I heard them words, my heart sank like a ton of bricks, and as I sat there, listening to the rumble of the footsteps galloping down the stairs, the lockers banging and clanging, and the guys laughing and shouting and making their way out of the building, I started to feel real shitty about losing my head and acting all crazy and stupid like I did. I guess I would've been a lot better off if I would've just swallowed the shit—like I always did.

Well, after about twenty minutes of twiddling my thumbs and worrying my ass off, Mr. Epstein finally came out of his office again.

"Okay," he said, "you may leave now, Joseph, but be careful. You don't know if that other boy could be lurking outside somewhere waiting for you. So go straight home—you hear me?"

"Yeah."

Before I went out into the street, I opened the door a few inches and peeked outside towards the corner of 116th Street. The coast looked pretty clear, so I took a deep breath and walked out. I lived only half a block away, and I knew I could try to make a mad dash and run home any time I wanted to. But I didn't want nobody to think that I was scared of that skeevy, rat bastard, so I took all my sweet time and walked down the steps real slow, nice and calm, just in case anybody was watching. But I wasn't stupid though; I kept my eyes glued to the corner every second.

Well, just as I got near the bottom steps and I thought I was home free, *boom!,* out popped fuckin' Chickie like the jack-in-the-box from hell, smiling that evil smile and looking like the Devil himself. And if that wasn't bad enough, he had Derrick and couple of his friends with him too.

I stopped dead in my tracks and froze like a statue. "Oh shit!" I said to myself, "what the fuck am I gonna do now?!"

Chickie and his boys were making a beeline straight towards me, bopping hard, and looking all mean and tough and everything. I didn't know what to do, so without even thinking, I started backpedaling and going up the steps of the school again—only backwards. I was really shitting in my pants by then, and just as I was about to panic and try to make a run for it, all of a sudden, out of nowhere, I heard the sweetest sound I ever heard in my life. It was the voice of my cousin Anthony. *Yes!*

He was hustling straight toward the moolies with a fuckin' baseball bat in his hand, and he had every single Redwood in Ben Frank right behind him.

"Hey, you!" he yelled, *"get the fuck outa here!"*

Well, maybe Chickie was one tough moolinyan, but he wasn't no damn fool though. When he found himself face to face with a bunch of crazy guineas coming at him with bats and chains, he didn't say peep. Nope, my man spun around and took off like a rocket.

The Redwoods chased Chickie and his friends all the way around the corner and up the block, almost to the corner of First Avenue. But after they threw a couple of bottles at them and missed, they slowed down to a walk, and finally gave up. 'Ey, those moolies could run faster than fuckin' lightning, and when they're scared, fuhgeddaboudit, you'd need a motorcycle to catch up with them.

177

Anthony was still huffing and puffing and all out of breath from the chase, and when I fell in step with him, I gave him a solid five with both hands. "Thanks a lot, Ant," I said, "you really saved my ass this time."

"Forget it, Junior, you'd do the same for me if ya could. Besides, I never liked that creep anyway, him and that dirty black rag he wears on his head."

"Yeah, he's a real slimeball. But where *were* you guys anyway? I didn't even see yuz at all."

"What'sa matter with you? We were all standin' right there by the park—right by the corner of Russo's restaurant. Ya better get your eyes examined, Junior."

I just shrugged my shoulders. "I guess I was too busy lookin' for Chickie up by the corner of 116th Street; I probably didn't even *think* about lookin' in the other direction."

"Well, it don't matter. The important thing is that we got to *them* before they got to *you*."

"You can say that again."

By now the rest of the guys were all crowding around us. There must've been about ten or fifteen of them in all, and they were happier than pigs in shit, laughing and goofing around, and bragging about how they'd scared the pants off the "eggplants".

I smiled and gave everybody five. "'Ey, thanks a lot for helpin' me out, guys. I never expected to see yuz come outa nowhere like that—right in the nick of time and everything."

Deek, a tall guy with pimples, grabbed me in a headlock and gave me a friendly noogie on my head. "C'mon, what did ya think we was gonna do? Stand around with our arms crossed and let a buncha niggas come in here and kick your ass? Forget about *that* shit."

"Yeah," Albie said, "that guy was twice your size for Chris'sakes. And he didn't even have the balls to come after you himself; he had to bring his buddies with him for backup."

Mario chimed in and gave Albie five. "That's right, that's the way it always is with them niggas: all talk—blah-blah-blah-blah-blah—all talk and no balls."

"What balls?" Dino grumbled, zipping up his Redwood jacket and flipping up the collar. "Moolies don't know nothin' about shit like that. All they know is how to pull the woof and throw around a lotta bullshit.

178

But let me tell ya, as soon as somebody calls their bluff, them spear-chuckers are the first ones to punk out, cop a plea, and shit all over themselves—every single time."

Butchie, the Redwood war counselor, had been staying pretty quiet up to then, but he put his two cents into the conversation too. "You got that right, Dino, them niggas don't even stick up for their own kind. I seen it happen a whole buncha times; they leave their own boys right there on the ground, bleedin' and getting' stomped and everything, while they go running away like a buncha pussies to save their own asses."

"You tellin' me?" Dino answered, holding out his hand so Butchie could slip him five. "They ain't nothin' but a lotta talk, a lotta talk and a lotta mouth—that's all. Nothin' but boo-coo nigga jive and no action."

"I don't know about that," I said, "them moolies sure looked like they were gonna kick the shit outa *me*."

Anthony waved me away with his hand, but then he grabbed me by the cheeks and looked over at the other guys. "Hey, did ya see the look on that creep's face when Joey hit him over the head with the fuckin' chair?"

"Hell yeah," Albie said, "that black bastard turned white as a sheet. He looked like he seen a ghost—just like Buckwheat on the 'Little Rascals'. Fuhgeddaboudit, you really shocked the shit outa that guy, Gimp—let me tell ya."

Frankie, the one everybody called "Pep", pushed his way through the guys and gave me some skin. "'Ey, not for nothin', but I really gotta hand it to you, Gimp. You really taught that jungle bunny a lesson. I been waitin' a long time for somebody to show some guts and stand up to that scumbag. He swears he's bad, but he ain't nothin' but a punk."

"Yeah," Anthony said, "that rat bastard deserved everything he got. I seen what he was doin' to you in the lunchroom, and let me tell ya, that was some wrong shit."

As soon as Anthony said that, I got an instant flashback of Chickie doing his stupid Walter Brennan imitation, and as soon as I remembered it and pictured it in my mind, I felt my face drop to the floor.

But before I could lower my eyes, Butchie came over and stood in front of me. He put up his dukes like he was play-fighting, and after he

179

gave me a make-believe jab to the chin, he looked me in the eye and said: "You got a lotta heart, kid...a lotta heart."

Well, maybe I had a "lotta heart" when it came to standing up to Chickie, but I sure didn't have a lotta heart when it came to facing up to Mom though. Are you kidding? I was shitting green and biting my nails just *thinking* about it. But after I rolled it around in my brain for a while, I started thinking maybe I should test the waters first by telling Grandma and Grandpa about everything *before* I dropped the bomb on Mom. Well, once I saw how quick they were to jump in my corner, I decided right then and there that my best bet would probably be to tell Mom the whole truth, exactly the way it happened, and just take my chances.

So that's what I did. As soon as Mom came home and we sat down for supper, I told her the whole story—with all the details and everything. I even told her about Googie and the stupid "shrimpy-gimp" shit, and Bobby Zito and all the bullying, so she could understand that something had been building and building inside of me, and I just didn't pick up a chair out of a clear blue sky and start hitting somebody over the head with it for no good reason. I wasn't crazy, I'd gotten to the breaking point, and I just couldn't take it no more.

"Are you tellin' me the truth, Junior?" she asked, looking me in the eye and holding up the feet of Jesus.

Without hesitating or nothing, I leaned over and kissed her fingers. "That's the truth, Ma— honest to God. And if ya don't believe me, you can ask Anthony; he was there in the lunchroom and he seen the whole thing."

Well, that's exactly what she did. Before you could say "Anthony Marino", she was already on the phone, calling Aunt Jean so she could get the scoop straight from the horse's mouth.

I didn't know exactly what Anthony told her, but he must've explained everything real good, because as soon as she got off the phone with him, she was in my corner one hundred percent.

"Sonuva*bitch!*" she yelled, gathering up the dirty dishes and slamming them into the sink. "What kinda piece of garbage is gonna pick on a poor kid just because he has a little problem with his legs? Stupid black bastard, he should rot in *hell!*"

"Celeste," Grandma said, "calm down. It's already finisha!"

180

"Well, it's not finished for me! Now my son has a black mark on his record, because of *chista bella razza.* Ya know, not for nothin', Ma, but these people got no respect, no respect at all—not even for God on the cross."

Mom was *pissed,* and it looked like she was gonna break a couple of plates the way she kept slamming them around in the sink and everything. "These people are nothin' but a buncha savages, that's all they are—*savages!"*

Jeez, I hadn't heard Mom say stuff like that since them moolies stole my bike over on Randall's Island. She was *boiling* and losing control, and I started to get a little worried about what she might do at that "hearing" thing. Yeah, the last thing I needed after all the shit that happened, was for Mom to get loud with the principal. Then I'd *really* be screwed.

Well, she faked me out again. Yep, as soon as she heard Doctor Morello say the magic words: "We're fully aware that the other boy was antagonizing Joseph, and that he was the instigator", she calmed down right away and acted just like the perfect lady. And Doc Morello acted like the perfect gentleman too, considering the situation and everything. He gave us a big speech about how "there's no room at Benjamin Franklin High School for such violent behavior", and even though he didn't seem too mad or nothing, he still suspended my stinky ass for three whole days.

Mom wasn't too happy about the suspension, and neither was I. But what ya gonna do? If you do the crime, you gotta do the time— that's all there was to it. So, for the first time in my life, I was officially suspended from school.

Mom looked real upset and embarrassed by the whole thing, and as we left and walked down the steps of the school, she really let me have it: "Well, I hope you're proud of yourself, mister; now ya got yourself suspended—just like a real juvenile delinquent. Happy now?"

I knew better than to answer, so I just kept on walking with my head down.

181

"Ya know, gettin' suspended doesn't mean this is gonna be a nice little vacation for you. If you think for one minute, that you're gonna be goin' downstairs and hangin' around with your friends and havin' a jolly ol' time, you got another think comin'. This is supposed to be punishment—understand? The only time you're leavin' the house is to go to Mass on Sunday. Outside of that, you're gonna be sittin' upstairs, staring at the four walls like a prisoner, 'til it's time for you to go back to school on Tuesday. Maybe this way you'll learn your lesson, and you'll think twice about the consequences of your actions, before you go flyin' off the handle and doin' something stupid like this again."

Well, with my rotten luck, the goddamn weekend fell right in the middle of my suspension, so instead of getting *three* days of solitary confinement, I was actually getting *five*. I didn't think it was fair, but I wasn't about to make no complaints about it. Are you kidding? I was lucky I didn't catch a beating from Chickie, and I was *double* lucky I didn't catch one from Mom, so if I had to spend five days cooped up in the house, the hell with it. Yeah, no matter how you sliced it, I still figured I was getting off easy, and I wasn't about to press my luck for nothing.

Chapter 14

I didn't know how it happened, but little by little, I found myself turning into a Redwood too, just like my cousin Anthony. I mean, I never got formerly initiated like he did, so I couldn't really say I was a member, but ever since I stood up to that scumbag, Chickie, the guys started treating me almost like I was one of them. I'd hang around with them over at the park almost every day, and it helped me to get a little bit of respect at school and around the neighborhood. Yep, once the word spread that I had backup with the Redwoods, a lot of them bullies who had been picking on me all the time, finally started to back off and leave me alone—'specially Chickie and Derrick. Are you kidding? After they got chased by Anthony and the guys that time, those two punks didn't even *look* at me no more—let alone open their mouths to start something.

Googie cooled it with me too. I guess he must've gotten the scoop through the grapevine, because he changed his tune *real* fast. He kept on calling me "Gimp", like everybody else—but at least he stopped with that "shrimpy-gimpy" bullshit.

Yeah, hanging out with the Redwoods really changed a lot for me, and little by little, I guess some of their stuff must've rubbed off on me. I even started smoking. I mean, I'd already tried cigarettes a long time ago—just to see what the big deal was all about—but I never got into it because I heard it "stunts your growth". But since I had pretty much given up on growing anyway, I figured: "what the fuck?". I never liked the taste of it that much, but it did make me look a lot older though. Every time I'd catch a reflection of myself in a store window or a car or something, I'd always scope out that snowy-white Newport dangling from my lip and think to myself that I looked ten times cooler than I ever looked before.

But I'd never smoke in the house though; I would've got my ass handed to me if I ever got caught smoking. That's why I'd always hide my smokes at the bottom of my toybox, and I'd always go around sucking on Sen-Sen or one of them violet mints to cover the smell of cigarettes on my breath.

183

That Sen-Sen and them violet things came in handy for covering up the smell of booze on your breath too. Not that I was a big drinker or anything, but whenever the guys would pass around some beer or wine over at the park, I didn't want to act like a doofus—so I'd take a couple of slugs. I didn't like the feeling that much—it can make you act like a real asshole—but what *really* turned me off was the idea of losing control of myself. That's why I'd only take a couple of little sips, just to show I was one of the guys and so nobody would goof on me.

But there was this one time when I did overdo it on the booze a little bit and got really fucked up. It happened at one of them hooky parties called "sets". I didn't want to go because I was afraid of getting snagged and getting in trouble, but Anthony talked me into it.

"Junior, you gotta come," he said, acting all excited. "Frankie Pep and Albie got a hold of some Spanish fly, and once we slip some of that shit to these slutty broads from Yorkville, they'll get so crazy and horny, they'll starting puttin' out like champs, and we're all *guaranteed* to get laid."

I guess I should've known better, but since I wanted to get lucky just as bad as the next guy, I figured "fuck it" and said yeah. But it didn't work out too good for me though. That's because there were five of us guys and only four broads showed up—so you know who the odd-man-out was, don't you? Me.

It really turned out bad because I had to sit there and watch, like a stupid little dingleberry, while everybody else was making out, tongue-kissing, and grinding their asses off to all these sexy slow-records they kept putting on. I didn't know where to put my face, and I didn't know what to do, so I started chugging down this nasty-tasting, orange shit they had there called "Tango". And that's how I got shitfaced.

When I started to feel all woozy and whatnot, I tried to get Anthony's attention, but it was no use. He was busy making out hot and heavy with this fat Irish broad over on the couch, and I knew wild horses weren't going to drag *him* away. So, without saying a word, I threw on my coat, slipped out the door, and stumbled out into the cold winter air.

I could hardly walk, and as I zig-zagged up First Avenue on rubber legs, I actually got lost along the way, and it took me a long time to get from Yorkville back to the neighborhood. I kept hoping and praying I

184

wouldn't get snagged by one of them truant officers. Are you kidding? Getting caught "on the hook" was bad enough, but getting caught playing hooky and being drunk was ten times worse.

Anyway, after I stumbled around for God knows how long, not knowing where the hell I was, I somehow made it to the park, and that was where Anthony and the rest of the guys found me, sprawled out on a bench. They made me use "the ol' finger trick", where you stick your finger all the way down the back of your throat and gag yourself to force yourself to throw up. I felt a lot better after I puked my guts out a couple of times, but once the guys started showing off their hickeys, and bragging about all the feels they'd copped off the chicks at the set, I felt ten times worse than when I was smashed.

Boy, thank God none of them bastards got laid, otherwise I would've never heard the end of it. That's because these guys were always bragging their asses off about all this wild and crazy shit they did with all these different broads and everything. Naturally, I wouldn't have too much to say, so most of the time I'd just stand there like a dingleberry and listen while everybody went on and on about how they "tongue-kissed" this one, "felt up" that one, and "finger-fucked" the other one. That's all these guys ever talked about: tits, ass, and pussy—for hours and hours and hours, all day long.

And they'd never get bored with the shit or keep anything a secret neither. Nope, any time one of them went out with a girl, they always had to come back and give the rest of us a blow-by-blow, play-by-play description of: where they went, what they did, and what they'd copped off the broad—right down to the last detail. And let me tell ya, when it came to shit like that, the rest of them nosy bastards would be all ears; they'd want to know *everything*. And they'd ask questions too: "So did ya grab her tits, or what?—"over or under the bra?"—"What kinda nipples she got?"—"Did she grab ya cock?"—"hand job or blow job?"—"Cop any pussy?"—"over or under the panties?"—"Finger smell?"—Fulton Fish Market or Bronx Zoo?" Fugeddaboudit, these guys were too much.

I figured half the stuff they'd always be bragging about was probably a big crock of bullshit anyway—I wasn't stupid—but no matter how you sliced it, listening to all that shit would always make me feel

185

kind of sad and messed up. Yeah, as much as I hated to admit, I guess I was a little jealous.

See, the other guys were able to talk to chicks, and whistle at them, and goof on them and whatnot, but not me. I was too shy. The only time I'd even open my *mouth* to a girl was if I knew her already, or if somebody introduced me to her—otherwise I'd just stay quiet. But not those guys. They'd always be howling, whistling, and yelling stuff at them from all the way across the park—just like it was nothing. And they'd never give it a rest neither. Nope, them horny bastards were always on the make, twenty-four hours a day, like a bunch of fisherman fishing for fish. And as soon as they'd spot anything wiggling its tail, *wham!,* they'd always have to throw out a line: "Hey, honey, how's ya bunny, makin' money?"—or "Shake it, don't break it, it took nine months to make it"—or the ol' Redwood favorite: "Whoa, that must be jelly, 'cause jam don't shake like that!".

From what I saw, girls didn't go for none of them stupid lines. They'd either ignore the guys, give them a dirty look, give them the finger, or just tell them to go fuck themselves. But these guys didn't care; they'd just grab their crotch, give them the *double-finger,* and shout: "Fuck you, ya little skank, I wouldn't want that keroded cunt if ya gave it to me on a silver platter!"

Well, I guess none of the Redwoods were ever going to win the "Gentleman of the Year" award, but they sure were a pisser though; and I had a goof hanging around with them. And let me tell ya, if it were up to me, I would've wanted to go "through the mill" and get initiated too, just like Anthony had. I even asked about it a couple of times, but every time I did, they'd just brush me off with: "You don't have to worry about that, Gimp"—or "Fuhgeddaboudit, Gimp"—or "It's alright, Gimp, you're with us, you know that"—so I didn't bring it up no more.

But to tell the truth, I never really felt like I was a real Redwood. I'd always feel like I was on the outside looking in, like I was still only Anthony's cousin, or a little pet that they liked to have around—sort of like a gang mascot or something like that. I mean, it was always cool for me to hang around and shoot the shit, or tell jokes, or to harmonize with the guys when they felt like singing, but whenever things would heat up and they'd go on one of them "japs" against the Viscounts, or

186

they'd have a bop with the moolies, that's when I'd always get left behind.

"Sorry, Gimp," someone would say, "we know you got the heart, ya just don't got the legs."

Well, as much as it hurt to admit it, I guess they were probably right.

See, a "jap" was like a quick, in-and-out raid on another gang's territory. The idea was to swoop in like bunch of crazy kamikazes— that's why it was called a "jap"—pick off a couple their guys when they didn't expect nothing, kick the shit out of them, and then tear ass before any of their boys could come and help them. It was a hit-and-run kind of thing, and you had to be able run your ass off. That's why whenever I'd get left behind, there wasn't too much I could say about it. I mean, I'd feel like shit on a stick, but I'd just have to lump it—that was it. And there was a time when I did an awful lot of "lumping", 'specially after the guys got into all that static with the Serpents. That's when they started going on japs almost every single day.

The Serpents was the biggest click in all East Harlem, maybe even in the whole city. They weren't gangbusting as much as they had been a few years earlier—most of the original Serpents were all junkies by then—but there were still enough younger guys bopping around in the green-and-black to keep the Serpent name alive. And it was pretty much the same thing with us. The original, old-time Redwoods had broken up a couple of years before Anthony joined, but the young guys in the neighborhood wanted to keep the name going, so they kept on with the stickball team, the football team, and the jackets and whatnot. But let me tell ya, whenever there was any static with the PR's or the moolies, we'd all go back to bopping full blast, hard and heavy, just like in the "old days".

Anyway, them Serpents were some really tough customers. I heard there were about five hundred or more in East Harlem alone: Apache Serpents, Demon Serpents, Young Magicians, Gallant Lords, Dorians— not to mention their "brother clubs" and all the "divisions" that they had all over the city: uptown, downtown, east side, west side, Brooklyn, Bronx, every-fuckin'-where.

And those motherfuckers were bad too. They weren't like the Redwoods—our guys prided themselves in fighting man to man, in hand-to-hand combat—but not them Serpents though; they didn't even

187

like to get their hands dirty. They'd go to a rumble all decked-out in their sharkskin suits, their stingy-brims, and all their diddy-bop shit, and nine times out of ten, they'd always be packing. That was their thing: pieces. And their favorite way of fighting was what they called "burning": walking right up to a guy, whipping out a piece, and "lighting him up" at close range—without even blinking an eye.

Most of them came from down around 103rd Street, and since they were always fighting with their mortal enemies from the uptown side of Spanish Harlem, the Viscounts, we never had too much trouble with them in our neck of the woods. But that was only until one of them got the bright idea to go diddy-bopping across Jefferson Park. That's when Butchie, Sammy Dee and Albie, surrounded the guy, kicked the shit out of him, and just to teach him a lesson, they took his green-and-black Serpent sweater right off his back and kept it as a souvenir. I knew that was Butchie's idea right away, because, from what I heard, he loved taking hats, sweaters, jackets, and anything he could after he kicked somebody's ass. He called those things his "war trophies", and he had them all hanging up on his bedroom wall—like it was a fuckin' museum or some kind of gang shrine or something. Pretty crazy, huh?

Anyway, I guess you didn't have to be Einstein to figure out that the Serpents wanted revenge. And they got it too, only a few days later. They caught one of our guys, Aldo, down by the Eagle theater near their turf, and a bunch of Serpents jumped him and kicked his ass. From what I heard, they put a shank in his face, made him give up his beautiful Redwood jacket, and for good measure, they stomped the shit out of him and fucked him up bad—right in front of his girlfriend.

Well, to make a long story short, all the guys got together for a meeting, and after everybody cursed out the Serpents for what they did to Aldo, and after they bitched and moaned about how the spics had no respect and were diddy-bopping in the park and all over the neighborhood, a decision was finally made about what our next move would be. We all knew that we couldn't risk a full-scale war, or even a war council with the Serpents—they outnumbered us by about 500 to 1—but nobody was going to back down or let them get away with what they did to Aldo neither. So, after everybody put in their two cents, Butchie made the official proclamation. And all he needed were four little words to do it: *"The shit is on!*

188

Well, when Butchie Pagano, the war counselor of the Redwoods, said "the shit is on", *the shit was on!*. Almost every night, bunches of our guys would cross over into Serpent territory with bats, chains, shanks, car antennas, homemade brass knuckles made out garbage-can handles, pipes, rocks and whatever else they could get their hands on. We knew we didn't stand a chance against the Serpents with all their divisions and whatnot, so we decided we had to limit ourselves to japping their brother clubs along the edges of their turf. That was all we could do.

I guess I shouldn't use the word "we" though, because the guys would never let me go along with them on none of them raids. I'd always be in the park with them when they'd go off to fight, and I'd be there when they'd come back, but while they were gone, I'd usually sit alone on a bench, smoke a couple of cigarettes, listen to my portable radio, and feel sorry for myself. Yeah, there was nothing worse than staying behind like a pussy, while all your buddies went off to fight like men.

I guess I finally got a taste of how my father must've felt when all his friends went off to fight in World War Two, and he had to stay behind because the Army thought he was too short to serve. Something like that can really mess with your mind, and make you feel mad at the whole fuckin' world, mad at God, mad at every-fuckin'-thing and every-fuckin'-body. And let me tell ya, little by little, I think one of them "chips" was starting to grow right here on my shoulder, probably just like the one my Dad must've had. I guess it was like father, like son—what can I say?

The shit with the Serpents kept getting worse and worse every day. One night, one of their brother clubs, the Gallant Lords, got us in an ambush over by the schoolyard on 108th Street, and they got us good. They came out "burning", Serpent style, and when it was all over, a few of our guys came back really messed up—'specially Albie and Gino. Albie got shot in the arm, and Gino caught a .22 bullet in his leg, up by his thigh.

"That's it!" Butchie growled, as he limped back to the park, all bloodied-up and madder than hell. "Now we gotta scrape up as many pieces as we can get our hands on: .22's, .25's, zip guns —any-fuckin'-

189

thing. If them scumbag motherfuckers are gonna use pieces, then *we're* gonna use pieces too. We gotta fight fire with fire."

So, everybody started looking for pieces. Butchie, Sammy Dee, Gino , Albie and Deek already had guns, but everybody else had to go scrounging around for something. A couple of the guys who had relatives in "high places" came through with some heavy-duty fire power: Frankie Pep with this cool, nickel-plated .25 that he got off his cousin, and Charlie Goggles with a fuckin' sawed-off shotgun he swiped from his uncle. But the rest of us who didn't have no money or no "connections", kept ourselves busy making zip guns.

All you really needed to make one was a piece of car antenna for the barrel, a couple of pieces of wood for the body of the gun, a strong strip of rubber from a bicycle inner tube, one of them "door-latch" things from the hardware store, and a lot of heavy-duty tape to tape the whole shit together. Mario showed me how to do it, and I made two of them in no time. And they both worked too! We took them across the highway and tested them by the river, and they both worked like a charm. All you had to do was place a little .22 bullet in the back of the homemade barrel, and when you pulled back on the piece of rubber—sort of like a slingshot—that door-latch thing would hit the back of the bullet, and *ping!,* it would come flying out of there almost like a regular gun—only without the loud noise.

I made another one and gave it to Anthony, and then I made a super-duper, deluxe model that I kept for myself. Hey, I didn't know if Butchie and Sammy Dee might change their minds and let me tag along on a jap someday, so I figured I had to be prepared—just in case.

Anyway, once we were ready to hit the Gallant Lords and get our revenge, the bulls showed up out of nowhere—like they had radar—and started breaking balls. They made a big production out of the whole thing, lining us up against the fence, frisking us, pushing us around, asking us a lot of questions about the static with the Serpents, and making a big pain-in-the-ass out of themselves. We didn't know whether they found out about the shit from the neighborhood grapevine, or whether one of them nosy Youth Board workers blabbed it to them over at the precinct or something. But no matter how they found out about it, they were on to something, and they started sticking to us like white on rice.

190

The bulls kept staking out the park to the point where we actually had to go over by the river to duck them, just so we could have a private war conference and plan out our next move.

As usual, Butchie did most of the talking, and the rest of us did most of the listening.

"Time's running out," he said, pounding his fist against the palm of his hand and spitting through his teeth. "We gotta do somethin', and we gotta do it *fast.*"

Sammy Dee slipped Butchie a quick five. "I'm with you, Butch, but we can't go over there all wild and crazy like last time; that's how they got us in that fuckin' ambush."

"Yeah, somehow they knew we were comin' before we even got there—almost like they were waitin' for us or somethin'."

"Hey," Deek chuckled, kind of half-kidding and half-serious, "who the fuck knows; maybe they got a spy feeding them information 'n' shit."

Dino waved Deek away with his hand. "Get outa here. What kind of stupid shit is that?"

Deek shrugged his shoulders and took a long drag on his cigarette. "Well, maybe nobody *got* no spies, but we'd be a lot better off if we *did* have one—ya know, somebody to scout out their turf and see what's shakin', before we all go running over there like a buncha gun-ho assholes."

All of a sudden Anthony's face lit up. "Hey, ya know somethin'? That ain't such a bad idea."

"C'mon, Anthony," Dino said, "Who we gonna use for a scout? They know every single one of us by sight already."

"They don't know *me!*" I said, jumping up and walking over towards Dino.

Anthony grabbed me by the arm right away and pulled me back. "C'mon, Joey, that's not somethin' for you."

"Yeah, Gimp, that's too dangerous for you."

"Whatta ya talkin' about?" I said, "I could do it!"

Anthony kept trying to pull me away from Butchie and Sammy Dee, giving me a cold, what'sa-matter-with-you? look. "We know you could do it, it's just too dangerous—that's all."

191

"That's right, Gimp," Butchie said, "if you get recognized, you'd have to tear ass like a bat outa hell, and I don't know if you could get outa there fast enough—ya know, with your legs and all. But thanks anyway, man."

"That ain't no problem, I could do it on my bike."

"On ya bike?"

"Yeah! They'll never catch me on my bike, and I could cover a lot more territory that way too. Fuhgeddaboudit, I could tell yuz what the Serpents are doin' all over the neighborhood—without them knowin' shit."

"Hmm," Butchie mumbled, scratching his chin and looking over at Sammy Dee. "Whatta ya think, Sam?"

"The kid's got a point, Butch, nobody's ever seen *him* before. Maybe it could work."

"Whoa!" Anthony said, standing in front of me and pushing me behind him. "Hold ya horses, Butchie. I don't want my cousin doin' any scouting or anything like that; that's way too dangerous for him."

Butchie stood up and stared Anthony down with a mean look on his face. "'Ey, who died and left *you* boss over here? *I'm* the war counselor, not you—and If I say the kid scouts, he scouts."

And so, it was decided, we were going to hit the Gallant Lords the following night, full blast, with everything we had. But before any of our guys would go over there, I was going to scout out the scene on my bike and report back to Butchie.

Just as I was about to head out on my scouting mission, Butchie pulled me to the side, and told me to wait for him for a minute while he went upstairs to his house to get something. I waited in front of his building, feeling excited that I was finally getting my chance to help out.

He came down with one of them stingy-brim, diddy-bop hats that he must've pulled down off the "war trophy" wall of his gang shrine. I couldn't believe this guy.

"Here," he said, handing me the hat, "wear this. It'll spic you up a little bit. They'll be less likely to peg you for a *paesan'* with one of these shits on ya head."

It was made out of velvety, black felt, and it looked practically brand new. The skinny, one-inch brim was pulled down in the front and

192

the back, diddy-bop style, and on the side was a single white pearl. I checked the hat for cooties and tried it on. It was a good fit.

"Sort of like a disguise, huh Butch? Like camouflage or somethin'."

"Yeah, camouflage," Butchie said, reaching over and taking the hat off my head. "But don't put the fuckin' thing on yet. Wait 'til you've crossed Second Avenue and you're a couple of blocks into their territory—*then* put it on. You don't wanna look too spicky around here; somebody might mistake you for a PR and throw a fuckin' bottle upside ya head—*capish?*"

"Gotcha."

So, as I knocked up my kickstand and swung my leg over my bike, Butchie put his arm around my shoulder, and gave me my last-minute instructions. He gave me my route in detail, told me the specific streets where I should pay extra-special attention, and told me exactly the type of things I should be looking for. "Alright," he said, "be careful, Gimp."

All the other guys crowded around me too, patting me on the back and wishing me luck, as I pushed off and pedaled away. I was scared, but it felt great to finally be able to do something to help out the guys after so many weeks of sitting on the sidelines.

Everybody was yelling stuff at me, but I could hear Anthony's voice a lot louder than anybody else's. "Jo-wee! Don't go past Lexington Avenue for *nothin'*—*ya hear?!*"

The water truck must've passed by not too long ago, because I was getting that clean, fresh smell that hangs in the air after it washes the gutter. The sun had gone down already, but the left-over light was painting the sky this pinkish-tangerine color. My heart was pounding, my mouth was dry, and I could feel the blood pumping through my veins, throbbing and sizzling through my body like electricity. I ain't gonna bullshit and say that I wasn't scared, because I was, but at least I felt *alive.*

When I passed 112th Street, I spotted the bulls, staking out the park and "cooping" with their coffee and donuts, keeping a careful eye on our activities. They gave me the once-over as I passed, but I kept my head down and watched them out of my rear-view mirror.

I followed the route that Butchie had given me, and I made mental notes along the way about everything I saw and where I'd seen it. The

193

fear I felt when I first left on my mission had faded away by then, and I didn't really get scared again until I had to pass through them skeevy, Park Avenue tunnels. Those were the pedestrian walkways that looked like they'd been carved out of the filthy black rock that held up the train tracks. Ever since I was a little kid, they always gave me creeps, so I pedaled a little faster and held my nose as I went through, trying to stop the stench of piss from knocking me flat on my ass. Yiiicchhhh!

When I got to 108th Street and made my turn, I knew right away I was in Gallant Lords' turf. They was a big painting on the schoolyard wall showing a top-hat, cane and gloves, and the words "Gallant Lords, 108 Street, D.L.A.M.F." (that meant Down Like A Mother Fucker), and under the emblem were the names of fifty or sixty gang members: Chino, Pipo, Cano, Speedy, Lefty, Chago, Abner, Tato, and on and on and on. I pulled my hat down a little to cover my face as I passed by, but I didn't see too many people on the street at all. My guess was that it probably was supper time and everybody and their mother was upstairs eating their rice and beans. But when I got to 109th Street, I hit paydirt. There they were, about a dozen of these creeps, playing stickball in front of the main entrance of the junior high school. They had a few of their broads with them, sitting on the steps watching the game, but I didn't think they were going to be too much of a problem. It was the perfect set-up.

"Alriiight! Wait 'til the guys hear about *this!*"

I made a quick U-turn so nobody would get suspicious, and then, after I made my right onto 112th, I pedaled my ass off back to the park.

I got back in no-time flat, and as I slammed on the brakes and swerved to a screechy stop, all the guys ran over and crowded around me.

"What ya see, Gimp?"

"How many are there?"

"See any Serpents?"

"What about the Gallant Lords?"

"Any cops around?"

"*Hold it!*" Butchie yelled, "We can't all talk at once over here! I'll ask the questions."

194

Everybody dropped their eyes and shut their mouths, as Butchie stood in front of me and asked the sixty-four-thousand-dollar question. "So, what ya see, Gimp?"

"Well, there ain't too much happening with the Serpents from what I could see. Small bunch of them over by that 'Federation' place on 106th, and a couple of Young Magicians down by 103rd, but outside of that, it looked pretty quiet."

"And what about the Gallant Lords?"

"Now's that's a different story. There's a buncha them playin' stickball on 109th between Second and Third, right in front of the junior high school."

"How many?"

"Only about ten or twelve maybe, and they got a couple of their broads with 'em too."

"*Perfect!*" Butchie yelled, pulling everybody together into a big, football huddle. "Alright, now listen up. When we get to Second Avenue, we'll split into two groups. One group will come at 'em from the Third Avenue side, and the rest of us will hit 'em from the Second Avenue side. We'll get 'em in a fuckin' Redwood sandwich and *destroy* them cocksuckers!"

"Hold up, Butchie!" I shouted, a little surprised at my volume. "There's bulls around."

"Bulls? Where?"

"Right there on First Avenue by 112th. They're sittin' there scopin' out the park."

"Fuck!" Sammy Dee said, "Them scumbags are probably lookin' to bust us with weapons. We can't go over there with all this shit on us; we'll be playin' right into their hands."

"I know, they'll snag us for sure."

Butchie stopped to think for a second, and then he scratched his head and turned to me. "Hey, Gimp, how were they dressed?"

"Who? The cops?"

"No, stupid, the Gallant Lords?"

"Oh! Uh, I don't know—just regular: dungarees, sneakers, stuff like that."

"Ah-*ha!*" he yelled, "that means they probably ain't packin'."

"What are ya drivin' at, Butch?" Sammy Dee asked.

195

"Well, if they ain't packin', then we don't need no pieces. Let's just go over there and kick their asses with our bare fuckin' hands!"

"I don't know," Anthony said, "you forgettin' what they did to Albie 'n' Gino last time?"

"I ain't forgetting shit!" Butchie answered, raising his voice. "I know these rat bastards, the only time they pack is when they're wearin' all their diddy-bop shit. If they're just wearin' dungarees and sneakers, it means they're just havin' a friendly game of stickball, and they ain't even *thinkin'* about fightin'. I say let's ditch the pieces and go in there clean—'cept for our usual bats and chains and pipes 'n' shit. That way if the bulls bust us, they ain't got shit."

"I don't know, Butch. You never know what these spics are gonna do; they can be some tricky motherfuckas."

Everybody stood around, thinking and mumbling and whatnot, 'til Butchie snapped his fingers and looked over at me again. "*I got it!* Those of you got bats and chains, keep 'em, but those of you who got pieces, zip guns or switchblades, give 'em to Gimp. He'll hide 'em in his jacket and follow half a block behind us on his bike. That way, if we need the shit, we got it; but if we don't, we're clean. Whatta ya say, Gimp?"

"I don't know, I...uh."

"Wait a second, Butchie!" Anthony shouted, "I don't want my cousin holdin' nobody's shit. Find somebody else."

Right away Butchie gave Anthony a cold, dirty look. "It ain't up to you, Ant', it's up to me. *I'm* the war counselor over here, remember? And it's up to the kid." Then he turned around and looked at me again. "C'mon, Gimp, whatta ya say? You'd be doin' us a real big solid."

"Well, uh I don't know...I..."

Before I could even finish my sentence, everybody was on top of me, handing me pieces, and switchblades, and zip guns, a box cutter, and all *kinds* of crazy shit. I didn't really know what to do, so I just took the stuff and started sticking it in the waistband of my chinos and in the pockets of my windbreaker. I guess I probably should've had my head examined, but what else could I do? The guys were counting on me, and seeing as how they all came through for me when I had that static with Chickie, I figured I owed them one—ya know what I mean? I knew right away it was probably a real dumb thing to do, but I just couldn't find it in me to say no.

196

Damn! That was a whole lotta shit I was carrying. I didn't know where to put it all. I even had to stuff a couple of switchblades in my socks because there was no more room for nothing anywhere else. Boy, good thing Charley Goggles didn't show up with that sawed-off shot gun of his. Where would I put that fuckin' thing?!

Anyway, as I wiggled and jiggled, trying to find a comfortable spot for each gun and knife so nothing would fall out on me, all of a sudden, crazy Butchie stuck out his arm and pointed straight ahead—just like George Washington crossing the Delaware. And as soon as everybody crowded around him, he yelled out the Redwood battle cry: *"C'mon! Let's get these bastards!"*

Well, what can I tell ya? As soon as those words came blasting out of Butchie's mouth, it was like yelling, "tally ho!" to a bunch of hopped-up, hunting dogs who'd just gotten a whiff of the fox. Everybody went apeshit, and before I could even push off on my bike to catch up, they were already bopping across the park twirling their bicycle chains, and taking these wicked cuts with their bats, like Mickey Mantle swinging for the bleachers.

There must've been about twenty of us, and even though all the guys had blood in their eyes, nobody was hollering, or shouting, or acting stupid. The last thing we needed was to attract attention to ourselves—least of all the attention of the bulls—and everybody knew it. So we circled over by the far side of the park, and then, as quietly as we could, we swung around onto 111th Street to go straight over to Puertoricanland.

I followed along on my bike. I didn't want to get too close, but I didn't want to lag too far behind neither. Nope, I was doing it just like Butchie told me: I was staying exactly half a block away—far enough away not to get pinched—but close enough to give the guys their weapons in case they needed them.

As I followed along, I started to get really scared. Hell yeah, I was shitting green-purple-orange and sweating bullets all at the same time. I couldn't even *imagine* what would happen to me if I got snagged; I was carrying a fuckin' armory on wheels for Chris'sakes!

When the guys got to the corner of Second Avenue, they put Butchie's plan into action and split up into two groups. Sammy Dee

197

went down the block and rushed one group up to Third Avenue, while Butchie stayed put, waiting with his guys. Then, when Sammy's group was in place, Butchie gave the signal, and both groups started hustling over toward 109th Street.

As they moved, I moved, always staying a half a block behind, checking out my rear-view mirror and looking to my sides, watching out for cops, or anybody else who could sneak up.

For some reason, I expected our guys to go running onto that block like a bunch of wild Indians and start attacking the PR's all at once. But that's not what they did. They strolled around the corner real slow, all calm and collected, and even though I couldn't see exactly what was happening too good, I heard it loud and clear. Those Gallant Debs started screaming and screeching so loud, you'd think they'd just seen an army of king-size rats.

"Redwoods! Redwoods! Aaaaaaayyyyyyyy!"

Everybody started opening windows and running towards the corner. I wanted to see too, so, without getting off my bike, I inched my way up to take a look. Holy shit! We were all over those guys, chasing them down the block and swinging at them with our bats and chains and pipes and everything—and the PR's were tearing ass like crazy.

Boy, them Gallant Lords didn't look so big-and-bad then. They looked more like Gallant *Chickens*, backpedaling, and throwing bottles and cans like a bunch of scared pussies. And as soon as they spotted Sammy Dee's bunch charging at them from the other end of the block, that's when they really started panicking. Their first instinct was to run and try to get away, but once they saw they were trapped, they had no choice but to stand their ground and fight it out as best they could. The shit was *on!*

Butchie and Anthony already had thrown some PR on the ground and were both stomping the shit out of him, while Sammy Dee had this other guy by the hair and was giving him a taste of his garbage-can knuckles. I saw a dark-skinned guy, scrambling to get away from Dino and Frankie Pep, but they cornered him against the schoolyard fence, and were coming in for the kill.

The only Gallant Lord who looked like he was holding his own was this tall, skinny guy who was swinging away with the stickball bat. He was able to get in a good shot and clip Deek right in the forehead, and

198

that gave him the chance to break free and work his way over to the steps of the school where the Gallant Debs were all huddled together and screaming their asses off.

"Negra!" he kept yelling, "the *piece! Gimme the piece!*"

At that moment, all our guys were busy kicking ass, and nobody had a bead on what the guy with the bat was doing, except me. So, without even thinking, I pedaled toward the middle of the block to see if I could help—or at least warn the guys or something. But I was too late. He was able to run over to one of the girls and grab something from her, and, all of a sudden, he had a piece in his hand.

I started yelling my ass off right away to try and warn the guys, but—*BAM!*—he started shooting all over the place. Everyone went fuckin' bananas and started scattering in all different directions. Then the guy with the gun started chasing Sammy Dee's bunch back up the block—*BAM! BAM!*—and once the guys saw what was happening, they all ran over to me.

"*Gimp! Quick! Open ya jacket! Pull out the shit! Hurry!*"

I unzipped my jacket as fast as I could, and everyone was all over me, reaching for their pieces, and pulling out—*BAM!*—whatever they could grab. In a flash, I had twenty panicky hands in my pockets and in my waistband, all at the same time, pushing and pulling—*BAM!*—reaching and grabbing for anything they could get their hands on. I heard police sirens. *BAM! BAM!* A couple of the guys already had their pieces in their hands and were running up the block and shooting back. *B' BAM!* I saw a PR fall to the ground and start rocking back and forth, holding his foot. *BAM!* Everybody was screaming and yelling. Dino's piece must've gotten stuck in the side pocket of my jacket, and as we were both fumbling to get it loose, I felt somebody grabbing me around my neck from behind. *Oh shit!* Then my arm got twisted behind my back, and I got pulled off my bike.

"*Bulls! Bulls!*"

I could hear everybody panicking and running, as the cop spun me around and slammed me against the police car.

"Put ya hands on the car!"

I did what I was told.

"Spread 'em. *Now!*"

199

I did what I was told again, and in the blink of an eye, these big, heavy hands were all over me, pulling out all the shit that was still left on me, piece by piece.

"Whoa! Whatta we got here? A twenty-two. Ho! A zip-gun. *Another* zip gun. Hey, Mike, looks like we got a real winner here. Jesus, Mary and Joseph, will ya look at all this shit?! A switchblade. *Another* switchblade. Hey, this is quite a stash ya got here, kid. What are you, a walking one-man army or somethin'? 'Ey, a box cutter! Terrific."

After he finished frisking me, he grabbed one of my arms, pulled it down off the roof of the cop car, and twisted it behind my back. Click. I felt this cold, hard metal around my wrist. Then he pulled my other arm down and around too, and when he did that, I lost my balance and—*owww!*—my face slammed into the roof of the car. Both hands were behind my back, and—click—I was handcuffed—just like a fuckin' criminal.

By that time all the guys from both gangs had split, and the only people left were the neighborhood nosybodies. I could hear more police sirens. Everybody was crowding around and staring at me. Off to my left, I heard a scuffle. I couldn't really see what was happening, but I could hear a familiar voice cursing out the cops. It was Butchie.

"Watch ya head, son."

They lowered my head so I wouldn't bunk it, and they shoved me into the back seat of the squad car. I was busted.

200

Chapter 15

The worst thing about getting arrested was seeing the look on Mom's face when she walked into that "interrogation room". The two detectives had been holding me there ever since they'd brought me to the stationhouse, and even though they hadn't really started in with the questions yet—I figured they were waiting for Mom to show up first—they still had me shitting some king-size bricks. For more than an hour, they'd been taking turns circling around me with this ugly gleam in their eye, licking their chops, like two hungry sharks getting ready for chow time.

But shitting bricks was one thing, and feeling cheap was something else, and once Mom was standing right there in front of me, staring me down, fuhgeddaboudit, I just wanted to crawl into a hole and die. I mean, I'd seen her mad at me lots of times, but I'd never seen that look of shame and disgust in her eyes before.

"What's all this gang fighting business about?"

"Nothin', Ma, I didn't do nothin'."

"Don't tell me you didn't do nothin'. Look at me! I wanna know what happened."

I just kept staring down at the table, biting my lip, and struggling not to cry.

"Answer me! I wanna know what this is all about, and I wanna know *now!*"

It looked like clamming up made Mom even more mad, because she blew a fuse right away and started yelling, and smacking, and punching me all over the place.

"I *told* you something like this was gonna happen. But did you wanna listen? *No!* You wanna listen to your stupid *friends! That's* who you wanna listen to, your stupid fr...."

One of the cops stepped in and grabbed Mom by the shoulders. "Whoa! Hold it, ma'am. Take it easy—just take it easy now."

Then, after he pulled her off me, he steered her to the other side of the room; I guess to try and talk to her and calm her down. But judging from the sneaky, half-smiles on both of their mugs, it looked like

201

they'd gotten exactly what they'd been waiting for. Yep, now that Mom was there, wiping her eyes and sniffling over in the corner, that was their cue to roll up their sleeves and take over the show.

It looked like they were trying to pull the good-cop bad-cop routine on me. One cop was playing it off like he was my long-lost buddy, while the other one did all he could to scare the living daylights out of me. Well, nice try, fellas, but I wasn't about to fall for no stupid shit like that. Are you kidding? That was one of the oldest tricks in the book; I seen them do that on "Dragnet" and "Naked City" a whole bunch of times.

"Hey, Pat," the good cop said, "look at the menu. What do we got this kid on?"

The bad cop started turning the pages of a big, thick book and talking out loud. "Hmm, let's see," he said, "Try six counts of criminal possession of a deadly weapon for openers,...plus inciting to riot,...disorderly conduct,...resisting arrest,...and if that Pawdarican kid that got shot in the gang fight don't pull through, he could be looking at accessory to murder too."

"*Murder!*" Mom gasped, jumping out of her chair, "Whatta ya talkin' about?"

"I'm sorry, ma'am," the good cop answered, "We're hoping that the wounded kid will be alright, but you never know."

"Yeah, right," I thought to myself, "What a crock of shit that was; I seen that guy get shot with my own two eyes, and he got hit in the fuckin' foot. What a couple of bullshit artists."

Ya know, not for nothin', but these cops will stoop to any-fuckin'-thing just to get you to spill your guts and cooperate with them. But I knew what them donkey bastards were up to: They wanted to scare the pants off me, so I'd try and save my own ass and pin as much as I could on Butchie. Well, they were pissing up the wrong tree with me; I wasn't no stool pigeon.

See, Butchie had gotten busted right along with me, and from what I could see, me and him were the only two guys out of both gangs who got snagged. I saw one of the cops patting his lip with his handkerchief when we were in the cop car, so I figured that Butchie must've slugged him while he was "resisting arrest". That's why they really had it in for Butchie, and even though we were separated, and I couldn't really say

202

for sure, I'd bet anything they kicked the living shit out of him after we got to the stationhouse.

Anyway, once the cops got the message that I wasn't going to tell them nothing about whose weapons I was holding, or about who had shot the Puerto Rican kid, they told my mother that they couldn't release me, and that I'd be going downtown to get "booked". Right way Mom started screaming, and crying, and going apeshit, begging the cops to give me a break and let me go. But them scumbags didn't want to hear it. Nope, they just pulled me away, and told her that she could see me on Monday morning at the "arraignment", and that it would be a good idea to get me an attorney

Well, what can I tell ya? That night was definitely the longest night I ever spent in my life. Every second felt like a drop of water plopping down off a slow, leaky faucet—drip, drip, drip—and all I could do was bite my nails, worry, and pace up and down that stupid cell like an animal trapped in a cage.

They'd brought me downtown to this place called "The Tombs", and they put me in an L-shaped cell in the juvenile section. There must've been about nine or ten guys in there when I walked in. Some were lying on a bench alongside the wall, and some were sitting curled-up on the floor. The toilet looked to be clogged, and there were puddles of piss, and raggedy pieces of wet toilet paper all over the place—and the smell of shit was so bad, you could hardly breathe. I tried to cop a squat over by the corner, but this big, fat moolinyan chased me away.

"Yo!" he growled, "What ya think you're doin'? That's my spot, you be sittin' in my spot, mothafucka."

I said "sorry" and went over to the other side of the cell as fast as I could. 'Ey, things were bad enough for me without getting into any unnecessary static with a close member of the Kong family. Are you kidding? That fat gorilla could've torn me apart with one hand tied behind his back—so I backed off, fast.

Anyway, besides King Kong's cousin and the smell of piss, and shit, and B.O. all over the place, the worst thing about being locked up was the "procedure" for taking a dump. First of all, there was no toilet paper in the cell, so if you had to do number two, first you had to yell out to one of the correction officers at the top of your lungs—just so you could

203

get a lousy piece of something to clean your behind with. And then, after he'd take all his sweet time and stroll all the way down to his desk at the end of the hallway, he'd roll out a couple of sheets of this hard, stiff toilet paper, wrap it around his hand, and shove it at you through the bars. Then, with a dozen strange guys who you'd never even seen before, staring at you, and listening to every little fart that came out your ass, you had to crouch down on that dirty, filthy toilet bowl with no seat, and do your business. Fuhgeddaboudit, I would've rather shit in my pants.

But it looked like I was the only one who was uptight about using the facilities though; nobody else seemed to care. Are you kidding? With the rest of those guys it was just "bombs away!", and they couldn't have cared less *who* was watching them. I'm serious! There was even this one goofy-looking, Italian guy who actually started reciting poetry while he was on the throne. I guess he must've been constipated or something, because after he sat there for a pretty long time, he came out with:

> "Here I sit
> all broken hearted
> Came to shit
> but only farted
> There is no need
> to wipe my ass
> I only peed
> And passed some gas."

There was nothing new about the first four lines—everybody and their mother had heard that one before—but it was the *last* four lines that really caught my attention. Yeah! Not only did they rhyme *perfectly*, but they really completed the whole idea. Hey, what can I say? I guess that dude was a poet and he didn't even know it.

Anyway, just the idea of doing number two in front of an audience really embarrassed me. That was why I didn't eat nothing after the first day so I wouldn't have to use the toilet again. Not that anything was very appetizing anyway. It was the same shit every day: a buttered roll

204

for breakfast, a baloney sandwich on stale American bread for lunch, and another baloney sandwich for supper. Fuhgeddaboudit, I wasn't able to eat none of that shit, and most of the time I traded it away for juice. Those little containers of apple or orange juice weren't half bad, and that was pretty much the only thing I put in my stomach since I got there. I guess I was too scared and upset to have very much of an appetite anyway.

Yeah, I found myself sinking fast. I felt like crying all the time, but I didn't want none of the other guys to think I was some doofy crybaby, so I just held it in as best I could. Well, at least in the daytime anyway, because when they'd shut off the lights at night, them tears would be rolling down my cheeks like there was no tomorrow.

The next day, the C.O. came and stood outside the cell, like he was going to make some kind of announcement or something.

"Shut the fuck up!" he yelled, as he looked down and started scanning his clipboard. "Listen for your name. And I'm only gonna say it *once*, so you can spend another three days down here if ya don't hear it—so listen up. Tyrone Johnson"

"Yo!"

"Hector Perez."

"Aqui!"

"Joseph Posella."

"Here!" I yelled, sticking my hands through the bars and waving to the C.O. "I'm here!"

"Alright, you got lawyers comin' in. Be ready."

Thank God! I'd been wondering if Mom was going to send somebody to help me.

After a while, a short, bald-headed man wearing a suit and tie walked up to the cell holding a briefcase.

"Joseph Posella?"

"Yeah, that's me."

Right away I felt a lot better; at least I knew I wasn't alone, and I finally had someone in my corner. He told me his name was Louis Villani, and from what I could see, he looked to be a really nice guy.

205

"Joseph," he said, touching my hand through the bars, "don't worry about anything. You have a clean record, you've never been any kind of trouble before, and there's no reason why you shouldn't be released by Monday. So just hang in there, kid. Okay?"

I had to look down at the floor, because my eyes were getting all watery 'n' stuff, and I didn't want anybody to see me crying.

He reached through the bars and gave me a little pat on the cheek. "Okay, Joey?"

"Okay, Mister Villani. Thanks a lot."

"Don't worry about it. I'm an old friend of the family, and I'm here to help you—*capish?*"

"Yeah."

"Good. Now come a little closer to me, belly to belly."

I didn't know what the guy was up to, but I did as I was told, and moved in closer so we were practically touching bellies. That was when I felt something jabbing me in my stomach.

"Here," he whispered, "take this. But don't go tellin' anybody I gave it to you. I had to smuggle it in, and you'd be getting me in a lot of hot water if you do?"

I looked down at my hand, and it was holding a Baby Ruth candy bar, my favorite.

"Thanks," I said, giving the guy a little smile.

"Bye, Joseph."

"Bye."

I waited 'til it was lights out, and then I unwrapped the Baby Ruth inside my shirt, real, real, slow, trying my best to open it without crackling the paper or making any kind of noise at all. I knew I had to be super quiet so nobody would notice it and try and steal it on me. Mmmm, that familiar chocolatey taste was delicious, and as I chomped down on the nuts, quiet as a mouse, I realized for the first time just how hungry I was.

When Monday finally came, everything turned out pretty much like Mr. Villani said it would. It was embarrassing as hell, to walk out into that courtroom and stand in front of the judge—'specially with Mom, and Grandma and Grandpa sitting right there in the second row. But once the judge saw that I had a clean record, he released me in my mother's "recognizance", and gave me a hearing date for six weeks later. I didn't really understand what that "recognizance" stuff was all about, but Mr. Villani told me I better not try and "fly the coop", because according to him, it meant that Mom was "legally responsible" for me, and if I didn't show up for the hearing, I'd be getting her into some serious trouble.

So, thanks to Mr. Villani, and the kind-hearted judge I lucked up with, I finally got my stinky ass out that shithouse they call "The Tombs". Glory hallelujah!

Well, maybe I was lucky enough to get out of the *shit*house, but I sure as hell didn't get out of the *dog*house though; Mom kept me buried in there for the next six weeks. Yep, I was a prisoner all over again, only this time in my own apartment. The only thing I was allowed to do was to go to school, and to Mass on Sunday—no friends, no park, no Redwoods, no going out, no nothing. And if that wasn't bad enough, I had to listen to hours and hours of speeches and lectures. That's what I hated the most, because Mom would go on forever and ever, harping on my "monkey-see monkey-do" attitude, and how I was such a "damn fool" for letting my friends play me for a patsy. But that was only the antipasto, the main dish was always the same four little words, stabbing me and cutting through me like a knife every time they'd come blasting out of her mouth: "I told you so."

But I had to lump it—what could I do? And the worst part of it, the part that would really burn my ass, was the fact that she was a hundred percent right. She knew it, and I knew it. She "told me so" a zillion times, but like she'd say: "it just went in one ear and right out the other."

Grandma would pull the "I told you so" routine on me too, only she was a lot slicker about it. She wouldn't nag me to death with it; she'd sugar-coat it and slip in the back door when I wasn't expecting nothing—sneaky style. Yeah, she'd wait 'til she'd see me all down in the dumps, looking out the window and wishing I could be downstairs with my friends, and then, like she was reading my mind, she'd sit down next to me, stroke my hair, and in her sweetest Grandma voice she'd say: *"medyu sulo e no mal acompagnatu"*. Well, what could I say? Nothing.

207

After spending two and a half days in The Tombs, smelling shit, eating garbage, and being caged up like an animal in a zoo, I learned that lesson good: "you're better off by yourself than with bad friends."

But the person who *really* made me feel cheap was Grandpa. He didn't have too much to say about the whole thing, but his silence and the look on his face hurt me twenty times more than anything else could. I'll never forget what he said to me that morning when we were walking away from The Tombs and heading for the subway.

"I wanna you know something," he said, stopping dead in his tracks at staring at me with a weird look that I'd never seen on him before, "In the other side, and in *L'America*, the first Posella to see the inside from the jail is *you*."

"But Grandpa...I..."

"I no wanna hear. Whatta you do was big mistake, big mistake and a big, big, *vergogna pe' tutta la famidya*."

Well, there wasn't too much I could say to that. When your own Grandpa calls you a "disgrace to the family", you know you've messed up *bad*.

So, there I was, standing in the courtroom again for that "hearing" thing, looking up at a mean old judge that had a mug like Frankenstein. And it wasn't just his looks neither; his name sounded almost the same too: Finkelstein.

And he was nosy too. He kept on asking all these questions about my family, my father, my father's disappearing act, my "leg length discrepancy", my friends, my marks in school, *every*-fuckin'-thing. The only thing he didn't ask me was what kind of underwear I wear, Fruit of the Looms or BVD's, but outside of that, he covered everything else.

Well, maybe some of those questions bothered me, but they sure didn't bother Mr. Villani though. Nope, this guy came prepared for everything. He brought in my report cards, my honor-roll certificates, my good-attendance certificates, all my art medals and art awards—the works! And he even had this big, long letter from Doctor Morello too.

Boy, you should've seen the way that judge perked up and stuck out his antennas when Mr. Villani stood up and read that letter out loud. I figured it was because him and Doc Morello both spoke the same language—with all them big, fourteen-karat words and everything.

208

Well, maybe that Judge Finkelstein understood that stuff, but I sure didn't. I could only pick out little bits and pieces of it. To me, the whole thing sounded like it was written in another language, like Greek or Chinese or something—'specially the last part when Doctor Morello kept talking about me being a "victim". That was weird. He said I was a victim of "ridicule", a victim of "harassment", a victim of "ostracism" (whatever the hell that meant), a victim of "circumstances", and a victim of my own "deep longing for peer acceptance". Fuhgeddaboudit, I had no idea what he was talking about—'specially that last thing. Why would I want to be "accepted" by a pier? I didn't even *like* going down by the docks; too many rats down there.

I guess Doc Morello's letter might have been a little hard for *me* to understand, but it must've really hit home with the judge though. Yep, that guy kept chomping on his pencil and scratching his head for the longest time, like he was concentrating and listening really carefully to everything—and thinking about it too. And when he finally put down the pencil and screwed up his face, it looked to me like the moment of truth had arrived.

"Would the defendant please rise" he said, frowning down at me with that mean-looking Frankenstein mug of his. "Joseph Posella, you have been charged with six counts of criminal possession of a deadly weapon, inciting to riot, and disorderly conduct, and in light of the evidence in this case, I have no choice but to find you guilty as charged."

As soon as I heard the word "guilty", my heart hit the floor like a ton of bricks, and an ice-cold sweat shivered up my spine. I was so sure I was going to get sent to jail, or to reform school, that I just closed my eyes and hung my head in shame. Goodbye Cholly, it was all over for me. But as I was standing there, trembling and wincing, and bracing myself for the bad news, all of a sudden, I heard the judge change his tone of voice. And then, after he coughed in his hand and shuffled a few papers around on his desk, I heard him say the most beautiful word I'd ever heard in my whole life: "however".

I opened my eyes right away, and when I did, I saw the judge staring back at me, burning a hole through my eyeballs.

"However," he repeated, "in view of the defendant's age, his clean record, and the sensitive circumstances surrounding this case, I will grant a suspended sentence."

209

I looked over at Mr. Villani, and I saw him smiling at me. And when I looked over at Mom, and Grandma and Grandpa, I could see them wiping their eyes and smiling back at me too. I was just about to smile right along with everybody else, when all of a sudden, I heard the judge's voice again. It didn't sound soft and friendly anymore; it sounded mean and cold like before.

"But let me tell you something, young man. If I ever see your face again in this court, I'm going to throw the book at you. So, I suggest that you think twice before you go making any more bad decisions like this again. Is that clear?"

"Yes, your honor."

Mom came over to me and gave me a big hug, and I could feel her tears wetting my face as she squeezed me tight and rocked me from side to side. And then Grandma got into the act, and before you knew it, all three of us were hugging and kissing like crazy.

Mr. Villani shook my hand and said "congratulations, Joey", and as I was thanking him for all he'd done to help me, I noticed Grandpa coming over to me out of the corner of my eye. He'd just finished wiping his glasses with his handkerchief and was adjusting them onto his nose. I felt scared to look him in the face, but as soon as our eyes met, he reached out and hugged me too.

"Sorry, Grandpa," I whispered.

He didn't say nothing, but as he broke off the hug, he gave me a kiss on the forehead—just like he always did.

Chapter 16

Ya know, life is funny. Sometimes the same shit that kicks your ass and knocks you for a loop, can actually turn out to be a blessing in disguise. I never thought I'd say it, or even *think* it, but in the long run, getting busted and going to jail was one of the luckiest things that ever happened to me. Why? Because that's the thing that finally changed Mom's mind about me working at the racetrack.

"Ya mean it?!" I said, doing a Jackie Gleason double-take. "Ya mean you're really gonna let me work at the track?!"

"Yeah, I mean it—but only for the summer though."

First, I hugged her, and then I gave her a big, noisy kiss on the cheek. "Thanks, Ma."

"Don't come thankin' me," she said, pushing my arms away and squirming out of my grip. "You can thank Mr. Villani."

"Mr. Villani?"

"Yeah, he told me if I don't get you off of the streets this summer and away from that gang of hoodlums you hang out with, chances are you're gonna wind up right back in jail again."

"He said that?"

"That's right. And let me tell you something, mister, that's the only reason I'm gonna go along with this stupid racetrack idea of yours. I still think it's too dangerous for a boy like you."

I watched as Mom walked over to the fire-escape window and looked down on the street.

I could tell she must've been upset, because I could see her lifting up her glasses and trying to push back a tear. "Ya know, Mr.Villani says you were real lucky this time, but if you get into any kind of trouble again, he says not even Perry Mason will be able to get you off the hook the second time around."

I didn't dare say nothing, and I didn't dare look Mom in the face neither. Nope, I knew everything she said was a hundred-percent true, so I just hung my head and picked at the oilcloth on the kitchen table.

211

"So," she said, sniffling and wiping her nose, "against my better judgement, I'm gonna let you do this crazy racetrack thing. But ya gotta promise me three things."

"Anything, what?"

As usual, she whipped out the ol' feet of Jesus and stuck them right in my face. "Number one: this racetrack job is gonna be just for the summer, right?"

"Yeah!"

"Number two: you're gonna go back to school and finish your education."

"Yeah, yeah."

"And number three: you gotta promise me you're never gonna go back to that park to hang out with those hoodlums ever again."

"Yeah! Whatever you say."

"Alright then," she said, holding her fingers up to my lips. "I don't have to tell you what this is, do I?"

"No."

"So go ahead, promise."

I leaned over and kissed her fingers. "I promise."

So...thanks to the Redwoods, the Serpents, the Gallant Lords, the N.Y.P.D., "The Tombs", Judge Finkelstein, Mr. Villani, Doctor Morello, and, of course, good ol' Uncle Rocco, there I was at four-thirty in the morning, riding the A-train to the "Big A", Aqueduct Racetrack. I hardly got any sleep the night before, because I kept tossing and turning, worrying that the stupid alarm clock wouldn't go off on time. The last thing I needed was to be late on my first day. Mr. Cardone only told Uncle Rocco that he'd try me out, but he said he couldn't make no promises or nothing. But no matter how you sliced it, it was still my big chance, and I sure as hell wasn't gonna fuck it up by being late.

It was still pitch-black outside as I got off the train and started walking toward the stable gate. Over toward the horizon, behind the airport, I could see a deep-blue glow, spreading in the sky, getting lighter and lighter and swallowing the stars one by one. The birds were just starting to wake up, and I could hear them chirping all over the place. The air smelled clean and fresh. I was a little surprised at how chilly it was—after all, it was July—but the cool, morning breeze felt

212

good, and as I made my way over to the little guardhouse where the Pinkerton man was standing, I was so excited, I felt like I was gonna jump right out of my skin.

"Can I help you, kid?" he said.

"Yeah. I'm here to see Sam Cardone in barn seven."

The Pinkerton reached into the guardhouse and pulled out a clipboard. "What's your name?"

"Posella, Joseph Posella."

He ran his finger down the list and stopped when he came to my name. "Okay, just wait inside over there. I don't think Sam is in yet, but I'll page his assistant, Tito, for ya."

A few minutes later, after the Pinkerton called out "Tito Lopez, barn seven, to the stable gate" a couple of times over the loudspeaker, a tan-skinned Puerto Rican guy with kinky hair and a thick Spanish accent stuck his head through the door.

"What'sa matter, boss?" he asked.

"Got a kid here to see Sam. Is it okay?"

"Yeah, we 'specting him—it's okay."

The Pinkerton handed me a yellow pass that said "Visitor" on it and told me to pin it on. I did like I was told and followed this Tito guy out the door. We walked across a small parking lot, up a couple of steps, and then through a swing gate in the chain-link fence that led to the stables.

"What's your name, kid?"

"Joey."

"Joey, ah? You ever work with horses before?"

"No, not really, but I'm crazy about 'em though. I wanna be a jockey."

Tito stopped and gave me the once-over. "Well, you the right size, that's for sure."

"Thanks."

As we walked over to barn seven, I got my first glimpse of the Aqueduct stable area. I thought it would look more like the Belmont stables, all nice and fancy with the shady trees and everything, but Aqueduct was different. The barns were these low, modern-looking things made out of that cinderblock stuff—and forget about trees. The only trees I could see were a couple of puny, little saplings, and a few

213

baby, weeping-willow trees that looked like they'd just been planted yesterday. The whole place had a kind of bare, empty look to it, but I didn't care; as long as there were horses there, that was good enough for me.

Anyway, by the light of the light bulbs, a few early-bird grooms were already moving around down by the other end of the barn. I could hear them talking to each other, and saying stuff to the horses, like "Ho!" and "Easy now, son", and stuff like that. A voice I couldn't see was singing a love song in Spanish, and as I listened to the melody, the damp smell of hay, liniment, and horse manure filled my nose with a warm, earthy smell. Most of the horses had their heads sticking out of their stalls and were stomping their feet and whinnying up a storm.

"They hungry," Tito said, as he bopped by and tickled a gray horse on his nose. "They want their breakfast."

I was about to say something, but all of a sudden, he ducked into a stall and came out with a feed tub. "Okay, okay," he said, talking to the horses. "Take it easy! Tito gonna give you breakfast, okay? Take it easy. I coming, I coming."

The horses squealed and pawed the ground, shaking their heads up and down, as they heard Tito scooping oats out of a big sack and dumping them into the tub.

"Looks like they know what you're doing," I said. "Pretty smart, huh?"

"You kidding? These horses are more smart than you or me. You don't see them betting on us, do you?"

Before I could say anything, I heard the voice of some Colored guy coming from inside the next stall. "Heh, heh, heh," he chuckled, "you sho' got that right Tito. That's why they say the back side of the track is a lot cleaner than the front side."

An old, wrinkled man the color of a Mounds candy bar stepped out of the stall and into the shed row. He frowned and winced as he struggled to duck under the webbing, but once he straightened up, he caught my eye and smiled. "You know why, son?"

"Uh-uh."

"'Cause the hoss's asses ain't back here in the stables, they're over in the *grandstand*."

214

We all laughed, and I guess the black filly in the next stall must've gotten the joke too, because she lifted her head and curled back her lip, like she was joining us in a big ol' horse laugh.

Tito wiped his hands on the side of his pants and came over to me. "Joey, I want you to meet Simon Green. If you want to be a jockey, this the man who can teach you everything. He used to be one of the *best*."

The old man waved Tito away and made a face. Then he stuck out his boney hand and gave me a warm, friendly shake. "Nice to meet ya, boy."

While I was shaking his hand, Tito pointed to me and said, "He going to be the new hotwalker."

"Oh yeah? Got any 'sperience 'round hosses, son?"

"Not really, but I been lovin' 'em ever since I was a little kid."

"Well, that's good, boy, 'cause you sho' gotta have a lotta *love* to work with these here hosses. That's right. They smart. They know who loves 'em and who don't. They can feel it in your touch and hear it in your voice."

I blushed and looked down on the ground. "Love" was probably not the right word to use, and I felt all stupid and embarrassed for having said it. I didn't want to sound like some doofy little schoolgirl who *loves* horses.

"Hey, Tito!" Simon shouted, grabbing a pitchfork and one of them big baskets that they use to pick up horse manure, "why don't we let this young fella get his feet wet. I need somebody to get that black filly outa my hair so I can muck out."

Tito scratched his head. "Well, Sam no here, but I guess it's okay. Give him a shank."

Simon handed me a long strap with a chain and one of them little hook-things at the end of it. "Here, son, now this here's a shank. C'mon, follow me."

As I followed Simon, I couldn't help but think to myself that it looked like I'd be needing to learn a whole new bunch of racetrack words if I was going to work at the track. Where I came from, a "shank" wasn't no strap with a chain on the end of it—it was a knife.

"See?" Simon said, holding the filly and clipping the hook part of the shank onto her halter. "First ya open up the hook and clip it over here. That ain't too hard, is it?"

215

"Naa."

"Okay, now remember: The most important thing about handlin' hosses is that ya always got to stay on their left side. That's call their 'near side'. Understand?"

"Yeah."

"Good. You always got to remember that, son. Never even walk by a hoss on their 'off side', their right side. That can be dangerous, you can get kicked like that. Got it?"

"Yeah."

"Okay. Now hold her by the shank like this and give her a little walk 'round the shed row while I muck out her stall. But be careful, now. Every time you turn a corner, you got to slow down a little and see if it's all clear first—'specially when ya get to the middle of the barn; that man on the other side of the shed likes to jog his hosses in here, so it might get a little crazy for a while. Just keep your eyes open and let 'em know you're comin' through."

"Okay."

"Alright now, go 'head, bring her on out. She nothin' but sweet lil' ol' baby girl, she ain't gonna give ya no trouble." Simon gave her a couple of quick pats. "Ain't that right, mama?"

I led the black filly out of her stall and started walking her down the shed row. It was really exciting, because there I was holding a real racehorse with my own two hands and walking it.

"Watch it now!" Simon shouted. "Keep your eyes open! And look out for that mean ol' chestnut hoss on the other side, third stall in. That sneaky som'bitch will try and take a bite outa you as ya walk by—so you be careful now, ya hear?!"

"Okay."

The black filly walked alongside me just like a perfect lady; she didn't give me no trouble at all. When I stopped, she stopped, and when I walked a little faster, she did too—without pulling ahead of me or tossing her head or nothing. And I didn't have to jerk down on the shank not even once. Nope, she was just like Simon said: "a sweet lil' ol' baby girl".

I asked Simon what her name was on my next lap around. He told me to look on her halter, and when I did, I saw this little metal plaque that read: Best of Show, Billings—April Moon. It was easy to see how

216

she got a name like Best of Show; she was a real beauty. She was the kind of horse Uncle Rocco would call a "picture horse".

After a few more laps with the black filly, I almost ran into Mr. Cardone as he ducked under the rail to come into the barn.

"'Ey, kid," he said, bopping into the barn with a cup of coffee and one of them 'guinea stinkers' in his mouth, "you Rocco's nephew?"

"Yeah."

"Joey, right?"

"Yeah, Joey Posella."

"Okay, Joey, you look like you're doin' fine. Finish up with that filly, and then we'll talk."

The best way to describe Mr. Cardone is to say that he looked a lot like the actor who played in that movie "Marty", that Borgnine guy— only a little balder and maybe a little fatter too. He even had that little gap in his teeth and everything.

Anyway, as soon as I finished with Best of Show, I hung up the shank and walked over to the tack room. From what I could see, it looked like the place where they kept all the saddles and bridles 'n' stuff, and I guess it doubled as Mr. Cardone's office too. When I knocked, he was fiddling around with a bridle, but as soon as he saw me, he stopped to shake my hand.

"Hi, Mr. Cardone."

"'Ey, how ya doin', Joey?" he said. "Got here real early this morning, didn't ya?—even beat *me* to the barn."

I lowered my eyes and felt myself blush. "Yeah, I wanted to be here on time—ya know, first day and all."

"Well, that's good. That's what we need, people we can count on— responsible people."

I didn't answer, I just waited 'til he finished with the bridle and looked back at me again.

"Looks like Tito put ya to work already, huh?"

"Yeah, that's a really nice filly."

"Best of Show? Yeah, great disposition on her—gentle as a baby. He sure picked the right horse to start you off on. But they're not all like

217

that; some of these sonuvabitches can be really rough. You think you could handle 'em?"

"I could try."

"You ain't afraid or nothin', are ya?"

"Hell no."

"Alright then. We're gonna be sending the first couple of horses over to the track in a few minutes. Your job is gonna start as soon as they come back."

"What do I gotta do?"

"Well, first you gotta hold 'em by the shank while the groom sponges them down. And then, you take 'em inside and you walk 'em around the shed row, around and around, lettin' them take little sips of water—but not too much—'til they're all cooled out and their coat is completely dry to the touch. *Capish?*"

"I think so."

"Well, don't worry about it. Just go 'head—Tito will show ya what to do."

"Alright, thanks a lot, Mr. Cardone."

As I walked out of the tack room, I almost bunked into this short Spanish guy wearing a jockey's helmet who was coming up the shed row. He looked like he was half-walking and half-dancing, and as he chugged along, he kept spinning around and doing these fancy mambo steps, clicking his fingers in rhythm, and singing some song in Spanish.

As soon as he saw me, he stopped singing for a second and said: "How you doing, man?"

"Alright."

"You new?"

"Yeah."

Without missing a step of his mambo, he stuck out his hand. "My name is Mongo, I'm Tito brother."

"Oh, yeah? Hi, I'm Joey,"

We shook hands, and Mongo went right back to singing his mambo song.

"You an exercise boy?" I asked, kind of falling in step with him.

"Um-hum. You?"

"I wish. Naa, I'm just a hotwalker. Today's my first day."

All of a sudden, Mongo stopped dancing and gave me a quick look up and down. "So, you wanna be jockey, ah?"

"Yeah! How'd you know?"

He shrugged his shoulders and did another mambo spin. "Lucky guess, my friend—just a lucky guess."

As we got near the end of the barn, we heard Tito's voice coming from inside of one of the stalls. He was cursing up a storm in Spanish, and it looked like he was having trouble getting the saddle on this big gray horse. Mongo started goofing on his brother, and that's when Tito got pissed.

"What so funny?" Tito growled, "If you so smart, why don't *you* come and put the saddle on this sonamabitche?!"

Mongo didn't answer, he just tucked in his chin, lifted up his fists like a boxer, and went back to twirling around and doing his mambo dance.

"Hey! What's this? The Arthur Murray Dance Studio, or what?"

I knew it was Mr. Cardone talking right away; I could spot that guinea twang a mile away.

"For Godsakes, Mongo, you here to ride, or you here to dance? Make up your mind."

"Sorry boss."

"C'mon, let's get this show on the road."

Tito finished with the saddle, and after he checked the bridle one last time and smoothed out the saddlecloth, he swung the gray horse out of the stall and onto the shed row. Then Mr. Cardone reached down and gave Mongo a "leg up".

"You ever seen a workout, kid?"

"Uh-uh."

"Well, c'mon. You'll have plenty to do when he comes back—don't worry about that."

So I fell in step with Mr. Cardone, and we followed Mongo and the big gray horse all the way down to the other end of the barn and out into the open air. The sun had already peeked out from behind the airport and was lighting everything up in a bright, rosy-gold glow. Over behind the grandstand, I could still see the full moon melting into the morning and fading away. The shadows were long and blue. There were lots of shiny, sun-splashed horses all over the place, snorting and

219

swishing their tails as they made their way up the ramp that led to the track.

Everybody I passed along the way said either "Hi", "Good morning", or "How ya doin'?", and they didn't even *know* me or nothing!

"What's his name, Mr. Cardone?" I said, struggling to keep up with him as he barreled his way up the ramp and left me two steps behind.

"He's called Olympic King. A son of Olympia. Yeah, this horse got a lotta speed. Only problem is, he runs out of gas all the time."

As we reached the top of the ramp, I got my first look at the track. And to a horse lover like me, it was paradise. There were horses everywhere. A few of them were jogging along the outside fence, going the "wrong" way up the track, while most of the others were galloping in the center part of the track, going the "right" way, counterclockwise. I could hear their hoofbeats and the rhythm of their breathing as they sailed by, snorting with every stride, hmmff, hmmff, hmmff...mouths open...necks bowed...tails arched. Some of the exercise riders were standing straight up in the saddle, whistling or humming a tune as they passed, enjoying the ride. But over toward the inside rail, I saw the horses who were *really* working out. Most of them were running alone, but a few were running in sets of two—like in pairs—matching strides and bounding along as a team, muscles rippling, manes and tails flying, hammering the ground with their hooves and drinking the wind, with their riders crouched down low, sitting chilly.

"C'mon, kid," Mr. Cardone said, "let's go to the viewing stand, we'll see better from there."

I followed him up the steps into a small wooden hut where a couple of men—probably trainers or clockers—were all scoping out the horses on the track. One of them was looking through a big pair of black binoculars, while the rest of them were staring at the track with cups of coffee or stopwatches in their hands. Mr. Cardone pointed to his horse as he galloped along.

"Look, kid, over there. He's almost to the half-mile pole; he'll take off in a second."

I watched as Olympic King bounded down the track. He looked like he really wanted to run, throwing his head up and down and shaking it from side to side, and when Mongo crouched down low, he took off. Mr. Cardone clicked his stopwatch, and without saying a word, the two

220

of us followed the big gray, as he sliced through the golden haze and scooted around the turn.

"What ya get him in, Al?" Mr. Cardone asked, looking over at the guy with the binoculars.

"Fourty seven and one."

"Yeah, that's more or less what I got too. Jeez, ya tell the boy to do an easy half mile in fourty eight or fourty nine and look what ya get."

As we hustled over to the gap where the horses come off the track, I could tell Mr. Cardone wasn't too happy with the workout, and when Mongo got back, he really let him have it.

"What'sa matter with you? Ya didn't eat your Wheaties this morning or what?"

"Sorry, boss," he answered, bouncing in the saddle as Olympic King trotted down the ramp, "he was pulling and fighting with me all the way. I couldn't hold him."

"Well, I hope you left a little gas in the tank for Friday; it's a nice spot and I don't wanna blow it."

"No worry, boss. He just feeling good—that's all. He be alright."

Olympic King wasn't like the black filly at all—he turned out to be little hard to handle—and when I first started walking him around the barn, I couldn't hold that sucker for nothing. No matter how many times I jerked the shank, he still kept walking two steps ahead of me and dragging my ass all over the place. Everybody was staring and chuckling to themselves, and when I passed the tack room, I even heard Mr. Cardone yell out: "'Ey, who's walkin' who over here? You walkin' the horse or is he walkin' *you*?!"

It was really embarrassing at first, but then I tried a little trick: I started singing to him. Yep, I hit Olympic King with a medley of my favorite doo-wop tunes, and little by little, I had the gray bastard eating right out of the palm of my hand. And everybody seemed to notice too.

"Attaboy, kid," Mr. Cardone said, sticking his head out of the tack room and giving me a wink and a thumbs-up sign, "that's the idea."

Well, after I finished with Olympic King and two more horses, Mr. Cardone seemed pleased with my work, and he told me I could take a

221

break and grab a bite at the "kitchen". The Aqueduct kitchen wasn't no fancy place—just a little help-yourself cafeteria with a few tables—but judging from the fat lady behind the counter and the cashier lady, everybody was wearing a smile and seemed to be real friendly. I got a cup of coffee and a doughnut, and while I was waiting for my change, I noticed an interesting sign on the wall. It read: Eat Your Betting Money, But *Never* Bet Your Eating Money.

A Colored guy in back of me must've noticed me checking it out, because as I stood there grinning to myself, he nodded over at the sign and said: "Man, ain't that the truth. Bettin' on hosses is worse than gettin' hooked on mothafuckin' *dope*."

Good thing I got my coffee to go, because for a dinky little joint, it sure was packed. There were a few exercise boys with helmets and windbreakers, sitting together at one table, shooting the shit, while next to them was a group of trainers talking quietly, studying their "condition books". Over on the food line, a couple of grooms were joking around and slapping each other five, telling the cook to "whip up a pair of eggs". Two Pinkertons were over by the wall, scarfing down pancakes, and at the next table was short guy wearing a green jacket who looked a lot like Pat Degnan, the jockey—but I wasn't sure though. And there were even a couple of big-shot horse owners in there too. They were all dressed up in suits and ties, but there they were, sitting in the kitchen, rubbing elbows with everybody else—just like it was nothing. I guess that was just the way things were over on the "backside", and even though all these people competed with each other in the afternoon, in the morning, they seemed to treat each other real nice, with friendship and respect—like one big happy family.

Well, by the time I finished my coffee, my next horse was already back from the track. It was a two-year-old chestnut filly named "Rusty". She was a little frisky and a bit of a pain-in-the-ass, but I thought I handled her okay. And I guess Mr. Cardone must've thought so too, because after she was put back in her stall, he told me to come into the tack room for a little talk.

"Joey, I've been watching you, and even though you're still green, I can tell you have a nice touch with a horse. So, if you want the

222

hotwalker job, you gotta be here every day, seven days a week, no later than six in the morning. Ya think you could handle somethin' like that?"

"Yeah!"

"Okay. The best I can do right now is fifty-five bucks a week, but as soon as I see that you've learned the ropes and you're starting to give Tito a little extra help, I'll throw in an extra ten. Good enough?"

"Sure."

"Alright then. I'm gonna take a chance on you and give you this job, but on one condition."

"What's that?"

He put his arm around my shoulder and gave me a squeeze. "That ya don't call me 'Mister Cardone' no more." Then he flashed a smile and stuck out his hand. "The name's Sam. C'mon, let's do down to the Pinkerton's office to fill out the papers and get you your badge."

"Gee, thanks, Mr. Cardone."

Right away he frowned and gave me a make-believe dirty look.

"I mean...Sam."

"That's better."

It took a pretty long time to get through all the red tape, and by the time I got back to the barn wearing my new "badge"—my backstretch employee I.D.—Tito, Simon and the rest of the grooms had already finished giving the horses their lunch and seemed to be knocking off the last of their chores. The sun had climbed up pretty high in the sky, and a quiet, peaceful feeling had settled over the shed row. Most of the horses had their heads sticking out of their stalls and were nibbling on their hayracks. A calico cat scurried around a corner. A sparrow flew in through an open window and nestled in the beams above the stalls. There wasn't anything left for me to do, so I just moseyed down the shed row, checking out the horses. Boy, they sure were beautiful. Best of Show let me run my hand along her long, silky neck, and stroke her soft, velvety muzzle. It got real quiet all of a sudden, and the only thing I heard was the sound of Simon's rake, as he smoothed out the dirt in front of the tack room.

"My, my, my," he said, looking over at me and Best of Show with a big smile on his face. "You sho' loves them hosses, don't ya, boy?"

223

I didn't answer, I just kept rubbing the black filly gently on her forehead and tickling her under her chin. I guess I probably looked like a doofus, just standing there petting the filly like that, but I didn't care. Besides, I knew Simon wasn't really making fun of me; he was a horse lover too—just like me. I could tell.

"Hey, Simon," I said, walking over to him, "is it true you were really a jockey?"

"Heh, heh, heh," he chuckled. "Yeah. I guess you can say it's true, but like the Injuns say: 'that was many moons ago'."

"Were ya good?"

"I win my share of races I guess, but only for a couple of years though. Weight got me. And I wasn't too good at the barrier neither. So, after a while, mounts stopped comin' in, and it came time for me to quit."

"What's a 'barrier'?"

Simon stopped raking for a second and pulled back his cap. "Well, son, back in the day when I was ridin', they didn't have no startin' gates like they have now—only the barrier."

"But what exactly was it?"

"The barrier was kinda like this webbing thing—sorta like a big tennis net. Hosses would line up behind that webbing, and then, when they were all in line, swoosh, that thing would fly up, and they'd be off and runnin'."

"Sounds like it wasn't too easy to get off to a good start in them days, huh?"

"Ooo-weee! Now ain't that the truth. Hosses be fussin' and fightin', and lunging, and rearin' up, and turnin' sideways... In them days, a lotta races were won and lost right there at the barrier. That's why if a boy wasn't no damn good behind that thing, nobody would wanna ride him." Simon grabbed his rake and went back to raking. "That's what happened to me."

"So, what ya do then"

"Well, then I just kept on bein' an exercise rider. Did it for more than fifty years."

"Really?"

"That's right. And I'd still be doin' it too, if this goddamn arthritis hadn't snuck up on me and started kickin' my raggedy ol' butt all over the place."

"Gee, that's too bad."

"Hey, what ya gonna do? Looks like the years is finally catchin' up to ol' Simon."

I didn't say nothing. I just watched as the old man leaned his rake against the wall and grabbed at the base of his spine, screwing up his face from the pain.

"But I'll tell ya somethin', boy, when I was in my prime, I was one of the best damn exercise boys around. Yas'suh, them trainers used to say I had a clock in my head. And I worked with some of the best of 'em too! That's right: Jim McCullough, Ben Higgins, ol' 'Hardboot' Wilson, Red Powell,...all of 'em. I was even the exclusive exercise rider for John Rowan at one time—ya know, the man who trained the Briarwood hosses for ol' man Marshall. Yeah, that sho' was one helluva job. Got to get up on some of the greatest hosses to ever look through a bridle: Colin, Sysonby, Exterminator, Regret... Hell, I was even John P. Grier's regular exercise boy. You know who John P. Grier was, don't ya?"

"Yeah, ain't that the horse that almost beat Man o' War?"

Simon started chuckling right away; I guess he didn't think I knew that much about horses.

"That's right," he said, "It was in the Dwyer Stakes at the old Aqueduct, July of 1920 to be exact. Ooo Lord, I remember that race like it was yesterday. Yeah, lil' ol' Grier sho made the big hoss sweat that day—almost win it too! Got his head in front between calls in the stretch and everything. But when Clarence Kummer called on him, Big Red dug down deep and came back at Grier, inch by inch, fightin' like a bulldog, 'til little Grier just couldn't take it no more and threw in the towel at the sixteenth pole. That's when Eddie Ambrose let up on him. Hell, the race was lost anyway; no sense in punishin' the hoss. But I'll tell ya one thing though: no hoss ever gave Big Red the kinda fight that Grier did that day. That John P. Grier was one helluva racehoss alright, just had the bad luck of bein' born the same year as Man o' War—that's all."

"Wow!"

225

Simon held his back with his hand and eased himself down onto some stacked-up sacks of oats, and as he sat there, he got the same faraway look on his face that Grandpa would get whenever he talked about *"Italia"*. The tractors had already started harrowing the track for the day's races, and as we sat there in silence, I could hear them humming away in the distance. Everybody had left the shed row by then—except me and Simon, and the horses.

It took me a while to get up the courage, but I finally took a chance and asked the question that had been on my mind ever since I shook Simon's hand. "Simon, you think you could teach me to ride someday. Ever since I was little, the only thing I ever wanted to be was a jockey."

He didn't answer me right away. He was busy pulling a handkerchief out of the side pocket of his overalls, but after he blew his nose and took a quick swipe at his eyes, he turned to me and said: "Let me see ya hands, boy."

I stuck out my hands, turning them palms-up and palms-down, as Simon studied them.

"Sick out ya feet."

I stuck out my feet, and Simon studied them too.

"Stand up for a second, son, let me get a good look at ya."

I felt a little weird, but I did as I was told, and I got up and stood in front of him, turning around slowly, so he could give me the once-over.

"How much you weigh?"

"About ninety-five, ninety-six pounds."

"How tall are ya?"

"Five feet. Well, really four eleven.

"Hmmm," he mumbled, frowning a little and scratching his cheek. "Why don't go in the tack room and fetch me one of them exercise saddles."

As I walked off to get the saddle, I could feel Simon following me with his eyes. If he hadn't noticed my limp yet, I *knew* he saw it then.

"Go on and throw that saddle up on that bale of straw over there."

I did as I was told again, a little surprised at how light the saddle was.

"Looky here," he said, walking over to the saddle and pulling the elastic strap that goes around the horse's belly. "This is the way you tie a cinch. You watchin'?"

226

"Yeah."

"First, you slip it through here, then ya pull it tight like this. You watchin', boy?"

"Yeah! I'm watchin'."

"Okay. Then, when it's nice and snug—but not too tight—you buckle it up like this, and you slip the end of the little strap through here. Go 'head, you try it."

I did it one-two-three. Piece of cake.

"Good," he said, "Now unbuckle the left stirrup, and make it about two inches longer than the right."

"How come?"

"That's called ridin' 'acey-duecy'. Almost all the jocks ride like that. See, when your left stirrup is a little longer than your right, it helps you keep your balance a little better, and it gives you leverage when ya lean into them turns at high speed. Understand?"

All of a sudden, I felt myself getting this weird, nauseous feeling in the pit of my stomach, and when I looked at my arms, I had goose bumps all over them.

"Y yeah,...b but...I..."

"What ya say? Speak up, boy."

"B...b..but...I..."

"What'sa matter, son? You alright?"

"Yeah, it's just that ever since I was born, I've had this problem with my legs."

Right away I could see that Simon was getting embarrassed. I could tell he'd been trying to play it off like he hadn't noticed it or nothing, but I knew he was bullshitting all along. Good thing his skin was that dark, chocolate color, otherwise he'd probably be blushing his ass off.

"What kinda problem?" he asked, coughing in his hand and looking down at his shoes.

"It's called L.L.D.—Leg Length Discrepancy."

"Never heard of that before."

"It's just a fancy way of sayin' that I have one leg shorter that the other—that's all."

Simon didn't say nothing at first, but I could see the wheels turning in his mind, and judging from the way he was looking at my legs and

227

starting to stutter, I could tell he wanted to say something, but he was probably just too afraid to say it.

"Well,...uh...uh."

"Go 'head, Simon, say it. It's okay."

"Well, I don't mean to step outa line or nothin', but is the right leg the...?"

"Yeah, my right leg's the shorter one. My left leg's always been about two inches longer."

I knew why Simon had asked me that question; me and him were already thinking the exact same thing. I lifted up my eyes and looked him in the face, and when the old man's eyes met mine, I saw him tremble and shake for a second, as if he'd just caught some weird kind of chill or something. All of a sudden, he started rubbing his arms up and down, and when he stopped, I looked down and saw that he had goose bumps all over them—just like mine.

"You know what that means son, don't ya?"

I didn't answer.

"You're a natural-born acey-deucy rider."

I kept looking in his eyes, but I couldn't say nothing.

"Yep, that's the ol' voice of destiny talkin' right there, boy. Looks to me like you were born to ride."

Chapter 17

And so, little by little, the racetrack became my life. I knew from the very first second I set foot on the backside, it was the place for me. I was at my happiest every minute I was there, and I felt drawn to it, like a fly to a light bulb. My only problem was convincing Mom. After all, I did promise on the feet of Jesus that I was going to quit in September and go back and finish school. Well, I figured I'd just have to cross that bridge when I got to it, because right then, I was too busy having fun and learning stuff to start worrying about that.

It's funny how things happen sometimes. About a week after I started working for Sam Cardone, I was talking with Tito at the track kitchen, and out of nowhere, I found out that he lived only a few blocks away from me. Yeah! I couldn't believe it, he lived right there on Madison Avenue between 110^{Th} and 111th Streets. We were practically neighbors. And after we talked for a while about some neighborhood stuff that we had in common, he was nice enough to offer to give me a ride to the track with him in the mornings. That meant that I had to get up a little earlier, because Tito had to be the first guy at the barn every day to give the horses their breakfast, but I didn't mind. Are you kidding? Anything was better than standing around that dark, empty subway platform at four in the morning, waiting for the A-train to show up. So, we made a deal: Tito would pick me up on 116th and Pleasant by the entrance to the FDR Drive, and I'd help him with the morning feeding. And it worked out great for both of us: I was getting a free ride, and he was getting a helping hand. I'd always offer to chip in a couple of bucks for gas, but Tito would never take it though. He'd just wave me away with his hand and say: "It no big thing."

Tito sure was one hell of a nice guy alright, and the more I got to know him, the better I liked him. He was a little hard to understand sometimes, because his accent was so heavy, but I got used to it. I even got used to the *pachanga* music he'd always be blasting on the radio— and I even started to like that after a while too. But whenever, Tito

229

couldn't find anything he liked on the radio, that was when I'd steer the conversation to my favorite subject: horses.

He knew a lot about the subject because he grew up right across the street from a little racetrack in Puerto Rico called "Las Casas", and by the time he was ten years old, he was already helping his older brother around the stable. Forget it, when it came to horse racing this guy knew everything. He'd tell me about all the top jockeys and trainers in Puerto Rico, and all the champion horses too—like that horse called *Camarero*, who won *fifty-seven* races in a row.

But the stuff I'd really find interesting was when he'd talk about all the slick tricks that they'd use in PR to win a race and make a score— like using drugs and stimulants 'n' stuff. He said the rules weren't that strict in Puerto Rico in them days—no saliva or urine tests—and that they'd do practically anything, even putting hot pepper, *"pica pica"*, up the horses' asses, and using *"baterias,* batteries. I guess I could understand giving drugs to the horses—even though it was a bad thing to do—but the idea of using one of them "battery" things on them seemed kind of cruel. Tito said the jockeys would hide it in their boot, inside a sleeve, or in the waistband of their pants, and when the time was right, they'd stick the metal prong-things from the battery against the horse's sweaty neck, and give them a fuckin' jolt of electricity that would scare the shit out of them and make them run like hell. That sounded like a real scuzzy thing to do. And in my mind, I made a secret promise to myself that if I ever get to be a jockey someday, I'll never stoop to using a battery on a horse, never ever—no matter what.

Anyway, I learned a lot just talking with Tito as we rode along, but once we got to the track, that's when my *real* horse education would start. Every day he'd teach me something new: like how to groom a horse and use all the different brushes and combs, how to take care of their legs by using poultices and rubbing them with liniment, how to use a foot-pick to clean out their feet, how to mix the morning feed, how to muck out a stall, how to roll bandages and how to put them on, how to get a bridle and a saddle on, how to tie up a tail for the mud.... Fuhgeddaboudit, this guy would teach me every-fuckin'-thing; it was like going to groom school for free. And I soaked up every little drop of information like a sponge.

After a while, Sam noticed how much I'd learned from Tito and how much I was helping him out, so he started letting me tag along whenever he'd run a horse in the afternoon. I'd walk right next to Tito and the horse, carrying the water bucket or the blinkers—if the horse wore blinkers—and when we'd bop into the paddock in front of all them people, I'd feel like a million bucks. And when Olympic King got loose on the lead one day and held on to win, I had the thrill of getting my picture taken in the winner's circle. I was so excited, my knees were knocking, and while Tito held the big, gray horse by the bridle, and Sam and Mr. Cerutti, his owner, posed at his head, I knelt down on one knee with my water bucket and smiled a big, nervous smile. It felt great to be a winner.

When August and the Saratoga meeting rolled around, instead of it being the usual curse that it had always been, this time it actually turned out to be a blessing in disguise. Sam called me and Simon into the tack room one day, and explained to us that the racing secretary hadn't assigned him enough stalls at Saratoga, and that he'd have to leave four horses behind, plus Jimbo, the stable pony, and he wanted to know if we could stay behind at Aqueduct and take care of them. Well, I guess what's bad luck for one guy is good luck for the other guy. See, for Simon is was bad luck; he loved Saratoga, and now he had to stay behind at hot, sweaty Aqueduct with four, broken-down horses and a stable pony. But for me it was good luck. Hell yeah! Mom wasn't going to let me go to Saratoga *anyway*, and now, thanks to the "shortage of stalls", I was getting the chance to continue my horse education right here in my own backyard.

With everybody and their mother up at Saratoga, almost overnight, the whole backside at Aqueduct had gotten real empty—'specially in the afternoons after all the morning work was done. The only people left after eleven o'clock were the Pinkertons, and a couple of lonely grooms who'd hang around the rec room, bullshitting, playing cards, or shooting pool. Me and Simon would be alone then, and in the still of those hot, muggy afternoons, when it was real quiet and hardly nobody

231

was around, Simon started to give me my first "riding lessons". Yep, I finally talked him into it.

Well, maybe Simon called them "riding lessons", but to me it felt more like we were playing that children's game: Simon-says. That's because this guy was real, real strict when it came to those lessons. Are you kidding? The only thing I was allowed to do was *exactly* what he told me to do—no more, no less. And God forbid I should jump the gun and do a little something extra, fuhgeddaboudit, I'd catch holy hell.

"Did Simon tell ya to do that, boy?"

"No."

"Well, then don't do it, you ain't ready for that yet."

Yeeesh, what a grouch! This guy was like fuckin' Hitler over here. I couldn't even throw a goddamn fart unless I had his permission first. For real! I'd have to tighten my ass and hold it in until he'd take all his sweet time and say: "Okay, Simon says fart."

Well, maybe I'm exaggerating a little, but I guess Simon had his reasons for doing it "his way". At the beginning, he didn't even let me get on the back of a horse, and I spent almost an entire week practicing my "seat" on an exercise saddle thrown over a bale of straw. But the special day finally came, and after he'd saddled up ol' Jimbo, the stable pony, he let me climb up on horseback for the very first time.

"Jimbo?" I said, disappointed that I wasn't gonna be learning on a real racehorse.

"That's right, son, you gotta crawl before you can walk. Jimbo's only a pony, but for learning your basic hossmanship, he'll do just fine."

The whole process took a pretty long time. At first Simon would lead Jimbo around the barn by the bridle, while I just sat up there smiling my ass off, getting the feel of what Simon called "hossbackin'". Then, after a couple of days, Simon let go of the pony and let me ride him around the shed row by myself—but only at a walk. And when we finally went outside and I was about to put my foot in the stirrup to get up on Jimbo, all of a sudden, Simon pushed me aside, and even though it was a struggle for him get in the saddle, he got up on him himself. Then he said for me to watch carefully, because he was going to show me how to "post".

232

"Watch me now," he said, giving Jimbo a little kick with his heels and setting him down to a slow trot. "See the way I lift my butt up 'n' down in the saddle to the rhythm of the hoss's stride? That's called 'posting'. It real important, son, 'cause if you can't post, you gonna wind up with a really sore butt from bouncin' all the time when you ride at a trot."

That "posting" stuff wasn't easy, and it took me a while to get the hang of it. But once I did, Simon stepped everything up, little by little. We went from trotting and posting to jogging, and from jogging, we went to cantering. And then, after I was riding okay at a canter, we got into galloping. And when I could hold my own at a gallop, he showed me how to signal Jimbo with my hands, knees, and heels to get him to change from one "gait" to another.

"Changin' gaits," he said, "should be just like changing gears in one of them new-fangled cars with an automatic transmission. Yas'suh, it got to be smooth—smoother than a lil' ol' baby's butt."

Fuhgeddaboudit, this guy taught me everything, and after only four weeks of playing Simon-says, I started to feel sort of proud of myself. I could ride a little bit.

Well, the proud feeling didn't last very long though. I guess Simon must've thought I was "feelin' my oats" and acting a little too "frisky" for my own good, because one day, out of a clear blue sky, he pulled the rug right out from under me.

"Alright, son," he said, watching me saddling up Jimbo, "why don't ya hike them stirrups up about six inches on each side; get 'em to exercise-rider length. Let's see how you handle that."

That sly old fox knew exactly what he was doing; riding with long stirrups was one thing but crouching down and balancing your ass in short stirrups was something completely different.

"How does it feel?" he asked, standing there grinning, watching me as I struggled to post and keep my balance all at the same time.

"I feel like I'm gonna fall off!"

"Heh, heh, heh…. Might as well get used to it now, boy, 'cause you ain't seen nothin' yet. Wait 'til we hike 'em up a few inches more, and we get 'em up to regular jockey length; then you're *really* gonna learn the meaning of the word 'balance'."

233

Yeah, that was Simon's way of doing things. First, he'd soup you up and make you feel like you were doing good, and then, when he'd see you were getting a little confidence in yourself, *boom*, he'd knock the wind out of your sails and drag you back to square one. But that was how the old coot would keep you humble, because even though I was starting to ride Jimbo all over the backside like it was nothing, I knew I still had a long, long way to go before I could actually climb up on the back of a racehorse.

But I was happy though; in only a month's time, Simon had taught me the fundamentals of riding, and now it was up to me sharpen my skills and practice, practice, practice. Only problem was, where was I going to practice? The end of August had already snuck up on us, and in a few days, Sam and the rest of the outfit were going to be back from Saratoga. That meant no more "riding lessons" for me; Sam Cardone was running a racing stable, not a riding academy.

Well, I guess practicing my riding should've been the least of my worries. Labor Day was right around the corner, and whether I wanted to or not, it was time for me to cross the bridge I'd been putting off crossing for the last two months: I was going to have to deal with Mom.

Ever since I started working at the track, she seemed pretty happy. I kept my promise about not hanging out with the Redwoods, every week I'd give her half my paycheck, and by seven thirty I'd already be conked out in front of the TV from getting up so early and working my ass off all day. But summer was over, and she wanted me back in school.

The problem with not keeping my promise wasn't about swearing on the feet of Jesus—I'd broken those promises before—it was about giving up the racetrack, 'specially after I'd gotten such a good taste of it. Working at the track had made me ten times happier than I'd ever been in my whole life, and there was no way I was going to stop and go back to that dull, boring school. It took me a while to get up the courage, but when I finally sat down with Mom to try and explain how I felt, she did what exactly what I thought she'd do: she hit the ceiling.

"I knew it, I *knew* you were gonna pull something like this! Ya see?! You can't be nice with you. If I give you my little pinky, you wanna bite off my whole goddamn arm!"

"But, Ma...I..."

234

"'But, Ma', *nothin'*. In case you forgot, you made a sacred promise to me, mister. Maybe *you* forgot, but *I* sure didn't. And I expect you to *keep* it!"

I kept on trying to explain the situation to her, but when I made the mistake of saying that I was seventeen and a half, and if she didn't let me continue at the track, I'd just have to quit school and move out on my own to do it. *Pow!* Right across the kisser. And it wasn't just one smack, it was a whole bunch of smacks—plus punches too.

Grandma jumped in and pulled her off of me, but she didn't do her usual lawyer number that time. Nope, she was sticking with Mom one hundred percent. She felt that the racetrack and my jockey dream was way too dangerous, and she wasn't going to budge.

Well, live and learn—that's all I could say. Once all the screaming and yelling was over, and Mom had calmed down and was sitting by the window, sniffling and wiping her eyes, out of nowhere, a new lawyer appeared on the scene: Grandpa. And this was really a shock to me, because Grandpa usually minded his own business, and never got mixed up in stuff between me and Mom. But there he was, pacing up and down in the living room with his hand in his vest pocket, looking like one of them country lawyers in the movies.

He started off by explaining that I didn't want to quit school just to be a bum, he tried to make Mom understand that I had *"ambizione"*, ambition, and the reason I wanted to stop going to school was to follow my dream. He compared it to him leaving school at twelve years old to become an apprentice at the tailor shop in his town, so he could learn a trade and make a living. But the thing that really hit home was when Grandpa started talking about *"la forza del destino"*, the force of destiny. He reminded Mom how I used to play with my horse-race game for hours and hours when I was little, how the only thing I'd draw were horse pictures, and how, little by little, it all turned into me wanting to ride. According to Grandpa, God gave me my love of horses for a reason. He said it was something that was meant to be, something that was too big and strong to fight against; it was *la forza del destino*.

I had a feeling that Grandpa's *"forza del destino"*, and Simon's *"voice of destiny"* were pretty much the same thing. And I didn't think it was just a coincidence neither. Nope, they both knew a lot about life

235

from having been around the block so many times, and I guess that's why old timers like them could really understand the true meaning of stuff like that.

I wasn't sure if it was Grandpa and *la forza del destino* that made Mom go along with me not going back to school. It might have looked like she understood and everything, but I never thought for one second that she was in my corner—because she wasn't. Far from it. And when November rolled around and the horses moved to Florida, she blew another fuse, and before you could even say the word "jockey", the shit was already flying off the fan in big, ugly globs.

"Are you crazy?!"

"I ain't crazy, Ma. The season's almost over. What am I gonna do for the next four and a half months, sit around here and twiddle my thumbs all day?"

"Well, Mr. Smart Aleck, maybe you should've thought about that before you went dropping out of school like a bum, so you could pick up horseshit at some stupid racetrack."

I bit my knuckle, took a deep breath, and tried to stay as calm as I could. It was time to drop the bomb, and I figured that my chances would be a lot better if I controlled myself and tried to act civilized.

"Look, Ma," I said, in a nice calm voice, "Mr. Cardone can't really take me to Miami with the rest of the crew anyway, but he got me a job working at a horse farm in this place called Ocala, Florida. He says it's the perfect spot for me. I can polish up my riding, get more experience, and learn a lot more of what I need to know to become a jockey. The manager of the farm is a close, personal friend of his, and he told me I'll get treated just like family."

"*Family?!* Your family is right here—in case you forgot—right here in New York, not a thousand miles away in goddamn Florida someplace."

"But, Ma..."

"'But, Ma', nothing. What makes you think you're ready to go gallivanting off to the swamps of Florida to break your neck riding a bunch of stupid horses?"

236

Cutting the apron strings and moving away from home was definitely the biggest tug of war I'd ever got into in my whole life. The harder I'd pull, the harder they'd pull.

I have to use the word "they", because as soon as Grandma found out about me wanting to go to Florida, she jumped right into Mom's corner and became her tag-team partner. Then they started double-teaming me—just like in them wrestling matches. While Mom would get me in a choke hold, strangling me with the good ol' apron strings, Grandma would sneak over and bash me over the head with her favorite weapon: *guilt*.

"What'sa matter you? You no like you family no more? You no love you Mama no more? You no love you Grandma no more? Ah? Why you wanna leave you house? You wanna make me cry? That's why you wanna go away? Ah? Or maybe you just wanna break my heart."

Fuhgeddaboudit, when it came to dishing out guilt, Grandma was the undisputed, heavy-weight champ. She was a real pro, and she'd keep piling it on, and piling it on, by the truckload, 'til she'd have you feeling so goddamn guilty, you'd feel like going to confession to confess shit you hadn't even *done* yet. That's why I figured it was time for us to have a little talk, to see if I could get her to cool it before I went completely bananas.

"Listen, Grandma," I said, sitting her down at the kitchen table and trying to reason with her, "I love you, I love Grandpa, I love Mom, I love my family, I love my house, I love everything and everybody. But I'm seventeen-and-a-half years old; in a couple of months I'll be eighteen."

"I no care how old you gonna be; to me you still my little Junior—always, all the time."

I rolled my eyes. "I know, and you'll always be my one and only Grandma too. But I'm growin' up, and I got an opportunity to work at a place where I can really learn, and practice, and get good at riding. I can't miss this chance. You understand, don't ya, Gram?"

She looked at me from the other side of the table as the tears rose in her eyes and clouded them over. And then, when there wasn't room for anymore, one by one, they spilled out and came trickling down her cheeks.

"C'mon, Grandma, don't cry. Please. It's only gonna be for a couple of months, I'll be back in no time."

237

"But, Junior, we gonna miss you."

"I know, Gram, I'm gonna miss you too, but it's somethin' I gotta do."

Seeing Grandma cry like that made me feel so shitty, I felt like forgetting about the whole thing and staying home. But I was in too deep and there was no pulling out. If I didn't take advantage of that opportunity, I knew I'd be kicking myself in the head for the rest of my life.

I still don't know if it was Grandpa's *forza-del-destino* stuff that kept kicking around in Mom's mind, or maybe it was me nagging her non-stop all day long, but she finally broke.

"Alright! I can't take it no more! Go! Go 'head, go! Do what ya wanna do—just leave me alone already!"

Grandma heard the yelling and jumped in right away. "Celeste! Calm down! Please!"

"I can't calm down, Ma, this kid is drivin' me nuts over here!"

I tried to say something to calm the situation. "But, Ma, I don't want ya to feel like I'm...."

"Oh, please. Stop it already, Junior—just stop it. You think you know so much? Then go. Go 'head. Do what ya gotta do. But don't come cryin' to me when you break your neck. Ya hear?"

I would've liked to go to Florida with Mom's blessing, but I guess it just wasn't in the cards. She had a nasty attitude that whole last week, and I could hardly talk to her at all. But when we moved into the last couple of days before D-day, the reality of the situation must've started sinking in, because little by little, her attitude changed and turned from mad to sad. Grandma and Grandpa had been getting sad about me leaving too, and so had everybody else once they found out about it— 'specially Ronnie.

She came upstairs to say goodbye and got emotional and started crying right away. She made me promise to write to her from Florida and call her on the phone. I crossed my heart and swore "scout's honor" that I would—even though I'd never been a scout—and that seemed to cheer her up and make her feel better. Then she gave me a big hug and

238

kissed me on the lips. I'd never been kissed by a girl before, and even though I knew it was sad occasion, I couldn't help but like the way it felt.

Ya know, not for nothin', but Ronnie had been growing up and was starting to look kind of cute over here. She was still only fifteen, but while I was busy with all my stupid shit, she'd been blossoming her ass off, right under my nose, and had turned into a little fox. She had this new sexy-dexy hairstyle, and she'd even started plucking her eyebrows and wearing make-up too. And forget about that little body. Holy shit! Where the hell did *that* come from?

But that's always the way it's been with me. Something good could be staring me right in the face, and I wouldn't even notice it because I'd be all wrapped up in my own bullshit. And then, when I finally woke up and smelled the coffee, it was usually too late.

Saying goodbye turned out to be a lot harder than I thought. I knew Mom and Grandma would probably break down and start crying and everything, but I had no idea it would be as bad as it was—not only for them, but for me too.

"My Junior," Grandma sobbed, holding my cheeks and kissing me all over my face. "What I'm gonna do without my Junior?"

I held her close and gave her a squeeze. "And what am I gonna do without my Grandma?"

Grandpa gave me a big hug too. I whispered, "thanks for helping me, Grandpa", in his ear. But he didn't answer; he just gave me his usual kiss on the forehead. "Goo'bye, Junior—*che Dio ti benedica*—God bless you all the time."

Before I could turn away from Grandpa, Mom was all over me, hugging me real tight, kissing me, and bawling like a baby. I could smell the Jean Nate' toilet water she'd always wear, and as her shoulders shook up and down, I felt the tears rubbing off her face and onto mine.

"Junior, I'm sorry if I acted mean to y..you. I c..can't help it. I'm your mother...I love you... and I don't wanna see you get h..hurt—that's all. Understand?"

"Yeah," I answered, pulling myself away gently and giving her a kiss on the cheek. "I understand. I love you too, Ma."

"You gonna call? Huh?"

"Yeah, yeah."

"Okay, don't forget your mother now?"
"I won't."

Chapter 18

The farm I came to work at was called Everglades Stud. It was in the heart of Florida's horse country, Ocala, and like the rest of the state, it was hotter and muggier than hell. The only thing I really liked about the joint were those beautiful, old trees they got there with that "Spanish moss" hanging down from the branches. That stuff was cool; it looked sort of like Christmas-tree tinsel, only instead of being all silvery, it was a dull, grayish-green color.

Anyway, this Everglades place wasn't no dinky, little farm. From what I was told, it was one of the biggest horse farms in the whole state. Rough 'n' Ready, Beau Gent, Tudor Prince, Gunflint, and some of the best stallions in Florida stood right there in the big stallion barn, and over in the broodmare barn, they must have had some thirty-five or forty, top-class broodmares in there, bellies all swollen, just biding their time and waiting to give birth in the next few months. The other two barns were filled to the brim with a whole bunch of yearlings and weanlings, and in the evenings when they'd get turned out for the night, you could see them running around and romping in the big, open fields like a crazy herd of wild mustangs.

The horses sure had a lot of room to graze and stretch their legs in Ocala. All you could see were acres and acres of emerald-green pastureland, dotted with oak trees and trimmed with freshly painted, white fence. Too bad the place was so fuckin' flat though. All it needed were a couple of hills and valleys here and there, just to break up the flat, boring lay of the land, and that place could've looked really beautiful.

The manager of the farm was this middle-aged, Irish guy with thick, gray hair called Tom Kerrigan. He lived in a fancy white house at the end of a long, tree-lined driveway at the entrance to the farm. He seemed nice enough, but he didn't treat me like "family" the way Sam said he would. Naa, he put me in this bunkhouse/barracks type place where the rest of the employees lived. But I didn't mind though; they kept the place clean and neat, and I had a whole lot of company over there—mostly young guys like me. Some were from nearby in Florida and some were from other parts of the country, but they all were cool, and it was easy to make friends.

The only bad thing about the set-up was the food. Mr. Kerrigan had his "Aunt Kathleen" cooking for us, and even though she was a sweet old lady, she definitely wasn't no Marietta Posella behind the stove—I'll tell ya that much. Aunt Kathleen didn't believe in making sauces or using spices, or herbs, or seasonings 'n' stuff. "All that fancy stuff just camerflages the natural flavor of the food," she'd say in her thick, Irish accent. Well, you could give me some "camerflage" any day of the week, baby. Are you kidding? *Nothing* she ever made had any taste to it. That was because, in her mind, "boiling" and "cooking" were fuckin' synonyms. Yeah! All she needed to make a "fine, tasty meal" was to boil a big pot of water, throw some meat and potatoes 'n' stuff in it, cook it, strain it, and eat it—no sauce, no gravy, no seasoning, no *garlic*—not even a lousy pinch of salt for Chris'sakes!

Well, "thank God for ketchup", that's all I can say. Yep, if it wasn't for my trusty, bottle of ketchup, I would've died of starvation the first week I was there. I'd blob and glob that stuff on everything they'd put in front of me; that was the only way I could sneak the shit past my taste buds and fool my food pipe into thinking it was actually *edible*.

I guess I shouldn't put down ol' Aunt Kathleen like that though—at least she tried. And her breakfasts weren't that bad—'specially when she'd whip up a batch of that "Irish soda bread".

That stuff was pretty good, and I guess you could say that when it came to Aunt Kathleen's cooking, that was about as good as it got.

My biggest problem was a bad case of homesickness though. It didn't really hit me until the second week, and I guess eating that Irish food every day, didn't help matters much neither. Everything I'd put in my mouth would remind me of how much I missed Grandma's cooking and being back in New York. But that's the way it goes; you don't miss the water 'til the well runs dry.

Like take Ronnie for instance, I never realized what a good friend she was 'til I went down to Florida. She'd write every single week, like clockwork, and let me tell ya, to a homesick guy like me, each one of those letters was like a frosty-cold, bottle of Mission soda in the middle of the Sahara Desert. Yeah, getting those letters really meant a lot to me. And along with the stuff she'd write, she'd always include pictures and newspaper clippings, and tell me all the important stuff that was happening in New York—plus all the latest gossip from the neighborhood. I'd always answer back and tell her what was going on with me and what I was learning at the farm. And you know something? Before long, I wasn't thinking of Ronnie as "the little girl from downstairs" no more. Nope, I found myself getting a little crush on her—'specially after she sent me that snapshot of herself from her birthday party. *Madon'*, this little chick was getting *fine*.

Unfortunately, there wasn't too much to report about what I'd been doing at the farm those first couple of months. Mr. Kerrigan had me working with the weanlings, mostly grooming them, feeding them, and bringing them out to the field and back in again. But I guess he must've noticed that I'd been doing a good job, because he finally took me to the side and told me that he thought I was ready to be part of the "breaking crew".

The breaking crew was a small group of young guys like me who'd been hired to "break" the yearlings. "Break" was probably a bad word though, because it had nothing to do with the way they'd "break" horses in the cowboy movies—like when they'd jump on one of them wild mustangs and hang on for dear life while the poor horse bucked like crazy 'til it was completely exhausted and would give up. It's not like that with racehorses. Are you kidding? Some of them Thoroughbred yearlings were worth boo-coo bucks, and it didn't make sense to risk hurting them just to save some time and break them "cowboy style". Mr. Kerrigan would always say: "When it comes to breakin' yearlings, there's only three ways to do it: slowly...slowly...and slowly".

First of all, each guy in the breaking crew got assigned three yearlings, but if any of the three turned out to be a "problem child", then the "green boys", like me, were allowed to switch and give the problem horse to one of the older guys with more experience. That worked out great for us "green boys", 'cause let me tell ya, we were learning our shit right along with the horses. It was like the blind leading the blind: boy teaches horse, and horse teaches boy.

Anyway, with the help of each yearling's groom, the first thing we'd do was to let each of them get the feel of the tack—the bridle, the bit, and the saddle and everything—and then, when they'd get used to that,

243

we'd lie across their backs on our bellies, slowly, without mounting them, so they could get their first taste of what a rider's weight felt like. Most of it was done right there in the yearling's stall where they felt safe and comfortable, and where there wasn't too much room for them to move around and kick up a fuss and whatnot. But to play it safe, we'd always remove their feed tubs and water buckets anyway—just in case any of them acted up. That way they wouldn't go banging into anything and hurting themselves.

There were a couple of yearlings that threw a king-size fit when we finally threw a leg over and mounted them, but with the way we'd do everything so slow and gentle, most of them handled it pretty good. And I was surprised too, because none of my three yearlings hardly even reacted at all. The whole shit was turning out to be a piece of cake, one-two-three, and there I was, sitting on the back of a real live racehorse.

Well, let me not jump the gun, because there was a lot more to breaking a yearling than just getting on its back; the next step was giving the horse its "mouth". That meant that the groom would unhook the shank from the bridle and would let the rider steer the horse using only the reins. It was a lot like taking the training wheels off a bike and learning to ride solo.

At first, they had us doing slow figure eights with them inside the stall, but after a few days of that, they brought all the mounted yearlings out onto the shed row, and we'd walk them around and around in single file. First, we'd go counterclockwise, and then, once they got the hang of that, we'd turn them around and walk them the other way: clockwise. We kept on like that for about a week, and then Mr. Kerrigan picked up the tempo a little and let us start circling them around the shed row at a slow jog—first counterclockwise and then clockwise. And then, when the yearlings, and also the "green boys", had gotten comfortable with that, he moved us out of the shed row and out into the open air.

Some of the yearlings got spooked a little when they found themselves out under the sky with a rider on their back, but my three horses were cool. Yep, I lucked up like a champ when it came to that; they had assigned me two chestnut fillies and a stocky bay colt, and each one was sweeter than pie.

We walked them and jogged them alongside a fence in an open paddock for a few days, and then we had them do figure eights for another week or so. Mr. Kerrigan was always right on top of us, smoking his pipe, scowling, scoping us out, and making sure nobody messed up or nothing; but after a while, when he saw how smooth everything was going, he divided us into two groups and sent us over to the training track.

Going to the training track didn't mean we were going to let the yearlings start running at top speed. Mr. Kerrigan would've had a heart attack if we even *thought* of something like that. These horses were still babies, and our job was just to school them and teach them what running around a track was all about—not to risk injuring their soft leg bones before they even had a chance to grow and develop.

So, we took it real, real slow—always with Mr. Kerrigan watching. Usually, we'd line them up ten abreast, and we'd walk, jog, and canter them around the track, and then we'd do an about-face and walk, jog, and canter them the other way, teaching them to "change leads", and how to control themselves and follow the group. Then sometimes we'd break them up into two or three smaller groups, and we'd line them up four or five across the track, changing places all the time, so each yearling got a chance to feel what is was like to be on the inside, on the outside, in the middle, in front of horses, and behind horses.

They had a starting gate there too, but we'd never actually break any of the yearlings from the gate or nothing like that. We'd just stand them in it a lot and let them sniff around and get familiar with it. Sometimes we'd walk them through it too, frontwards and backwards, over and over again, so they wouldn't be scared of it and go apeshit every time they'd get near one of them things. It was a slow process, and as Mr. Kerrigan would say: "There ain't no short cuts when it comes to trainin' a racehorse".

Fuhgeddaboudit, we taught them babies everything, and as they were learning, we were learning too. Yep, I was greener than the yearlings when we first started, but as the months passed, little by little, I thought I was turning into a pretty good rider. Even Mr. Kerrigan said I had a "good seat" and a "nice, light touch" with a horse, so I started thinking: I'll keep working real hard and practicing my ass off through the rest of the summer, and when September rolls around, maybe I can

245

go back to New York, take out my exercise-rider's license, and start working at the track again—only this time *galloping* horses instead of just walking hots.

It took me about a month of serious thinking, but I finally decided it was time to make my move. I wasn't completely sure I was ready to be an exercise boy yet—I knew I still had a lot to learn—but I just couldn't take Florida no more. I'd already had it with that place. So, I gave Mr. Kerrigan my two-week's notice, and after I said "thanks" to everybody and had a few "goodbye beers" with the guys in the bunkhouse, I packed up my suitcase, and got ready to head back to New York, "the Big Apple", home sweet home.

When I walked into the house, I got a big shock. Grandma had the place looking like it was Thanksgiving or Christmas or something. Yeah! The big table was all set up in the living room for a feast, and everybody and their mother was there: Aunt Jean, Uncle Rocco, Anthony, Carmela, Frankie—even Ronnie too. Holy shit! I felt like a hero coming home from the war.

Well, after Mom squeezed me half to death, and Grandma showered me with a hundred little kisses all over my face and hands and everything, everybody else gathered around to give me a welcome-home hug.

Ronnie gave me a big, long hug too, and a kiss on the cheek for good measure. "Oh, Joey, I missed you."

I didn't say anything back to her, because with everyone standing around watching, I felt a little embarrassed. But a few minutes later when I was able to catch Ronnie's eye, I gave her a look that let her know that I'd missed her a lot too.

Anyway, once everyone had patted me on the back and told me how good I looked and how great it was to see me again, little by little, we all sort of drifted over to the table to sit down. Yep, it was time to put on the ol' feedbag, and I could hardly wait. *"A mangiara!"*

Wow! I could hardly believe my eyes; every single thing on the table had been custom-cooked, 'specially for me. Grandma really outdid herself, she made an entire meal out of all my favorite things: a huge

246

platter of antipasto with all the goodies that I loved, a big pan of eggplant parmigiana with lots of extra sauce, and if that wasn't enough, she put out a big plate of my favorite pork chops and green peppers, fried in garlic and vinegar—just the way I liked them. Fuhgeddaboudit, that was a feast, fit for a king—and the king was me.

I've never been a big eater, and I still had that problem of getting full right away after I'd take a couple of bites of something. But after eating Aunt's Kathleen's *boiled* meat, with *boiled* potatoes, and *boiled* vegetables every day for God knows how many long months, every bite of Grandma's food tasted like paradise.

Once I started scarfing all that delicious stuff down, the whole table started staring at me. Yeah! From the minute I opened my mouth and took my first bite, everybody was chucking their asses off and goofing on me—'specially Uncle Rocco, Anthony and Frankie.

"Whoa! Slow down, Joon, nobody's gonna take it away from ya."

"Yeah, why don't ya come up for *air* for Chris'sakes. You're gonna choke yourself like that."

"You tellin' me? Hey, Junior, when's the last time you ate anyway—last year?

But I didn't pay them no mind, I was way too busy attacking those pork chops and peppers to worry about those three clowns.

Well, the whole scene but a big smile on Grandma's face. There was nothing that gave her more happiness and satisfaction, than having the whole family together and watching us going bananas over her cooking—'specially me. And as I chomped away, rolling my eyes, kissing my fingertips and mumbling "delicious" with every bite, she just sat there, smiling big, golden sunbeams at me, saying: "*Va bene*, I'm glad you like."

Mom was happy too. She sat right at my elbow through the whole meal, stroking my hair and kissing my face, while I tried to juggle eating and carrying on a conversation. And it wasn't easy because I had her on one side of me, and Ronnie on the other, and they were both yapping away at the exact same time.

But nobody was as happy to see me as Grandpa. He just kept smiling his ass off and filling up our glasses with his special, holiday wine. And then, out of nowhere, he even stood up and made a toast.

247

"To Junior!" he said, as everybody lifted their glasses. "He come back to his house. *Che Dio lo bendica!*"

I was kind of surprised to see him give me and Anthony full glasses of wine, instead of our usual "two fingers" worth—like Frankie was still getting. And I guess it surprised Mom too.

"Papa!" she gasped, watching him fill our glasses for the second time. "Whatta ya doin'?"

Grandpa touched his fingertips together. "What I do? I give my grandson some wine—that's what I do."

"Yeah, but Papa!"

"*Lasha l' stara!* They both eighteen years old. If they old enough to go to fight for the Uncle Sam, they old enough to drink a little glass of wine. Leave them alone."

Mom and Aunt Jean rolled their eyes and mumbled and grumbled to each other as they gathered up the dishes and brought them to the kitchen, but me and Anthony just looked at each other and smiled. Yep, for us it was sort of like a victory. We knew right then and there, that in Grandpa's eyes at least, we weren't boys no more, we were men.

Chapter 19

I took a little vacation and hung around the house for a while, mostly sitting on the fire escape catching up on old times with Ronnie and sitting at Grandma's kitchen table catching up on my eating. But when I got on the bathroom scale and saw that I'd put on *four* pounds in only *three* days, I knew right away it was time for me to get back to work. There's nothing more dangerous to someone who wants to be a jockey than packing on extra weight; every little pound is like the kiss of death.

Anyway, as soon I got back to the Big A, I went straight to barn seven to see Sam. It was great to see that grumpy ol' bastard again, and all my buddies too: Simon, Tito, Mongo, Eddie, Floyd, and all the rest of the guys—'specially Simon. I was anxious to show him all the stuff I'd learned in Florida. But all that would have to wait; the first thing I had to do was talk with the boss, to see if he'd be willing to give me a shot as an exercise boy.

He was a little skeptical at first, but once I galloped a horse for him and he saw with his own two eyes that I'd really learned to ride, he helped me to get my exercise license right away. And after that, he kept me more than busy jogging horses around the shed row and taking them over to the track for long, slow gallops.

He'd never let me breeze a horse though—he kept saying I wasn't ready for speed yet—so whenever he needed somebody to work a horse, he'd stick with Mongo and this new exercise boy he'd hired called Carlos. But I didn't mind, I figured I'd just keep on practicing and polishing up my skills, before I'd even worry about being ready to breeze a horse. I was happy just to be on horseback, galloping them nice and slow, feeling the cool, fresh, morning breeze kissing my forehead as I'd go bouncing along, singing a tune and watching the sunrise.

Yeah, there's something really special about that early morning light at the racetrack. It's hard to describe, but sometimes it would feel like something magical, something almost holy. 'Cause let me tell ya, you could take the ugliest thing you could think of, like a dried-up blob of dogshit, and if that sunrise light would be shining on it, it could make

249

it look just like a million bucks. Everything would take on a beautiful, rosy-gold glow, like God himself was smiling at you from deep inside the sun, and even though I'd seen hundreds of sunrises since I started working at the track, I'd never get bored with them or take them for granted. Nope, sunrise was my favorite part of the day, and as soon as I'd spot them first golden rays rising up from behind the clouds, gobbling up the stars, and swallowing the moon, I'd feel like I was an eyewitness to a miracle. Sometimes the shit was so beautiful, I'd just stop and stare at it with my mouth open. But most of the time I'd make the sign of the cross—like Grandpa would do when he'd feed the pigeons at sunset in his "church" in Jefferson Park.

But don't go thinking that every morning at the track was all hunky-dory, with a storybook sunrise and little birdies of happiness chirping all around. Are you kidding? On some of those nasty, gray mornings when the rain is slamming you in the face and the wind is blowing you out of the saddle, you'd curse the day you ever *thought* of getting up on a horse—let alone leaving your nice, warm bed at four in the morning to go riding around some dark, muddy racetrack. That's because horse racing is nothing like baseball, tennis, or golf, or none of them other pussy sports; there's no "postponements" or "rain dates" in this game. We're just like the fuckin' mailman: rain or shine, we still gotta deliver.

Yeah, working at the track wasn't always a bed of roses, but in spite of all the bad stuff, I loved it, and I wouldn't have traded places with nobody. And little by little, with all the tips and pointers I was getting from Simon, and all the practice I was getting by riding every morning, I was becoming a real, honest-to-goodness exercise rider.

Well, I still hadn't breezed a horse yet, but I guess I must've been doing something right, because when November was almost over and everyone was packing up and shipping out to their winter headquarters, Sam didn't give me the pink slip like before. Nope, he called me into the tack room, and with a big smile on that Ernest Borgnine mug of his, he said: "Pack ya bags, kid, you're goin' to Florida".

Holy moly! I couldn't believe my ears. I'd only been galloping horses for him for a few months, and even though I was still green and had a whole lot to learn, he still had enough confidence in me to take me along for the winter and make me a permanent part of his team. Hey, this Sam Cardone sure was one hell of a guy alright—and I owed him a lot.

Cutting the apron strings was a little easier this time. That's because I used the thing with the draft board to my advantage. I'd gotten my "greetings" letter from Uncle Sam about a month before, and when I went down to Whitehall Street for the physical, they took one look at me and gave me a "4F" faster than you could say "L.L.D.". I knew that sooner or later the good ol' Leg Length Discrepancy would come in handy for *something*, and I knew a whole bunch of guys who'd give their right eye to be limping around in my shoes, 'specially with that Vietnam bullshit heating up.

Well, anyway, even though Mom was really happy about me getting off the hook with the Army, she still put up a big stink about me going to Florida—right along with Grandma, her tag-team partner. It was still the same old story.

But Grandpa was cool though; he just put his hand on my shoulder and said: "You no more boy, you a man. You pick you trade, and now you gotta do what you gotta do. God bless you."

So, with Grandpa's blessing, and Mom's and Grandma's tears still tugging away at my heartstrings, I hopped on the van at Aqueduct with the rest of Sam's crew, to head south for the winter racing season. Bye-bye cold, hello sun.

Miami was a lot flatter and uglier than Ocala was. All you could see was what was standing directly in front of you—no hills, no valleys, no "vistas", no nothing—just miles and miles of flat, ugly land, filled with gas stations, diners, and hundreds of tacky-looking motels, one after the other, as far as the eye could see.

Sam's base of operations was Tropical Park. It wasn't as fancy as Gulfstream, or as beautiful as Hialeah, but it was a nice, little track though. The backside was small, sort of like Aqueduct, but it was nice and clean, and the room I shared with Tito, Simon and Mongo was a lot better than what I'd expected.

251

The first few weeks down there were a little rough—our team had won only one race—but little by little, things began picking up, and we started to get in the groove. The following week we won three races—not to mention a few seconds and thirds—and by the time the racing shifted over to Hialeah, the whole crew was ready to kick ass.

Sam seemed pretty happy with my riding, and when Carlos got fired for showing up late too many times, I lucked up and got my big break: He finally gave me the chance to breeze my first horse, an old gelding named Kid Creole.

"Hold him now, Joey! He's gonna try and run off with ya. Remember, all I'm lookin' for is a nice, slow half in forty-nine or fifty. So keep your feet in the dashboard—*capish*?"

"Okay, Sam."

Well, all I could say was *"wow!"*. There just weren't any words I could've used to describe what it felt like to ride a racehorse at top speed—the mane flying in your face, the head bobbing up and down, the drumming of the hoofbeats, the vibrations tingling up through the stirrups, going right through your feet and up your legs, making your whole body tremble with the speed and the power in every stride. Fuhgeddaboudit, there was nothing like it. Nope, you could ride a motorcycle at forty miles an hour, or ride the merry-go-round at double or triple speed, or get in a convertible and go speeding with the top down, but none of that stuff would even come close. Those things are just machines and they don't have no life in them. But a racehorse is a living thing, with a heartbeat and a personality, and let me tell ya, when I was sailing around that turn and bounding down the homestretch on Kid Creole, I felt ten times more alive than I'd ever felt in my life.

Only problem was, I knew right away that shit was going to be more addicting then dope. Yep, before I'd even brought the horse back to the barn, and I was already thinking about when I could do it again. I was hooked.

Sam seemed pleased with the way I handled Kid Creole, and after that, he started letting me breeze at least one or two horses every morning, along with my regular jogs and gallops. Most of the time I'd do okay, but there were a few times that I messed up like a champ.

"Forty-six and change?! I told you to *hold* this sonuvabitch! What'sa matter with you?"

"I'm sorry, Sam, he was doin' it so easy, I guess I didn't realize how fast he was goin'."

Getting a handle on calculating time was definitely the hardest part about being a good exercise rider. I mean, when Sam would say he wanted a "half mile in forty-eight", or "three eights no faster than thirty-six", or "five furlongs in a minute and change", he *meant* it. I'm telling you! You needed a fuckin' *stopwatch* in your head to please that guy.

I tried counting Mississippis, to give myself an idea of how fast I was going, but according to Simon, that Mississippi shit was just a big waste of time.

"When you're up there ridin', boy, ya gotta be concentratin' on a whole bunch of stuff: your balance, your seat, your hands, your touch, your timing, the feel of the hoss under you. You ain't got time to be countin' no goddamn Mississippis."

"So how can ya tell how fast you're goin'?"

"Well, there ain't no short cuts when it comes to ridin', son. You just gonna have to get out there and do it, do it, do it, over and over again, and then, after a while, that little ol' clock will start tickin' inside your head without you even realizin' it."

So, that's what I did, I rode as much as I could. And even though I made a lot of mistakes, little by little, I felt like I was starting to control a horse a lot better and stick a lot closer to Sam's instructions.

Too bad I had that stupid accident—'specially after I'd been making so much progress. Yeah, talk about fucked-up luck, that shit really took the cake. It happened while I was breezing a green, three-year-old filly out of the gate. The wind must've blew a piece of paper in her path or something, because, *ba-da-boom!,* all of a sudden, the stupid bitch spooked and went slamming into the rail. I lost my balance and went flying into the infield. At first, I thought I was okay, but when I tried to get up, I felt a sharp pain in my neck. They took me to the hospital in an ambulance, and after the X-rays were done, the doctor told me that I'd broken my collarbone and that I'd have to stay "out of action" for at least five or six weeks.

Man! Talk about shit on a stick?! When I heard those words come out of that doctor's mouth, I felt like a dried-up turd that had just gotten squashed to smithereens under the wheels of a twenty-ton Mack truck.

Well, I guess I looked pretty fucked up, because when I got back to my room at Tropical, Tito and Simon tried every trick in the book to cheer me up and make me crack a smile.

"Congratulation, Joey," Tito said, "now you baptized."

"Baptized?"

"That's right," Simon chimed in, "A rider that ain't broke his collarbone at least once can't even call hisself a rider. *Shoot*, I musta broke mine 'bout four or five times already."

"For real?!"

"Why sho! That ain't no big thing, you'll be back in the saddle in no time."

Well, maybe is wasn't "no big thing" to Simon, but it sure was one hell of a big thing to me. Hell yeah! And it would've been even a *bigger* thing if Mom, or Grandma or Grandpa would've found out about it. I felt guilty about lying to them and keeping the whole thing a secret, but knowing how high-strung Mom and Grandma were, I figured the best thing for everybody concerned—'specially me—was to just keep it on the Q.T.—ya know, what I mean? 'Ey, why rock the boat, right? Everything had been going great until that stupid filly went bananas and fucked the whole shit up on me. So why say anything to Mom? All she was going to do was worry. And besides, the last thing I needed then was to hear her voice over the phone, screaming: "I told you so, I *told* you were gonna break your neck, *didn't I?*" Fuhgeddaboudit, that would've been a bigger pain-in-the-neck than breaking my neck in the first place—believe you me.

The days dragged by in slow motion—it felt more like six *months* instead of six *weeks*—but, little by little, everything worked out pretty much like Simon said it would. I was real down in the dumps for a while there—not being able to ride and all—but after I finally got out of that stupid sling and got back to work, I was singing "Back in the Saddle Again"—just like Gene Autry.

254

It took me a while to get the kinks out of my neck and get back into the swing of things, but Sam was real patient with me. He'd only let me jog horses for that first week back, but after I got my strength back and was in riding shape, he had me go back to galloping horses and breezing them.

Sometimes he'd send out me and Mongo to work some of the younger horses in sets. We'd never push or pump our horses to try and beat each other—that would've been stupid—but just having another horse and rider next to me gave me the feeling of competition, and that was exciting to a new guy like me. I was hoping that Mongo might start helping me out a little, seeing as how we were working horses together, but he pretty much kept his shit under the cap. I mean, he was friendly enough, and would goof around with me and make small talk and whatnot, but when it came to showing me some of the little tricks of the trade and stuff like that, I got the feeling he really didn't want to be bothered.

The person who really helped me with that stuff was Simon. We'd gotten to be good friends ever since we worked together that summer at Aqueduct, and after we spent the whole winter living together as bunkmates, we got even tighter. He became almost like a second grandfather to me, and let me tell ya, when it came to "hossbackin'", I couldn't have had a better teacher. He'd been on the backs of racehorses for more than fifty years, and just by explaining and demonstrating stuff to me, he taught me practically all the basics of "race riding". And after he'd observed me for a few months with his super-critical eye, he surprised the shit out of me one day and actually said I was doing "pretty good".

Well, those two little words, were really encouraging to me, 'specially coming from Simon; that old dude was stingier than Jack Benny when it came to giving out compliments.

"You're doin' pretty good," he said, "Just keep doin' what ya doin', and maybe by the fall you can start thinkin' about taking out your jock's license."

"You serious, Simon?"

"Sho I'm serious. All ya need is 'bout six more months or so. Then you're just gonna have to jump in the water and get your feet wet. It'll be sink or swim after that, so you better be ready."

So, I followed Simon's advice. I kept on doing what I was doing, and when the fall came, and after I had given it a lot of thought, I approached Sam with the idea. He pulled the guinea stinker out of his mouth, frowned, spit on the floor, thought about it for a second, and then he said: "Why not?"

Well, if Sam Cardone thought I was ready, I figured "what the fuck?", and I went down to the track office and picked up an application form.

After I filled out the papers, one of the stewards had to come out one morning to watch me break a horse from the gate, along with the starter. They do that with all the jockey applicants to make sure that the new rider can handle himself in the gate, and also to be sure that he's not going to be a danger to himself or the other riders. But that wasn't a big thing for me. Nope, once they saw me break out of there, one-two-three, nice and smooth, with no problem at all, they gave the OK, and in a few days, I had my license. I was now officially an apprentice jockey—better known as a "bug boy".

It sounds like a crazy name, but all it really means is that an apprentice rider gets a special weight allowance called "the bug", and that's why they call them bug boys. I heard that people started using the word "bug" because of the asterisk that appears next to the apprentice's name in the track program. I guess somebody, way back when, thought that the asterisk looked sort of like a fly, or a beetle, or some kind of insect or something, so they started calling the apprentices "bug boys". I never knew whether that story was true or not, but I'll tell ya one thing though: thank God for the "bug", that special weight allowance, because without that, an apprentice would probably *never* get a chance to ride.

See, at the beginning when an apprentice first starts riding and doesn't know his ass from his elbow—like me—they start you off by letting you carry ten pounds less weight than what you're really supposed to be carrying in a race. Then, after you've won five races, they make it seven pounds less, and after you've won thirty races, they lower it to five pounds off; and that's the way you stay for one complete year starting from the date of your thirty-fifth win. When that year is up, you're no longer an apprentice; you become a 'journeyman", and there's no more weight allowance after that.

256

The reason for the weight allowance was so that trainers would have a reason to give mounts to apprentices and help them get started—otherwise *nobody* would give you a horse to ride. Why should a trainer put a bug boy on his horse when he could have an experienced, veteran jockey ride his horse at the exact same weight? So that's why they invented the "bug system" to level out the playing field and give us young guys a way of getting our foot in the door.

And thank God they did, because I needed all the help I could get. I thought that once I had my license, Sam was going to be giving me a lot of horses to ride in the afternoon, but it didn't work out like that at all. Nope, I had my license for two whole months, and Sam hadn't given me not even one mount.

But that finally changed when we got back to Tropical Park for the winter season. It happened right away on the third day of the meeting, and when Sam told me he was going to put me on something and give me a shot, I practically *kissed* the ugly bastard. That was a really big day for me. I'd been working toward that moment for so long, and when I finally found myself inside the jock's room, putting on the silks, and rubbing elbows with all the big-time pros, fuhgeddaboudit, I had to pinch myself in the leg to see if I was dreaming or if it was really happening.

The horse I rode was Mister Big Shot. He was one of them "professional maidens" who'd run about fifteen times and still hadn't won his first race yet. But I guess Sam figured the ten-pound bug allowance might help him, so he put me on. Well, Mister Big Shot ran more like Mister Big *Shit* if you ask me; we beat only two horses in a field of twelve. But it was still real exciting though. Are you kidding? All I ever dreamed about since I was a little kid was riding in a real live horse race, and after I did it, I felt like I was floating on air.

I was so excited, I bought four programs that day: one to keep as a souvenir, one to send home to Mom, and Grandma and Grandpa, one for Ronnie, and, of course, one for Uncle Rocco. The program read: Mister Big Shot, owner—Albert Cerutti, trainer—Sam Cardone, odds—45 to 1, jockey—*Joseph Posella**! Wow! I never thought I'd see my name in a racing program next to the word "jockey", but there it was, in black and white: jockey—Joseph Posella*.

257

Well, now that I'd had the thrill of being in the jock's room, putting on the silks, bopping out into the paddock, and riding in my first race, the next thing on my agenda was to get into that winner's circle. Yep, just riding in a race wasn't good enough for me anymore—I wanted to win.

Sam was trying to help me as best he could, but the only horses he'd ever put me on were these hopeless longshots—and even those mounts were coming few and far between. I'd spent the entire winter season going from Tropical, to Hialeah, to Gulfstream, and in the whole four months, I don't think I'd ridden more than a dozen times. I came in fourth once on a lazy old mare named Gilly's Girl, but that was nothing to write home about—so I didn't.

But it wasn't Sam's fault. I knew he was under a lot of pressure to win races for his owners, and using some green, ten-pound, bug boy wasn't exactly in the game plan. That's when he told me about this friend of his, Ollie McClellan, who trained on the New England circuit and had a reputation for being good at developing young riders. Sam even told me that he was very important in developing Vinny Vaccaro and helping him get started. Well, as soon as I heard that, I decided it was time for me to make a move.

So, when the Gulfstream meeting ended, and everybody was packing up to head back to Belmont and Aqueduct, I'd already made arrangements through Sam to work for Ollie McClellan and try out the New England circuit. I knew that the quality of racing up there was nowhere *near* as good as in Florida or New York, but I figured: you gotta start someplace. And if plan-A don't work out, then you just gotta go with plan-B.

Before I went to Boston, I had to make a pit-stop in New York. I'd been away from home for a pretty long time, and I was dying to see everybody—'specially Ronnie. And when I saw her, I flipped. She sure wasn't "little Ronnie from downstairs" no more; she'd turned into a full-grown woman. Maybe a little *too* full grown if you ask me. I didn't know how or when it happened, but she was about three or four inches taller than me. But I didn't mind though. I mean, I felt a little stupid looking

258

up at her, but I really didn't care how tall she was; it was just great to see her again and hang out together. She seemed to be pretty happy to see me, and since she was already old enough to go out with a guy alone—Mr. Spinale finally gave in—me and her went out a few times. We went to the movies, went downtown to eat at Chinatown, had some pizza at Patsy's—and took a couple of nice long walks in Central Park too.

One day I even tried to make out with her under a big, flowering tree near the reservoir, but she turned her face away and said she thought it'd be better if we stayed "just friends". I felt real shitty and embarrassed for misreading the signals and thinking, like a shithead, that maybe she liked me in a boyfriend-girlfriend kind of way. Yeah, making that move and going for that kiss was one of the stupidest things I'd ever done in my whole life. I didn't know why I did it. Maybe I had a touch of spring fever or something...or maybe I just wanted to see what it would feel like to kiss a girl. But whatever the reason, it was dumb. Good thing Ronnie just kind of brushed it off and didn't make a big production out of it. I felt bad that she didn't feel the same way about me as I felt about her, but I still didn't want to lose her as a friend.

Anyway, while I was in New York, I decided to do something I'd been wanting to do for the longest time: I went downtown with the money I'd been saving and bought myself a pair of them special "corrective shoes". I had to go back to the place twice to get them though. The first time, after they measured the exact length of my L.L.D., I had to stick my feet in this gooey plaster to make a mold so that the shoes would fit me perfectly—just like a glove. I guess that's why they were so expensive because they were custom made and all. But let me tell ya, they sure were worth the money though. Hell yeah. I couldn't believe how I looked bopping around in those shoes; they cut down my limp by about fifty percent at least. I mean, you could still notice that I had a little dip when I'd walk, but, hey, at least I wasn't waddling around like a fuckin' duck no more—ya know what I mean?

Yeah, those shoes worked out fantastic. Too bad I couldn't ride in them or use them around the track or nothing. The thick platform on my right shoe was never going to fit through a stirrup iron; I would've had to get a special, custom-made stirrup to do that, and even if I could,

259

I still wouldn't have been able to use them anyway because of the weight. That right shoe alone must've weighed a good two pounds at least, and there was no way in hell I could carry extra weight like that. After all, I was a ten-pound bug boy, and I had to make weights like 103 or 102 all the time, so I had to forget about that idea fast. And besides, jockeys don't ride in shoes anyway; they ride in boots.

I would've *loved* to be able to wear them when I was riding though, because for me, the worst thing about the whole routine was duck-waddling into the paddock with all those hundreds of eyes on me. Forget it, I'd get so embarrassed I'd want to run back to the jock's room and hide. But, hey, what can ya do? You can't have everything, right? And even if I couldn't wear the shoes when I was riding, I was still happy just to *have* them.

I figured they'd come in real handy for special occasions and for going out 'n' stuff, and that's why I decided to splurge and buy myself a new suit too. It was still embarrassing as hell to go shopping for clothes—I always had to go to the boy's department to find something that'd fit me—but I was able to find something in a gray sharkskin, and I guess it looked okay.

Gee, too bad there wasn't enough time to wear my new suit and my new shoes on one of my little dates with Ronnie—'specially my new shoes. She would've been tickled pink to see me walking around almost like a regular person and everything. But since I had to leave right away, I figured I'd just have to surprise her next time.

So, with Grandpa's blessing, and after Mom and Grandma had cried, and sobbed, and heaped their usual twenty-five pounds of guilt on me for leaving home so soon, I packed up my stuff and headed down to Port Authority to catch a bus to Boston. Yep, look out Beantown, here I come.

Ya know, not for nothin', but I could never figure out what the big deal was about them Boston baked beans anyway? I'd tasted better beans at the automat for Chris'sakes—not to mention Grandma's delicious *pasta e fagioli*. Forget it, the only thing them Boston baked

260

beans were good for was gas. And them "Bostonians" had a funny way of talking too: "Paak ya caah in Haavud Yaad". Get the fuck outa here.

Anyway, Suffolk Downs wasn't no fancy racetrack like Belmont, or Hialeah, but it was okay. And after I met my new boss, Mr. McClellan, he turned out to be an okay kind of guy too. He came on a little strong at the beginning—all tough and big-and-bad—but after he'd scoped me out for a few days and saw that I knew my shit when it came to riding, he lightened up a little and started giving me a few breaks. Yeah! I couldn't believe it, I hadn't even cashed my first paycheck yet, and I'd already started riding a couple of horses in the afternoon. They were still the usual, sore-legged bums who didn't have a chance of winning, but I didn't care—I was happy just to be riding.

There was this one horse, a speedy filly named Wee Bonnie Lass, who ran pretty good for me the first time I rode her though. According to Mr. McClellan, she was a "habitual quitter", one of those horses that always goes to the lead, opens up, and then chucks it in the stretch. Well, from what I saw in the form, she'd been tiring and fading out when she'd been ridden by other jocks, but when *I* got on her, she didn't chuck it too bad for me. Nope, she held the lead all the way down to the sixteenth pole, and if it wasn't for that fast-closing, son-of-a-bitch that snuck up on me on the outside, she could've hung on for second money.

Mr. McClellan seemed happy with the way the filly ran, and he promised me he'd give me another shot on her next time around. I would've liked to think that she ran good because of my excellent riding ability, but I wasn't nobody's fool; I knew the ten-pound weight allowance had a lot to do with it. Are you kidding? That was the only reason Mr. McClellan had even *given* me the mount in the first place. He probably figured that if the filly carried ten pounds less, maybe she wouldn't run out of gas so fast and might hold on a little longer.

Well, I guess Mr. McClellan really knew what he was doing, because the next time I rode the filly, we lucked up and caught a sloppy, speed-favoring racetrack, and fuhgeddaboudit, she was long gone. I gunned her out of the gate, just like Mr. McClellan told me, and once she was out there winging on an easy, uncontested lead, she got so goddamn

261

brave, she forgot to stop 'til we'd already crossed the finish line three lengths in front.

I stood up in the irons and punched the sky with my fist. I'd finally won my first race. *Glory hallelujah!*

When I got back to the winner's circle, Mr. McClellan was waiting for me with a big smile on his mug. "Nice ride, Joey," he said.

I reached down and shook his hand, and then I smiled and patted Wee Bonnie Lass on the neck as the photographer snapped the picture.

Well, it had taken me almost six months to do it, but I was finally, and officially, a winner.

Chapter 20

Ever since I got that first win, everything started to fall in place for me. Within a couple of months, I'd already won the four more races I needed to go from a ten-pound bug to a seven-pound bug, and by the time the racing shifted over to Rhode Island for the Narragansett meeting, I was riding at least five or six horses a week. It might not sound like a lot, but to a guy like me who had been riding five or six horses a *month*, it felt like I was in the big time.

And the Narragansett meeting didn't turn out too bad for me neither. I won another seven or eight races down there, and when we moved up to the cool, green hills of New Hampshire for the Rockingham meeting, I felt like I was riding a hell of a lot better. With each race I was polishing up my skills and taking more and more of the stuff that Simon had taught me and putting it all into practice. That's because learning to be a jockey was kind of like learning to be a pilot; you could talk about it 'til the cows come home, but until you're sitting in that cockpit and the clouds are whizzing by, none of that blah-blah-blah meant shit. And when it came to race riding, it was the exact same thing: the only way to learn it was by doing it.

So that was my plan, and I was doing it, doing it, doing it, as much as I could—just like Simon said. I didn't care if my horse was 2-1 or 200-1, as long as the horse had four legs and a tail and could make it into the starting gate, that was good enough for me. That's because for an apprentice like me, even if you ran dead last on a horse, there was still something you could learn from each and every race you rode. And let me tell ya, little by little, just by practicing stuff over and over again, I was learning all the little tricks of the trade: like grabbing a handful of mane in the starting gate to help me keep my balance lunging out of there....or how to "rate" a horse and hold him back without strangling him or making him sulk....or how to "scoot 'n' boot" and scrub on a horse's neck so that my movements flow with the rhythm of his stride....or how to shift my weight in the saddle coming off the turns to get my horse to "change leads"....how to pull down my goggles on a sloppy track, one pair after the other, so I could actually see where the fuck I was going....how to gun a horse out of the gate and try to win wire to wire, "on the Bill Daley"....how to hold back a horse and make one run with him....how to shake the reins and "throw a cross"....how to pick up a horse and hold him together in the stretch when he's running out of gas and struggling to hang on....how to whip right-handed....how to whip left-handed....how to "switch sticks" and slip the whip from one hand to the other without dropping it or messing up my hand ride....how to "fan" a horse, by shaking the whip alongside his head so that it buzzes in his ear....how to "slap" a horse on his shoulder to get him to reach out when he's slowing down and shortening stride....how to pull him in when he's trying to bear out....how to pull him out when he's trying to lug in....how to warm him up before a race....how to pull him up after the race....how to keep him calm in the post parade.... Fuhgeddaboudit, I could've gone on from here to *doomsday*, and I still couldn't cover even *half* the shit I'd learned in only those first few months of riding. Yep, I might've been a "city boy" from New York, but let me tell ya, I'd learned a hell of a lot about riding in a hell of a short time.

But being a jockey was weird though, because you could learn every trick in the book, but if you didn't have no confidence, forget it, none of that shit was worth a plugged nickel. Nope, those horses were extremely sensitive, and without you even realizing it, they'd pick up on every little move you'd make, and every little thing you were feeling too. If *you* were scared and nervous, *they'd* get scared and nervous, and if *you* were steady and confident, *they'd* be steady and confident too. That's why the same horse would run different sometimes for two different jocks. I'd see it happen every day; I guess they feel your personality through your touch, or pick up your vibes or something like that—who the hell knows? But I definitely learned one thing for sure: confidence was the key. And it wasn't easy to come by neither. At the beginning, that confidence thing keeps slipping out of your grip and taunting you, but once you nail that sucker, it becomes your best friend—and your best weapon too. Yep, it was like having the keys to success right in the palm of your hand, because when you had confidence, you had everything.

Well, at least that's the way it was with *me* anyway. Once I got a little confidence in myself, and I wasn't shitting in my pants no more

264

during the running of a race, those horses started to move pretty good for me. I guess they must've felt the confidence flowing through my hands, or my legs, or something, because, all of a sudden, I had the magic touch. For real! I couldn't believe it! Without even knowing what I was doing half the time, or how I was doing it, I started bringing in all these big, fifty and sixty-to-one longshots, one after the other, like it was nothing. Square biz! I was shocking the shit out of everybody and their mother, *including myself*—and I was the guy who was *riding* those bums.

Well, as soon as I started bringing in them longshots, a whole bunch of those same trainers who wouldn't even give me the time of day when I first came around, started patting me on the back in the morning and giving me a couple of horses to ride in the afternoon. I even got myself an agent too, a guy named Carlo Trignano. Well, that was his real name, but everybody around the track called him either "Trigger", or "Trig" for short.

Me and Trigger were cool, and we hit it off right from the start. And not just because we were both Italian, but because we both put our cards on the table from the beginning, without any bullshit. Trigger wanted the usual twenty percent of my earnings, plus a one-year contract. I didn't mind the twenty percent, but I told him right from the jump that my dream had always been to ride the bug in New York, and I didn't want to get tied up with no contracts or nothing. He didn't like the idea at first, but when I explained that I was kid from Manhattan and all my family and friends were there, he seemed to understand, and we reached a "gentleman's agreement": Trigger would be my exclusive agent, but I'd be free to "walk" whenever I felt like I wanted to try my luck in New York.

So, with a handshake and a toast for good luck, me and Trigger became bug boy and agent. It was almost like a marriage, because a jockey and his agent had to work close together, just like a team, otherwise neither one of them would even get to first base. But me and Trigger were a good combination, like meatballs and spaghetti, and once he started to rustle up some live mounts for me—instead of the hopeless longshots I'd been riding—I started winning some races. Yep, by the time the Rockingham meeting ended, and we went back to

265

Suffolk for the last few months of the season, I was only *nine* winners away from earning my five-pound bug.

Trigger was happy to be back in Boston. He was a Boston boy, and he knew the place inside and out, like the palm of his hand. He drove me around and gave me the "royal tour" a couple of times, but on the weekends, he'd always take me to the North End, the Italian part of the city. Trigger was from an old-fashioned Italian family, like me, and he knew how important those lazy Sunday meals were to us guineas. So, on Sundays, he'd usually pick me up and take me to Benigno's, a great Italian restaurant, where the food was so good, sometimes I'd close my eyes and think I was eating Grandma's eggplant parmigiana right there at the kitchen table.

Boy, good thing I'd finally won those last few races I needed to go from a seven-pound bug to a five-pound bug. Those Sunday trips to Benigno's were starting to take their toll on my weight, and sometimes, when I'd get on the scale on Monday mornings, I'd have a fuckin' *heart attack*. That's why I was happy to have those extra two pounds to play around with. Hell yeah. There was nothing I hated more than getting into that hot box and sweating my ass off.

Anyway, me and Trigger hadn't done too bad at Suffolk, and when the season ended, we didn't think twice about packing up and following everybody down to the Fair Grounds. Yep, while the New York stables were all heading out to Florida or California, the "leaky roof" circuit from New England was making its way down to its own winter headquarters: "The Big Easy", New Orleans, Louisiana.

Trigger was excited about our chances down there.

"The bug always rides hot at Fair Grounds, Joey. All we gotta do is play our cards right, and we could come home with a barrelful of moolah."

"Ya think so?"

"I *know* so. Ever since I can remember, there's always been some bug boy that pops up out of the woodwork and wins everything in sight down there."

"Really?"

"Shit yeah! Ever hear of Eddie Oakley?"

"Of course."

"Well, he got his start at Fair Grounds and wound up being leading rider in '58 or '59, and with any kind of luck at all, maybe this year it could be us."

I watched as Trigger rubbed his palms together and smiled a big, greedy smile. But I didn't say peep; I just stuck out my index and pinky fingers and made the *malocchio* sign behind my back and mumbled: "from your mouth to God's ears".

Well, I guess God must've finally gotten around to cleaning the wax out of his ears with some heavy-duty Q-tips, because I think he heard every single one of Trigger's words. Yep, as soon as I got started at Fair Grounds, it was bim-bam-boom, winners, winners, winners. In only a couple of months, I'd become hotter than a whore's pussy on sailor day.

By the way, talking about pussy, New Orleans had to be the poon-tang capital of the United States of America. They had unbelievable broads down there, and each one was finer than the next. And let me tell ya, they didn't call it The Big *Easy* for nothing. Are you kidding? All you had to do was *look* at one of them babes down by the French Quarter, and they'd grab you by the hand and practically *drag* you into a hotel.

I got to see the bright lights for the first time with this cute, little mulatto chick I picked up at this place called "The Lucky Bear". That was the best-known place for pussy in New Orleans, and as the guys in the jock's room would say: "If you can't get lucky at The Lucky Bear, you can't get lucky no-damn-where!". And they weren't bullshitting neither; the entire place was nothing but wall-to-wall broads.

Anyway, that mulatto chick was really fine. She has this creamy, cinnamon-color skin, and an ass on her that belonged in a fuckin' *museum*—and her hair was silky smooth and soft. I didn't get a chance to really enjoy the shit the way I should have though. Naa, as soon as Mr. Johnson got his first taste of paradise, ba-da-boom!, he goes exploding his ass off, one-two-three, and before you knew it, the whole thing was over. I didn't know if he was a little too anxious for his own good, or just plain horny, but no matter how you sliced it, it was a blip. That's why I started trying out Trigger's trick: he said he'd do algebra

267

problems in his head while he was balling, to hold back his nut and enjoy the shit a little longer. Well, seeing how I was never very good at math, I just started thinking about whatever came into my mind—like who invented the scumbag. Yeah! I mean, everybody and their mother knows who invented the light bulb, and the telephone, and automobile, and the polio vaccine.... How come nobody knows who invented the scumbag? For real! Here's something that's controlling the population of the world, protecting people from diseases, changing the entire history of modern civilization, and nobody even knows who the fuck invented it.

Well, anyway, while my mind was busy contemplating the invention of the scumbag—and a lot of other crazy stuff I can't even remember no more—my johnson was busy having the time of his life, playing hide-the-salami with a whole bunch of broads. And since practice makes perfect, after I had a couple of nookies under my belt, I started stroking like a champ.

And I was *riding* like a champ too. In spite of a couple of real stupid mistakes, like getting dumped at the gate and spraining my ankle, and a five-day suspension I got for "careless riding", I was doing great. The meeting wasn't even half over, and I'd already won *thirty-six races*, and was almost tied with that veteran, Cajun jock, Greg Beauchamp, for the title of leading rider.

Ronnie was excited and proud once she found out how good I'd been doing. We'd always write to each other whenever I was away from home, and when I answered her last letter, I slipped in a copy of an article that they'd written about me in The Morning Telegraph. I figured she'd get a kick out of it. The title was, "Hot Apprentice Takes Fair Grounds by Storm", and it had my picture in it and everything. I made a few extra copies: one for my scrapbook, one for Mom, and Grandma and Grandpa, and one to send to Uncle Rocco too. Yep, it had taken me a few years to do it, but little by little, slowly but surely, I was putting the Posella name right up there on the map.

Ya know, it's funny how things happen, because that little write-up in The Morning Telegraph really changed my life. Only a few days after it came out, all of a sudden, completely out of nowhere, I got *the call*.

"Hello?"

"Is this Joseph Posella?"

"Yeah. Who's this?"

"How ya doin', Joe? My name's Max Bloom. I'm a jock's agent, and I'm callin' from New York."

Well, fuhgeddaboudit, as soon as I heard that, I started dancing around like a moolinyan on welfare who'd just hit the fuckin' number—I'm tellin' ya! But I didn't let none of my excitement slip into my voice though. I ain't *that* stupid. I answered the guy real cool, calm, and collected, and even though my hands were trembling, and my knees were knocking, I still played it off all blasé-blasé 'n' shit. "Oh yeah?" I answered, "What can I do for ya?"

Well, after this Max Bloom guy threw the small talk around for a few minutes, he finally cut to the chase. The guy wanted to know how much time I had left on the bug, and when I told him I was good until November 19th, he practically creamed in his pants.

"Really?" he said, trying to hide the excitement in his voice but not doing too good a job of it. "That means that you're gonna be only a week short of being able to ride the entire New York season as an apprentice. Ever think of ridin' in the Big Apple, kid?"

"Sure. But I never really got the opportunity before."

"What? You're under contract?"

"Who me? Naa, me and my agent just have an understanding—ya know, like a gentlemen's agreement 'n' stuff.

"Nothing in writing?"

"No."

"So? Why not take a shot at the big time? You only get to ride the bug once ya know. And let me tell ya, kid, with your talent and my connections, we could set New York on its *ear*. Whatta ya say?"

"Sounds great, but what's the deal?"

"Exclusive contract 'til you lose the bug, plus the usual twenny-five percent."

"Twenny five? I've only been payin' twenny over here."

"Hey, kid, we're talkin' about New York, the crème de la crème; I gotta take twenny five to cover my expenses."

"Well, I don't know. Let me think about it."

"Ya wanna think about? Think about it. But don't waste too much time thinkin'; they're already startin' to trickle in from Florida, and if I'm

269

gonna start hustlin' up mounts for you for the beginning of the meeting, I've gotta get started right away."

"Okay, Mr. Bloom, I'll try an...."

"Why so formal, Joey? Call me Max."

"Okay...Max. I'll get back to you as soon as I can. Thanks for callin', okay?"

"You bet, kid. Lookin' forward to hearin' from ya."

Well, I'd been waiting for a call like that for the longest time, and even after I got it, I *still* couldn't believe it. And I couldn't believe I actually played hard-to-get and pulled that "think it over" bullshit with that guy neither. Yeah. On second thought, maybe that was a stupid move; maybe I should've grabbed at the chance right away, before the whole thing slipped through my fingers and I wound up with shit. Hey, you know what they say about opportunity: that fickle, little bitch only knocks once, so you better answer the door fast, before she goes knocking on somebody else's door—ya know what I mean?

But, after thinking about it for a while, I realized I probably did the right thing. After all, Trigger had been real cool with me, almost like a big brother, and without him and all the success we'd been having those last few months, this Max Bloom guy wouldn't have known me from a hole in the wall. So, before I made any kind of move, the right thing to do was to sit down with Trigger and see how he felt about everything. I owed it to him.

I was feeling kind of scared that Trigger might fly off the handle when I told him about the call and the offer to ride in New York and everything. But I was wrong. He didn't even let me finish explaining; he just stuck out his hand and gave me a warm, friendly shake.

"Congratulations, Joey. Knock 'em dead."

Well, what can I say? That showed me the kind of guy Trigger was. He loved to make money as much as the next guy, but he knew he'd made a deal with me, and when I got my chance to grab for the gold ring, he wasn't about to stand in my way and welch on it. Nope, that was one thing you could say about Trigger: he was a real slick dude when it came to business, but he was always a man of his word—and he'd always been one hell of a friend too.

Talking about friends, I figured I should give Sam a call over at Tropical to see if he could give me the scoop on Max Bloom, before I got in too deep with him and signed a contract.

"Max Bloom called *you*?!"

"Yeah."

"Get outa here, Joey."

"For real! He called me the other day and says he wants to handle my book and help me ride the bug in New York and everything. What's the deal with this guy, anyway? Is he legit?"

"Joey, Max Bloom is one of the top agents in New York! If he wants to do somethin' with you, go for it. This guy's been around forever, and he's handled some of the best jocks in the business: Paulie Tompkinson, Rick Donato, Pat Degnan.... He even had a few bug boys too. Remember when Stevie Collins had the bug a couple of years ago and got red hot?"

"Yeah."

"Well, who do ya think his agent was?"

"Max?"

"You got it."

"Oh shit. But what kinda guy is he? Ya know, what's he like?"

"Well, he's short, he's fat, he's got an ugly-lookin' Jew mug, smokes cheap panatelas, dresses like a *cafone*...and he's a real pushy bastard."

"Pushy?"

"Yeah, but don't worry about that. That's good. When it comes to agents, the pushier the better."

"Thanks, Sam. You've given me a lot to think about."

"Well, don't think too long, Joey. He's powerful and very well-connected, and if anybody can help you squeeze the juice out of the bug, Max Bloom is the man."

Well, after I'd gotten the seal of approval from Sam, the only thing left to do was to talk to Grandpa about it. I knew he didn't know his ass from his elbow when it came to horses and racing, but he knew a lot about life and a hell of a lot about human nature and all kinds of shit. And besides, he was my Grandpa, and I never made any big decisions without consulting with him first. He was my *consigliere*.

The first thing Grandpa asked for was a description of this Max guy. I told him more or less what Sam had told me, and when I did, the thing

271

that caught Grandpa's attention was the fact that Max was Jewish. Grandpa knew about Jewish people because he'd spent more than half his life working alongside them in the garment district, and he knew what made them tick.

The first thing he explained to me was that, in their eyes, I wasn't a guy—I was a "goy"—and when push came to shove, or when I wasn't needed to help them make money anymore, I wouldn't get the same loyalty and respect that another Jew would get—I'd just be disposable.

"So, Grandpa, are you saying you don't think I should do business with this guy?"

"I no say to no do *bisinissa* with him. Most of the Jewish are very nice people, and very honest people too. What I say to you is to watch you step, keep you eyes and you ears open, all the time. No let you'self be *pidyatu pe' fesso*—no let him take you for a fool. Remember, with this kind of people, you gotta be *furbu*—like the fox. You undastand?"

"Yeah."

So, with Sam's seal of approval, and Grandpa's warning ringing in my ears, I found myself getting ready to call Max Bloom and tell him that I was ready to go for the deal. I still wasn't sure whether I was doing the right thing or not. After all, I *was* doing really good at Fair Grounds and on the New England circuit, and you know what they say: "A bird in the hand is worth two in the bush". But even though the shit was risky, I still couldn't pass up the chance. It was like a dream come true for me. I mean, maybe I'd become a star, or maybe I'd wind up falling flat on my face and making a stupid jackass out of myself. Who knew? But I was definitely sure about one thing though: I had to try. Because no matter how you slice it, the guy who's afraid to swing the bat, never hits a home run.

272

Chapter 21

When I got back to New York and met Max Bloom in person I really had to laugh; Sam's description had been right on the money. He *was* short (only a couple of inches taller than me),...he *was* fat (made Jackie Gleason look like Twiggy),...he *did* have an ugly mug (only I didn't know how "Jewish-looking" it was),...he smoked cheap panatelas (but they couldn't have been much cheaper that Sam's guinea stinkers),...he *definitely* dressed like a *cafone* (tacky, plaid sport jackets with striped ties),...and he *definitely* was a "pushy little bastard". The only thing Sam left out was that he had the personality of an *assbag*, otherwise he had him down to a T.

And Grandpa had him pegged pretty good too—'specially when he told me to watch my step with the guy. Yeah! Because instead of giving me a nice, simple-dimple contract, he came handing me a big, long, ten-page stack of papers all written in lawyer-talk. Well, seeing how I wasn't nobody's damn fool, I told him I couldn't sign anything until my lawyer looked it over first. Hey, I might've been a hungry young guy looking for a break, but I wasn't about to sign my soul away on the dotted line just for a chance to ride in New York. I wasn't stupid.

Anyway, as soon as I showed the contract to Mr. Villani (he did me the favor of looking it over), the first thing out of his mouth was that it was "obscene". He went over it with a fine-tooth comb, and when he was finished, he said there were a couple of clauses that "definitely had to go". One had something to do with "power of attorney" and the other one had to do with "life insurance". According to Mr. Villani, the "power of attorney" clause gave this Max Bloom guy complete legal control over me, and the "life insurance" clause would give him the right to take out a life insurance policy on me with him being the sole beneficiary. That meant that if I should break my neck and get killed before the contract ran out—or even *after* the contract ran out—he could still make money off me after I was dead by collecting on the policy.

Max Bloom didn't seem too thrilled with the idea of getting rid of his two favorite clauses, but I stood my ground. I told him that if the

273

power-of-attorney bullshit and that skeevy, life-insurance angle didn't go, the deal was off. Hey, I could've been cutting off my nose to spite my face, but at that point, I really didn't care. Nope, the way I felt about it, life was way too short to let some nervy prick play me for a damn fool over here. Fuck that shit.

Anyway, I guess I must've given Max some heavy-duty *agida*, because even though he hemmed and hawed, and bluffed and bullshitted for three long days, I just stuck to my guns and refused to budge. I guess when he finally realized that he was dealing with a complete stonehead, he figured he had no choice but to give in, remove the clauses, and close the deal. 'Ey, this guy might've been slicker that grease on glass, but he was dealing with a *Calabrese* over here, and when it comes to being stubborn, we make a mule look like a fuckin' diplomat.

So, with a sneaky little smirk on his face and his rat-bastard tail stuck deep between his ass cheeks, Max Bloom stuck out his hand, and we became jockey and agent. I guess I should've been happy and excited because it was such a big opportunity and all, but after all the slick shit he tried to pull, and the tug of war over the clauses, I was left with a really bad taste in my mouth—and a lot of regrets and second thoughts too. But I knew it was way too late; I was just going to have to lump it and hope for the best. As Simon would say: "Once the egg is fryin' in the skillet, there ain't no way to put it back in the shell."

Yeah, that struggle to close the deal was a big turn-off, but the thing that *really* turned my stomach was the way he tried to turn on the sugar faucet afterwards and be all buddy-buddy and palsy-walsy with me— like nothing had ever happened. Well, maybe that phony bullshit worked with some of the other guys he'd dealt with, but it sure as hell wasn't going to work with me. Are you kidding? Hell would have to *freeze* before that creep would ever be *my* friend. Forget about *that* shit, when it came to me and Max...it was strictly business.

Well, maybe Max was a little weak in the personality department, but when it came to taking care of business and getting me horses to ride, he definitely had his shit together. On opening day alone, without anybody knowing me at all, he somehow managed to con four trainers into giving me mounts. 'Ey, I had to hand it to the guy—he hustled.

274

So, there I was, bopping into the walking ring at the Big A, shitting bricks and sweating bullets all at the same time. Not only because I was "the new kid on the block" in a jock's room full of big-name pros, but also because I was a new face to the fans too. And some of those horseplayers could be downright cruel sometimes—'specially when they lose—and I was worried that some asshole might make a crack about my limp and embarrass me in front of everybody.

See, at the beginning when I started riding in New England, no one even noticed me, but once I got hot at Fair Grounds, I started catching a whole lot of shit from some of them redneck sore losers. I got called everything in the book, from a "cripple-ass, wop mothafucka" to a "lame, dago bastard", and everything in between too. And let me tell ya, it hurt. That's why I was so nervous about walking into that big, sunken paddock at Aqueduct for the first time. I was hoping for the best...but bracing myself for the worst.

I was really uptight, but once I spotted Uncle Rocco, Mom, and Grandma and Grandpa in the crowd, waving at me and calling out my name, all my fear disappeared, and I felt like a million bucks. It was like I was in the middle of a dream—only it was real—because there I was, sitting on top of a racehorse in the middle of the walking ring at the Big A with my whole family cheering me on.

Gee, too bad Ronnie couldn't make it. She said she had a big exam at school and couldn't take off, but she called me the night before to wish me luck though. I figured she was probably real busy after she got accepted into the "pre-med" program at City College, and I couldn't have been happier for her. Becoming a doctor or a nurse was always Ronnie's dream, and little by little, she was going after it—just like me with the horses.

I wish I could've given my family the thrill of seeing me in the winner's circle, but I didn't have any luck that day. I came in the money twice out of three tries—close, but no cigar—but nobody seemed to mind though. Uncle Rocco was proud as a peacock, and every time he'd see me in the paddock, he'd give me the hi-sign and yell out: "Go get 'em, Joon!" And forget about, Mom and Grandma, whenever they'd spot me, they'd start jumping up and down, waving, and blowing double-barreled kisses at me—like two teeny-girls who'd just seen the Beatles.

275

But the coolest of the whole family was Grandpa. He didn't call out to me or jump around and wave like Mom and Grandma. That wasn't Grandpa's style. He'd just wait for me to pass right in front of him, and then, when he'd catch my eye, he'd give me a wink and a nod, and a great big smile.

When I started at Aqueduct, I had almost all my bases covered: I had an agent backing me up and getting me mounts, and I had my family in my corner, cheering me on too. The only thing that was missing was a valet. Every jock has a valet, someone to take care of their equipment, get their silks ready, and also to help with the saddling of the horses. This guy called Kevin had been "doubling up" and giving me a helping hand—just until I could find someone—but I needed to find my own guy as soon as possible.

Well, sometimes the answer to your problems could be right under your nose, and you don't even know it. That was what happened one morning when I went to Sam's barn to work a horse for him. As usual, I hung around for a little while, catching up with Sam, and checking out Tito and the guys. But when I asked for Simon, Sam told me that he'd quit.

"What happened, Sam?" I asked, "You and Simon had a fight or something?"

"No, Joey, no fight. He just felt he couldn't do the work no more. His arthritis was bothering him pretty bad when we were in Florida, and once we got to New York, it got worse."

"Really?"

"Yeah, poor guy, it probably gets affected by the cold, or the dampness in the air or something. Either that, or maybe he's just getting too old for this type of strenuous work."

"Well, what happened, he just split? No phone number, no address, no nothin'?"

"No, he doesn't have a phone. But he's living with his sister in Brooklyn—Bushwick I think. Hold on, I'll get you the address."

Well, with Simon's address in hand, I hopped on the train one day, and went out to see him. I was a man with a plan. Whether it was going

276

to work or not, was something else, but I thought it was worth a shot though. I knew Simon was probably miserable being away from the track, just moping around the house doing nothing, so my plan was to ask him if he wanted to help me out in the jock's room. I really didn't care that much about him actually being able to do all the work of a valet—Kevin told me he'd pick up the slack if necessary—I just missed the ol' coot, and I thought the valet thing was as good as excuse as any for us to be together again.

It took me a while to get up the courage to pop the question—I was worried he might get offended or something—and when I did, I pretty much got the answer I expected.

"Aw, shucks, Joey," he said, rubbing his hands and holding them up for me to see them. "I'd love to help ya, but my hands keep crampin' up on me all the time now. I don't know if I'd be able to handle the silks— let alone polish boots and take care of saddles and such?"

Right away I whipped out a bottle of "Esquire, self-shining liquid wax", and I held it up right in front of the old man's face. "I had a feeling you were gonna come out with somethin' like that. I'm way ahead of ya."

Simon took one look at the bottle of liquid shoe polish and cracked up. And then, after we both finished laughing, I knew I not only had a valet, but I had myself a teacher, an advisor, and one hell of a friend.

Boy, good thing I had Simon with me in that jock's room; I was nervous as hell in there. Every time I'd turn my head, I'd find myself surrounded by some of the best jockeys in the business. And let me tell ya, to a young, bug boy like me, that could get scary sometimes. That's because some of the same guys I was sharing a locker room with, or shooting pool or playing ping-pong with, were my *idols*. For real! I'm talking about guys like Sidney Brookhouse, Bill Dorman, Rick Donato, Johnny Mullane, Ron Lutz, Freddie Oakley, that hot Canadian jock, Tom Roquette—not to mention the guy who practically *owned* Aqueduct: Ray Mallory, the man who used "Mallory's alley" to win race after race. And if that wasn't enough, then you had all the great Latin jocks too, like: Candido Carrera, that serious, Inca-looking rider,...Benito Sanchez, the guy that had a great touch with fillies,...Ruben Otero, the young Puerto Rican dude who rode just like his idol, Vinny Vaccaro,...Ruben's

277

"compadre", Jaime Hernandez,...and that other Panamanian jock that always wore his helmet cocked to the side like a pimp, Samuel Peraza. And on top of all that, you had the South American crew: Heriberto Ramirez and Reynaldo Sosa from Chile, and Dario Medina form Peru. Fuhgeddaboudit, I felt like I was the water boy for the Green Bay Packers over here!

Me and this other guy, Edwin Nazario were the only two bug boys in the place, and if it hadn't been for a newly arrived jock from Puerto Rico, Jose Laracuenta, and a French guy, Jean Vuillard, me and Edwin would've felt like the two lowest dingleberries on the totem pole.

And that was only the local crew, because on Saturdays some of the big guns from the west coast would blow into town to ride in some of them big stakes races. I'm talking about guys like Ramon Garay, Denny LaFarge, and Bob "the Watch" Watchmaker.

Boy, I'll never forget the day when I first met Watchmaker. It was only my second week in the jock's room, and there he was, only a few feet away from me, rubbing some Ben-Gay on his knee. Hey, I'm talking about one of the all-time greats over here. And he wasn't called "the Watch" for nothing. Nope, he was such a good judge of pace, they'd say he had a fuckin' *stopwatch* buried inside his brain. But the thing I liked best about him, was his light touch and his gentle approach. He'd never try to bogart a horse or muscle a horse; he'd just sweet-talk them, pat them on the neck, hum to them, keeping them nice and calm and relaxed, so they could save every last ounce of energy for the final stages of the race. Yeah, that Watchmaker sure was one hell of a rider alright—a living legend.

It took me a while to get up the courage to approach him, but when I did, he turned out to be a really nice guy.

"Uh, Mr. Watchmaker," I said, inching a little closer to him, "my name is..."

"Bob, call me Bob."

"Okay...Bob...uh... My name is Joe Posella, and I was...wondering... What kind of advice would you give to a young guy like me—ya know, somebody who's just startin' out?"

He smiled and scratched his cheek, and then he said: "Well, I could tell ya two things: number one, horses are like snowflakes; there's no two of them the same. And number two, save your money and don't

278

spend it, 'cause when you lose that bug, the whole house of cards is gonna come crashin' down on top of you."

I wasn't so sure I understood that first thing about the snowflakes and whatnot, but Bobby the Watch hadn't been the only guy to warn me about that second thing though. Nope, ever since I first walked into the jock's room, all I'd be hearing was: "Save for a rainy day", "Don't go crazy spendin' your money", "Be stingy", "Put something aside for when you lose the bug"....

Fuhgeddaboudit, I hadn't even *made* the money yet, and everybody and their mother was already telling me how to *spend* it. Yeesh! Give a kid a break for Chris'sakes.

But I knew their intentions were good. I figured it was the voice of experience talking, so when I decided to take my ass off the subway and get some wheels, I didn't go splurging like crazy. I wound up buying a used T-bird. It was a couple of years old, but it was in pretty good condition inside and out, and it would get me where I'd want to go.

Anyway, the advice about saving money wasn't the only thing I learned from those veteran riders. I'd watch every little move they'd make, inside the jock's room, out on the track, in the post parade, in the gate, during the running of a race... Forget it, I was like a walking sponge over here.

Most of the guys were nice to me, and they'd point out my mistakes and give me tips and pointers every now and then, but there were a couple of real scumbags in the joint too. And as usual, it's always your own people, the *paesans,* who'd treat you the worst. I'm talking about guys like Chuck Sabatino, Rick Donato, and that real scuzzball, Skip Fusillo. Those creeps didn't even want to be bothered saying hello, let alone taking a minute or two to help a young guy out. Naa, those bastards were nothing but a bunch of conceited assholes, and as the days went by, I found myself hanging out more with the Latin jocks— 'specially that new guy from Puerto Rico, Jose Laracuenta.

Since Jose means Joseph in Spanish and we almost had the same name, this guy would call me "Tocayo" all the time. (That's the special word they got in Spanish for someone who shares a name with you.) And instead of me calling him Jose, he told me to call him by his nickname: "Cheo". He didn't speak English that good, but he was a nice guy, and little by little, we'd become pretty good friends. I guess it was

279

because we were both new and were kind of on the outside looking in— ya know what I mean? But for whatever reason, it felt good to have a buddy and somebody to talk to and pal around with—besides Simon.

But the friendship between me and Cheo, Italian with Spanish, was more of the exception than the rule, because from what I'd been observing, the whole jock's room was divided into these little clicks. In fact, it reminded me a lot of the lunchroom in high school: Spanish with Spanish, Irish with Irish, Italian with Italian, country boys with country boys, old-timers with old-timers. That's pretty much the way it was. And those little clicks of friends would help each other out sometimes too. I mean, on the racetrack it was usually every man for himself, but there were times when a couple of guys would work together to box in a heavy favorite to make a score and win a bet. And there were times when some guy might even kamikaze his own horse and go on a suicide mission, just to trap the heavy favorite into a speed duel in order to tire him out and get him out of the money. But everything was hush-hush and strictly on the QT, and the only way you'd even pick up on stuff like that, was if you had your antennas out, or by eavesdropping, or by observing and watching shit out of the corner of your eye.

I wouldn't say there was a *lot* of betting going on, but there was some though; and it was mostly the older, over-the hill jockeys, who were involved in it. Yeah, that jock's room sure wasn't no Sunday school, and I was only a bug boy, an outsider; I didn't know *half* the shit that was going on.

But the thing that turned me off the most was all the "flipping". Yeah! Practically every time I'd go into the bathroom to take a leak, I'd usually hear the sound of some guy sticking his fingers down his throat and gagging himself to throw up. That was something that was very common in all the jock's rooms I'd been in. See, some of the guys— 'specially the ones who have a weight problem—use the ol' finger trick, to bring up whatever they've eaten so that it doesn't stay in their stomach and make them go up in weight. Nobody likes to throw up, but nobody likes to suffer heavy-duty hunger pangs neither. That's why a lot of guys would rather eat and vomit, than not eat at all—and *starve*. I guess the word "vomiting" sounded kind of gross, so the jockeys made up a nicer-sounding word for it; they call it "flipping". But whether you

280

call it "flipping", or "vomiting", or "heaving", or "puking, or "barfing, or whatever, it's still the same shit on a different plate.

Anyway, even though I'd never had a weight problem, I'd still have to watch my weight and watch what I'd eat as much as the next guy. Only difference was, I had my own little trick. See, whenever I got tired of eating lettuce, and vegetables, and salads 'n' stuff, and I had a bad craving to eat something delicious and fattening—like a piece of chocolate cake or a big bag of potato chips—I'd never pull the scarf-and-barf routine. Nope, I'd just take big bite of whatever I felt like eating, roll it around in my mouth, chew it, enjoy all the taste of it and everything, but instead of swallowing it, I'd just spit it out. I got the idea from these gourmet, wine-taster guys I saw on television one time. They'd taste glass after glass of wine, but instead of swallowing it, they'd just swish it around in their mouths, and then spit it out into a fancy, gold bucket. Well, as soon as I saw that, I figured if those hotsy-totsy, gourmet guys, could do it right there on TV, why couldn't I? So, that became my own secret trick, and while the other jockeys were busy scarfing and barfing, I was having a ball, "grittin' 'n' spittin'".

The other thing the jocks would use to keep their weight down was the "hot box". That's when you'd shut yourself up in a "human oven" or one of them sauna things to sweat your ass off—'specially if you were a few pounds over and you had to make weight. I tried it couple of times after I'd overdone it at Benigno's in Boston, but I couldn't take it. The high heat would make me feel dizzy and I'd get panicky, not to mention the way it would zap all the strength out of me and leave me feeling like a total douchebag. Later for that shit.

Anyway, starving, and flipping, and taking laxatives, and sweating in the box, weren't the only things those guys would do to keep their weight down. I wasn't a hundred percent sure or nothing, but I had this pretty strong feeling that some of them were taking drugs too. There was a little click of Latin Jocks over in the corner of the room, and they'd always be whispering to each other, real secretive, and saying stuff in Spanish like: "Tiene algo?" or "Necesita algo?" or "Quiere algo?"—ya know, shit like that. I didn't know too much about that stuff, but you didn't have to be a drug expert to figure out what was going on over there. All you had to do was observe. Because one minute you'd see these guys slouched in the corner, looking like douchebags from

281

starving themselves and from shitting and flipping all the time, and then, five minutes later, after they'd come back from the bathroom, ba-da-bing!, all of a sudden, they'd be bouncing around the room, playing ping-pong, fooling around, and gabbing their asses off with a big fuckin' smile on their mugs. Get the fuck outa here. 'Ey, I wasn't born yesterday—ya know what I mean?

Yeah, there was definitely something going on alright. At first I thought they were taking "ups"—ya know, pills—but my friend Cheo told me it was something else. He said they were probably using "perico". (That's the Spanish word for cocaine.) I'd never seen it before, but Cheo explained that it was this white stuff that looked like talcum powder or flour or something, and the guys would take it by snorting it up their noses. Yiiicchhh, that sounded kind of gross if you ask me, but Cheo said a lot of them like it because it gives you a quick jolt of energy, and it kills your appetite and helps you control your weight too.

Well, I wasn't about to mention any names or nothing, but I was pretty sure I knew who the ringleader of that little "perico" click was. I'd seen him over in the parking lot a few times, talking all hush-hush with these two chocolate-colored skeletons that looked exactly like Heckle and Jeckle—ya know, the cartoon characters, the two blackbirds that look just like twins. Anyway, "Heckle and Jeckle" and this jockey would always be blabbing away in Spanish, and even though I couldn't understand what they were saying, the whole thing looked suspicious. I'd always see them looking around and casing out the parking lot, real sneaky-like, and then, when they thought nobody was looking, all three of them would pile into this jock's Caddy, and they'd just hang out in there, doing God-knows-what.

'Ey, I'd be the first one to admit that I didn't know shit from Shinola when it came to drugs and stuff like that. But from what I knew about the street, I'd bet anything that all the "perico" that was floating around the jock's room, was all coming from the exact same place: Heckle and Jeckle.

Well, from the very beginning, my motto was always: see no evil, hear no evil, and speak no evil. I wasn't in the jock's room to be no cop, I wasn't in there to be no nosybody, and I wasn't there to be worrying about what this guy and that guy were doing over in the corner. I was there to concentrate on only one thing: winning races. And if those

282

other jocks wanted to fuck themselves up by puking their guts out and taking drugs all the time, that was their business—not mine.

Chapter 22

When May rolled around, I didn't get a chance to live my dream and ride at Belmont. They'd torn down the grandstand a couple of years ago, and the while the place was under reconstruction, we stayed at Aqueduct and ran the Belmont meeting there. But I guess Aqueduct was just as good. And it was, because as we moved into the final week of the long, spring/summer meeting, I'd already won fifty-three races in four months, and was ranked sixth in the jockey standings.

The other bug boy, Edwin Nazario, hadn't really impressed too many people, so whenever a trainer wanted those all-important five pounds off, he'd usually call Max and give the mount to me. And business was booming; I'd usually ride about five or six horses a day. Yep, with a little bit of luck and a lot of hard work, the team of Max Bloom and Joey Posella had been turning quite a few heads; I'd become New York's leading apprentice, the hot new bug boy.

The fans even gave me a nickname too: "JoJo". It's funny how the whole thing got started. One day, as we were passing the grandstand side of the walking ring, this loud, Jamaican dude in a big, bubbly cap, started yelling at me at the top of his lungs: *"Come on, JoJo! Gotta win wit' dis blood clod! Bring 'im in, mon! Bring 'im in, JoJo!"*. Well, as luck would have it, I happened to win with that horse—and at a big, juicy price too. So that's when that same guy and all his Jamaican buddies kept on with the "JoJo" this, and the "JoJo" that, 'til before you knew it, it spread around the track, and everybody and their mother started calling me "JoJo". I wasn't too thrilled with the name—I thought it sounded a little doofy—but I felt kind of proud that the fans had actually come up with a nickname for me. I guess it probably meant that I was starting to get noticed, because all the top riders had nicknames—and now I had mine.

At first, I felt a little funny about my new nickname, but after a while, it grew on me. It was a hell of a lot better than "Shrimpy Gimp", and it definitely boosted my ego and gave me a lot more confidence too. And with only a few more days left to go at Aqueduct, I felt like I had the world by the tail. Hell yeah. Everything was going great for me: Max was getting me live mounts, I was winning races at a steady clip, I was making money, the fans were cheering and yelling "JoJo" all the time, and I was finally getting accepted in the jock's room and getting treated like one of the guys. Fugeddaboudit, things couldn't have been going any better. And then, for the cherry on the ice-cream sundae, after all the years of dreaming about the place and always getting left behind, I was finally going to get my chance to check out the crème de la crème, the big-time of the big-time: Saratoga.

Well, from the moment I set foot in that town, I felt like the curtain was going up on the best four weeks of my entire life. I loved everything about the place: from the tall, leafy elm trees that line the streets and make everything cool and shady, to the clean, fresh mountain air that fills your lungs with summer and makes you feel glad to be alive. Yeah, Saratoga Springs sure was the place to be in August alright. And let me tell ya, after sweating through July at hot, muggy Aqueduct, I felt like I died and went to heaven.

I could never figure out what was so wonderful about that stupid mineral water—it tasted like piss if you ask me—but outside of that, Saratoga was definitely the most beautiful track I'd ever seen—'specially the backside. I'd seen a lot of pictures of it, but to actually be there was something else. Sometimes the shit was so fuckin' gorgeous, I'd just have to stop what I was doing, look around, take a deep breath, and say "wow!". It even made me wish I hadn't been so quick to give up drawing and painting, 'cause let me tell ya, that place was an artist's paradise. Hell yeah! Every time I'd turn my head, I'd see one beautiful scene after the other: the rising sun burning through the mist over by the Oklahoma training track,…the hotwalkers cooling out hots in the shade of the big, tall trees,…the steam rising from the backs of horses as their grooms sponged them down in the cool, morning air,…sets of frisky two-year-olds jogging through the long, blue shadows at Horse Haven,…exercise boys guiding their mounts across Union Avenue to test them for speed on the famous main track, "The Graveyard of Favorites",…the smell of the pines, the chirping of the birds…. Forget it, I'd seen the backsides of some nice racetracks—Belmont, Hialeah, Fair

285

Grounds—but I'd never seen nothing that could stack up to Saratoga though—at least not for beauty anyway. Nope, when it came to that, the "Spa" was in a class all by itself.

The only thing I wasn't crazy about was the layout of the joint. Now don't get me wrong, the thing about saddling the horses under the trees, right in front of the people, was a cool idea, but the thing that would bug me was the long walk we'd have to take before every race, from the jockey house, through the crowd, all the way to the walking ring at the other end of the paddock. Sometimes it would be fun because kids would run up to you and ask you to sign their programs— can you imagine *me* giving out *autographs?*—but most of the time it was a big, pain-in-the-ass. Yeah, every time I'd have to hike through the crowd, I'd feel like everybody in the place was following me with their eyes and pointing at me, whispering behind their programs and making comments about the way I walk 'n' stuff. But, hey, what could I do? I'd just have to take the bad with the good—ya know what I mean? I was happy just to *be* there, so if I had to feel self-conscious and uncomfortable getting to the paddock, I figured it was a small price to pay.

Anyway, in spite of the fact that bug boys usually don't do too good at Saratoga—the fancy, old-money stables up there "prefer" to use more "experienced" riders on their horses—I hadn't been doing too bad. I'd won eleven races, and let me tell ya, if it hadn't been for that nasty spill I took, the whole month would've been straight out of a storybook.

It happened on a sloppy racetrack, just as we were approaching the quarter pole. My horse has shown a little speed earlier in the race, but by the time we hit the turn, he'd thrown in the towel and was dropping back. That turned out to be a bad thing for me, because all of a sudden, out of nowhere, this horse that was moving up the rail under Bill Dorman, stumbled and went down. The jock in front of me tried to swerve to avoid him, but his horse went down too. I only had a spit-second to react and to try and steer my horse out of the way, but there wasn't enough time. My horse tried to jump over the fallen horses and riders, but his legs got tangled up, and *whap!* he fell down too, throwing me face-first into the gray Saratoga mud. I was lucky nobody was behind

286

me; that was what saved my ass. I mean, I still got banged-up and bruised, but seeing as how I didn't get stomped on by no oncoming horses, I was able to wipe the mud off my face and walk away from that shit. But the other two jocks weren't that lucky though. Reynaldo Sosa, the guy who'd gone down in front of me, got up holding his wrist like it was broke or something, and the other guy, Bill Dorman, the jock whose horse had started the whole chain reaction, wasn't able to get up at all. He was taken away unconscious on a stretcher, and from what I could see before they sped him off in the ambulance, he looked like he was hurt *bad*.

I felt real shitty about the whole thing—'specially since my horse was one of the two that had trampled the guy—but when I got back to the jock's room, everybody was rubbing me on the back and telling me not to worry about it or beat myself up over it. And they were probably right too. At first, I tortured myself with that shoulda-woulda-coulda crap, but after a while, I realized that wasn't going to accomplish nothing—except to drive me fuckin' nuts. I had only a tenth of a second to react, and there was nothing I could've done anyway. That horse on the inside just took a bad step and broke down; that was all there was to it. Those were just the fucked-up breaks of the game—what can I tell ya?

But I learned something though. I finally found out what that thing was, that glue, that bond, that binds all of us jocks together like brothers—even though we're always competing against each other out there on the racetrack. It's the same thing we deal with every day, the same thing that makes some guys cross themselves when they're out there riding: the danger of it all.

I was left feeling kind of sore and shook up, so I told Max to cancel my next-day's mounts. He only had me booked on two horses anyway; and seeing as how it was the last day of the meeting, I figured I'd get an early start and beat the rush back to New York. Besides, I knew Mom and Grandma were probably still upset about the spill. I'd called right away to let them know I was okay, but knowing them, they weren't going to stop worrying 'til they saw me walk in the door with their own eyes, safe and sound.

287

Ever since I'd hit Yonkers on the Thruway, I started to hear a weird, clicking sound coming from my engine. I wasn't able to stop and check it out on the highway, but once I got to the block and parked in front of the house, I popped the hood to take a look. Holy shit! No wonder that shit was clanking like crazy; I hardly had no oil! I guess I must've had a leak or something, because I'd checked the oil only a few days before, and it was fine.

Anyway, while I was still checking stuff out under the hood, all of a sudden, a black Caddy pulled up alongside me, and when I turned to look, I saw a familiar-looking old man easing his way out of the passenger seat. I recognized him right away, not so much from his trademark hat with the brim turned up all the way around, but from his gigantic nose. It was Carmine *"U Nasu"*, the guy everyone in the neighborhood called "The Nose".

Nobody would dare call him that to his face though; The Nose was a big-time Mob boss, and everybody and their mother was scared shit of him. I'd heard that his last name was Stigliano or Stigliani or something, but nobody really knew anyway. Those Mob guys avoided last names like the plague; that's why they were always called by their nicknames or by the first letter of their last names—like "Vinnie Bee" or "Tony Cee" 'n' stuff like that. I guess they figured the less people knew about them, the less likely the chances of getting themselves fingered to the bulls. And a lot of them didn't like calling attention to themselves by wearing fancy clothes and jewelry 'n' stuff—'specially somebody like The Nose. He'd dress plain and simple, and if you didn't know who you were looking at, you'd probably think he was some ordinary old man from the neighborhood.

But you didn't have to be a genius to figure out that The Nose wasn't just some ordinary guy from the neighborhood. All you had to do was open your eyes, observe, and read between the lines, and then everything became crystal clear. I remember one time I saw him coming out of Russo's restaurant around the corner on Pleasant Avenue. He was strolling along and talking with one of them big-shot wiseguys in a fancy silk suit, when all of a sudden, he stopped dead in his tracks, threw his foot on the bumper of a parked car, and without even breaking his conversation or even looking at anybody, *boom!*, three of his boys came running and tripping over each other to tie his fuckin' shoelace. What

288

can I say? The Nose might've dressed like some ordinary guy from the neighborhood, but he definitely wasn't no regular joe.

Anyway, I used to see him around the block all the time when I was growing up, but once I started riding in New York, I started seeing him even more than when I lived right across the street. I guess the guy must've been a really big racing fan, because before we went up to Saratoga, I'd see him and his cronies almost every day at Aqueduct, hunched over the railing on the clubhouse side of the paddock, checking out the horses as we'd circle the walking ring. I'd usually watch him out of the corner of my eye as I'd ride by, but I'd never look him square in the face or make any kind of eye contact with him. I'd heard too many stories about The Nose, and I wasn't about to make him feel uptight or get myself in any kind of hot water by letting him catch me staring. I wasn't *that* stupid. But he'd always look at me though—I'd snagged him doing it a whole bunch of times—and while I was fiddling around under the hood of my car, I couldn't believe Carmine the Nose was standing right next to me.

He was only about two feet away, and he kept staring at me and scratching his forehead. I guess I should've been a little shocked or surprised, but for some reason I wasn't.

"'Ey, kid," he said, nailing me with his cold, beady eyes, "where do I know you from?"

I slid the dipstick back into the crankcase and looked up. "I don't know, around I guess."

He kept looking at me for a few more seconds, but when he couldn't place me, he shrugged and walked away. I thought I was home-free, when all of a sudden, I heard his voice again coming from over my shoulder.

"The track!" he said, turning around slowly and pointing his crooked finger at me. "That's where I know you from. You're that bug boy,...that Posella kid,...the one they call 'JoJo'."

I blushed a little, feeling kind of flattered that a big provolone like The Nose would actually recognize somebody like me. But before I could open my mouth to say anything, he'd already turned his back on me and was calling over his driver/bodyguard.

"'Ey, Nino, *veni ca*. Look who we got here, that Posella kid, the jockey."

289

A big, stocky guy with a twenty-inch neck walked over and studied my mug as he picked something out of his teeth with a matchbook cover. "Get outa here, Carmine, that ain't him."

"Whatta ya mean 'it ain't him'? I'm tellin' ya, it's him!

The Nose waved him away and then turned to me. "'Ey, kid, what's ya name?"

"Posella," I answered, sticking out my hand to shake. "Joey Posella, nice to me...."

"See?!" he said, spinning around and leaving me hanging. "I told ya it was him; I never forget a face."

This Nino guy didn't answer; he just shrugged his shoulders and grinned—like he just got snagged in the act of being dingleberry.

"C'mon, kid," he said, nodding over at the social club, "come inside and have a cup of coffee."

"Well, uh...I'm working on my car over here and I...."

"That can wait. C'mon, we can talk about the horses. Maybe you can give me some tips."

I tried to take a polite excuse—real diplo-diplo, like Grandpa had taught me—but since this guy wasn't going for it, I had no excuse but to swallow the lump in my throat, sneak a quick look up at the living-room window, and follow him inside. Thank God Grandpa wasn't looking out the window at that moment—that's all I can say—otherwise he would've had a heart attack.

The inside of the place looked pretty much as I expected: dark, quiet, some card tables, a shiny espresso machine, an American flag, a big map of Sicily on the wall, plus a couple of winner's-circle photos from the racetrack—which surprised me a little.

I was led to a small table in the back, and The Nose ordered "two coffees" from a young guy wearing an apron.

"So," he said, "I hope you know you cost me two large with that shitty ride you gave Shirley's Pet the other day. Remember that race?"

I felt the blood drain right out of my face and my insides turn to jelly. "Yeah, I remember. But if that hole along the rail hadn't closed up on me, I could've won going away."

"If" he growled, pulling out a cigarette. "If my aunt had balls, she'd be my uncle. What are ya talkin' about 'if'."

290

I squirmed in my seat and looked down at my hands. "Gee, I'm sorry Mr. Carmine, if ya lost money on me...but sometimes ya take a chance in a race, and things just don't work out the way you expect 'em to—ya know what I mean?"

The Nose leaned back on his chair and chuckled as the guy with the apron came back and served us two little cups of espresso. "Relax, kid, I'm only breakin' ya balls a little. Ya might've looked like a crock of shit on Shirley's Pet, but you sure looked like a million bucks when you brought in Bold Dynasty...and Crafty Marilyn...and Cardone's horse, that gray filly. What's 'er name? Ball of something..."

"Twine. Ball of Twine."

"That's it. Ball of Twine. That's the name."

"Ya know, not for nothin'" he continued, leaning over the table like he was telling me a big secret. "but that was one helluva score. That filly paid forty-somethin' dollars that day."

"Forty-two."

"'Ey, ya got a good memory, kid. You're right, she went off at twenty to one."

I felt the knot in my stomach loosen a little, as I watched The Nose sip his coffee.

"So, you see, even if I did lose my ass on Shirley's Pet, I'm still way ahead of the game backing your horses. I've been doin' pretty good with you, kid."

As soon as I heard him say that, I sighed like somebody who'd just gotten off the hot seat. "Thanks. I mean, I'm glad things have been workin' out okay for ya."

The young guy came back and laid a plate of cookies on the table. But I didn't take none.

"So,' The Nose said, reaching for a cookie and taking a bite. "what brings ya around here?"

I wanted to give him as little information as I could about my family, so I just took a sip of coffee and said: "Visiting."

"'Visiting' huh? That's funny. I got this friend of mine that's always tellin' me you're the grandson of the *Calabrese* from across the street, the sharp-lookin', old guy that always wears a vest. I'd always tell my friend he was full of it, but seein' you here like this, I guess he was right all along. Small world, huh?"

Jeez, that's when I finally understood what the people in the neighborhood meant when they'd say: "The Nose knows". Because without me giving this guy not even one little shred of information, somehow, he already knew my story.

Well, seeing as how the cat was already half-way out of the bag anyway, I figured it didn't make much sense to risk angering The Nose by bullshitting him, so I just told him the truth.

"Yeah," I answered, "that's my grandfather."

"Really?" he said, trying to play dumb and getting all slick and cagey with me. "Ya see that? All along I thought my friend was pullin' my leg. Gee, I guess I owe this guy an apology."

(Yeah, right. I could really picture Carmine the Nose *apologizing* to somebody.)

"It's true, I grew up right here on the block—I even went to Benjamin Franklin."

"Get outa here."

"Serious."

"Well, how come I've never seen ya around before? What'sa matter? You're such a big-time jockey now, ya don't got time to come around and visit your family?"

"I come around all the time, but I usually come on Sundays—that's my day off."

"Hmm," he mumbled, "I guess that's why I've never seen ya around before."

"Probably. I've noticed that you guys usually keep the club closed on Sundays."

"'Ey, we got families too ya know. Besides, ya gotta keep the Lord's day holy over here. Right or wrong?"

"Right," I answered, chuckling to myself and picturing Carmine *u' Nasu* kneeling at the communion rail with his fuckin' tongue sticking out.

We kept on bullshitting for a while, talking about horses, trainers, jockeys and this and that, but little by little, the conversation seemed to be shifting in the direction of my personal business for some reason. Yeah. Real sneaky-like, The Nose was getting a little nosy. Well, if it would've been anybody else poking around in my business, I would've just shut down and cut them off, but seeing as how it was Carmine the

292

Nose doing the prying, I figured I'd be better off just answering the questions.

"So, I guess you have a pretty good agent, huh?"

"Yeah."

"What's his name? If ya don't mind my askin'."

"Bloom. Max Bloom."

"Oh! Max Bloom. I heard about him before. He used to handle Rick Donato's book a few years back. Yeah, chubby little Max. You happy with this guy?"

"Yeah, I guess."

"Well, if you're happy with the guy, you should stay right where ya are. But in the future—ya know, if you should find yourself in a situation where ya feel like ya might be lookin' to make a change or somethin'—I got somebody who could help you out."

"Ya mean a jock's agent?"

"Yeah, a jock's agent. What do ya think I'm talkin' about over here?"

As I shrugged my shoulders, The Nose got up from the table and walked over to the closet, and then after he rummaged through a shoe box for a minute or two, he came back and handed me a business card.

"Here, stick this in your wallet. Ya never know when it might come in handy."

I took the card and read it to myself. It said: Phil Stigliano—personal management.

I'd never really heard of the guy before, so I looked up at The Nose and in a very polite way I asked: "Are you sure this guy's a jockey agent?"

"Sure, I'm sure," he answered, looking a little annoyed. "He's my own cousin for Chris'sakes, and he's one of the best too."

I wasn't about to argue with Carmine the Nose, so I just slipped the card in my pocket and said thanks.

Anyway, seeing as how The Nose hadn't sat back down at the table to continue our conversation, I picked up on the cue and stood up to leave. "Well, it was nice talkin' to you, Mr. Carmine—and thanks for the coffee."

"Any time, kid," he said, giving me a light tap on the side of my face. "You just keep bringin' in them winners; I'm gonna be watchin' for you."

"Okay."

As I turned to leave the club, somebody came in and walked straight to the back. The guy looked kind of young—only a couple of years older than me—and he wore his hat with the brim turned up all the way around, just like The Nose. As we passed, our eyes met. He didn't seem to recognize me, but I remembered him.

Chapter 23

Ever since we got back to Aqueduct, I got right back in the grove. In only two months, not only had I won thirty-two more races, but I was clicking with an unbelievable twenty-two percent of my horses. 'Ey, a .220 batting average might not be nothing to write home about for a baseball player, but for a jockey it was fantastic. I even had a shot at winning the Turf Writer's Award for "Best Apprentice of the Year". My closest competition was a bug rider from California called Craig Simmons. Only problem was, while my bug ended on November 19th, he had his all the way into the following year; so that meant I had to try and hustle my ass off and build up as big a lead as possible.

Max sure had his sights set on winning that Turf Writers Award alright. He kept saying that if we could win it, the "prestige factor" alone could be a big help in getting me through the big nose-dive that every apprentice takes when he loses the bug and becomes a journeyman. That's because without getting those all-important five pounds off, a lot of trainers and owners just toss you aside and stop giving you mounts. There was no way around it. I knew the fat lady was already warming up to sing "The Party's Over", so I figured I'd better squeeze every last drop of juice out of the bug before I lose it forever.

So, I kept riding my ass off trying to win that best-apprentice award, hoping that the little bit of fame and the prestige that it would bring might help me to survive losing the bug. It was a long shot, but I was giving it my best. And things were going really good until the day I got that terrible call.

I was in the jock's room, just back from a race, when Tex, the Pinkerton, called me over and handed me the phone. I got scared right away, because jockeys weren't allowed to receive any calls unless it was a heavy-duty emergency.

"Alo? Junior?"

"Yeah, who's this?"

"Junior, this Mrs. Minetti. You gotta come home right away."

"Why? What happened, Mrs. Minetti—what'sa matter?"

295

I heard a pause, and as she cleared her throat to answer my question, I could hear somebody crying in the background.

"You Grandpa, he have an accident."

"An accident? What happened?"

"Well, he go downtown to buy a suit...and he have a heart attack."

"A heart attack? Well, what happened? Is he alright, is he in the hospital? What?"

I heard another pause, longer than before, and the sound of crying was louder.

"Junior...you Grandpa...he pass away."

I dropped the phone like it had just burned my hand, and then I staggered over to the wall, feeling the words spreading from my ear to my brain like and ugly, black cloud.

"No!" I yelled, grabbing my helmet by the chin strap and flinging it against the wall. *"No!"*

I could feel people gathering around me, but I couldn't see them or hear them though. It was like I had just caught a bullet in the heart, and as I struggled to breathe and keep my knees from buckling underneath me, all I could do was mumble to myself and shake my head.

Simon came running over right away and started shaking me by the shoulders. "Joey! What'sa matter? What'sa matter, son? Talk to me."

But I couldn't answer, I just twisted myself out of his grip and stumbled over toward my locker, ripping off my silks and pulling off my boots. Then, with trembling hands, I grabbed my street clothes, threw them on any which way, and flew out the door.

I had no idea how I got home; it must've been a miracle or something. I was so goddamn shook-up, I couldn't remember walking to the parking lot, starting the car, driving home or nothing. How I got home all the way from Aqueduct will always be a mystery to me. But I guess somebody up there likes me, because somehow, through the grace of God, I made it.

The first thing I saw when I walked into the living room was Mom sitting on the couch with our neighbor, Mrs. Minetti. She was crying full blast while Mrs. Minetti held her and rocked her in her arms. Over toward the window, Grandma was slumped back in Grandpa's chair. It looked like she must've just come to from passing out or something,

296

because Aunt Jean was still fanning her with an envelope, and Uncle Rocco was hovering over her with a bottle of smelling salts in his hand. I didn't know what to do, so I just plopped down on the arm of the couch, stunned.

But as soon as Mom saw me, she started crying out: "Junior! Oh Junior! Junior!"

I took her in my arms right away. I didn't really know what to say or do, so I just hugged her and rubbed her back. She was sobbing away like crazy, but little by little, she seemed to be calming down and getting a grip on herself. Then, after she wiped her eyes and sniffed up her tears, she took me by the hand and led me over toward Grandma.

"Mama, look. Junior's here. Junior's here, Mama—look."

Once Grandma heard the word "Junior", she shook her head and started twitching, like she'd just been hit with an electric jolt or something. She was still white as a sheet and her eyes looked all groggy and half-closed, but I could see the color slowly starting to rise in her cheeks. It took a lot of squinting and rubbing for her to get her eyes in focus, and when she finally made me out, she reached out for me right away.

"Junior!" she wailed, "My Junior! My Junior! Oh, my Junior!"

I hugged her real tight, feeling her body tremble as she sobbed and choked on her words.

"You lose...you b' best friend in the whole world today, m' my poor, J' Junior. You lose you... b' best friend."

"I know, Grandma. I know."

We decided to lay Grandpa out at Anselmo's, the funeral parlor over on 116th Street. Mom, Grandma, and Aunt Jean had been holding up okay, considering the circumstances, but when we walked into that big, empty room and saw Grandpa lying there like that, they broke down and really lost it. I got all choked up and felt like I was going to lose it too, but I knew I had to control myself and be strong. Yeah, all three of them were basket cases, plus Carmela, and I knew it was up to me, Uncle Rocco and Anthony, to try and hold them together.

The worst of everybody was Grandma. She kept throwing herself on top of the casket, wailing and screaming and carrying on, to the point where Anthony had to pull her away and sit her down because she looked like she was about to knock things over. Good thing Uncle Rocco remembered to bring those smelling salts; he had to use them twice on Grandma, and once on Mom too. And when it took such a long time for Mom to react to the smelling salts and snap out of it, it gave us all a really big scare. You kidding? For a moment there, we didn't know *what* to think.

Well, thank God the Belcuores started to trickle in from Jersey. Grandma, Mom and Aunt Jean would break into hysterics as each new relative walked in, but after they'd hug and cry together for a few minutes, they seemed to have soothing effect on them—'specially the women. Yeah, having Aunt Frances, Aunt Rose, Aunt Connie, and some of the other aunts and cousins nearby really helped out, and let me tell ya, that was a big load off our shoulders, because once the women had each other, it gave us guys a chance to go out in the hallway and have a smoke.

Ya know, not for nothin', but from the time I first heard the story about how Grandpa died, the whole thing sounded a little fishy to me. I mean, according to what I was told, Grandpa had gone downtown to buy a suit at one of them wholesale places, and then, after he had found something he liked and was just about to pay for it, *ba-da-bing!,* out of nowhere, he gets a heart attack and drops dead right there in the store—just like that. That might've been all there was to it, but I had a feeling that Grandpa must've gotten into some kind of argument or something. I'd seen it happen lots of times. Grandpa would walk into a clothing store, nice and calm and everything, but as soon as one of them pushy salesmen would try to bullshit him about the merchandise or talk down to him with one of them snotty attitudes, he'd get upset and lose his cool. And with good reason too. Grandpa had more knowledge of tailoring in his little pinky than any of them stupid salesmen had in their whole freakin' body. He even had his own little trick—I called it his "wool test"—where he'd pull off a couple of loose threads from one of the inside seams, and he'd light them up with a match and let them burn. Then, by holding the burning fibers up to his nose and smelling them, he could tell you if the shit was really one-hundred-percent wool or whether it was one of them cheap, imitation blends. Yep, you had to get up pretty early in the morning to pull the wool over Grandpa's

298

eyes—'specially when he already knew whether it was 100% virgin, 40% worsted, or pure polyester. That's why I thought there must've been some kind of static or an argument or something. Who knows? Maybe some snotty salesman snagged him with a lit match in his hand, doing his wool test, and he made a big production out of it. Could be. 'Ey, something like that made a lot more sense to me than him just keeling over and croaking like that; Grandpa didn't even have heart trouble or nothing.

I told Uncle Rocco my theory, but he thought I was wrong. He said that him and Aunt Jean talked to the police when they went to the morgue to identify the body, and according to them, nobody from the store had said anything about any kind of argument or nothing like that. Well, maybe Uncle Rocco and Aunt Jean believed that story, but I sure didn't. Are you kidding? If I were some scuzzy salesman and I had gotten wise with Grandpa and ticked him off so bad that I actually made the poor guy have a heart attack, I wouldn't go blabbing it to no *cops*—I'll tell ya that much. Hell no! I'd keep that shit buried so deep under the cap, not even the *cooties* would be able to find it. And that's probably exactly what he did too—the rat bastard. Maybe he was able to fool the cops, and Aunt Jean and Uncle Rocco with that bullshit, but he sure as hell didn't fool *me*. Get the fuck outa here. "Heart attack" my ass! I'd bet anything Grandpa was *provoked.*

But I guess it was a little too late to be worrying about that; what's done is done, and all the theories in the world, whether they were right or wrong, weren't going to bring him back. He was gone forever.

Anyway, while the women were huddling together and comforting each other, the men were out in the hallway smoking and telling Grandpa stories. Uncle Tony and Uncle Sam Belcuore had a couple of really good ones, and we all had a few laughs, but it was our neighbor, Andrew, from upstairs who made us serious again.

As we were standing around talking, Andrew came over to me, and after he shook my hand and patted me on the back, out of nowhere, he came out with something that brought a tear to everybody's eye.

"Joey, I want you to know somethin'. I was raised by my father never to lower myself to kiss another man's hand, no matter *who* he is—not even the *Pope*. But I just kissed your grandfather's hand—and I kissed it once when he was alive too. Ya know why? 'Cause your

299

Grandpa was the only *true gentleman* I've ever known in my whole life. I really mean that, Joey."

"Thanks a lot, Andrew."

The second day of the wake was a lot better for all of us. The rest of the Belcuores who hadn't made it the day before, came in from Newark, and since Grandpa didn't have any real family of his own, it meant a lot to all of us that they'd come all the way from Jersey just to pay their respects. But it didn't surprise me though; they all loved Grandpa, and even though he wasn't a Belcuore by blood, they'd always considered him one of the family.

But the Belcuores weren't the only people that showed up to see Grandpa, a lot our friends and neighbors had come too: Ronnie and DeeDee and their parents, Mrs. Minetti and her son from all the way out on Long Island, Mrs. Dellarocca and her daughter, Sally Pork, Nicky Specks, a couple of Anthony's old buddies from the Redwoods, the people from the building, the ladies from church, everybody—even Simon, Tito and Sam. And they didn't even *know* Grandpa. But I guess they wanted to show respect for me, and let me tell ya, when you're hurting, it means a hell of a lot to know you got people who care about you.

I wish I could say the same for Max though. You know what that scuzzball did? Instead of coming to the wake in person and showing a little bit of respect and consideration, he actually had the nerve to call me at the funeral director's office, and after he mumbled a couple of quick words about "I'm sorry" and this and that, right away he wanted to start talking business—right there on the phone. For real!

Well, what can I say? I guess I must've gotten pissed and raised my voice a little louder than I thought, because all the people standing around nearby got the picture loud and clear, even though they could only hear one side of the conversation.

"Max! This is neither the time or the place to talk business, okay?—

"I don't care what ya tell 'em! Tell 'em anything ya want; I can't ride right now!—

"Hah? When I'm ready, that's when—

"Whatta ya mean, '*only* a grandparent'? What'sa matter with you, don't you got no respect at all?!—

300

"Yeah, yeah, I know—

"Well, the hell with it then! The hell with the Turf Writers Award, the hell with the riding title, and the hell with *you* too!"—

Click. And I hung up the phone.

Mannaggia! I couldn't believe that guy, right there in the funeral parlor, with my poor grandfather lying in a coffin only a few feet away from me. Jeez! What a *scumbag*.

Well, I guess I got a little more carried away than I thought, because when I stormed out of the funeral director's office, all red in the face with smoke coming out of my ears, a few of my cousins crowded around me.

"Uh-oh," cousin Sonny said, slipping an arm around my shoulder, "sounds like you were just dealing with one of 'The Chosen Ones'."

"Yeah! How'd you know?"

"C'mon, Junior, who else would be nervy enough to call somebody at a goddamn *funeral parlor* to talk business. These people got no respect for God on the cross, how they gonna have any respect for you and me?"

Cousin Lenny pulled out a pack of Pall Malls out of his pocket and offered me one to calm me down. "You got that right, Sonny, the only people that count, the only people that mean anything at all to them, are their own kind. If you ain't one of them, you ain't worth shit."

I took a long drag on my cigarette, and then, almost as if I was thinking out loud, I turned to my cousins and said: "Ya know, it's funny, but Grandpa had this guy pegged from the very beginning—almost like he had E.S.P. or mental telepathy or something. He said that when push came to shove I wouldn't be a guy; I'd be a "goy"....and I'd be disposable."

"Well," Sonny said, "looks like you beat him to the punch on that one. You just disposed of *his* stinky ass before he had a chance to dispose of *yours*."

"Yeah, I guess I did. Well, too bad, so sad. I ain't gonna lose any sleep worrying about that piece of shit."

"Fuck 'im," Lenny said, "You're better off without him."

"I guess so. Time will tell."

I tried my best to show respect and go along with the program when Father D'Amiano came in to console the family and pray for Grandpa. He didn't know Grandpa very well at all—Grandpa never went to church—but he still found some nice things to say about him, and I know it meant a lot to Grandma and to Mom to have a priest present at the wake. Everything was moving along fine until Father D'Amiano said "let us pray", and started leading the mourners in the rosary. I didn't want to make any waves, so I stayed put and tried to pray along with everybody else, but no matter how hard I tried, I kept remembering what Grandpa used to tell me about God not being deaf, and how He didn't want "prayers by the pound". And the more I thought about it, the more bugged and pissed off I got. I mean, there we were at Grandpa's wake, and instead of respecting his religious ideas, we were rattling off those mile-a-minute Hail Maries like a bunch of zombies at a sleepwalker's convention. I had this strong urge to interrupt and explain to everybody exactly how Grandpa really felt about stuff, and how they were doing the exact opposite of what he would've wanted. But I knew I wasn't going to accomplish anything by making a scene—except embarrassing my family—so I just left instead. I walked around the block a few times, smoked a couple of cigarettes, and by the time I came back, the rosary was over.

I'd been able to hold myself together all through the wake and the funeral Mass and everything, but when we were in the limousine, taking that final ride to the cemetery, I just couldn't fight it no more. But I didn't start slobbering out loud and carrying on like some stupid broad or nothing. I just sat there, real quiet, staring out the window, checking out the rust-colored trees and the gray November sky—not even bothering to wipe my tears away. What for? That wasn't going to stop them anyway.

Chapter 24

After we buried Grandpa, I decided to spend some time at home with Mom and Grandma. I knew they could've used the company, and besides, seeing as how I'd lost my agent and my bug, both at the same time, I wasn't in a hurry to follow the horses down to Florida anyway. The only real possibility had to look forward to down there was an exercise-boy job with Sam Cardone, and after being the top apprentice in New York, that wasn't exactly what I'd call a "step up".

But staying home for a while turned out to be a good move though. Just having me around seemed to cheer up Mom and Grandma a lot, and by sticking together like a family, we were able to struggle through the first few weeks of grieving. The only bad part of being home, was Grandma shoving food down my throat. And not just any food; I'm talking about all my favorite things. Fuhgeddaboudit, I was afraid to get anywhere *near* a scale. I must've put on four or five pounds, at least, and that was already becoming a problem.

See, without me realizing it, all the riding I'd been doing the last couple of years had filled me out and made me a lot more solid and a lot more muscular. Those days of being able to make 102 or 103 were long gone. Are you kidding? Towards the end of the season, I was having trouble making 109 or 110, and after two weeks of pigging out on Grandma's goodies, I didn't know if I could've made 114 anymore.

I knew I had to make a move fast. The strain of the Grandpa's funeral had me feeling like I'd just gone fifteen rounds with Sonny Liston, and I knew if I didn't get out of the apartment quick, I was going down for the count. The guilt was really kicking my ass though. I mean, leaving Mom and Grandma alone at such a bad time was probably not the right thing to do. But I had no choice. It was either that or turning into Haystacks Calhoun or the Goodyear Blimp over here. So, with my heart all black and blue, and a stomach full of guilt, I decided to pack my bags, say my goodbyes, and head down to Miami.

As soon as I hit the backstretch at Tropical Park, I knew the party was over. The very same trainers that were standing in line only a few weeks ago to put me on their best stock, were ducking me as if I had leprosy. It wasn't: "Hey, Joey, how ya doin'?" anymore. It was: "Sorry, kid, can't help ya". Some of them wouldn't even let me work their horses in the morning, even when I'd offer to do it for free, just because they didn't want to feel obligated to give me the mount when they ran the horse in the afternoon. But I guess I couldn't blame them though. Why should a trainer give a mount to me, someone who's only been riding for a year and a half, when they could put an experienced, veteran rider on the horse at the exact same weight and get tons of experience in the bargain. 'Ey, who could argue with logic like that?

Well, maybe *I* couldn't, because it was tacky and embarrassing to try and sell yourself and blow your own horn, but an agent could. Hell yeah, an agent could answer these guys back with stuff like: "C'mon, don't be like that. My boy won twenty races for ya this past year; how you gonna drop him like a hot potato, just because of the lousy five pounds? That ain't right." See, sometimes when an agent would talk to a trainer like that, he could embarrass the guy and make him feel so cheap, and guilty and shitty about everything, that he'd finally break down and throw you a few crumbs every now and then. But when you don't have anybody to represent you and speak up for you, all you're left with is shit. That's why if I had any chance of getting back in the ball game, I needed an agent, and I needed one right away.

Only problem was, since I got to Florida a little late, all the jocks and the agents were all paired-up already. It was like walking in on the tail end of a game of musical chairs; everybody had a seat except me.

Well, one morning while I was at the kitchen, my luck changed. I ran into this agent that I knew from Aqueduct named Manny Garcia. He said he was handling the book of a newly arrived Panamanian rider called Eulalio Echevarria, but seeing as how the guy was a complete unknown in the U.S. and he wasn't getting such a hot reception, he told me he might be able to take me on too. I figured I might be getting sloppy seconds—from what I heard this Eulalio guy was a hell of a rider and a big star in Panama—but since hustling on my own had only gotten me three mounts in two weeks, I figured I had nothing to lose. Nope, playing second fiddle sounded better than playing no fiddle at all. So,

304

with a simple handshake and a clink of coffee cups, I had myself a new agent, Manny Garcia.

Manny and Max were as different as night and day. Manny tried to hustle mounts by getting all chummy-chummy with the trainers and turning on the ol' Latin charm. I guess it must've worked sometimes, but Max's approach would get more results. That pushy little bastard would nag everybody half to death and make such a big a pain-in-the-ass out of himself, nine times out of ten, these trainers would go along with anything, just to shut him up and get rid of the guy.

By the way, talking about Max, I ran into him the other day in the parking lot. He tried to come on like my long-lost buddy, but I gave him the cold shoulder and kept on walking. As usual, he made believe he didn't get the message, and by the time I could pry his clammy paw off the sleeve of my jacket, he'd already slipped me the scoop about Craig Simmons winning the Turf Writer's Award for "Best Apprentice of the Year"—just in case I hadn't heard about it. Gee, thanks a lot, Max, you're a real prince.

Anyway, Manny and his sweet-talking tactics, didn't seem to be working out too good for me. The best mounts would always go to his boy "Lalo", the Panamanian guy, and the table scraps and leftovers that would trickle down onto my plate were nothing but a bunch of sore-legged longshots that didn't have a prayer. I'd only been riding one or two horses a day, if I was lucky, and when the racing shifted over to Hialeah, I started to get worried. I'd already ridden in fifty-something races since I'd been in Florida, and the best I'd been able to do for all my trouble was two crummy seconds and a third. Yep, JoJo Posella, the red-hot, bug boy from New York, was 0 for 53 as a journeyman.

Well, you didn't have to be a genius to figure out that the whole ugly mess was starting to get me down. Are you kidding? I hadn't seen the winner's circle in almost three months, and not only was I running out of *confidence*, but I was running out of *bread* too. Yeah, the money I'd chipped in for Grandpa's funeral took a big chunk out of my savings, and since I hadn't been bringing in no new winnings or nothing, I was starting to walk on some really thin ice.

305

Boy, good thing for Sam Cardone. If it wasn't for him and what I'd make from exercising his horses in the morning and riding a few of them in the afternoon, I would've been up Shit's Creek.

My situation had gotten as serious as a heart attack. I even had to check out of my motel and go looking for a cheaper place, because the rent I was paying there was getting a little too hard for me to handle. Not to mention the windshield on my T-bird; that shit had been cracked for more than a month, and I still didn't have the money to get it fixed. Yeah, my whole stinking life was floating down the tubes, right before my very eyes. And to make matters worse, I started to have problems with my weight.

I couldn't understand it. As soon as I got to Florida and started riding again, I'd dropped those four or five pounds I'd put on at Grandma's house like it was nothing, but I guess, little by little, I must've put them back on again because, all of a sudden, I was having trouble making 113 or 114 over here. I didn't know if it could've been the drinking—I'd like to cool off with a couple of brews after the races—or some of the stuff I'd been eating, but whatever it was, I was really starting to get worried—'specially when Manny would put me on some of them bums that hadn't won since God-knows-when, and I'd have to make 109 or 110.

Well, as soon as I noticed my problem, I knew I had to do something fast. And since I could never stomach the idea of puking, or taking laxatives, or sweating my ass off in the goddamn hot box, I started checking out these diet pills. They weren't no big thing or nothing, just some over-the-counter stuff called Slim-a-Dex, but they seemed to work pretty good though. Yep, all I'd have to do was take one little capsule in the morning, and, *boom*, it would curb my appetite all fuckin' day. Only problem was, after I'd been taking them for about a month, they didn't seem to be working as good as they had before. I didn't know if my body had been getting used to them or what, but I was starting to feel like I needed something a little stronger.

My friend Danny had been telling me all along that the Slim-a-Dex was bullshit, so last week I tried a couple of them little red pills that he was using. He called them "bennies" or something like that. I didn't know where he'd get them, but I knew you needed a prescription for

306

them though, because any time I'd run out, I'd have to keep going back to him to get more. But let me tell ya, those bennies worked twenty times better than that stupid Slim-a-Dex did. Shit yeah! With the bennies, I could go all day on one slice of toast and a cup of coffee. And they weren't even that expensive neither. They'd only cost me a few bucks a day, and with the way they'd blast my hunger to smithereens, I figured them shits were a bargain.

I'd been taking some of those Vatrix pills too every once in a while, but they made me piss too much and I didn't go for that. Naa, I didn't like the idea of taking a leak every five minutes like I had a fuckin' bladder problem. But a lot of guys in the jock's room swore by them though; they'd say that with the Vatrix they could piss away the pounds instead of flipping or sweating them off in the box.

Well, I guess it made pretty good sense, but there was just something about that Vatrix stuff that I didn't like. I didn't know why, but it would make me feel all weak and drained out and whatnot, so I pretty much stuck with the bennies, or the "black beauties", or them green-and-white "dexies, or "greenies", or whatever else happened to be around.

And I never went in much for that "speed" stuff neither. I tried it once, but I got so fucked up, I swore I'd never take it again. Are you kidding? That shit had me up all fuckin' night! And when it finally wore off, *ba-da-boom!*, I came crashing down so goddamn hard, I felt like I was riding the Cyclone at Coney Island. For real! And that's not all, after you come down off that shit, it would make you so damn tired and groggy, you'd want to sleep your ass off like fuckin' Rip Van Winkle. Square biz. I'd even have to pop a greenie just so I could stay awake and ride my two horses that afternoon. Naa, that "speed" is full of shit; that's why I just stuck with the stuff I'd get from Danny.

Well, since I'd already been taking all those pills and whatnot, I figured I might as well try some other stuff. But I didn't take no acid though. I'm scared to death of that shit—'specially after seeing all that stuff on TV about them hippies having "bad trips", and "flashbacks", and going all fuckin' nuts and everything. Later for that shit. Besides, I never went in much for that hippie bullshit anyway—ya know, sitting around like a bunch of zombies, "grooving" on Sergeant Pepper or that loud,

307

irritating, Janice Joplin broad ... love beads ... long hair ... granny glasses ... bell-bottoms.... Get the fuck outa here; that was all paddy shit anyway.

But I did try some pot at a party over in Fort Lauderdale. It was alright I guess, but it made me fuckin' hungry though. Yeah! Before I knew it, I'd already eaten an *entire pint* of vanilla- fudge ice cream all by myself. That's when I knew right then and there that pot wasn't for me. Are you kidding? There I was, busting my ass dieting and popping pills just so I could control my appetite and keep my weight down, and then I was going to smoke some shit that would make me *hungry?!* That didn't make no sense, no sense at all.

Well, maybe smoking pot could give you the "munchies", but snorting coke didn't. Nope, that shit was tailor-made for us jocks; it killed your appetite and really helped you to control your weight. But instead of it getting you all edgy and grouchy like the "ups" did, it would make you feel nice. And on top of that, it would give you tons and tons of confidence—and a whole lot of energy too.

I got to like it a hell of a lot better that the pills—that's for sure. And even though it was a lot more expensive and a big pain-in-the-ass to cop, I still thought it was worth it. Besides, from what I heard, those ups could become habit-forming, but not coke though. Naa, coke was just the kind of thing you could take when you needed a little pick-me-up— that's all. But when you didn't, you could just leave it alone—ya know what I mean? Yeah. I looked at it like that: sort of like a tool, or a trick of the trade, something to help you get it up when you'd have to ride some shitty, sixty-to-one shot—even though you felt like a fuckin' douchebag. But that's all it was, just a trick of the trade. And besides, I didn't use it that much anyway—only once in a while.

Ya know, not for nothin', but that coke really did the trick—at least for me anyway. I'd slip into the bathroom to powder my nose, and *vroom!,* I'd be ready for any-fuckin'-thing. Hell yeah! I even won a couple of races too. Yep, it had taken me seventy-six tries to win that first one, but once I'd finally broken my cherry as a journeyman, I started to get a little lucky every now and then. I didn't know if it was the coke giving me back my confidence, or whether it was the fact that good ol' "Lalo" finally went back to Panama and Manny started getting me some better-quality stock to ride. But whatever the reason, it felt great to finally climb out of that awful slump and get back into the winner's circle again.

Only problem was, since I'd won a few races and I had a couple of bucks in my pocket, I started to cop more coke. I didn't know if it was because I was getting used to it or what, but it got to the point where I really didn't feel much like going out there to ride anymore, unless I had a little something before the race—ya know what I mean? 'Ey, it might sound a little sick and fucked-up and everything, but what can I tell ya? That's the way it was with the coke; it sneaks up on you. Yeah, little by little, I was starting to realize it was nothing but a big tease. In the beginning, it would just be "take it or leave it", but after a while, after you get *"el gustito"*, as the Spanish guys would say, you *wanted* that shit—and you'd be thinking about it all the time too.

The worst thing about it was copping though. You'd have to deal with all these scuzzy, lowlifes who controlled the shit, and sometimes you'd get some stuff that had been smuggled in by somebody who'd swallowed some little condoms full of it to get it through customs, and when you'd go to take a blow, the stuff would smell like *culo*. Eeuuww, I'd hate that. I didn't mind that funky gasoline smell it usually had, but that smell of ass would make me want to puke. But that wasn't nothing, sometimes the stuff would be cut up with so much lactose and baby laxative, that as soon as you'd feel that freeze tingling in the back of your throat, *ba-da-boom!,* you'd have to go running to the toilet to shit your ass off. And that would really scare the living daylights out of me, because I was a jockey, and all of us jocks had to wear *white pants.* Oh my god! Can you imagine having an "accident" while you're out there riding a race? Forget it, I'd fuckin' *die!*

But the thing I hated the most about the coke wasn't so much the smell of it, or the shits, or the runny nose, or the way it would lock your jaw and make you look like fuckin' Frankenstein. That stuff could be a pain-in-the-ass sometimes, but I would usually be able to handle it. The thing I *really* hated was the way it would loosen up your tongue and make you want to run your mouth. Hey, they didn't call it "perico" for nothing—that's the Spanish word for parrot—because that's exactly what it would turn you into: a goddamn parrot.

309

See, I'd never been the kind of guy who likes to put his business out on the street—'specially with people I don't know that good. But sometimes, after I'd take a couple of hits of some really good blow, I'd find myself blabbing my ass off about a whole bunch of shit that really should've stayed under the cap—if ya know what I mean? Yeah, I didn't know what it was about that stuff, but a lot of times I'd feel like I'd just taken an injection of truth serum or something. For real! Because as soon as that shit would hit my brain, I'd get this uncontrollable urge to *express* myself and communicate my true feelings—ya know, like to get all fuckin' deep and everything. I'd hate that. And when the shit would finally wear off, I'd always want to give myself a big kick in the ass for acting like such a dingleberry. But what could I do? I guess maybe I just had too much stuff bottled-up inside of me, because sometimes, without me even realizing it, I'd find myself spilling some of my personal beans all over the place.

That's why I'd splurge once in a while and have a long talk with Ronnie long distance. She was a really good listener, and even though I never told her nothing about the pills, or the coke, or none of the other stuff, she'd always seem to understand what I was going through, and just talking to her would make me feel a whole lot better.

She was taking this psychology course in college where they teach you all about the human mind 'n' stuff. Sometimes she'd come out with some big, fancy words that I didn't understand, but she'd always break it down into everyday language for me.

"Dee-who?" I said, scowling at the phone like it had just insulted me.

"Depression, Joey. Depression."

"Depression? What the hell is that?"

"It's when you walk around feelin' sad all the time, and you lose your taste for life and everything—like when you have a bad case of the blues."

"Oh."

"Yeah...sometimes they call it melancholia too, but...."

"Mellon-what?"

"Me-lan-cholia. It's more or less the same thing as depression, only sometimes melancholia can be triggered by a personal tragedy or the death of a loved one or something."

310

"Ya mean you think I..."

"'Ey, your grandfather passed away only a couple of months ago—God rest his soul—and maybe you're still grieving for him without even realizing it."

"Ya mean ya think I could be..."

"Look, I know you, Joey—and I know how close you were to your grandpa. He might not be in the front of your mind, but I'll bet ya anything he's always in the back of your mind."

"C'mon, Ronnie, don't ya think you're taking this psychology stuff a little too far?"

"Okay, if that's the way you feel about it, fine. But remember: 'denial' ain't no river in Egypt, Joey. It's a state of mind, and it can stop you from healing yourself and moving on with your life."

"Alright. So let's say, for argument's sake, that I do have that mellon-whatchamacallit thing. How can ya get rid of it once ya got it?"

"Well, I don't think you can get rid of it just like that, one-two-three, but you can do things to help yourself snap out of it though—ya know, little by little."

"Like what?"

"I don't know. Maybe in your case...taking up drawing and painting again. You were always good at that stuff."

"I guess."

"Or maybe like playing an instrument, or writing poetry, or songs...or even writing letters to yourself, or just talking to somebody, anything—anything that keeps your mind occupied and helps you to externalize your feelings."

"Externalize?"

"Yeah, externalize. Ya know, like gettin' stuff out, bringing out your feelings—unburdening yourself."

"Ya mean sort of like Ex-Lax for the soul."

"'Yeah! That's a very good analogy, Joey. 'Ex-Lax for the soul', I like that. That's exactly what you gotta do: give your soul a heavy-duty laxative, and flush all that clogged up shit straight down the toilet."

I had to chuckle at Ronnie talking about "shit" and "laxatives" and whatnot; she was always so prim and proper about everything. "So, Ronnie, you think If I start drawing and painting again, or writing poems 'n' stuff, you think I'll actually get shit out and start feelin' better?"

311

"I can't say for sure, Joey, but it's worth a try—don't ya think?"
"Yeah, I guess so."

Well, to give Ronnie the benefit of the doubt, I tried to paint a little something. But instead of it relaxing me, it had the opposite effect: It got me so aggravated and pissed off, that I wound up smearing the shit with a rag and smashing up the canvas. I guess that's why a lot of artists, like that Vincent Van Gogh guy, wind up killing themselves. 'Cause let me tell ya, if you're serious about trying to capture the beauty of nature in a painting, it can be frustrating as hell. That's because you're trying to compete with God, and no matter how good of an artist you are, or you *think* you are, in the end...you're always going to come up short.

Well, I guess painting didn't work out too good as a way to "externalize" my feelings, but I *was* able to write a little poem though. I came up with it driving home from Florida. It was a nice, sunshiny day, the beginning of April, the smell of spring in the air, and all that corny stuff. I had a lot of time on my hands, and since it was such a beautiful day and all, I decided to take a detour and make a stop in Washington DC along the way. I'd always wanted to see the sights, but for one reason or another, I'd never gotten the chance to. So, after I checked out the Washington Monument, The Lincoln Memorial, and the National Gallery of Art, I found myself in this beautiful botanical-garden type of place with lots of flowering cherry trees.

The sun was getting kind of low in the sky, and as it streamed through all those sweet-smelling blossoms, it lit up little patches of lime green all around my feet. I was just leaning up against a tree, smoking a cigarette, and as I was standing there, scoping out a blue jay who was pecking at a puddle, all of a sudden, out of nowhere, I got the idea for the words to a poem—almost as if it had already been written for me. It was just some dinky, little poem I put together in a couple of minutes, and since I'd never written anything like that before, it probably sucked too. But anyway, it was called "Spring, Wait for Me."

Spring...wait for me!
My eyes can hardly see your bloom
Spring...wait for me!

312

My ears can hardly hear your song
Spring...wait for me!
My nose can hardly smell your scent
Spring...wait for me!
My heart's not ready for your joy.

Chapter 25

All the way home from Washington, I kept thinking about how good it was going to be to see Ronnie again. I was a little embarrassed that I didn't have no paintings to show her, but since I *did* write that little poem, at least I felt like I'd done *something* to externalize my feelings. And Ronnie was right: getting stuff out in the open really had made me feel better. It was weird, but as soon as I'd come out with that little poem, I started feeling real calm and peaceful inside.

Well, I guess that peaceful feeling was good while it lasted, but after I got to New York and pulled onto 115th Street, I saw something that blew my mind so goddamn bad, I knew I'd never be the same again. It took whatever was left of my heart and smashed the whole fuckin' thing into a million pieces.

It all happened so fast I didn't know what hit me. I had just parked the car across the street near the social club, when all of a sudden, I saw Ronnie coming out of the building all dolled-up and looking really pretty. I was just about to stick my head out the window and yell "'Ey, Ronnie!", when I saw this big, husky guy walk out onto the sidewalk two steps behind her. At first, I didn't know whether the two of them were together, but when Ronnie twirled around on her tiptoes to give him a quick little peck on the lips, I knew what the deal was right away.

My jaw hit the floor, and as I sunk behind the wheel so nobody would see me, I could feel my heart sinking too—all the way down to my knees. I guess I'd always known that Ronnie would probably find a boyfriend sooner or later, but to actually see the two of them together like that, with my own two eyes, walking down the street holding hands, all lovey-dovey and whatnot, fuhgeddaboudit, that was a real tough pill to swallow.

Well, what can I say? I didn't get out of the car for a real long time after that. I just sort of sat there, slumped behind the wheel, paralyzed like a frozen dingleberry, and if it hadn't been for Mom's voice yelling, "Junior! Junior!" from the window, I think I might've stayed there all night.

314

When I saw Ronnie the following day, she at least gave me the respect of not trying to bullshit me. After we talked for a while, she told me that she'd met this guy at school and the two of them were "going out" 'n' stuff. I tried to act all blasé-blasé about the whole thing, but since I've never been a very good actor, I guess a few drops of disappointment must've shown on my mug, because Ronnie picked up on it right away.

"Joey," she whispered, holding my face in her hands and looking into my eyes, "this doesn't change anything. I love you—I'll always love you. It's just that...well...seeing as how we grew up together, and we're almost like family, I guess I love you more like a big brother—ya know what I mean?"

I didn't dare look her in the face because I knew she'd probably see right through me anyway, so I just kept looking down at my hands. "Yeah, I understand."

"C'mon, Joey, don't be like that. You and me can still be friends; that's something that's *never* gonna change."

I nodded and tried to play it off like everything was all hunky-dory and whatnot, but in my heart, I knew things would never be the same—at least not for me anyway.

The thing with Ronnie still had me feeling like shit on a stick, but since I couldn't do anything about it, I tried to block it out of my mind, and I'd tell myself it was no big thing. Besides, I was used to holding the short end of the stick; that's the story of my life.

Anyway, in spite of the big down I was on, I couldn't help feeling a little optimistic about the start of the new racing season—'specially with the brand-new, reconstructed Belmont opening up in a month's time. That was going to be exciting. But in the meantime, I was back at my home track, Aqueduct, and even though I'd had a rough time in Florida, I felt psyched. Hell yeah. I'd won more than a hundred races here last year, and I was hoping that some of my old clients would remember me and give me some live horses to ride.

After a few weeks of making the rounds, kissing ass, and working horses for free, trying to stir up some business, I started to realize that

315

things weren't going to work out like I thought they would. I guess horse racing is a lot like show business. Nobody gives a rat's ass about what you did last year—or even last month—the only thing anybody cares about is: "What have you done *lately?*" And if you didn't have a good answer to that question, forget it, you might as well kiss your ass goodbye, because you weren't going no-damn-where. Yep, that's the way it works around the track: when you're hot, you're hot...and when you're not, you're not.

Well, I guess I must've been colder that yesterday's mashed potatoes, because I couldn't even get myself arrested. I'm serious. Me and Manny had been out there every single morning, rain or shine, making the rounds at Belmont and Aqueduct hustling our asses off and offering our services to any trainer who'd be polite enough to listen. But nobody would give me a play—nobody except Sam Cardone that is.

Yeah, good ol' Sam, he'd been sticking with me through thick and thin, and let me tell ya, even though I knew a lot of his owners really didn't want a washed-up, ex-bug boy riding their horses, he'd still manage to twist a couple of arms and get me on something.

Only problem was, I was getting more mounts on my own through Sam than what I'd been getting through Manny. Yeah, Manny was a hell of a nice guy and everything, but he hadn't been coming up with very much at all. He knew it, and I knew it. I guess maybe that was why he was dropping all those little hints about calling it quits. Hey, that was fine with me; I didn't want to feel like anybody's burden anyway.

Well, that the way the Tootsie rolls. I'm back on my own again, no agent no nothing, and things went from bad to worse *real* fast. I tried scuffling around for a while, but when I started to get the feeling that some of the trainers were only throwing me a few crumbs because they felt sorry for me—seeing me limping around the backside every morning, all by myself, scrounging around for mounts—I dropped that shit like a hot potato. Hell yeah, I wanted to ride horses because people believed in me, because they had confidence in my talent and my ability, not out of pity. Later for that, I didn't need pity from nobody. But I wasn't all stubborn and stupid about it though. Naa, when I'd see that somebody was offering me a helping hand because they were

316

really my friend and they wanted to help me out, I wasn't too proud to accept a favor and say thanks.

That was what happened when my buddy, Cheo, offered to let me move in with him. Cheo hadn't been doing too good either, and when he heard me say that I was going to get thrown out of my apartment in Franklin Square because I was behind in the rent, he figured it was a good idea if I moved in with him, like roommates, so we could split expenses 'n' stuff. I felt a little funny sharing an apartment with somebody, but since we were both in the same boat, and things didn't look like they were going to get better any time soon—for neither of us—I figured I really didn't have much choice. Nope, it was either take Cheo up on his offer, or go back home to live with Mom and Grandma and commute to the track every day. And I couldn't do that; I was already used to the bachelor life. Besides, that would've been a big step backwards

A funny thing happened while I was unpacking my stuff at Cheo's place; I came across that business card that Carmine the Nose had given me in the social club that day. That shit hadn't crossed my mind in months, but since I was only two steps away from the poorhouse, I figured I should try and find out about this guy—or maybe give him a call. What could I lose, a lousy dime?

Cheo had never heard of him before, but when I mentioned his name to Sam, he seemed to know him pretty good.

"Phil Stigliano? Of course, I know him. He used to be Skip Fusillo's agent for years."

"Really?"

"Sure. Skip did real good with him too—'til he got mixed up in that race-fixing thing and got ruled off for a while. Then, when Skip came back on the scene again, he had this new guy handling his book—same guy he has now, Benny Ziegler. Jeez, I always wondered what happened to Phil. Nice guy. Where did you run into him anyway?"

"I didn't. I mean, somebody told me about him. Said he was a pretty good agent, but I never met him or nothin'."

I knew better than to mention the fact that this guy was Carmine the Nose's cousin. Are you kidding? I was real tight with Sam, and I

317

trusted him with pretty much anything, but when it came to shit like that, I'd always remember my cousin Anthony's favorite joke:

"Why is dealin' with the Mob the same like eatin' pussy?"

"I don't know, Anthony. Why?"

"One slip of the tongue and you're in deep shit."

Well, what can I tell ya? I'd been walking around with Phil's card in my wallet for quite a while, but when I found myself hanging around the jock's room every day, like some pathetic asshole, hoping someone would get sick or have an accident so I could scavenge myself a "pick-up" mount, I started to think: fuck it, maybe I should give this guy a call. I knew Grandpa was probably turning over in his grave at just the *thought* of me getting involved with a cousin of Carmine the Nose. But sometimes, when your back is nailed to the wall, you just gotta do what you gotta do.

Phil sounded like a pretty nice guy over the phone. Maybe a little cold and suspicious at first, but once I told him that The Nose has recommended me, he got friendly real fast. I met him at this bar called "The Railbird" over in Ozone Park, right near Aqueduct. He said he was co-owner of the joint, along with the bartender, an old friend of his named Pete. I had a couple of beers and we shot the shit for a while, and when it came time for me to leave, I left with a pretty good feeling.

First of all, me and this guy Phil had a lot in common: Not only were we both Italian, but we both came from the same neighborhood. Phil was from right there on 109th Street, right around the corner from St. Ann's. For real! He even told me he used to hang out with the Devil Tots too, except he was gangbusting in the late fifties when the shit was really heavy. We had a blast talking about the Serpents, and the Viscounts, and the rumbles, and all the big-money stickball games and whatnot. And when I bullshitted a little and told him I'd been a Redwood, that's when we really got tight.

Anyway, to make a long story short, Phil told me he hadn't handled anybody's book for almost two years, ever since he broke up with Skip, but he thought his connections were still strong, and when I told him I was in the market for a good agent, he said he might be able to help me

318

out. I was still kind of leery about getting involved with him—mainly because he was The Nose's cousin—but since I was already up Shit's Creek anyway and I didn't have a pot to piss in, I figured: "How can things get any worse? Maybe I should take a shot with this guy."

But ya know something? It really wasn't being broke that was making me do it. That was just the excuse I gave myself. The *real* reason was that I missed that feeling, the feeling of being a winner. Yeah, once you've gotten a taste of that winning feeling, you're hooked for life. 'Cause let me tell ya, you could take all the fuckin' drugs in the world, and the high would never even come close to the feeling you get when you're turning for home, sitting on a ton of horse, just waiting to straighten out into the lane, so you can release all that raw power and energy and storm down the track like a raging river busting through a dam. Fuhgeddaboudit, there's nothing like it, nothing in the whole wide world.

Well, against my better judgement, I got hooked up with Phil, and as soon as me and him started to make the rounds at Belmont and Aqueduct, I realized right away that he wasn't bullshitting about all the "connections" he had. Nope, everybody was so happy to see Phil back in action, it was like Audie Murphy coming home from World War Two.

Not really "everybody" though. Phil didn't have any connections with none of them bigshot trainers that worked for them fancy, high-class owners. People like that didn't want to have nothing to do with guys like Phil—or even with *me* for that matter. I learned that lesson when I first came on the racetrack: If your name ends in a vowel, you can pretty much forget about riding for any of them old-money, WASP outfits. But when it came to the little guy, the type of trainer who had some cheap, claiming horses, the kind of guy who was behind in the feed bill, scuffling, trying to make a score so he could pull himself out of a hole and get back on his feet again, forget it, those guys welcomed Phil with open arms.

And it didn't take me very long to figure out what Phil's angle was, and why everybody was so happy to see him neither. All you needed was half a brain and a little bit of street-smarts, and all the pieces of the puzzle fell right into place. See, the way it was looking to me, Phil was a jock's agent in name only. That was his front, his license to roam the

319

backside and mingle with all the owners and trainers—and with the jockeys too. It was the perfect cover. Nobody could call Phil an "undesirable", because he had a legitimate reason for being wherever he was: he was a jockey's agent, and he was there taking care of business.

Well, if Phil Stgliano was a bona-fide jock's agent, then my name was Wilt "the Stilt" Chamberlain. Phil's *real* occupation was professional gambler, and from what I could see, he didn't look like no small-time hustler neither. Nope, he had boo-coo bucks behind him, and he had big-time backup too. My guess was that Phil was the middleman, the guy who'd make all the arrangements and set everything up so his "people" could throw their weight behind him and make a nice little "investment". I got the picture right away, as soon as we started making the rounds together. We'd walk into somebody's barn, and when the greetings and the small talk were over, I'd usually be left standing there like a stupid dingleberry, while Phil and the trainer would walk off to the other side of the shed row—or into the tack room where nobody could hear their conversation—and then they'd start mumbling to each other out of the sides of their mouths, like two ex-cons planning a bank heist. 'Ey, I wasn't stupid. I could put two and two together; they were probably setting up some heavy-duty score or something. Of course! 'Cause let me tell ya, Phil wasn't getting up at the crack of dawn just to watch the sunrise—or to make a lousy commission off some dinky little jock's fee. Are you kidding? That was chump-change to a guy like Phil. He was in it to bring down the *big* bucks, and even though I wasn't a hundred percent sure yet, I had the feeling that the key to the door to Fort Knox was going to be yours truly—little ol' me.

Well, it looked like I really had that guy pegged, because ever since I started riding a few of the horses he'd booked me on, he didn't waste any time before he called me into his "office" (his cream-colored Lincoln), to "discuss a little business".

"Joey," he said, slicking back the sides of his DA in the vanity mirror, "you and me gotta have a little talk over here."

"About what, Phil?"

"Well, you know Harry Bickel's horse that we're riding today in the fifth?"

320

"Yeah."

"Well, Harry don't want ya to try with him yet."

"What do ya mean, 'he don't want me to try with him'? I got a good shot to win that race."

"Just what I said, the guy don't want ya to try with him. Not yet anyway. He's got a better spot for him a couple of weeks down the line, and...uh...ya know...he wants to darken up his form a little so we can get a good price on him when we're ready to let him run."

"You mean ya want me to stiff him?"

"Look, kid, I don't give a fuck what you wanna call it, just make sure you finish up the track with this horse. Alright?"

"But Phil, I thought the reason we got together was to win races 'n' shit."

Phil took a long, deep breath like he was running out of patience. "Let me refresh your memory a little. You came to me sayin' you were tired of being broke, and you wanted to make some money. Right or wrong?"

"Right."

"Well, in this business, sometimes ya make the money by winning, and sometimes ya make the money by losing. It don't matter, the main thing is that ya make the fuckin' money. *Capish?*"

I took a slow drag on my cigarette and gazed out the window. "Whatever you say, Phil."

I wasn't too thrilled with the situation I'd gotten myself into, but since I'd made my bed, I was just gonna have to lie in it. So, even though I felt like a real, lowlife scumbag doing it, I stiffed Harry Bickel's horse that day. And I made sure I finished up the track with him the next time he ran too. But when I got the green light from Phil and Harry, fuhgeddaboudit, I rode my ass off and brought that horse in at *twenty-five to one.*

Madon', what a score! I couldn't believe it; I had money coming out of my ass over here. For real! Phil had put a hundred on the nose for me, and with the jock's cut of the purse, I made almost *three grand* on the deal. Phil was even happier than I was, and when Saturday night rolled around and I didn't have to ride the next day, he invited me down to The Railbird for a little celebration.

Holy Mother of God, did I have a ball that night! Phil introduced me to this really fine Spanish broad called Evelyn, and while I was having a few drinks and making time with her and whatnot, he called me over to the bar and slipped me a hefty gram of some heavy-duty blizz.

Well, once Evelyn had a couple of snorts under her belt, she went fuckin' bananas. Yep, I'd gotten laid in New Orleans by some real pros, but they weren't nothing compared to Evelyn. You kidding? When it came to doing freaky shit in bed, that broad was unbelievable. My favorite thing was the way she'd run the tips of her fingernails up and down my back, and whisper stuff in Spanish while we were slipping and sliding and humping our asses off.

"Ay, Yoey! Ayy! Ay, Yoey! Yoey! Ayyy! Asi, Yoey, asi! Asiii! Ay, Papi! Ayyyyy!"

Fuhgeddaboudit, let me stop; I get turned on just remembering that shit.

But things weren't peaches and cream all the time. Sometimes I'd fuck up, or the horse would fuck up, or there'd be some kind of accident or slip-up or something, and the whole fuckin' score would float straight down the toilet. 'Ey, that's why they call it horse racing.

Yeah. Like the time I dropped the battery in the middle of this race at Aqueduct. Holy shit, I thought Phil was going to kill me. See, we'd been getting ready to put over this cheap claimer, Duke's Revenge, for the longest time. The trainer of the horse, Mike Reilly, even had me doing dry runs in the mornings so it wouldn't be a complete shock to him—pardon the pun—when I'd give him a little taste of it during the running of a race. (It was always important to test these horses out with the battery beforehand, because some of them would bolt when they got the jolt, and if a jock wasn't careful, he could find his ass hanging over the outside fence.)

Anyway, Phil and Mike had the whole thing hooked up. The pony boy, this guy called Stan, was going to hold the battery 'til we got near the starting gate on the backside, and then, when nobody was looking, he'd slip it to me and I'd go into the gate with the shit cupped right there in the palm of my hand. Well, the gate opened, I gave Duke's Revenge a little jolt, he jumped out in front by three, I'm sitting chilly hugging the rail, we hit the turn, Duke started running out of gas, as usual, I go to

322

give him another jolt to keep him going, and *boom*, all of a sudden, I dropped the fuckin' thing right there at the quarter pole.

Oh my God, I'd never seen Phil that pissed; he had molten lava coming out of his ears. And forget about Mike Reilly; two Pinkertons had to pull him off me after the race, because the big donkey bastard wanted to kick my ass right there in the paddock.

But I guess I couldn't blame them; I fucked up like a champ. And to make matters worse, even with all the money that Phil and his "people" were pouring in on the horse—in dribs and drabs so it wouldn't attract attention—that son-of-a-bitch still went off at *thirty to one*. That sure would've been one hell of a score. Mike Reilly could've paid off the feed man for an entire year with that kind of bread. But what can ya do? It's not like I *meant* to drop the battery; it was a fuckin' accident. 'Ey, nobody's perfect ya know.

Well, anyway, after Phil cooled down and gave some excuse to his "people", little by little, he seemed to forget about the fumble, and we started concentrating on our next move. But I guess the fuck-up left its mark, because he didn't want to mess around with no more batteries after that. He said it was "way too risky", so he stuck with his usual stand-by angles, like cooking up his favorite dish: the filet of "drop down" with a side order of "insurance". That was when we'd get together with a trainer who had a high-class, allowance horse that he wanted to use to make a score. We'd stiff him and give him a few bad races to dirty up his form, and then, after Phil would pay off the clockers to make his workouts look really dull, the trainer would pull the "drop down", and enter the horse in a cheap, claiming race with shitty competition. The "insurance" would come in the form of some "fiery jack", a hot, cayenne pepper mixture that would be put near the horse's butthole, and also a nice little "speed cocktail"—a shot of a stimulant that would help him tear ass like crazy. Usually the trainer, or sometimes Phil, would get a hold of a drug that was so brand-new, there was no way for it to show up in the urine test after the race. How could it? The lab guys hadn't even *heard* of the shit yet—how could they have a test for it?

If any extra insurance was necessary, Phil would take care of that personally by spreading enough cash or promises around, to turn the whole thing into a "boat race". That was when the other jocks in the

323

race were "taken care of". They'd hustle the last part of it and put on a show for the stewards, but everything was arranged beforehand and they weren't going to mess anything up. The ones who'd fuck up the shit sometimes were the bug boys. Yeah, them apprentices were way too "green" and way too "clean" to be brought in on the score, and let me tell ya, I'd seen a few perfectly-planned boat races that were ruined by some gun-ho bug boy who hustled a little too hard for his own damn good.

'Ey, but what ya gonna do? That's just the way it was when you were trying to set up a score. You could try your best to cover all the angles, but there were never no guarantees. Sometimes you wind up getting over like a fat rat in a cheese factory, and sometimes you'd wind up stepping on your dick and pissing in the wind. A lot of it would depend on luck.

But I'll tell ya one thing though: good ol' Phil would spend a hell of a lot more time eating *cheese* than he would eating *crow*. Hell yeah. And as long as I was playing ball with him and doing what I was told, I didn't have to worry about money, I didn't have to worry about blow, and I didn't have to worry about broads neither. Nope, Phil had all three bases covered, and let me tell ya, I was having the time of my life.

Only problem was, sometimes I'd get a little carried away. There were a few times when I overdid it on the coke, and after the stupid shit sent my dick into a fuckin' coma, in spite of how horny I was, I wouldn't be able to play hide-the-salami with Evelyn. Talk about embarrassing, I wanted to disappear. But the thing that *really* blew my mind was the night when my heart went apeshit on me. That sucker started pounding away so goddamn fast, I thought it was going to pop right out of my chest. Square biz. That's when Cheo had to rush me to emergency.

Now that was crazy. I'd been chugging down straight shots of rum trying to bring down my high, but no matter how much I drank, my heart just kept banging away, faster and faster—like a fuckin' time bomb that was getting ready to explode. The doctor at the hospital called it "acute cocaine poisoning", but I called it being just plain greedy. Yep, instead of taking a couple of "one and ones", bim-bam-boom, nice and cool, I had to be a hog and kill a whole gram all by myself. Thank God for Cheo—that's all I can say. He really saved my ass that night. Shit yeah, if it hadn't been for him, who knows what could've happened. Not only did he jump in his car and drive me all the way to the hospital at five in the morning, but he waited right there in the emergency room, all fuckin' night, 'til they finally released me at two in the afternoon the following day. Now that's what I call a friend—ya know what I mean?

"Listen to me, *Tocayo*," he said, in his thick Spanish accent. "You keep hanging aroun' with that sonamabitche, Phil, and he gonna take you straight down the toilet."

Well, Cheo really hit the nail on the head that time. And the proof came only one week after I had that close call at the hospital. That's when I found myself doing one of the scuzziest, most disgusting things I'd even done in my whole life. Fugeddaboudit, I get ashamed just *thinking* about it.

It happened on the day before Grandpa's birthday. It was a Sunday, and I had promised Mom and Grandma that I was going to drive into the city, have dinner with them, and then take them to the cemetery out on Long Island to plant some stuff on Grandpa's grave. Well, instead of laying low and resting at home like I should have, I wound up going over to the fuckin' Railbird again, and I drank and snorted my ass off 'til the wee hours of the morning. Naturally, I was way too wired to go to sleep, so by the time I broke night and made it into the city, I was feeling like shit on a stick—and I must've looked like it too.

"Junior," Mom said, feeling my forehead to see if I had a fever, "are you alright? You don't look so good."

"I'm okay, Ma—just didn't get too much sleep last night. I think I must've eaten something that didn't agree with me."

"Well, maybe it's gas. Why don't try and do number two, maybe you'll feel better."

Well, I went to the bathroom, but I didn't go in there to do number two; I went in there to powder my nose. I still had some blow left, and I knew if I took a couple of hits, I'd be able to straighten out my head and stop myself from crashing—'specially since I had that long drive to the cemetery ahead of me. Anyway, when I whipped out the folded-up piece of aluminum foil, I noticed that the coke had caked up into these clumpy little rocks, and since I had left my keys on the kitchen table, I started looking around the bathroom for something to chop it up with. I couldn't find anything around the sink, so I opened up the medicine cabinet—and that's when I saw Grandpa's stuff: his shaving mug, his

325

shaving brush and his razor. (Grandma probably hadn't had the heart to get rid of it yet.) Well, I felt really shitty doing it, but since I needed a hit bad, I unscrewed the razor and took out the blade. Then, after I'd chopped up the little rocks into a loose powder, I scooped up some of it on the corner of the blade and held it up to my nose. I was just about to snort it up, when I caught a glimpse of myself in the mirror. Holy shit! I couldn't hardly recognize myself. I had purple circles under my eyes,...my skin looked all yellow and clammy and rubbery,...I had the shakes,...my fuckin' jaw was sticking out on the side and had frozen into this weird position like I had lock-jaw or something,...I had little blobs of white spit at the corners of my mouth,...my nose was all red and crusty,...my face was fuckin' twisted.... Fuhgeddaboudit, I looked like something straight out of a horror movie. But no matter how fucked-up I looked, I still leaned over the sink and brought my trembling hand closer to my nose.

I guess I probably would've snorted up the shit, one-two-three, if I hadn't looked down and seen the words "Wilkinson Sword" written across the razor blade. Well, I didn't know how or why, but as soon as I read those words, something really weird happened to me. All of a sudden, I had this crazy flashback, and I felt like a little boy again. I could actually see Grandpa in my mind, and hear the sound of his voice, talking to me, clear as a bell—like in one of those real vivid dreams.

"Junior," he said, taking some money out of his wallet and putting it into my hand, "take these five dollars and go to the drug store on First Avenue. Buy me 'na butiglia di Aqua Velva, and small package razor blade."

"Okay, Grandpa."

"Remember, I no wanna Gillette, I no wanna Gem, I wanna Wilkinson-a."

"Got it, Gramp—Wilkinson."

Well, what can I tell ya? As soon as I heard myself mumble the word "Wilkinson", I looked down at my hand, and when I saw Grandpa's very own razor blade with that skeevy little mound of white powder sitting at the corner,...my stomach turned,...and a cold, freaky chill went up my spine. I took a quick look at the ugly, twisted mug in the mirror, and then, without thinking twice, I dropped the blade, the blow, the aluminum foil, everything, straight in the toilet, and flushed it all away.

Grandma had trouble bending down, so I got on my hands and knees and helped Mom to plant the two bushes of yellow flowers on Grandpa's grave. Then, after I sprinkled them with some water, the three of us stood in front of the headstone in silence. I read the words that were chiseled on the stone to myself: Domenico Posella, 1889—1967, *Riposa in Pace*. And then, after I said a real slow Our Father, Grandpa style, I closed my eyes and made a secret promise: "Grandpa, I swear on your grave, I'll never take any more drugs for the rest of my life."

When I opened my eyes, I saw Mom and Grandma sniffling and wiping their noses with their crumpled-up tissues. I went over and put my arms around both of them, and as we stood there, huddling together, our tears flowed for Grandpa. Theirs out of sadness, mine out of shame.

Chapter 26

I knew right away that keeping the promise I made on Grandpa's grave wasn't going to be as easy as I thought it would, 'specially with all the temptation around me in the jock's room—plus Phil inviting me to The Railbird all the time "for a little taste of somethin' good".

Sometimes he'd even bring the shit to the track with him and try to force it on me. And I ain't just talking about blow neither; I'm talking about broads too. Yeah, Phil really knew my weakness alright. If he couldn't get me with the coke, he'd just dangle some pussy in front of my face, and *boom*, I chomp down on that bait like a hungry fish who's never seen a hook before.

"Joey, 'c'mere. I want ya to meet a friend of mine, Vivian."

"Hey, Joey boy, come over here and say hello to Wendy. She's dyin' to meet ya."

"Joey, this is Lulu. Lulu, this is the best goddamn jockey in New York, Joey Posella."

Fuhgeddaboudit, keeping my nose clean was one thing, but keeping Mr. Johnson under control, now that was something else. I can't deny I wound up banging a few of those broads, but I didn't take no coke off them though—not even when they offered it to me and teased me with it. Hey, I made a sacred promise over here, and I wasn't about to break it for nobody.

But that was the thing I could never understand about Phil. I mean, it wasn't like I didn't play ball with him—I'd *always* do what I was told, no matter *how* I felt about it—but I guess that just wasn't good enough for him. Phil was like a lot of them racket guys; they can never be happy unless they got you by the short hairs—owing them something. But what could I do? I knew I was in way too deep to even *think* about pulling out. Are you kidding? I could wind up in the weeds someplace with my brains blown out. But by the same token, I couldn't just keep on the way I was going neither. I mean, there I was, struggling my ass off to stay clean and turn over a new leaf and everything, but no matter what I did, this guy just kept trying to drag me down the sewer with him. The whole thing was turning into one big dilemma. I didn't want to bite the hand that feeds me, but I sure as hell didn't want to feed the mouth that bites me neither—ya know what I mean?

Anyway, in spite of all the changes I was going through with Phil, plus fighting temptation and trying to keep my weight down without the help of no drugs or nothing, something really cool happened to me right around that time: I finally convinced Sam to give me the mount on this fiery, little two-year-old he had in his barn by the name of Red Rebel.

I'd been begging and pleading with him to let me ride the colt ever since I first got on him in the morning and got a taste of all that raw speed and talent he had. But the owner of the horse, this moving-and-storage guy from the Bronx, Frank Gargiulo, never wanted to give me a shot. Sam kept telling me that the guy had some really high expectations for the horse because he was so well-bred and everything, and that's why he only wanted to use a top, veteran jock on him, like Ray Mallory or Candido Carrera.

Well, I guess I couldn't blame him; I knew that little red colt was something special from the first minute I laid eyes on him. Yep, you didn't have to be an old Kentucky hardboot to see that he was one-hundred-percent racehorse. He was a little on the smallish side, but he was put together real well tough. He had beautiful conformation, and a perfect balance on him too. He reminded me a lot of his sire, Never Yield, only Never Yield was a sleek, seal-brown color, and Red Rebel was this bright, orangey red—sort of like the color of burnished copper. And the unusual thing about him was that he didn't have no white on him like most chestnuts do. Nope, not a speck: no star, no strip, no blaze, no white stockings—not even a little white coronet band around the rim of his hoof...nothing. He was just a solid-red ball of fire.

But the thing I liked best about him was that beautiful head of his, and the way he'd carry it, real high and proud, like he was fuckin' royalty or something. Yeah, he sure had one hell of a mug alright: real wide between the eyes, with a small, finely chiseled muzzle, and these sharp, pointy ears. He looked kind of like an Arabian if you ask me, because he had the "dish", that slight concave line to his profile. But he didn't have that soft, gentle eye like most Arabians have. Not that guy. He'd always have this strange, faraway look, like he was searching for something way beyond the horizon somewhere, in another time, in another place,

329

in another world. I'd get goose pimples sometimes when I'd see him stare off into space like that and get that weird look. But I could never take my eyes off him though; he was definitely a "picture horse', as Uncle Rocco would say. Yeah, from head to tail, that little guy was nothing but pure class.

Only problem was, the horse was a fuckin' nut job. Either that or he was "just plain ornery", as Simon would say, or "*un hijo de la gran puta*", as Tito would say. And they were both right, 'cause let me tell ya, he didn't get his name, Red Rebel, for nothing. Nope, that son-of-a-bitch hated everything and everybody. All you had to do was get a little too close for comfort, and *bing!* he'd pin his ears back, his eyes would change colors, and he'd try and bite the living shit out of you. And when he wasn't biting like a snake, he'd be kicking his ass off like a Missouri mule. The horse was fuckin' nuts—I'm tellin' ya. The only way you could control the little bastard was to run a stud chain across his nose and under his top lip, so it would dig into his gums and make him respect you when you'd yank down on the shank—otherwise, forget it.

But the weirdest thing I'd ever seen him do was when he ran his first race at Saratoga; that shit taught me a whole lot about Mr. Red Rebel alright. Carrera was up on him that day, and after Red burned himself out by blazing a wicked half mile in forty-four and change, he actually reached over and tried to bite the shit out of the colt next to him when he got collared a little bit past the quarter pole. For real! I saw that shit with my own two eyes, and I still couldn't believe it. See, one horse trying to bite or "savage" another horse during the running of a race is rare enough to begin with—I think I'd only seen it once or twice—but to see some green, two-year-old do something like that was practically unheard of.

Yeah, I'm tellin' ya, that little red bastard was as mean as they come. At first, I thought maybe somebody had mistreated him when he was a weanling or a yearling or something, and that was why he had such a big chip on his shoulder and hated people so much. But Simon told me the whole thing was most likely in his blood.

"Son," he said, as he was taping up a whip for me in the jock's room, "it's a miracle anybody can even ride that som'bitch."

"How come, Simon?"

330

"How come? Just look at his breedin', boy: Never Yield out of a War Admiral mare. That sho' is one helluva combination alright. He got that mean, nasty-ass attitude from Never Yield's daddy, Nasrullah. And if that ain't enough, he got another wild-'n'-crazy streak on his mama's side too. You can trace that from War Admiral, to Man o' War, to Fair Play, all the way back to his great, great, great granddaddy, Hastings."

"Hastings? Who's he?"

Simon chuckled to himself like he knew some kind of inside joke. "Hastings was one of the meanest som'bitches to ever look through a bridle—that's who Hastings was. Born with a bug up his ass. Never did care for nobody sittin' on his back, tuggin' at him, and tellin' him what to do 'n' such. No suh, not Hastings. That hoss wanted to be free—just like one of them wild mustangs."

"Ya mean you think Red got his mean streak from Hastings?"

"Could be. It's a long way back on the ol' family tree, but the mix with that Nasrullah blood mighta kicked it back up again. I don't know who thought of puttin' *them* two bloodlines together; that's like mixin' a barrel of TNT with a keg of dynamite. Only thing you gonna get out of a combination like that is a goddamn explosion."

Simon put down the roll of tape and started rubbing his fingers like his arthritis was acting up on him. "But he sho got that Hastings color though."

"Really?"

"Shoot, I seen Hastings, Fair Play, Man o' War, all them hosses with my own two eyes, and I can tell ya for a fact: Red Rebel got that same exact bright-red chestnut color. A lot of them Hastings hosses got it— runs in the family."

"Hmm."

"Yas'suh, it all comes from Hastings—even that proud way he carries his head, and the look of eagles he got in his eye."

"Ya think he has the look of eagles?"

"Sho do."

"Not me. I think he got the look of a wolf."

Simon screwed up his face like he was trying to picture Red's mug in his mind, then he chuckled. "Ya know som'n, boy? You might be right at that. He do have the look of a wolf...a little red wolf...heh-heh-heh...a lil' ol' red wolf."

331

Ya know, not for nothin', but all that stuff that Simon told me about Red's family tree really opened my eyes to a few things. I started thinking that Red might have the same problem that Hastings had; he just didn't want to be ridden—plain and simple. I'd bet the only reason he'd even let me get on his back in the morning was because he knew I was going to let run—otherwise he probably would've dumped me on my ass a long time ago and stomped my fuckin' brains out. And every time I'd breeze him, it would be the same old story: I'd grab a real tight hold, set my feet square in the dashboard, pull back on the reins with all my might, and he'd *still* run off on me—like a runaway freight train. And the more I'd pull, the faster he'd go. I'd bet anything if that red bastard could talk, he probably be saying something like: "Oh yeah? Ya wanna pull on my mouth? Ya wanna stop me from runnin'? Yeah? Well then watch *this!*". *Zoom!* And off he'd go, charging down the track like a wild fuckin' maniac. If I didn't know any better, I'd swear that sonuvabitch did everything out of spite—*"dispetto"* as Grandpa used to say. 'Ey, I know it sounds crazy, but that's exactly the way he'd act; he just wanted to fuck with you. And it wasn't just with *me* neither. He'd pull the same shit on everybody, and nobody could control him— nobody. That's why he ran so bad those first two times. Each race was a carbon copy of the other. He'd break good, streak straight to the lead, run an unbelievably fast half mile, and then, after he'd exhausted the shit out of himself, he'd come staggering down the lane like a drunken sailor.

Well, after hearing all those stories about Hastings, plus the Nasrullah temperament that he got from Never Yield, I decided to do a little investigating on my own: I talked to Sammy Peraza one day in the jock's room. He was Never Yield's regular rider, and he told me all about his personality and all his freaky little habits in detail. That's when I got the idea to try an experiment. I knew I was going out on a limb, and I knew that I'd be guaranteed to get a serious tongue-lashing from Sam if my plan backfired, but since I had a strong, gut feeling about it, I took a chance.

So, one morning, instead of grabbing my usual stranglehold and fighting Red tooth and nail like I always did, I tried some "reverse psychology", and did the exact opposite. I just gave him his head and rode him on a long, loose rein, nice and easy, with a real light touch—

332

just to see what would happen. Well, naturally, he took off like a rocket. But instead of panicking and putting on the brakes right away, I just sat there, chilly, still as a statue, trying to fool the bastard into thinking that he was running free as a bird and he didn't have no stupid human on his back, busting his balls and trying to control him.

Well, what can I tell ya? I guess I must've been doing something right, because, all of a sudden, instead of him running off and getting all wild and crazy, I actually felt him starting to slow down and relax under me. Yeah! That's when I took another gamble, and I inched up on the reins, ever so slightly, little by little, real sneaky-like, 'til I finally had him under a firm but loose hold.

Holy Mother of God! I couldn't believe it. Instead of him going apeshit and bolting down the track like some hopped-up speed freak, he just kept chugging along at a nice, relaxed clip—just like I hoped he would. And when I got him nice and mellow and started singing to him, forget it, he just cocked his ears back and twitched them around like he was really digging the shit. Yep, as soon as I started crooning, that little red bastard calmed right down and started going about his business like a real professional racehorse.

Well, I guess Sam must've been watching the workout very closely, because when me and Red bounced down the ramp, he was waiting for us with a great big grin on his face.

"Attaboy, Joey," he smiled, reaching up and slapping me five, "ya finally got this little ballbuster to relax. Man, that was beautiful."

"Thanks. He looked smooth out there, didn't he, Sam?"

"Yeah! What the hell did you do to him anyway?"

I was just about to blab the whole thing to him when I remembered how stingy Grandpa used to be about giving away his little sewing secrets, the things he used to call his "tricks from the trade"—so I decided to think of myself for once, and I played it off all dumb and stupid. "Gee, I don't know, Sam, nothin' special—just a different touch maybe."

"Well, it must've been the *magic* touch, 'cause let me tell ya, I've never seen that pain-in-the-ass act like that before."

I felt great that Sam liked the way I handled the colt, so when we got back to the barn, I figured I might as well put in a little plug for myself. 'Ey, it's the squeaky wheel that gets the grease—right or wrong?

333

"Listen, Sam," I said, swinging my leg over the colt and jumping down from the saddle, "I've been meaning to ask you. You know that maiden race ya got lined up for next week?"

"Yeah."

"Well, do ya got a rider yet?"

"C'mon, Joey, we been through this a hundred times already. You know if it was up to me, I woulda given you a shot a long time ago, but I don't have the final say in the matter. Frank's the owner of the horse, not me. He's the guy that pays the bills and he's the boss. What can I do over here?"

"Well, can't ya talk to him or something?"

Sam pulled the stubby De Nobili out of his mouth and flicked off the ash. "Alright, I'll talk to him, but I can't promise ya nothin'—ya hear?"

"Yeah, yeah."

"Don't 'yeah yeah' me, Joey. I'm tellin' ya, this guy Frank has got a one-track mind. All I can do is put in a good word for ya and explain to him what I saw out there on the track just now. But if he don't buy it, I don't want ya to feel bad."

"I ain't worried. All ya gotta do is turn on that greasy guinea charm, and I know I'll be in like Flynn."

Sam jerked his arm into the up-yours position. "Look who's talkin'."

Well, this guy Frank must be part *Calabrese* or something, because he was stubborn as a mule. He didn't want to take Sam's word for anything, so he came out to the track, personally, to see Red's next workout for himself.

In a way I was glad he did, because when Mr. Gargiulo saw me spin that firecracker around the turn, nice and smooth, like a little red sports car, forget it, his trap opened so wide, it looked like the inside of the Holland Tunnel. Hey, if that guy didn't give me the mount after what he'd just seen out there, then he didn't know shit about horses.

Well, as it turned out, Mr. Gargiulo was nobody's fool, and when I brought the colt back to the barn and jumped down, he was the first one to come over to me and give me a pat on the back. "You handled the colt really good out there," he said. "You think you could do the same thing in a race."

"Sure! All I need is somebody to give me a shot."

Mr. Gargiulo held out his hand and gave me a warm friendly shake. "Well, you got it, kid. I can see you've done a helluva job with this horse."

"Gee, thanks Mr. Gargiulo, thanks a lot."

"Don't mention it—just bring him in. We've been overdue for a long time already."

"Tell me about it."

It definitely wasn't easy to get the mount on Red Rebel, but once I had it, it was up to me to prove I deserved it. Put-up-or-shut-up time had finally come.

I probably should've been all nervous and excited, but I wasn't. I felt nice and calm, because once I discovered my little trick to settling Red down, I knew there wasn't another two-year-old in New York that could even come close to him—not when it came to natural speed and talent anyway.

And it looked like I wasn't the only the one who thought that way. Those killer workouts of his had let the cat out of *that* bag a long time ago, and everybody in the know had been buzzing about Red for quite a while already. Well, everybody except John Q. Public. Yeah, it's really hard to hide talent on the backside, but the only thing the regular horseplayers knew about him was that he'd fizzled out twice at Saratoga, and that he had a couple of good works under his belt. Outside of that, they probably had him pegged as a "morning glory", one of them freaky horses that breaks clocks in the morning, but always winds up chucking it in the afternoon.

Well, all I could say was "thank you, racing fans", because I as I stood there in the walking ring, scoping out the odds board, I couldn't believe my eyes. Little ol' Red was going off at a juicy *eighteen to one*. I looked for Phil, and when I saw him in his usual spot, standing there with that sneaky, little smile on his face, drooling and giving me the hi-sign, I knew right away he'd probably bet a yard or at least fifty on the nose for me. Not that it mattered much; I'd been waiting for that chance for months, and I was going to ride my ass off even if I didn't have a penny on the race.

335

The only thing that had me a little worried was Sam. After he'd seen how I got him to relax in the mornings, he'd been toying with the idea of rating Red, holding him off the pace at the beginning part of the race, and then making a big run at the end. But Tito talked him out of it. He'd been saying from day one that Red was a stone-cold *"puntero"*, a front-runner, and to try and do anything else with him would just be going against his nature.

Well, I guess Sam must've thought it over and wound up taking Tito's advice, because before he gave me a leg up, his only instructions were: "Let him roll, Joey...just let him roll."

The hardest part of the whole thing was getting Red to the starting gate without the help of a pony boy. (He hated ponies so much, he'd always try to bite the living shit out of them.) But once I got him warmed up and loaded in the gate, I knew half the battle had already been won; the rest would be a snap. I could feel it in my bones.

Wham! As soon as we broke, we got the jump on everybody and shot out to lead by three. That was fine with me; I wasn't about to try anything new. I was just going to give him his head like I'd been doing in the mornings, relax on him, sit chilly, sing to him, ride him on a loose rein with a relaxed hold, conserve his energy and nurse his speed as best I could. Well, by the time we hit the turn, I pretty much knew it was going to be "Goodbye Cholly"; we were already in front by five or six, and Red hadn't even broken a sweat yet. And then, once we straightened out into the lane, instead of running out of gas like he always did, that little guy pinned his ears back, changed leads, dug in and *tore ass*. Holy shit! I'd never felt nothing like that before: the speed, the power, the thrill, the rush.... Fuhgeddaboudit, I snuck a peak under my arm, and nobody was even close. Nope, me and Red were long gone. Home by ten.

336

Chapter 27

The big win with Red had me bopping into Sam's barn like I was sitting on top of the world. Naturally, I was expecting to find everybody else happy too, but as soon as I spotted Tito in front of Red's stall with a long face on, I knew something was up.

"What happened, Tito?"

Instead of answering, he turned his gloomy mug to the inside of the stall and pointed to Red with his mouth. "Look like buck shin to me."

"Bucked shins? Don't tell me that."

I took a peek and saw Red standing toward the back of his stall with his head drooped down in the corner. He kept trying to touch the front part of his legs with his nose, and it was easy to see he was in pain.

"When did this happen?"

"I don't know," Tito answered, leaning over the webbing of the stall and shaking his head. "He cool out perfect after the race, but in the morning we find him like this."

"Where's Sam?"

"He go to get the vet."

"Damn, of all the dirty rotten luck."

Tito shrugged his shoulders. "What can you do?"

As soon as Sam came back with the vet, we knew right away that Tito had hit the nail right on the head. It was bucked shins alright, a bad inflammation of the tendons along the shin bone. Most two-year-olds get it at some point in their first year of racing. I guess their tendons and ligaments just aren't ready for all that strenuous running yet. It's probably like training a ten or eleven-year-old kid to run track in the Olympics; their bodies just can't handle it.

But it wasn't the end of the world though. Usually there ain't no permanent damage or nothing like that; just a pain-in-the-ass and a big setback. Yeah, when a two-year-old shin bucks, it can knock them out of action for a while. And then, once the horse is ready to start training again, it isn't like you can just pick up where you left off. Nope, you pretty much have to go back to square one and start all over again, easing them back into condition little by little.

Sam looked like he was real upset about the whole thing. "Can you believe this shit?" he growled, kicking the dirt on the shed row. "We finally get this son-of-a-bitch in the winner's circle, and now this happens. *Fuck!*"

"Sorry, Sam," the vet said, ducking out from under the webbing of Red's stall. "I know how hard you've been struggling with this colt. Tough break. I guess he overextended himself yesterday; that sure was one helluva race he ran."

"Yeah, looks like the little bastard bit off a little more than he could chew."

"You can say that again."

Me, Tito and Floyd stayed in front of Red's stall for a while, just checking him out. And it was hard to believe we were actually looking at Red Rebel. He looked like a completely different horse. All the fire and the spirit were gone; all that was left was a mopey-looking horse in pain.

Sam had left to walk the vet out of the barn, but when he came back, he hustled down the shed row clapping his hands. "Alright, hands off ya cocks and pull up ya socks! Let's go, we got work to do around here. Joey, 'c'mon, let's get a nice blowout into this gray filly."

I fell in step with him right away. "Jeez, I can't believe the timing on this, Sam—just when we were starting to get somewhere with this colt."

"'Ey, what ya gonna do? No sense cryin' over spilt milk now—what's done is done. You know how it is with these horses, Joey. They're like strawberries, they spoil overnight."

"Yeah, ain't that the truth."

As it turned out, the least of our worries was getting Red's tendons to heal; mother nature was taking care of that, slowly but surely. The *real* problem was dealing with his mean, nasty attitude—'specially once he started to feel a little better but wasn't ready to hit the track and go back to training again. Forget it, that horse got to be *impossible.*

I couldn't believe what he did to Tito, and I was standing right there. Tito was trying to get the shank chain under Red's lip so he could take him out and walk him around the shed row, when, all of a sudden, *bam!* Red bites him on the arm so damn bad, they had to take him to get stitches and everything. For real! That nasty bastard actually broke the skin and drew blood from the guy.

Well, as soon as Sam saw what Red had done to Tito's arm, he blew a fuse. "That's it!" he yelled, "I've had it with this son-of-a-bitch. I'm calling Frank right now to see if I can convince him once and for all to have this horse gelded. That's the only solution to this problem: cut his motherfuckin' *balls* off!"

Sam went storming off to the tack room, huffing and puffing, and cursing up a storm, with me and Floyd tiptoeing behind him to see if we could eavesdrop on the conversation.

"Frank Gargiulo please—

"Sam Cardone—

"Yeah, I'll hold—

"It's me, Sam—

"Fine. Listen, Frank, I wonder if you can spare a couple of minutes; I gotta talk to you about the situation with this colt over here—

"Who else? Red Rebel—

"Well, he's going fuckin' bananas, that's what'sa matter. He just bit my assistant, Tito, so bad on the arm, they had to take him to get stitches—

"Because he's knockin' the fuckin' walls down! He's dyin' to get out on the track to blow off some steam, but you know we can't work him yet. If I start galloping this horse before them tendons are fully healed, we're settin' ourselves up to get *really* screwed—

"What? Yeah! Of course! That could cause permanent damage—

"Tell me about it. I mean, if we were dealing with a *normal* horse, then maybe I could take a chance and pony him, but I can't get a pony boy to come anywhere *near* the horse, let alone *work* the horse—

"Why? 'Cause he a fuckin' nut job, Frank—that's why! This son-of-a-bitch ain't just satisfied with biting the shit out of the pony, he wants to go after the pony boy and take a bite outa *him* too! Yeah!—

"I *tried* a muzzle. He started rearing up and kicking so bad, the pony boy had to bring him back to the barn 'cause he just couldn't handle him—

"Frank…I've been tellin' ya the solution to the problem for the longest time already, but you don't wanna listen. We gotta cut this horse, geld him. That's the only way to go at this point. He's been way too studdish from day one. The only thing he wants to do is bite, and kick, and chase pussy and make everybody's life miserable around here. Let's face it, he's a rogue—that's all there is to it. If we geld him now, we still might have a chance to settle him down and turn him into a real racehorse next year. Otherwise, forget it; you're just pissing your money away, and I'm wasting my time over here. 'Cause let me tell ya, the writing is on the wall, Frank. Sooner or later this bastard is gonna hurt somebody bad—or even worse, he's gonna hurt *himself*. And then whatta ya got? *U' cazz!*—

"Hah? As soon as possible. He's already on the shelf with the bucked shins; might as well take advantage of the situation and do it now. It'll be like killin' two birds with one stone—

"Yeah, Frank, I know how well-bred he is, and I know you paid a pretty penny for him at the sales—

"Stud potential? Who's to say? His fancy breeding ain't gonna cut the mustard as far as that's concerned; he's gotta prove himself on the racetrack before he can even be considered as a serious stallion prospect—

"Yeah, yeah, I know he could turn out to be any kind of a horse; I'm not gonna deny that. But I got a lot of experience over here, and I'm tellin' ya: this horse should definitely be gelded—

"I know…I know…. Look, we're goin' around in circles. Why don't I set up a meeting with the vet, Doc Newman, and this way you can ask him all the questions you want—ya know, to discuss all the pros and cons and this 'n' that. Maybe he can help ya come to a decision—

"Friday? Alright. Let me check it out with the doc, and I'll call you back to confirm—

"Yeah…okay…Let's see what happens. I'll be talkin' to ya, Frank. Alright…*ciao.*"

Overhearing that conversation really blew my mind. I mean, it wasn't like somebody was planning on cutting *my* balls off—God forbid—but still, just the idea of doing something like that to a horse, or any other kind of animal, really bugged the shit outa me—'specially

340

a horse like Red. What was his crime? Being himself, doing what came naturally, having a little too much *coglioni* for his own damn good? And it wasn't like we were dealing with a goddamn *plow horse* over here. Red had some hot, high-strung blood flowing in his veins; he was bred to run and born to fight. And to expect a horse like him to stay locked up in that little, jail-cell of a stall, all day long, like a prisoner, forget it, that was like living in fuckin' Fantasyland. Hell yeah! Anybody with half a brain could see that the horse was gonna go apeshit sooner or later and lash out at someone. It was only a matter of time.

Now don't get me wrong, I felt as bad as the next guy about what happened to Tito, but cutting the poor horse's balls off didn't seem like a very smart way of dealing with the situation. That would be like cutting off James Brown's legs because he dances too much, or amputating Sandy Koufax's arm because he pitches too fast—ya know what I mean? The whole thing was fuckin' stupid.

I hadn't been invited to sit in on the powwow between Sam, Frank and the vet, but when Friday rolled around, I wound up getting called into the tack room anyway. I guess Mr. Gargiulo must've spotted me walking by or something, because it was him who waved me in.

Right away I played it off like I didn't know nothing from nothing, and as I stuck my head in the door and saw the three of them sitting by Sam's desk drinking coffee, I just said "good morning" to everybody with a blank look on my face.

"Joey, c'mere for a second," Mr. Gargiulo said, smiling and waving me inside. "What do you think about this whole thing? You probably know the horse better than anybody; what's your opinion?"

I could see Sam didn't seem too thrilled with the idea of me being brought in on the deal, so I kept on playing dumb.

"About what?"

"You know, whether or not Red should be gelded."

"Oh. Well, Mr. Gargiulo, I don't know as much about stuff like that as Sam and the Doc do, but I'd say: If God wanted Red Rebel to be a gelding, he would've been *born* a gelding."

"Whoa!" Sam laughed, "Don't go bringin' God into this; we got enough problems on our hands without Him stickin' his two cents in."

341

Everybody got a chuckle out of Sam's wisecrack, but I just stood there with a serious look on my face. "Go 'head and laugh, but I'd bet anything He's probably lookin' down on us right now, right this very second, and he's sayin': 'Who died and left you boss?'"

"Aw, for Chris'sakes, Joey," Sam said, "anybody would think you just came on the racetrack yesterday. You getting' soft on us? You know how this works; horses get gelded all the time. It's no big thing."

"That's right," Doc Newman added, popping a Lifesaver in his mouth and offering one to Sam, "the whole procedure is relatively painless, and in the long run, you're actually doing the animal a favor."

"A favor? How can ya say somthin' like that, Doc?"

"C'mon, kid, you know the score; it's common practice. Look at the meat industry; where do you think all the steaks and hamburgers come from? Steers."

"Well, I'm sorry, Doc, but we ain't talkin' about no shitty-ass cow over here. We're talkin' about a finely-bred racehorse, who not only runs with his four legs, but with all his heart, and with both of his balls too."

(Jeez, just the idea of comparing Red to some stupid meat-cow showed me what an asshole that Doc Newman was. But, hey, he was still a bigshot veterinarian, so I guess I should've shown a little more respect and changed my tone of voice.)

"Just take Red's first race up in Saratoga," I continued, trying my best to make my point without sounding rude. "Remember the way he tried to savage that other colt when he got hooked in the stretch? How many times have ya seen a two-year-old do somethin' like that? I'm tellin' ya, this horse has got one helluva fighting spirit; he's got the will to win. What's gonna happen to that when he's left without no balls?"

Before Doc Newman could even answer, Mr. Gargiulo started nodding his head and pointing his finger at me. "The kid's got a very good point. How will his racing attitude be affected?"

"Well, it's been my experience that most colts retain their aggressiveness and their competitiveness on the racetrack after they've become geldings, but if you're concerned with that, I could cut him proud for you."

"'Cut him proud'? What the hell is that?"

342

"That's when we remove the testes with the scrotum, but we leave part of the seminal vesicle in place. Some of these geldings can act studdish when they're cut like that. I've even seen a few who can actually get half a hard-on if they happen to see a cute filly pass by."

"Get outa here."

"It's true. They can still have some sexual desire left, just can't do very much about it—that's all."

Sam and Mr. Gargiulo chuckled a little when the Doc said that, but for me it was one of the most disgusting things I'd ever heard. Hell yeah, how can somebody be vain enough to fuck around with nature like that, like they're playing God or something? For Chris'sakes, if you're going to geld a horse, at least have the consideration to do it right; don't torture the poor animal with that "cut him proud" bullshit.

Well, I guess Doc Newman must've said something that clicked on a switch in Mr. Gargiulo's mind, because before I could open my mouth to say anything else, he'd already stood up and was putting on his raincoat.

"Let's do it, Sam," he said. "Make the arrangements with the Doc over here—okay? I gotta get back to the Bronx."

As everyone was saying their goodbyes, I just stood there like a frozen dingleberry with my mouth hanging open. I couldn't believe it; they were actually going to do it.

Sam seemed pleased with the way everything turned out, and I guess I should've minded my own business, but I couldn't hold in my feelings no more.

"Listen, Mr. Gargiulo, I know this is your horse, and you have the right to do anything ya want with him, but I just gotta tell you: I think you're making a very big mistake.

"Joey, I...uh..."

"Please, just give me a few minutes, let me explain."

"Gee, I'd like to, kid, but I'm running late. I've got a business to run over here."

"For God's sake, Mr. Gargiulo, remember me? I'm the guy who figured out what makes this horse tick and brought him into the winner's circle for ya. You're tellin' me you can't spare a couple of minutes of your time?"

343

Mr. Gargiulo didn't answer, but when he sighed and crossed his arms, I got his "hurry-up-and-make-it-snappy message" loud and clear.

Out of the corner of my eye, I could see Sam glaring at me and shaking his head. He was scaring me, but at that point, I didn't give a shit. It was my time to say what was *really* on my mind, and I was gonna say it—whether he liked it or not.

"Look, I know you're in a hurry, so I'll put the whole thing in a nutshell for ya."

"Shoot."

"The Aqueduct stable area is the prison...barn seven is the cell block...that shitty little ten-by-ten-foot stall is the jail cell...Sam is the warden...Tito is the C.O....and Red Rebel is the prisoner. *Capish?*"

"Hmm...maybe I do. Go on."

(I had this big urge to say: "Have you ever been behind bars, Mr. Gargiulo? Because I have, and I can tell ya, it's the most fucked-up feeling in the world". But I then I dug myself, and I figured it was probably better to keep my personal shit under the cap.)

"Well, it's like this, Mr. Gargiulo. With the exception of the hour or so they get for their exercise and when they go to the track to race every couple of weeks, these horses are cooped up in their stalls all day and all night, seven days a week, all year long. That's like a prisoner who's been given solitary confinement. Now most of them can handle it, but some of them can't—'specially a high-strung animal like Red. A nut-job like him needs a little extra yard time. You give it to him, and I guarantee you're gonna see a big change in this horse."

Right away Sam touched his fingertips together and twisted up his face. "'Yard time'? What the hell is 'yard time'? C'mon, Joey, stop talkin' in riddles over here."

Mr. Gargiulo seemed to get what I was driving at. "You mean 'recreation time', or something like that. Right?"

"Exactly. Even the worst prisoners who are in solitary confinement get some free time in the yard—all the prisoners do."

Sam crossed his arms with a real sarcastic look. "Well, who—pray tell—is gonna give this crazy maniac of a horse his 'recreation time'?"

"Me."

"You?!"

344

"Yeah! I could stop by every day after the races. I'll take him out of his stall for a walk around the stable area. I'll let him look around, let him graze a little, let him be a horse. I'll talk to him...sing to him...pamper him—ya know, give him a little extra attention and whatnot. Just give me two lousy weeks—that's all I ask. And if you don't see a change after that, then do what ya gotta do, and you won't hear me say peep. Just give me a chance, Mr. Gargiulo. I promise ya, I won't let ya down. Please."

Mr. Gargiulo shrugged his shoulders and looked over at Sam, but when he saw him corkscrewing his finger by the side of his head, he scratched his head and looked me in the eye. "Why do you wanna do something like this anyway?"

Sam didn't give me time to answer. "'Cause he's in love with the horse—that's why."

"Get the fuck outa here, Sam; I ain't in love with shit."

"Well, what else could it be then?"

I could feel my blood rising. Sam was really pissing me off with his smart-ass attitude. But he was still my boss, so I just took a deep breath, sucked my teeth, and tried my best not to blow my cool. "Look, Sam, the guy who was up on Red's back when he broke his maiden by ten lengths was me, not you—okay?"

"So?"

"So?! In case you hadn't noticed, this horse ran the fastest six furlongs that day of any two-year-old in New York this entire season, 1:09 flat, and I didn't even ask him to run or show him the stick or nothin'—he did it all on his own. And when he crossed the finish line, that little bastard had so much gas left in the tank, I think he could've gone around again."

"Get outa here," Mr. Gargiulo said, his eyes lighting up like flashbulbs.

"For real! Whatta ya think, I'm kiddin' ya? You don't know what you got, Mr. Gargiulo; this could be a once-in-a-lifetime horse—I swear to God."

"Really?"

"Hell yeah! That's why I don't want ya to touch him or do anything to him. 'Ey, if it ain't broke, don't fix it—ya know what I mean?"

"I don't know...I..."

345

"C'mon, Mr. Gargiulo, just give me two weeks; let's see what happens. What do ya got to lose?"

"Two fuckin' weeks—*that's* what we got to lose."

"Aw, for cryin' out loud, Sam—give me a break already."

Mr. Gargiulo screwed up his face and looked over at Sam. Mr. Wiseass didn't make any more hand gestures this time; he just rolled his eyes.

"Alright," Mr. Gargiulo said, putting his hand on my shoulder, "you came through for us once already, so I guess you deserve a chance with this too. But if we don't see a big change in this horse after two weeks, it's gonna be…." Mr. Gargiulo didn't finish his sentence; he just made a scissor motion with his fingers.

I stuck out my hand right away. "Fair enough…and don't worry, I won't let ya down."

He nodded and took a quick look at his watch. "Holy shit! I was supposed to be in the Bronx half an hour ago. Let me get outa here. I'll see ya, Sam."

"Ciao, Frank."

"Bye, Joey—and good luck. You're gonna need it."

"Thanks a lot, Mr. Gargiulo."

I could feel Sam burning a hole through the side of my head as we stood there and watched Mr. Gargiulo hurry off to his car. I knew he must've been really pissed at me for ruining all his plans, 'specially after he'd already gotten what he wanted—but what could I do? Somebody had to stick up for Red—right or wrong?

"You're gonna thank me someday, Sam—just you watch."

"Yeah yeah, I'm holding my fuckin' breath over here."

Chapter 28

Giving Red his yard time every day really wasn't no big thing. It would usually take only about an hour of my time, and, seeing as how I didn't have a roommate no more—Cheo finally gave up on New York and went back to Puerto Rico—it gave me something to do besides going home and staring at the four walls.

I was still struggling to keep my mind off the drugs and to stay clean like I promised, and with the exception of Phil tempting me all the time, my worst enemy was definitely boredom. That's because when my mind was occupied, I was usually okay. But when I'd find myself alone in the evenings, with nothing to do and nobody to talk to, that was when temptation would sneak up on me, grab me by the throat, and start kicking my ass. I didn't give in to it or nothing, but there were a couple of times when I came pretty close to falling off the wagon. One time I even drove hallway to The Railbird, before I finally dug myself and turned back. Yeah, I guess I had no choice but to take it real slow, one day at a time—what else could I do?

Anyway, I wish I could say that everything had worked out all hunky-dory with me and Red, but that wasn't what happened—at least not at the beginning anyway. See, like a shithead, I started out with the goofy idea that I was going to conquer the horse with kindness—ya know, like in one of them corny, horse movies where the little boy tames the wild stallion by sweet-talking him and petting him, 'til he gains his trust and has him eating right out of the palm of his hand. Well, maybe shit like that worked in the movies, but it sure didn't work in real life though. Are you kidding? The first time I reached over to give Red a little pat on the neck, the crazy bastard locked his teeth on my forearm so bad, if I hadn't whacked him real hard over the nose with the shank chain, I don't think I would've ever gotten loose. Good thing I was smart enough to wear some thick gloves and my leather jacket, otherwise I would've gotten bit to shreds.

But little by little, he seemed to catch on to the game plan though. Those first few days I had to fight with him for almost twenty minutes, just to get the fuckin' chain through the halter and over his nose, but

347

once he figured out that I was coming to take him out of his cell and give him some yard time, the son-of-a-bitch started to change his tune. 'Ey, Red Rebel might have been as mean as they come, but he wasn't stupid though. Nope, once he got familiar with the routine, he'd already be hollering and pawing the ground as soon as he'd spot me bopping into the barn, all the way down by the other end of the shed row.

"Alright, alright," I'd tell him, "keep ya shirt on. I'm gonna take ya outside for a nice little walk. Just let me hook up this shank and we'll be in business—okay? Calm down now. That's it. Easy boy, easy."

Yeah, that little Red bastard sure loved getting out of his stall and going outside in the open air alright. At first, he'd get so excited, he'd practically drag me around the stable area, and I'd have to give him a couple of quick smacks on the shoulder with the shank strap, just so he'd cool out and start respecting me. But once the newness of the shit had worn off and he'd gotten used to everything, he really didn't give me that much trouble. I'd usually walk him down to the end of the stable area near the maintenance yard, and then I'd double back and let him graze for a while on a patch of grass behind the receiving barn. It was a nice spot. There was a row of weeping-willow trees alongside the slope that leads up to the racetrack, and at that time of the day, you could usually scope out the sun as it dipped behind the clubhouse. Red seemed to like that place a lot, and in between bites of grass, I'd always see him staring off into the sunset with that strange, faraway look in his eye.

Sometimes I stay quiet and listen to the sound of the breeze and the squawks of the seagulls as they'd comb the parking lot for little scraps of food, but most of the time I'd find myself singing. Hey, I wasn't no horse psychologist or nothing like that, but it was easy to see that Red really seemed to dig it when I'd sing to him—'specially when I'd hit him with a couple of my favorite bossa-nova songs. Yep, I couldn't figure out what it was with Red and that bossa-nova stuff, but every time I'd hum him one of those tunes, he'd stand still as a statue, raise his head real high, prick his ears, and listen—like he was grooving to the most beautiful sound on the face of the earth.

It was funny how I got into that Brazilian music in the first place; the whole thing happened completely by accident. One night I was lying in bed, trying to fall asleep—just kind of flipping through the dial on the radio—when all of a sudden, *boom*, I heard this voice. At first, I couldn't believe my ears; it was like hearing Grandpa singing on the radio. I swear to God! It was the exact same voice; only instead of singing in Italian, like he always did, he was singing in this strange foreign language that I'd never heard before. Well, as soon as I heard that voice, goose pimples started to pop up all over my arms and down my spine. I know it sounds crazy, but it was almost like Grandpa was with me again, right there in my bedroom, singing this beautiful song, just for me.

When the record finished, the dee-jay said the name of the tune was "Corcovado", and the singer was some Brazilian guy by the name of Joao Gilberto. I'd never heard of the dude before, but the people in the record store knew who he was right away. They had three of his albums there, and after I bought all three of them, I took them home and gobbled them up with my ears. I didn't have the foggiest idea what the guy was singing about—all the words were in Portuguese—but I didn't really give a shit. Nope, just the sound of that guy's voice, whispering them soft, velvet melodies was good enough for me.

Anyway, seeing as how Red would always perk his ears up any time I'd sing one of them bossa-nova songs, I got the idea that maybe I should give him a taste of the real thing. So a few days later, I borrowed a little record player and a long extension cord from a friend of mine, and after me and Red came back from one of our walks and he was back in his stall, I whipped on a couple of Joao Gilberto records, just to see what he'd do. Holy moly! I couldn't believe the way he lapped that shit up. I couldn't tell if it was the guy's voice, or the melodies themselves, or that slow samba groove that turned him on, but whatever it was, Red definitely dug it. Yep, I even snagged him closing his eyelids and taking a little catnap—just like a sleepy little baby nodding out to a lullaby.

Once I discovered the bossa-nova angle, I milked that shit to the max. Any time I wanted to calm Red down, I'd just croon him a couple of those tunes, and that grouchy bastard would get so mellow, he'd turn into a pussycat right before my eyes. Well, maybe I'm exaggerating a little; you still couldn't put your hands anywhere near his head or his neck, or try to pet him or anything like that, because he'd bite the shit outa you in a heartbeat. But in spite of his usual unfriendly attitude, I was starting to see a noticeable change in his personality and his

349

behavior. Yep, I didn't know if it was the extra yard-time, or the bossa-nova tranquilizer, or what, but something must've worked, because when we reached the end of the two weeks, I was looking at a different horse.

Everybody in the barn noticed the change too, 'specially Sam, and I guess he must've said something to Mr. Gargiulo about it, because a few days later, he popped in to check things out and get the scoop for himself—straight from the horse's mouth.

"So, what's the deal, Sam?"

"Frank, I don't know what this kid's been doing to the horse, but to tell ya the truth, he does seem to me acting a little better."

"Really?"

"Yeah! I mean, he's still a pain-in-the-ass and everything, but for some reason, he doesn't seem as dangerous as before."

"So, whatta ya think, you still wanna geld him, or what?"

"I don't know. Maybe we should take a wait-and-see approach. I mean, who knows? Now that his tendons are healing and he's ready to get back to the track again, maybe the exercise will calm him down even more. Why don't we play it by ear and see what happens?"

And so, it was decided, Red was granted a stay of execution—I mean castration—at least for the time being anyway. And I felt great about the whole thing—'specially since it was my faith in him, and my hard work, and my patience that made the difference. That's why if the day should ever come, somewhere down the line, that Red finds himself living the life of Riley on some fancy Kentucky stud farm, playing hide-the-salami every day with a whole bunch of fine-looking mares, I hope he'll know who his guardian angel was.

It had taken almost three months of steady training in Florida to get Red back to the kind of shape he was in before he shin-bucked, but once he was ready, he became unstoppable. Sam put him in an allowance race at the end of the Hialeah meeting, and he *destroyed*. I just gave him his head coming out of the gate, and rode him on a nice, relaxed, loose rein, and *zoom!*, he ran away and *hid* from those horses. Won by seven lengths in 1:09 and change, eased up.

Mr. Gargiulo must've gotten excited about Red's win, because the very next day when he called Sam on the tack room phone, it sounded

350

to me—from what I could overhear from one side of the conversation—that he was actually thinking about pointing him for the Triple Crown.

"Whoa, Frank!" Sam said, "I know you're really high on this horse, and so am I, but let's not get carried away. For all we know, he could be nothin' but a sprinter—

"I know. Yeah. We know he's got a lotta natural speed, but whether he can carry that speed for the classic distance of a mile and a quarter, or a mile and a half, like in the Belmont, now that's a different story—

"Huh? Sure, we can. You're the boss, Frank. If you want me to start stretchin' him out, we'll stretch him out. But we gotta do it little by little, step by step—otherwise forget it. You can't turn a sprinter into a stayer overnight ya know—

"How long? I don't know, a couple of months of steady training maybe—it's hard to say. But ya can't rush me on this, Frank; ya gotta cut me some slack over here. Just let me do what I gotta do, okay?"

So, Sam started shifting the focus of Red's training from speed to stamina. Instead of giving him those short, quick works to sharpen his speed, he began giving him lots of long, slow gallops to build up his legs and his lungs and to put a real solid bottom on the colt. And when he found a nice, non-winners-of-two allowance race at Gulfstream, he put him in to see what he could do at seven furlongs.

We all were a little worried that Red might run out of gas and wouldn't be able to handle that extra eighth of a mile, but he passed the test with flying colors. Yep, he bounced out of the gate, grabbed the lead, and drew away from that field like they were standing still. Covered the seven panels in 1:22 flat, wire to wire, one hell of a fast time for a green three-year-old who was still learning the ropes.

Red sure turned a lot of heads with that performance, and with the Triple Crown races only a few months away, everybody and their mother was shopping around for an up-and-coming three-year-old that could be molded into a derby contender. Sam told me that some rich, newspaper guy from Chicago offered him $75,000 for Red after the race, but after he checked with Mr. Gargiulo, he turned him down.

"Sorry," he told him, 'we can't even *think* about sellin' this colt 'til we try him in stakes company."

351

Yep, that was going to be the real test. If Red could handle two turns and carry his speed beyond a mile against some top-class stake horses, then we'd know if we really had a genuine, Triple Crown prospect on our hands, or just a flash-in-the-pan sprinter. The time had come to separate the men from the boys.

Sam didn't want to bite off more than Red could chew, so he took his time and searched the condition book 'til he found a spot that looked like it wouldn't come up too tough, the Fountain of Youth Stakes at a mile and a sixteenth. It wasn't one of them big-money prestige races, like the Flamingo or the Florida Derby, but it was still a stakes race though; and to a young jock like me who had never even *ridden* in one before, it was definitely the most exciting thing that had ever happened to me.

I was psyched—and I even called home to tell Mom and Grandma about it. Mom was over at Mount Carmel playing bingo, but I got a chance to talk to Grandma though—and she told me something very interesting. As soon as I told her that the race was on Wednesday, March 19th, she completely freaked out.

"Junior", she said, all excited, "Wednesday is the feast from *San Giuseppe*, Saint Joseph. This the saint from you name. How you gonna lose?"

"Well, from your mouth to God's ears—that's all I gotta say."

"No you worry. I gonna go to the church and light a big candle to *San Giuseppe*—special for my Junior."

Well, once I knew I had Saint Joseph in my corner, I was ten times more psyched than I was before. 'Ey, I knew it was bad luck to count my chickens and everything, but I just couldn't help myself. I knew me and Red were going to win that race, and as far as I was concerned, the Fountain of Youth Stakes was in the bag.

Mr. Gargiulo must've felt the same way, because for the first time all winter, he came down to Miami all the way from the Bronx, just to see the race.

352

"This is the moment of truth, kid," he said, shaking my hand in the paddock and introducing me to his wife, Marie. "It's gonna be make it or break it now."

"I ain't worried, Mr. Gargiulo, I know we got the best horse. With a little bit of racing luck, I'll see yuz in the winner's circle."

"Hope you're right, Joey."

Well, not only was I right, but I was uptight *outa sight!* Hell yeah! I'd never seen Red run like that before; it was like riding an express train. First, we outbroke the field,...then we outran everybody to the first turn,...I grabbed the lead with no problem,...Red changed leads like a pro,...we were three or four lengths in front on the backside,...Red was relaxing and pricking his ears like he was going for a stroll in the park,...we swung around the turn,...I shifted my weight in the saddle and Red changed leads again like it was nothing,...we straightened out into the lane and poured it on,...and then, all them hotsy-totsy, stake horses choked on our dust, all the way down to the wire.

We made mincemeat out of them bastards, and when I looked up at the board to see the time of the race, I couldn't believe my eyes; that little son-of-a-bitch had just run a mile and a sixteenth in 1:41 and 1— only a couple of ticks off the track record. Yep, not only had we both won our very first stakes race, but we won it together, like a team— looking sharp.

"*Vayaaa*, Joey!" Tito shouted, as he slapped me five and swung Red around in the winner's circle so Mr. and Mrs. Gargiulo could pose at his head for the picture. "You really kick some *culo* today!"

Mr. Gargiulo couldn't wait to celebrate, so after I'd changed into my street clothes, he took us all out to eat at this fancy Italian restaurant on Biscayne Boulevard. Man, we sure had one hell of a time that night, eating and drinking, and making plans to run Red in the Triple Crown. Fuhgeddaboudit, that had to be the best Saint Joseph's Day of my whole life. The only thing that was missing was a creamy, delicious *sfinghi* from Cincotti's bakery (the pastries we always eat on St. Joseph's Day), but outside of that, everything was right on the money.

Chapter 29

Red came out of the Fountain of Youth in such great shape, Mr. Gargiulo actually wanted to run him in the Florida Derby the following week. Sam told me he was tempted, but he thought ten days rest wasn't enough for the colt—'specially since he'd just gone a distance of ground for the first time.

"A racehorse is like a bar of soap," he said, "the more you use it, the less you got."

"Yeah, I guess you're right."

So, after he had a little conference with Mr. Gargiulo, it was decided: We were going to skip the Florida Derby, take Red back to New York, and point him for the Wood Memorial. I got a little lump in my throat when I heard the words "Wood Memorial". Are you kidding? That was the most important prep race for the Kentucky Derby on the entire east coast, and I knew we'd be going up against some really stiff competition. But the more I thought about it, the better I liked the idea. If we were going to take on the big guns, the best three-year-olds in the east, what better place to do it, than at our home track, Aqueduct.

As soon as I got back to New York, I made my usual stop to see Mom and Grandma—and to see Ronnie too. I guess she must've found out that I was coming back from Florida, because she came upstairs to say hello. I was glad to see her, and after we hung out for a while, we made a date to catch a flick and have some pizza at Patsy's

As it turned out, Ronnie had broken up with that dude she'd been seeing, but it didn't affect our relationship very much. We'd always have a good time together, but it was always more buddy-buddy than boyfriend and girlfriend—'specially ever since I saw her standing on her tippy toes like a little schoolgirl, kissing that big guy on the mouth. That was when everything changed for me. I guess that's the funny thing about love; once it fades away, wild horses can't bring it back. Nope, that shit was gone with the wind—like a splash of fancy French perfume

354

that evaporates in the air and floats away with the breeze—gone forever.

But I guess it all turned out for the best though. I really didn't have no time to be worrying about no broads anyhow. I'd finally found my ticket to the Kentucky Derby, little Mister Red Rebel, and that was pretty much all I could think about.

I guess I must've been getting a little carried away with Red and everything, because Phil was already starting to get on my case about all the time I was spending over at Sam's barn.

"C'mon, kid, use your head for once in ya life. Ya got sixty-something barns at Belmont, chock full of horses to ride, and only a dozen lousy barns at Aqueduct. Now where is the business at, where are the customers at—Aqueduct or Belmont?"

"Belmont, Phil, but Sam wants me to...."

"Fuck Sam! I'm your agent and you're my jock! And I say you belong with *me* every morning, making the rounds and hustling up mounts, at *Belmont*—not over there at Aqueduct, brown-nosing Sam all the time."

Jeez, I couldn't understand why Phil had such a big bug up his ass about me riding Red Rebel and doing business with Sam. He was getting his twenty-five percent; you'd think the guy would be happy for Chris'sakes. But it wasn't about money, it was about control. It just burned Phil's behind, that I'd gotten the mount on Red on my own, without no help from him, and every time I'd book myself on the colt without "consulting" him, he'd throw a shitfit. What was there to "consult"? Sam would give me a date to ride the colt, and I'd tell him "yeah". What was I supposed to do; tell him that I'd have to check with my agent first, and I'd get back to him? Get the fuck outa here! Me and Sam went back a lot longer than me and Phil did, and I wasn't about to play no head games with him, just so Phil could feel like the big provolone and have the upper hand. Later for that shit.

The whole thing was getting ridiculous if you ask me. Every day Phil would act like a big baby and make a real jackass out of himself, all because of one thing: jealousy—plain and simple. He knew Red was a zillion times more racehorse that any of the broken-down bums he'd ever put me on. And it wasn't just the jealousy bullshit that was starting to turn me off about Phil; the thing I *really* couldn't stand, was his whole

355

fucked-up style of doing business. Yeah! I was just sick and tired of all the scams, the scores, the fixed races, all the sneaky crap he'd force me to pull out there on the racetrack, the lying, the cheating.... I just couldn't take it no more. I mean, sure, I was making good money with him, but I'd just gotten to the point where I felt that there was more to life than making a buck—ya know what I mean? I wanted to wake up in the morning and feel *good* about myself—not to get nauseous every time I'd look in the mirror.

But the worst part of dealing with Phil was his refusal to accept the fact that I was finished with the goddamn drugs, and I didn't want to have nothing to do with it no more. He just didn't want to hear it. And every day it would be the same old story:

"Ey, Joey, why don't ya come down to The Railbird tonight and have a little taste of somethin' good? C'mon! All work and no play make Jack a dull boy. And besides, Evelyn has been asking about ya. I'm running out of excuses; I don't know what to tell her no more."

"For Chris'sakes, Phil, how many times I gotta tell you? I'm off the shit. I've *been* off the shit for more than six fuckin' months already! Why don't ya get the message once and for all and leave me the fuck alone already."

"Well, excuse *me!* I didn't know we were so touchy-touchy all of a sudden."

Madon! What a creep. This guy just couldn't accept the fact that I was really trying to clean up my act and get my shit together. He'd just keep dingling and dangling the stuff in my face, every chance he'd get. If it wasn't pills, it was blow, and if it wasn't blow, it was pussy. And I ain't talking about no nice clean pussy neither; it was usually some scuzzy cokehead like Evelyn, or Vivian, or Lulu, who'd only be throwing me a piece of ass because Phil probably promised her a gram if she'd fuck "the little guy with the limp". Hey, I might've been horny as a motherfucker, but I sure as hell didn't need no mercy fucks though. Later for that shit; I'd rather take a swim in a cesspool than get laid like that.

But just because I'd lost my taste for pre-arranged pussy, didn't mean I'd lost my taste for blow. Are you kidding? Every time Phil would say those magic words: "Railbird" and "a little taste of somethin' good", my nose would start twitching and my mind would run off on me. Yeah,

356

once you had a taste for that shit, you *always* had a taste for it. No matter how hard you'd try to distract yourself and forget about it, the memory of that coke-high would always be right there in the back of your mind, gnawing away at your brain, teasing you, and fucking with you.

But I shouldn't complain though. Even though I had to deal with Phil every day and all his lowlife, rat-bastard bullshit, I still had a lot of good things going for me—like riding Red Rebel and having a chance to go to Louisville for the "Run for the Roses". Yeah, just the thought of it had me feeling like I was the luckiest guy alive.

Well, I might've been lucky up to that point, but with the Wood Memorial only a few days away, I felt like all my good luck had flown right out the window. It was like somebody whipped the *malocchio* on me, and I'd bet anything that the evil eye was coming straight from Phil. 'Cause as soon as I got a look at those entries, I knew we were going to be up against it.

First of all, the race came up a lot tougher than any of us expected. The field was filled to the brim with the toughest, most hard-knocking three-year-olds on the east coast, and every single one of them had a lot more seasoning than Red did. I'm talking about a whole bunch of experienced, high-class stake horses, horses that had either won or placed in some of the most important Derby preps—like the Florida Derby, the Flamingo Stakes, the Louisiana Derby.... Fuhgeddaboudit, every single horse in the race was a *monster.*

And then, as if the competition wasn't bad enough, when they did the post-position draw, we had the rotten luck coming up with the *eleven hole.* Oh my god! That could be the kiss of death in a mile-and-an-eighth race at Aqueduct. Yep, we'd be running one complete lap of the track, starting from the finish line, and with such a short run to the first turn, if you didn't break good and get position right away, you could get carried out so wide, you could find your stinky ass all the way out in the *parking lot!*

Well, by the time Wood Memorial Day arrived, it was way too late to worry about the competition *or* our shitty post position. We were in

357

it to win it, and we had no choice but to play the hand we were dealt. And let me tell ya, in spite of all the obstacles we had to overcome, Red blew everybody's mind and came through like a champ.

I've never been that good with words, so instead of me trying to describe what happened, I'd rather just read what that turf writer, Vic Morris, wrote about us in the *Daily News*. I'd never had my name in the paper before, so that article was a really big thing for me.

Red Rebel Takes Wood
By Vic Morris—Daily News Sportswriter

In an unbelievable display of pure grit and determination, Red Rebel turned back several challenges and survived a prolonged stretch duel with Assuredly to win yesterday's Wood Memorial at Aqueduct. Ridden by his regular rider, Joseph "JoJo" Posella, and trained by the veteran conditioner, Sam Cardone, Red Rebel shocked the crowd of 38,000 fans and paid a hefty $32.60 for the win.

Stumbling to his knees at the start, Red Rebel had to overcome and extremely bad post position and an extraordinarily wide trip into the clubhouse turn before he could assume command entering the backstretch. Then, under constant pressure from Canada's Brigadier General, Red Rebel held onto the lead tenaciously, until he was collared at the head of the stretch by the favorite, Assuredly.

At one point, it appeared as if Assuredly had actually passed Red Rebel, and was about to pull away, but responding to a vigorous hand-ride from jockey Posella, the chestnut colt came on again valiantly in the final strides to snatch victory out of the jaws of defeat.

It is the opinion of this writer that New York's racing fans have rarely witnessed such a brilliant exhibition of sheer courage and gameness from such a lightly raced three-year-old. Overlooked by many as being a notch below the others in the field, Red Rebel's gutsy performance has now placed him squarely in the middle of the Kentucky Derby picture.

A fiery chestnut colt by Never Yield, out of War Queen by War Admiral, Red Rebel races in the colors of Frank Gargiulo's Blue Sky Stable. When asked if any plans have been made to send the colt to Kentucky for the "Run for the Roses", a jubilant Mr. Gargiulo replied,

"We'll see how he comes out of the race, and then I'll talk things over with Sam and we'll make our decision. But if it were up to me, I'd say: 'Lookout Louisville, here we come!'"

Well, that Vic Morris guy pretty much said it all, and his description was right on the money. Red Rebel showed everybody his class that day. We were actually headed by that Assuredly horse at the top of the stretch, but Red fought back like a bulldog, and just refused to lose. He was all heart, and I was really proud of him.

It didn't take very long for Mr. Gargiulo to consult with Sam and make the decision about the Derby. No time at all. As soon as they both saw how Red ate up his dinner that night, and how fresh and frisky he looked the next morning, it was a no-brainer. We were going to Kentucky.

And not as no hopeless longshot neither. When Monday's newspapers came out, *The Daily News* had us rated fifth in its "Kentucky Derby Forecast", and in The Morning Telegraph, they made us the fourth choice at six to one—only a few points behind Shoot the Rapids, the winner of the Florida Derby, Assuredly, the horse we'd beaten in the Wood, and the morning-line favorite, the horse everyone was calling "the best in the west": Bold Sultan.

I was so psyched and excited about the whole thing I could hardly sleep at night. All I'd do was lie there, looking up at the ceiling, imagining myself in the jock's room at Churchill Downs, rubbing shoulders with all them big-time riders, bopping into the paddock in front of that big, Derby day crowd, climbing up on Red's back and guiding him through the tunnel and onto the track, while he hot-stepped underneath me, dancing to "My Old Kentucky Home". Jeez, not for nothin', but I'd get a lump in my throat just *thinking* about it. Yep, win, lose or draw, I knew I was going to have the time of my life.

I even had it all planned out: I was going to leave for Louisville a couple of days early so I could make a little side trip to Lexington and check out the breeding farms. Ever since I was a kid, I'd always wanted to see all the great stallions, and to watch the broodmares and their

359

new-born foals, sunning themselves in the warm, spring air, and munching away on that famous Kentucky bluegrass.

Well, I guess I must've jinxed myself by making plans and counting my chickens, because out of a clear blue sky, out of no-goddamn-where, the unthinkable happened: Red pulled up lame after a workout. I didn't know what to say or what to think; the whole thing was a big, freaky mystery if you ask me. Red was sound as a bell of brass, and while he was breezing, I didn't feel him take a bad step or nothing. But after the work, when I was bringing him back to the barn, I started to feel him favoring his left front foot a little.

Sam must've noticed it too, because as soon as I jumped down, he stomped out his cigar and called Tito over. "Hold him for a second, Tito, I wanna check something out over here."

"What'sa matter, boss, you see something?"

Sam didn't answer; he just bent down and lifted up Red's foot, checking out the underside of his hoof and then feeling his ankle for any sign of heat. "Feels a little warm to me,...and his hoof looks a little tender over here on the right side near the frog."

I leaned over to get a closer look. "What do ya think it could be, Sam?"

"I don't know. Looks like it might be some kind of bruise."

"A bruise? How do ya think something like that could've happened?"

"Hard to say. Maybe he stepped on a stone, or a pebble, or a piece of twig or somethin'—or maybe he just put his foot down wrong. Who knows? But the timing on this couldn't be any worse."

Well, that had to be the understatement of the year; with the Derby only two weeks away, the last thing we needed was Red coming up lame with some kind of foot problem. Hey, what can I tell ya? As they say on the racetrack: no foot, no horse.

Sam called Doc Newman right away. He checked everything out carefully, and even though he thought it was only a "stone bruise", he still took a couple of X-rays anyway, just to play it safe. Lucky for us, he didn't find any fracture or nothing, but he did find a small abscess along the inside wall of the hoof though.

360

"I'm going to have to lance that abscess, Sam, and then in a few days, after it's completely drained, we can put a protective patch on there, and put him in a bar shoe temporarily."

"But, Doc, how long could the whole process take?"

"Can't say for sure. With these injuries you just have to play it by ear and see how things develop. But you can pretty much forget about the Derby. Sorry, Sam."

I watched as Sam chomped on his cigar, struggling to put on a brave face and hide his disappointment. "Ey, what ya gonna do?" he said, "That's the way it is in this game. One minute you're sittin' on top of the world, and the next minute you're eating shit by the shovelful. Go figure."

Gee, I wish I could've been as good a sport as Sam, but I just couldn't find it in me to fake it.

Not that time. Nope, that wasn't one of those "wait-till-next-year" type of situations that you could just brush off and keep on going. That was a now-or-never, once-in-a-lifetime opportunity, and I knew it was never going to come again—not for me anyway.

So, when the first Saturday in May came, instead of riding in the "Run for the Roses", I just sat there, like a dingleberry, watching it on TV from the jock's room at Belmont. And that was nothing; the worst part of the whole thing was listening to Phil gloating about it. Boy, talk about shit on a stick, I hadn't felt that bad since I was a teenage wallflower, watching everybody grinding their asses off at them CYO dances. Fugeddaboudit, if disappointment were water, I was up to my eyeballs, drowning in the Pacific Ocean.

And to add insult to injury, who snuck up the rail and won the Derby at twenty-two to one? Humberto Nova's horse, Idaho, the same jughead that we beat by seventeen lengths in the Wood Memorial. 'Ey, what can I tell ya? When your ass cheeks are dipped in gold—that's all you need.

But time heals all wounds, and little by little, it healed Red's hoof too—'specially after Sam took off the bar shoe and had him shod in regular racing plates again. Yeah, even though he had that big setback

361

and missed the Derby, he got back on track pretty fast and started improving in leaps and bounds. I was even hoping he might be ready in time to take a shot at the second leg of the Triple Crown, the Preakness, down at Pimlico in Baltimore. But Sam decided against it. I guess the stupid stone bruise must've set Red's training schedule back a little farther than he expected, so the new game plan was to skip the Preakness and start pointing him for the Peter Pan Stakes at Belmont the following week.

The Preakness turned out to be another blip—'specially since it was that Canadian horse, Brigadier General, who won the thing. I had no idea how he did it, but maybe with Red on the sidelines, there was nobody to fight him for the lead, and he got loose and stole the race. Our old friend Assuredly, and the California colt, Bold Sultan, both came flying at him at the end, but the lucky bastard had just enough gas left in the tank to hold them off and win by a neck in a blanket finish. Jeez, I couldn't help but think what would've happened if Red would've been in it. We'd already run the pants off that cheap-speed, piece of shit in the Wood; who's to say we wouldn't have kicked his ass all over again in the Preakness?

Aah, fuhgeddaboudit, all that shoulda-woulda-coulda crap was nothing but a big waste of time anyway. Yep, as far as I was concerned, the Derby and the Preakness were both ancient history—dead and buried. And I wasn't talking no sour grapes neither. Nope, sooner or later, every dog gets his day in the sun, and I knew Red's was waiting for him right around the corner.

Everybody expected Red to win the Peter Pan Stakes—we went off as the even-money favorite—but nobody expected us to win by nine lengths, eased up. That shocked the shit out of everybody, including me, and I was *riding* the horse.

Yeah, I guess the way Red won must've turned a lot of those doubters into some heavy-duty believers, 'cause let me tell ya, before Red could even get back to the receiving barn to cool out, the bookies and the railbirds were already laying down odds and making him the favorite for the big race coming up in two weeks, the third leg of the Triple Crown, the Belmont Stakes.

I felt pretty good about Red's chances, but I've got to admit, I was a little worried about him being able to get the distance though. After all, he hadn't even gone a mile and a quarter yet, let alone the grueling Belmont distance of a mile and a half. But the distance question didn't stop none of them turf writers from making him the big, pre-race favorite. Nope, once they saw how he destroyed that field in the Peter Pan, combined with the unbelievably fast time he won it in, everybody and their mother started jumping on the bandwagon with both feet, touting Red as the greatest thing to come along since Citation. And they even gave him a couple of nicknames too! Vic Morris started calling him "The Red Blur", and this other turf writer for The Morning Telegraph called him "The Red Rebellion".

And they weren't just writing stuff about Red, they were writing stuff about Sam, and Mr. Gargiulo—even me! Yeah! All of a sudden it was "JoJo" this and "JoJo" that; I became an instant celebrity overnight—just like Red. I even got a call from some guy called Matt Marcus, a reporter from *Sports Digest*, the biggest sports magazine in the country, saying that he wanted to do a feature story on me. He said he wanted to do an "in-depth, human-interest article" with lots of pictures 'n' stuff, and if me and Red should be lucky enough to win the Belmont, he was talking about maybe even putting me on then cover.

At first, I felt all souped-up and flattered—nobody ever wanted to interview *me* before—so I automatically agreed to do it. Are you kidding? I was tickled pink, proud as a peacock, and happier than a pig in shit, all at the same time. Until I started thinking about what the guy meant by "human interest article". I didn't know why, but I had the sneaking suspicion that the "human interest" angle had something to do with my L.L.D., and how I overcame my handicap and was able to become a jockey in spite of it.

I was even about call the guy to cancel everything, but after I thought about it for a couple of days, I figured it wouldn't be fair to jump the gun; I should at least give the guy the benefit of the doubt—ya know what I mean? So, I showed up for the interview and the "photo shoot" at some photographer's studio downtown. The interview part was cool; he asked me questions about my background, my family, my

363

neighborhood, how I got interested in horse racing, how I became a jockey—shit like that. But everything changed when the *finocchio* with the camera started taking pictures. Yeah! At first he took a whole bunch of "head shots", which was okay with me, but then, all of a sudden, out of nowhere, the guy started taking pictures of my legs and close-ups of my feet—he even wanted me to take off my right shoe, so he could "get a good shot of the platform". Well, that's when I realized that my first instincts were right all along, and that's when I told both of them to "kiss my ass", and I walked out.

Chapter 30

Well, here I am at the track for the big day, and after the bad time I had with Carmine the Nose last night—plus no sleep at all—I'm feeling like pure, unadulterated shit on a stick. And I guess I must look like it too, because now that I've dragged my ass into the jock's room, the first thing out of Simon's mouth is: "Oooo, Lordy Lord! Look what the cat drug in."

I mumble hello and plop myself down on the bench, burying my head in my hands.

"You alright, son? You don't look too good."

As much as I trust Simon, I'm not about to let him know all the ugly shit that's going down, so I just answer: "Yeah, I'm okay, just didn't get too much sleep last night—that's all."

"Nervous, huh?"

"Yeah, I guess."

"Bet you was up all night worrying about the rain and everything."

"Rain? What rain?"

"Where you been, boy? Didn't ya hear the weather forecast? They talkin' 'bout some serious thunderstorms late in the afternoon. Hope it holds off 'til after the big race though."

"Oh shit."

"What'sa matter, son? That red colt of yours can run in the mud, can't he?"

"I don't know, he never really ran on it before. I mean, I worked him on an off-track a couple of times, and he seemed to handle it good enough, but ya never know 'til you try 'em in a race."

"Yep, that's true. But don't you be frettin' about it none—ya hear? Ain't no sense if sayin' hello to the Devil 'til ya looks him in the eye— that's what I always say. Shoot, for all we know, it might not even rain at all."

"Well, from your mouth to God's ears, Simon. I got enough to worry about, without dealin' with no stupid rain."

As I walk out of the jock's room for the first race, I can't believe how packed the paddock is. I've seen some pretty big crowds here at Belmont since it reopened last year, but this looks like the biggest *I've* ever seen. Looks like half of New York has come out to see the big race, and if there's a threat of rain, I'm not seeing anything yet. Maybe a couple of clouds floating around here and there, but outside of that, it looks like a beautiful, sunshiny day.

I guess I should feel more excited about riding Bill Sheldon's filly in the first—she *is* the even-money favorite—but I feel so fuckin' shitty, both physically and mentally, I can't get into it. I got this really bad headache, and I'm so goddamn weak and nauseous, I feel like I'm gonna keel over any second.

Oh shit, is that who I *think* it is?! Yeah, that's him alright: Carmine the Nose, along with my "pal", Phil—plus Irv and Marty, the roly-poly bookies, and the rest of the crew from last night. Yep, there they are, leaning over the railing on the clubhouse side of the paddock like a flock of vultures, scoping me out and whispering out of the sides of their mouths. Damn! Just what I need right now.

I try not to look at them, 'specially not at The Nose, but I can feel his cold-blooded stare burning through his sunglasses and piercing me like X-rays. My guess is that he wants to hit me with one last dirty look to put the fear of God into me—just in case I'm having any second thoughts about what I'm supposed to do.

Well, I guess there's not enough stress and confusion showing on my mug, because before I can ride by, The Nose pulls off his shades, nails me with his eyes, and starts giving me some weird hand gesture. Out of the corner of my eye, I can see that it's the same scissor-motion that Mr. Gargiulo made when he was talking about having Red gelded, only this time it's got nothing to do with no *horse*; it's got to go with a *human being*—namely *me*.

This must be The Nose's final threat—and it's working. Those evil eyeballs and them two fingers clicking together have got me feeling like I've just been condemned to death. 'Cause let me tell ya, when a guy like The Nose says that he'll cut your balls off, he ain't making no idle threats, and he definitely ain't bullshitting—he would actually do it. These wiseguys don't fuck around; they say what they mean, and they mean what they say.

366

Well, it's time for me to get up on this filly. Bill Sheldon, her trainer, just gave me a leg up, along with some instructions. But they went in one ear and out the other; I'm way too shook up to pay attention. I just nod and try my best to smile.

And in spite of how crappy I feel, as I ride around the walking ring, I'm still able to enjoy the thing I've always liked best about riding: looking down on people. Yeah, all my life I've had to look *up* at everybody—even after I got to be an adult. But once I'm perched up here on the back of a horse, I ain't no shrimpy four-foot-eleven no more; I'm ten-feet tall, and everybody and their mother has to look up at *me* for a change—even Carmine the Nose.

Well, I guess Bill Sheldon's filly must've picked up every single one of these bad vibes, because she ran exactly how I feel: shitty. I don't know what happened to her, but she had no speed at all—didn't lift a hoof. Might've bobbled a little coming out of the gate, but that's no excuse; she ran like a pig—beat only one horse.

Jeez, good thing I spotted Mom in the crowd, waving at me after I stepped off the weigh-out scale. She popped up just in time, because a few of these sore losers are really giving me the business, and it's getting embarrassing.

"Hey, JoJo! Why don't ya go back to the bush tracks where ya belong!"

"Yeah! Who told ya *you* knew how to ride?!—ya gimpy little scumbag."

"Stiffed another one, huh, JoJo?"

"Booooooo!"

Boy, good thing Mom is here—at least I have someone to talk to, and I can play it off like I'm not hearing these jerks. She looks great as usual. Too bad she's still dressing in black and doing that *luto* number—that makes her look a lot older—but she's wearing her pearl necklace and a beautiful, lavender-color orchid, and they're perking things up a little.

I lean over the fence and give her a kiss on the cheek. "Hi, Ma, when ya get here?"

367

"Just now. Uncle Rocco's parking the car, and everybody else is with Grandma up by that bench. But I saw you on the track, so I came running to say hi. Did ya win?"

"Naa, stupid horse ran next to last—and it was the big favorite too."

I feel her fingertips running down my cheek. "Well, don't worry. It's only the first race, things'll get better."

"I sure hope so."

"Say, Junior, are you feelin' alright? You look a little pale. Did you get any sl..."

"Ma, I gotta go. Let me get away from these guys."

This is definitely the worst thing about Belmont: the long walk back to the jock's room, 'specially when you got assholes like this razzing you.

"Boooo! Call the garbage truck and sweep this little turd off the racetrack!"

"Great ride, JoJo, just great! You're a real winner, ya crippled little prick."

"Boooo! Throw the bum out!"

Boy oh boy, I sure wish I was back in Aqueduct now. Over there it's just a hop, skip and a jump back to the jock's room. Over here it's a hike and a half.

Anyway, as I start to go up the incline toward the tunnel, all of a sudden, I hear a sweet voice calling my name. I don't even have to look; I know it's Ronnie right away.

Yep, there she is, running over to me with a big smile. "Joey! Joey!"

She looks nice. Her hair is pulled back in one of them French-twists, and she's wearing this pretty, light-blue dress. I jump on the fence and give her a kiss.

"Hi!" she says, giving me a hug, "How ya doin'. Bet ya didn't expect to see *me* here today."

"No...I mean... Yeah!"

She wipes some clumps of dirt off my face. "C'mon, Joey, shame on you. This is the biggest day of your life, your graduation into the big time. I wouldn't miss this day for the world."

"Thanks for comin', Ronnie. But I gotta go. See ya later."

"Bye, Joey."

My next mount is Harry Bickel's horse, Roman Law. He went off as the big favorite too, but I didn't have any luck with him neither. Naa, he's a one-run, come-from-behind type of colt, and when I tried to sneak through between horses with him, I got blocked all the way down to the eighth pole. After that it was a case of "too little, too late"; the horse on the lead held on to beat us by a neck. Well, at least this mount wasn't as embarrassing as the first one, but it's the second one of Phil's "mortal locks" to go down the tubes.

I wish I could say that I redeemed myself in this race, my third mount of the day, but that didn't happen either. Nope, I'm starting to feel like I'm drowning in quicksand over here, and the more I struggle to get free, the deeper I sink. This was another favorite that flopped, but it really wasn't by fault. His name was King of the Blues, but they should have named him King of the Snooze, because he fell asleep in the gate and broke really bad, losing all chance.

The hecklers are having another field day with me but thank God Uncle Rocco is coming over.

"Forget about these chumps, Joon, they're just a bunch of sore losers—no class. And block these last three races out of your mind too. They're nothin' but ancient history now; you gotta concentrate on the big race."

"Yeah, I guess you're right, Uncle Rock."

"Of course, I'm right. Listen, go in that Jock's room and take a nice cool shower; wash everything outa ya hair. Refresh yourself. Pysch yourself up. Get yourself ready. 'Ey, this is a once-in-a-lifetime shot ya got here. Don't let these assholes mess with your mind."

"Yeah."

"Alright, now do what I told ya; go in there and take that shower. Relax. Distract yourself. Shoot some pool or play some ping-pong. But remember: a winner never quits, and a quitter never wins. Right or wrong?"

"Right. Thanks Uncle Rock."

Well, I went into the jock's room and I took a nice cool shower, just like Uncle Rocco told me, but it didn't do no good though. I still feel like

369

shit on a stick, and with the pressure mounting and the big race less than an hour away, I'm turning into a basket case. It's like I got ants in my pants, and I can't sit still for nothing; all I can do is pace up and down like an animal in a cage, chain smoking, mumbling to myself, and racking my brains out, still trying to come up with the answer to the sixty-four-thousand-dollar question: What the fuck am I gonna do?

I guess the tension must be really getting to me, because as I stare up at the clock, watching time drip-dropping away, I'm starting to feel like my mind is playing tricks on me. I can't concentrate on nothing no more; my mind keeps racing a mile a minute, bouncing around from one thing to another like a pinball in a pinball machine. For real! One second I'm thinking about Red Rebel, then I'm thinking about Carmine the Nose, then I'm thinking about Sam, then I'm thinking about Mr. Gargiulo, the I'm thinking about getting turned into a gelding, then I'm thinking about my family, then I'm thinking about Phil, then Irv and Marty, then Uncle Rocco, then The Nose again, then I'm thinking about ways to win, then I'm thinking about ways to lose... Fuhgeddaboudit, good thing Simon is tapping me on the shoulder and handing me my silks; another few minutes of this shit and they'd have to carry me out of here in a straight-jacket and throw me in the looney bin.

As I'm standing here, looking in the mirror and buttoning up my shirt, I can't help thinking to myself how beautiful Mr. Gargiulo's racing colors are, and how proud I always feel every time I put them on. They're plain and simple, not all loud and tacky like some of them other ugly shits I have to wear. Just a solid, sky-blue shirt, and a solid, sky-blue cap—simple-dimple, understated, reserved, classy. Nobody would ever guess that these fancy silks belong to a moving-and-storage guy from the Bronx—but they do. Mr. Gargiulo named his racing stable after his business: The Blue Sky Moving and Storage Company. And to keep everything consistent, he picked these sky-blue silks, so they'd match with his fleet of moving vans. (They're all painted sky-blue too.) Sounds crazy, but it's tr...."

"C'mon, son," Simon whispers, interrupting my little daydream and handing me my whip, "it's time. Good luck."

"Thanks, Simon."

370

I finish tucking in my shirt, and now I'm following the rest of the riders through the tunnel and out into the paddock.

Wow! Something really strange must've happened between races. All of a sudden, the sun has completely disappeared, and the sky has turned a dark, gloomy gray. The smell of rain is in the air, and I can feel a damp wind hitting my face and whipping through the crowd. I watch as the ladies hold onto their hats, and the men grab at their ties and tuck them back into their suits. Thousands of cigarette butts and little scraps of paper are swirling around all over the place, looking like snowflakes in a blizzard, while the leaves in the trees are making this tingly "ssssssh" sound. I can feel my no-sleep, shit-on-a-stick body dragging behind me, weighing me down and pulling me back like an anchor, but my mind is speeding two steps ahead, tight as a drum, edgy as a cat.

"'Ey, how's it goin', Joey?"

"Hi, Mr. Gargiulo," I answer, shaking his hand and taking off my helmet to greet his wife. "Hello, Mrs. Gargiulo. How yuz doin'?"

"The question is not how *we're* doing, Joey, it's how *you're* doing. You're the man of the hour—not us. How ya feel, ready to win the big one?"

I open my mouth to answer, but before I can get a word out, some TV reporter sticks a microphone in my face and starts interviewing me. "JoJo Posella, your horse, Red Rebel, is the overwhelming favorite here today. How do you see your chances? Do you think your colt can get the distance?"

"Well, I guess that remains to be seen. A lot of it is gonna depend on how the race is run—ya know, the pace and everything. But we're in it to win it."

"Thank you, JoJo Posella. Best of luck."

"Thanks a lot."

Right then I see the horses being led into the walking ring. Red had drawn the number-one post position, and he's leading the parade.

"Ooooh, Frank!", Mrs. Gargiulo sighs, "don't he look bewdeeful?"

Mr. Gargiulo crosses his arms and admires his horse as if he's looking at a painting in a museum. "Yeah, Sam's got him fit as a fiddle. Look at the shine on him, and the way he's all tight and cut-up and everything. That's one helluva good-looking animal."

371

Well, Mr. Gargiulo sure is right about that; Red's never looked better. He's grown a lot over the spring, and he's filled out and gotten a lot more muscular too. I'm kind of surprised at how calm and relaxed he looks—considering the crowd and all the excitement—because instead of making his usual entrance, bouncing on his toes and swishing his tail around, there he is, cool as a cucumber, head down, neck bowed, ears pricked, tail arched, bopping hard and mean like a bulldog—all business.

"Did you feel a drop, Frank?" Mrs. Gargiulo says.

"I don't know. Why? Did you?"

Mrs. Gargiulo sticks out her hand, palm up, and looks at the sky. "Yep, it's starting to drizzle."

"Shit! Just what we need—and it don't look like no quick, little shower neither."

"Nope, it's getting' ready to pour; look at how dark it got all of a sudden."

"Did ya bring an umbrella?"

Mrs. Gargiulo touches her fingertips together. "What umbrella? I saw the sun shining, so I figured it was gonna be a nice day over here!"

"Shit! Shit! Shit! *Shit!*"

"What are you 'shitting' about, Frank?" Sam says, chuckling and walking over to us with a big grin on his face. "This is great, I hope it comes down in *buckets!*"

Mr. Gargiulo pulls his head back and looks at him like he's crazy. "What'sa matter with you, Sam? We don't know if this horse can run in the mud."

"Don't worry about it," he answers. "Even if it pours, it ain't gonna be mud by the time they run this race—it's gonna be wet-fast."

"Wet fast? What are you talkin' about?"

"Wet, but fast. Ya know, like when the water lies on the surface of the track in puddles, but it hasn't had a chance to really sink down into the dirt and make mud yet."

"That's good for us?"

"Of course! With any luck, Joey'll make the lead, and we'll be out there winging, splashin' gallons of goop all over the rest of the field. And besides, this track is mostly sand, and you know how sand gets when it's wet."

372

"I don't know. How does it get?"

"Well, the moisture packs it down and makes it a lot less deep and a lot less tiring. It's kind of like jogging at the beach along the wet strip of sand by the water's edge. That's a helluva lot easier than running in the deep, dry stuff—ain't it?"

"Yeah! I never thought of it like that."

"Sure! Let me tell ya, Frank, if this horse is ever gonna get the distance and hang on for a mile and a half, a wet-fast racetrack is the perfect kind of track to do it on."

"Well, what are we waitin' for? Let's put on our war bonnets and go into a rain dance over here!"

Mrs. Gargiulo grabs her husband's arm and cuddles next to him. "I don't think we have to. Look."

Before we can even lift our heads, the little drizzle has already turned into shower, and by the time I hear the paddock judge shout "Rider's up!", the shower has turned into a full-fledged thunderstorm."

Holy shit! I haven't seen it come down like this in a long time; it looks like the end of the world over here.

Booooooommm! A gigantic clap of thunder roars and rips open the sky, sending shivering sheets of rain all over the crowd. In a couple of seconds, it's already coming down in cats and dogs, and dogs and cats, and every-fuckin'-thing. Everybody's running for cover, including Sam and Mr. and Mrs. Gargiulo, and as we circle the walking ring, only a couple of people holding umbrellas, and a handful of the real, hard-core fans have stuck around to watch what's left of the post parade.

I can feel my silks clinging to my skin as the machine-gun rain drums down on my helmet and slithers down my neck. Red's getting soaked too, but he looks like he's loving it though. Yeah! All the other horses are trudging along, with their ears pinned back and their tails tucked deep between their ass cheeks, swinging their heads from side to side, like a bunch of tired, old work-mules, but not Red. He looks like he's really getting turned on by this shit, bucking and squealing, and dancing around like he's having the time of his life.

I wish I could say the same for Tito though. Poor guy. He doesn't even have a hat on, and as he leads us out of the walking ring and up toward the tunnel, I can hear him cursing his ass off in Spanish. *"Fucking lluvia. La fucking lluvia cabrona. Me caso en la fucking hostia, carajo!"*

But now that we're in the tunnel, things are a lot better—if only for a few minutes. Tito seems a lot happier, and so am I—now that I'm hearing all this cheering and clapping. I look to see where it's coming from, and *boom,* there's Mom and Grandma, and Aunt Jean and Uncle Rocco and everybody, calling out my name and waving at me.

"Junior! *Junior!*"

I smile and wave back as I ride by, feeling happy and proud, and sad and embarrassed all at the same time.

Mom's beaming with pride and keeps mouthing the words "I love you", over and over again.

Grandma's leaning over the fence, blowing kisses at me with both hands, mumbling "God bless you, Junior. God bless you, Junior."

Uncle Rocco's making the V for victory sign, shouting, "Go get 'em, Joon!", with Frankie standing next to him, grinning his ass off, and Aunt Jean and Carmela, jumping up and down like a couple of high-school cheerleaders.

Mrs. Minetti, Mrs. Dellarocca, and the other ladies are all shaking their little white hankies at me, like I'm the Pope or something. And now, as I'm passing Ronnie, she's looking up at me and pointing to her light-blue dress. "Look! We match! That means good luck!"

Boy, this is some cheering section. Everybody and their mother is here—everybody except Anthony that is. Yeah, he didn't luck up too good in the draft-lottery. The last time we heard from him, he was in a rice paddy in Vietnam, dodging bullets. Gee, I hope to God he makes it out of that mess in one piece—that's all I can say.

And I hope *I* make it out of *this* thing in one piece too. But it doesn't look too good though. Nope, any way you slice it, I'm getting fucked. With a cheering section like this, it's gonna be real hard to lose, but with The Nose's scissor-fingers still fresh as a daisy in the front part of my brain, it's gonna be even harder to win.

Well, there's no way to put off the moment of truth now; I'm already out here on the track, and as much as I hate to do it, I guess I have no choice but to get myself beat. I know I'm gonna be letting down Red, and Sam, and Mr. Gargiulo, and my family and all my friends and everybody —not to mention all the fans who've bet their money on this horse—but, hey, we're not just talking about losing the family jewels;

374

we're talking about *bleeding* to death and probably getting *killed* over here.

Nobody has to tell me I'm the lowest piece of slime on the face of the earth; I know it already. I feel guiltier than fuckin' Judas over here. But what else can I do? Time is running out, and if I don't come up with something fast, I can pretty much kiss my ass goodbye.

I figure my best bet is to pull the backstretch-burnout routine. All I have to do is give Red his head and urge him on a little in the beginning stages of the race, specially down that long, straightaway on the backside. That way he'll run his eyeballs out for the first mile or so, burn up all his energy, and then fizzle out in the stretch. It's a little risky, but I know I can't be seen putting on the brakes or doing anything suspicious once we turn for home and head into the lane. Are you kidding? If I get caught doing anything shady in a race like this, I'll be ruled off the track for the rest of my life.

Anyway, now that we're slowing down to a walk and approaching the starting gate, all of a sudden, something really weird is catching my eye. It's this short little guy who's just rushed out onto the deserted apron in front of the grandstand, waving his arms around in the rain, yelling out loud, and acting like a real maniac—no umbrella, no hat, no jacket, no nothing. Looks to me like he's some shitfaced drunk, or just another one of them nut-jobs, because the guy's getting soaked to the skin and he don't even give a fuck. But now that I've been scoping him out for a few seconds, I'm starting to realize that he's on some kind of a mission. He's not just strolling around in the rain for the fun of it, he's making a beeline straight for me! What the fu.... Who the hell is this lunatic, and what does he want with me?

Well, I ain't about to let Red get spooked by some fuckin' wacko, so I'm swinging him around and getting him away from the outside fence as fast as I can. But now the guy's hollering my name at the top of his lungs—like he knows me or something.

"Joey! Joey! Joey! Joweee!"

I'm just ignoring the guy, but now that he's screamed out my name ten times already, I'm starting to notice something strange—like there's something familiar-sounding about the voice.

"Joey! Joey! Joweee!"

375

Without thinking, I spin around to take another look at the guy. *Holy shit!* It's like seeing myself in the mirror, only older—like at about forty-five or fifty. For real! The exact same mug.

"Joey!" he cries, reaching out for me over the top of the fence. *"It's me, Joey! It's me!"*

The rain is still pouring down in sheets, but through it all, somehow, I can tell he's got tears in his eyes, and they just keep rolling down his face. Naa, it can't be. How could it?

"Joey! Joey! I love you, Joey! I love you!"

Oh shit! You don't think it could...

"Joey! Don't ya recognize me! I saw your picture in the paper, and I knew it had to be you! I came to see ya! It's me!"

Oh my God...don't tell me...

All of a sudden, some fat guy with a big umbrella is running toward him, yelling at him, and calling him by name. *"Shorty! Ey, Shorty! C'mon, what the fuck ya doin' out here? You're gettin' soaked! C'mon, get under the umbrella for Godsakes, what are you, fuckin' crazy?!"*

It's my father.

I tug on the reins and pull Red to a stop. Our eyes meet. And here we are, staring at each other in the rain, like two assholes—father and son. I feel my mouth opening to say something, but I just keep stuttering, and before I can get a word out, the assistant starter is already grabbing Red by the bridle and leading us toward the starting gate. I spin around and look over my shoulder, but all I can see is the back of the fat guy, struggling to get "Shorty" out of the rain.

"Joey!" he screams, tearing himself loose and running back toward the fence again. *"Joey! Joweee!"*

They just brought in the two-horse and that's blocking my view. All that's left now is the sound of his voice, sailing above the shouts of the gate crew, the squeals of the horses, and the clinks and clanks of the starting gate.

"Joey! Joweee!"

In comes the three-horse....and the four.

"Joweeeee!"

Then the five, and the six....and the seven.

"Joweeeee!"

The eight-horse still don't wanna go in.

376

"Joweeeee!"

Now, finally, all eight horses are in the gate and standing in line. Everybody around me is hollering and shouting, and a couple of the colts are snorting, and stomping, and raising a ruckus. I sneak a look up at the starter and get tied on. He's got his hand on the button. I feel time freeze.

"Joweeeeee!"

I'm a zombie now, going through the motions and using my instincts—like I'm running on automatic pilot or something. Don't know who I am, and I don't know what the fuck I'm doing no more neither. Everything is one big blur. I feel hypnotized, paralyzed, lost in the sound of a voice, stunned by the sight of a memory.

Riiiiinng! Red leaps out from under me like a lion pouncing on its prey, grabbing the ground with his hooves, ripping through the rain and biting the wind. All I can do is hang on and bury myself in his mane. I got no plan. I got no scheme. I'm lost, tossed on a sea of circumstances, like a leaf on a runaway wave. The pilot has become the passenger, and as we swing into the first turn, I can feel Red dragging me to the lead, splishing and splashing, skipping and skimming over the slop as if he has wings on his feet. The reins hang loose in my hands, and as I rock to the rhythm of his stride, I can feel myself spacing out like a junkie, nodding out in the saddle, high off the hoofbeats, high off the heartbeats, drunk from drinking too much wind and too much rain. Who knows how fast we're going? Who knows if there's enough gas in the tank? Who cares? Red sure don't, and I don't either. We're inside time, inside the zone, running free, soaring, sailing, spinning, speeding, shaking loose, slipping and sliding in the joy of the moment—like two cons busting out of jail.

If you ask me what happened on the backside or around the turn, I don't think I know. I'm still numb, reeling from the shock of seeing my father after all these years ... looking into his face ... hearing his cries ... remembering.

But now that we're at the top of the stretch, I can feel something happening. I can't really describe it. All I know is that, now, for the first time since the beginning of the race, I feel like my mind is starting to clear on me, and I can actually pick out the rhythm of the horses' breathing behind me and the pounding and the splashing of their hoofbeats. It keeps getting louder and louder, and now that I'm taking

377

a peek under my armpit, I can see the rest of the field, gaining on me, like seven, shit-covered wolves coming in for the kill.

I know Red's running out of gas; I can feel him shortening his stride and huffing and puffing, but I ain't going down without a fight. *Fuck Carmine the Nose!*

"C'mon, Red," I whisper, crouching down real low, throwing a cross, and slapping the reins against his rain-soaked neck. "C'mon, Red! You can do it. You can do it, Red."

Well, I guess me and this horse must speak the same language, because now that I'm calling on him, he's putting his head down and starting to dig in with all his might. I know he's tired, and I can feel him struggling, but I don't even *think* about hitting him. I just keep hand riding, flexing my body to the flow of his stride, pumping and pushing, chirping and whispering, hoping and praying...begging and pleading.

Well, I have no idea where the fuck it's coming from, but all of a sudden, somehow, out of somewhere, Red's finding another gear...a second wind...one more drop of courage.

"That's it, Red. That's it. Shovel in the coal and let the dry wheels *roll!* C'mon, baby. C'mon! C'mon, Red."

I see the black-and-white eighth pole whizz by, and as I sneak another peek under my arm, I can still see the same seven, shit-splattered horses chasing me—but now they look a lot smaller than before. I can still hear their hooves pounding, the mud splashing, the jocks shouting, the whips cracking, but it's not nearly as loud as it was only a few seconds ago. We've pulled away, we've given them the slip, we're *gone!*

"Attaboy, Red! Now you're cookin'! C'mon, baby! C'mon, Red! I *knew* you could do it!"

We're flying past the sixteenth pole, and I'm setting my sights on the wire. I hadn't noticed the roar of the crowd before, but now that we're coasting home, free as a bird, I can hear an ocean of screaming voices, thrilling my ears and rocking my soul.

"We got it, Red! It's all over! You're gonna win The Belmont Sta...."

Out of nowhere, I hear the horrible crack of bone breaking in two, and in a flash, I feel Red going down like he's just been hit with a bullet right between the eyes. I feel myself flying through the air and landing

378

face first in the mud. I made a desperate try to roll out of the way of the oncoming horses, but it's too.....

Chapter 31

On the inside of my eyelids, I'm watching a movie about the story of my life. In only a few seconds, it's all flashed in front of me, twenty-three years of life all squashed together into two and a half seconds: from riding my scooter around the block, to riding Red Rebel in the Belmont Stakes—and everything else in between.

But now it's like somebody turned on the lights, and I feel myself tumbling back to reality—like I just stepped off a cloud. Only it's not really reality anymore—not like I knew it anyway. My mind has opened up as wide as the sky, and instead of having to focus on only one thing at a time, now I can see, and hear, and smell, and touch, and taste a million things at once. I feel like a bird that's just been set free from a cage, flying over everything, dipping and gliding, sailing, free-falling, looking and listening, understanding the real nitty-gritty of stuff, just by stealing a few bits and pieces of a conversation or taking a quick snapshot with my eyes.

The first thing I notice is how quiet everything has gotten. All the moans and groans have died out now, and a big hush has fallen over the crowd. Thousands of nosy fans are opening up their umbrellas and rushing out into the pouring rain to check out the show and get a closer look at the "accident". Some of the people have a real look of concern on their faces, but most of them have this ugly gleam in their eye, like a bunch of jackals that have just been turned on by the sight of blood.

As I look over at the track, I can see myself lying there, face down, my beautiful sky-blue silks all covered in mud. An ambulance has just stopped next to me, and two paramedics are jumping out and scrambling over in my direction with worried looks on their faces. I'm not moving.

Sam and Tito are running toward me too, but when the ambulance guys wave them off, shouting, "We got it covered, help the horse!", they run over to Red instead. He's standing in the mud, only a few feet behind me, hobbling around on three legs and tossing his head in pain, his right front leg snapped forward and shattered at the shin. I can even see the tip of a piece of white bone, splintered at the spot where it

380

broke, sticking out from the back of the leg, the ankle and the hoof just hanging down from it, held together by a muddy shred of torn skin. It's the ugliest, most gruesome sight I've ever seen.

But nothing is as bad as seeing Mom freaking out over by the gate near the winner's circle. She's screaming and pounding her fists on the chest of the Pinkerton who's trying to stop her from running out onto the racetrack.

"Let me go! That's my son out there! That's my son!"

All of a sudden, Uncle Rocco and Frankie join in the struggle too, and before the Pinkerton can fight off all three of them, Mom slips his grip and ducks under his arm. Her high heels are giving her a lot of trouble in the mud, so she just kicks them off and keeps running toward me, tearing ass as fast as she can in her stocking feet, the Pinkerton chasing after her.

"No. *No!* Junior! Oh my God! Oh my God! *Junior!"*

One of the ambulance guys is pounding on my chest with his fist, while the other guy is holding an oxygen mask over my face. Mom slides down next to me, splashing mud all over her black dress, shrieking and screaming, tugging at the roots of her hair. But now that she's seen the blood all over my face, her cries are turning into sobs, and she's just kneeling there, rocking back and forth and mumbling my name, as the paramedic keeps banging away at my chest, trying to jump-start my heart and bring back my pulse.

The Pinkerton who had chased Mom out onto the track is trying to pull her away, but she's so wild and hysterical, and so close to the ambulance guys, I guess he's figuring it's probably better not to risk making matters any worse by fighting with her—'specially in the rain and on the slippery footing. So now he's just letting her stay kneeling at my side, and he's positioned himself in front of us with his arms stretched out, looking toward the clubhouse turn, getting ready to shield us from any returning horses who might get spooked by the sight of Red and his broken leg.

But as the paramedics run back to the ambulance to get a stretcher, Mom moves in closer. The ambulance guys already warned her not to touch me or move me, but she's sticking by my side though, kneeling in the mud, still rocking back and forth and sobbing like crazy. The rain is coming down even harder than before, and I can see big, heavy drops dotting her glasses and curving through her hair like rivers, rolling down her forehead and mixing with her tears. I can smell the familiar scent of her Jean Nate', and I can smell her corsage too, the soft petals brushing against my cheek.

"Junior! My poor Junior! Oh, my poor *Junior!*"

All of a sudden, I hear the click-click of a camera from the other side of the rail. It's that same reporter guy from the interview, Matt Marcus, and his photographer friend. They must've been covering the race from the infield, and then they ran over. I watch him scribble something on a notepad. It says: "Rainy Racetrack Pieta'". I guess he's got his "human interest" story now.

A few feet behind me, two men are placing a big, blue, V-shaped screen in front of Red. I guess the idea is to block the ugly sight of the suffering animal from the fans, so they won't get grossed-out. I wish they would set up another screen to block my view too, but I can feel myself hovering only a couple of feet above Red's head, and I can see and hear practically everything—a lot clearer than I want to.

Somehow, he must've lost his balance and fell down, 'cause now, instead of hobbling around on three legs, he's lying flat on his side in the mud. Tito is lying across his neck, stroking him and whispering to him, trying to keep him calm, but at the same time leaning against him with all his weight so he won't be able to get up and hurt himself even more. But Red is already in a complete state of panic, and he just keeps flailing away and thrashing his legs around, squealing and whimpering in pain, fighting with all his might to push Tito off and get back on his feet again.

I can see the track veterinarian huddling with Sam off to the side. He has a syringe in his hand.

"I'm gonna have to put him out of his misery."

Sam bites his lip and nods. "Go 'head, Doc, do it."

As the tip of the needle disappears into Red's neck, I see him shake and shudder as if he's having some freaky seizure or some weird muscle spasm. But only a couple of seconds later, he goes stiff, and his muddy body slumps to the ground and stays there, still, motionless. A minute or two later, the emergency van rolls up to take him away. I watch as they lower the platform and haul him into the dark insides of the truck, his long red tail dragging behind him. Tito breaks down and starts crying, and so does Sam.

When Red died, a part of me must've died too. I can feel myself slipping into that peaceful, dream-place where I was before—only now, a strange light is surrounding me, lifting me up and pulling me away, higher and higher, as if it were a huge electro-magnet, and I'm nothing but a puny, little paper clip. At first, I got scared, but now that I've been inside it for a while, it's making me feel so calm, and warm, and happy, I find myself letting go and surrendering to it.

I've never felt anything like this. All of a sudden, I'm part of everything, and everything is part of me. There are no more boundaries, no more barriers, no more names, no ranks, no titles, no nothing. A tree, a leaf, a rock, a sparrow, a cloud, a horse, a man, a blade of grass, a worm, a woman, a bee, a child, the sun, the sky, the rain...everything is all one—just different parts of the same thing. I feel so happy and peaceful, I could stay right here inside this light forever. But little by little, in spite of all the joy, I'm starting to feel like I'm losing myself— like my identity is slipping away. The light just keeps pulling me and pulling me, swallowing me up, to the point where I don't really know who I *am* anymore.

"Hold it! Wait! Wait! *Wait!*"

As I fight against the light, I feel myself starting to fall again. But I haven't fallen all the way down though. It's like I'm suspended in mid-air, hovering over everything, reaching out like a blind man without a cane, desperate to grab a hold of reality before it slips through my fingers.

The rain is trickling down to a drizzle now, and I can see the sky starting to clear over in the distance. Mom is still at my side, stroking my hair and holding my hand as the paramedics strap me onto the stretcher and lift me into the ambulance.

"I love you, Ma. I love you."

I don't expect her to hear me—I haven't moved my mouth or said anything—but as soon as I *think* the words, I feel her soft lips on my forehead, and I hear her whispering the same thing back at me—almost like an echo.

"I love you, Junior. I love you."

Simon is standing next to the ambulance in back of Mom. His face is all twisted, and his two boney fists are crammed inside his mouth like he's trying to stifle a scream. I try to call out his name, but I guess he can't hear me. He just keeps standing there with that sad look on his face, and as they close the doors on the ambulance, I can see the tears spilling from his eyes...one by one...drop by drop.

Ronnie is standing by the fence near the edge of the track. She's got her head buried in Mrs. Minetti's chest, sobbing "Joey! Joey! Joey!", over and over. It really hurts to see her like that. I wanted her to see me in the winner's circle, smiling, with a big bouquet of flowers in my arms—not lying face down in the mud, all trampled, like some broken little ragdoll.

"Sorry, Ronnie."

But the worst of everybody is Grandma. She's looks like she's out cold, and even with Aunt Jean and Uncle Rocco fanning her with their programs and slapping her, she's just lying there on the bench with her arms drooping down at her sides. There isn't any expression on her face, and all you can see are two white slits instead of her eyes.

Aunt Jean is starting to lose it. "Mama! *Mama!* Oh Rocco! What are we gonna *do?!*"

"Don't panic, Jean, she's coming out of it. Look! She's gettin' a little color in her face."

I watch as she slowly starts to open her eyes and move her head from side to side. I guess the shock of everything was way too much for her.

I try calling out to her, but it's no use. The rainbow light has lifted me so high, she's beyond my reach—and I'm beyond hers. All I can do is take one last look at her face, and try to remember the sparkle in her eyes, and the golden glow of her beautiful, Belcuore smile. I don't know how or why, but I find myself focusing on her hands, zooming in on

384

them, as if I were looking through binoculars. I can see them real clear, and I just keep staring as she lifts them up and clutches them to her heart, her black, *luto* dress making them shine like two pearls in a black, velvet jewelry box. I can see every vein, every wrinkle, every split-nail, every bit-cuticle, every beauty mark, all the little, brown, age-spots, the gold wedding ring, the crumpled-up tissue peeking out from between her fingers...everything.

"Bye Grandma. *Ti voglio ben' assai.*"

I try looking for my father, but I can't seem to find him. Maybe "Shorty" flew the coop, just like he did when I was a kid. Who knows? Your guess is as good as mine. But I can still hear his voice though, and it keeps haunting me and ringing in my ears, even louder than before: *"Joey! Joweeeeee!"*

My "pal", Phil, is sitting with Carmine the Nose, and Irv and Marty, and the rest of the crew. They're all looking down on the scene from The Nose's box up on the second floor.

"Serves him right," The Nose grumbles, flicking his fingers under his chin at the ambulance as it speeds away down the track. "He shoulda been an abortion—the little rat bastard."

"C'mon, Carmine."

"'C'mon' *nothin'*! His piece-of-shit father should've jacked off in the sink; we would've all been better off."

"Take it easy, Carmine."

"'Take it *easy'*?! Did you see the way this little prick was pumpin' and drivin' in the stretch? He sure didn't look like a jock who was tryin' to lose to me. Shit, if that horse hadn't taken that bad step and gone down like that, he woulda *won* the fuckin' thing."

Marty, the fat bookie, just shrugs his shoulders and scarfs down the last bite of his hot dog, wiping the mustard from the corners of his mouth with his napkin, and then smoothing out his moustache with his fingers. "Don't give yourself any more *agida*, Carmine. The kid's horse ran out of the money, that's all that matters to us. Whether he was trying to win, or whether he was trying to lose, it's all a moot point now anyway."

Carmine the Nose waves Marty away with disgust, and then stands up to leave.

Phil is right behind him, but before he walks away, he turns to Marty and grabs his crotch. "Moot *this* over here."

****